Father Ralph

GERALD O'DONOVAN

FATHER RALPH

BRANDON

Published in 1993 by
Brandon Book Publishers Ltd
Dingle, Co. Kerry, Ireland

First edition published 1913

British Library Cataloguing in Publication Data
is available for this book.
ISBN 0 86322 174 2

Front cover illustration, detail from Charles Conder's "William Orpen, Artist", is reproduced by permission of the National Gallery of Ireland.

This book is published with the financial assistance of the Arts Council/An Chomhairle Ealaíon, Ireland.

Cover design: The Graphiconies, Dublin
Printed by Colour Books Ltd, Dublin

Introduction

By John F. Ryan

Though born in Co. Down, Gerald O'Donovan considered himself a Corkman. His father, Jeremiah, and mother, Margaret Regan, were married in Enniskeane church on 11 February 1860. The O'Donovans, of Breachna, Desertserges, near Bandon, were tenant farmers on the estate of the Earl of Bandon with a holding of sixty-eight acres. The Regans, also tenant farmers, lived in the adjoining parish of Enniskeane with a lease on thirty-four acres in Farrannasheshery, on the estate of Henry Beamish.

After their marriage Jeremiah and Margaret lived in Desertserges. Their first child, Julia, was born in 1861; Daniel, Margaret, Patrick, and Mary followed at two-yearly intervals. In 1867, on the recommendation of John E. Barrett, land agent for the Beamish estate, Jeremiah, who worked as a building contractor, was appointed clerk of works for the Board of Works on the building of Bantry pier. On the completion of the project in October 1870 the O'Donovans moved to Kilkeel, Co. Down, where he was similarly employed. Their sixth child, Gerald,[1] was born in Newry Street on 13 July 1871. It was thus as the son of a minor government official that the young O'Donovan spent most of his formative years.

The family moved around the country as work became available on pier construction. In 1873 they were in Courtmacsherry, Co. Cork, and three years later at Ballyvaughan, Co. Clare. When not under contract, O'Donovan and family spent intermittent periods in Desertserges. Gerald attended National School in Cork, Galway and Sligo, in all of which he received what he later described as a poor education. The move to Enniscrone was crucial to his career. While here he enrolled as a student at Ardnaree College, the old seminary for Killala diocese before the present St Murdeach's, where he received all of his secondary education.

In September 1889, O'Donovan entered St Patrick's College, Maynooth, for Killala diocese. After a year of rhetoric and two of philosophy, he commenced studies in theology in 1892. The only award he won during this period was when he earned first prize in History of the Old Testament. During 1893 he left the college, with the permission of his bishop, to join the Jesuit Order. Six months later, on the nomination of Bishop John Healy, he was readmitted for Clonfert diocese. After an average to mediocre performance, O'Donovan was ordained on 23 June 1895. He was first appointed curate for Kilmalinoge and Lickmolassy and then to the diocesan seminary at Esker. Transferred to Loughrea in 1897, he remained there until October 1904.

The town, and most of the surrounding grazing lands, was the property of the notorious absentee landlord, Clanricarde, with results all too evident in the local workhouse. Its social problems were highlighted by Bishop Healy in 1900 when he described the "squalor, poverty and chronic wretchedness" there and recorded the decline in its population in living memory from eight thousand to less than three thousand.

By contrast, the elaborate Maynooth centenary celebrations in the year of O'Donovan's ordination bore witness to the power and wealth of his church. O'Donovan believed that the college did not prepare its students for the social responsibilities of the ministry. He urged that economics should be part of their training and was critical of the standard of Irish language teaching there. His aim was to equip the priest, who should remain aloof from party politics, to contribute to the Irish revival then taking place. In an outpouring of national enthusiasm, organisations such as the Gaelic League, founded in 1892, the Irish Agricultural Organisation Society, founded in 1894, the Irish Literary Theatre, founded in 1899, and several others had set about the task of nation-building, a social and cultural activity which was believed to transcend the divisiveness of politics.

Imbued with these ideals, O'Donovan tackled the social problems in Loughrea by founding St Brendan's Total Abstinence Society for men. With a library, reading room and gymnasium, it had a membership of over three hundred in 1901. As its president, he made it the focal point for all local efforts at regeneration by bringing the language, literary and industrial movements under its aegis. He also rented rooms in the Mercy Convent and founded St Raphael's Home Industries Society to train women in lacemaking and embroidery. The extent to which he involved his parishoners in the revival belied the fact that in national terms the movement was a minority one.

O'Donovan saw the building of St Brendan's Cathedral in Loughrea, then underway, as an opportunity to engage the church in an artistic and industrial revival by employing Irish artists and craftsmen in its decoration. He was critical of the practice of importing inferior art for the extensive church-building programme of earlier decades. Supported by Edward Martyn, who considered him as a leader of opinion in the country, he campaigned to highlight what he saw as a lack of patriotism and forcefully put the case in lectures to the National Literary Society in 1901, and to the annual meeting of the Maynooth Union in 1902. Bishop Healy was already converted to the cause and appointed him administrator of the parish that year, with a free hand to commission the artists. By the time of his departure the work, which was to initiate a renaissance in Irish art, was underway. He had engaged the sculptor, John Hughes and stained-glass artists, Sarah Purser and Michael Healy, and had given the first large commission for banners to the Dun Emer Guild, a craft studio founded by the Yeats sisters and Evelyn Gleeson.

The myriad activities undertaken by O'Donovan in Loughrea were but part of his involvement at national level where he saw the various organisations interlocked in a broad movement for regeneration. His efforts won wide approval. The editor of the *Leader*, D. P. Moran, judged him to be one of the most vigorous and gifted men of his day. The *United Irishman* confidently predicted that his efforts to rebuild Irish Ireland would endear his name to future generations, while the *Irish Catholic* saw him as a "very distinguished ecclesiastic" with whose fame as a patriot priest all Ireland was ringing.

O'Donovan was inspired by the ideals of the literary revival, first formulated at nearby Coole Park. Writing on "The Celtic Revival of Today" in the *Irish Ecclesiastical Record* in 1899, he sought to promote their work, largely an Anglo-Irish phenomenon, among his fellow clerics. He pleaded for a literature which would have as its source the history, legend and folklore of ancient Ireland. With W. B. Yeats, Lady Gregory, Douglas Hyde, Jane Barlow, and others, he contributed a number of short sketches of Irish life to the *Celtic Christmas*, an annual publication of Irish art and literature. Written in romantic idiom, they achieved a fruitful conjunction between mythology and history, dealing with such contemporary issues as emigration and the revival in terms of the old Celtic legends.

The Gaelic League journal, *An Claidheamh Soluis*, was critical of O'Donovan's efforts to promote a "Celtic" literary revival. But soon afterwards it published his radical suggestions, which foreshadowed those of Patrick Pearse, for recognition of the subjective and national elements of education in the National School. Though unable to speak Irish, he was soon a leading propagandist for the League, presiding over the first Raftery Feis in Killeneen, giving public lectures in the Rotunda, and promoting the movement in America. In all cases he campaigned for its educational demands and underlined the failure of his fellow clerics, as school managers, to support it. In 1903 he was elected to its governing body where he served until 1905.

During 1899 also, Horace Plunkett, founder of the Irish Agricultural Organisation Society, noting O'Donovan's promotion of technical training for girls in the *Irish Ecclesiastical Record*, saw him as a "young cultured gentlemanly priest" and hoped he would educate the clergy about the co-operative movement.[2] He was soon promoting it in the *New Ireland Review* and in the *Leader* and, attracted by its pronounced social as well as economic character in Connacht, was actively involved there. Its educational possibilities appealed to him and a campaign, with A. E., to establish village libraries was his most enduring achievement. Elected Connacht representative on the executive committee in 1901, where he remained until 1908, he was one of the few priests in Ireland to be involved in the ideological side of co-operation.

A prominent and able controversialist on aspects of Catholic thought and action, O'Donovan was invited to address the annual meeting of the Maynooth Union of former students three times. In his work for the Revival he had embraced liberal and secular views, particularly on education in which he had a special interest, and his plea for a more practical and democratic approach was not well received by his church. His disaffection was also evident in his discomfort with the stress on the pietistic side of religion at the expense of its intellectual and social dimension. But his view, which had to await the sanction of Vatican Two several decades later, that the laity should be involved in the church's internal decision-making process, underlined the extent to which his thinking was out of tune with that of his contemporaries.

In October 1904, O'Donovan advised Plunkett that he had "thrown up the ministry" and, referring to Dr. O'Dea, who had replaced Dr. Healy in Clonfert, confided that he was unable to put up with his bishop who had "no knowledge of life whatever".[3] While O'Dea left no record of the affair, it is believed in clerical circles that he had given his administrator an ultimatum to reduce his lecturing and travel commitments and concentrate on his parish duties and, rather than conform, O'Donovan resigned. But, if the bishop was dissatisfied with his performance, the laity and some of the clergy took a different view. A public function to mark his departure was described in the *Western News* as one of the most spontaneous outbursts of genuine regret witnessed in the town for a long time.

George Moore, whose novel *The Lake* later depicted a priest's escape to freedom and who undoubtedly drew on these events, wrote to his publishers introducing O'Donovan as "a young priest... of great ability". Moore spoke of his excellent knowledge of literature and hoped that Unwin might give him some literary work to do.[4] Yeats and Lady Gregory also tried to get employment for him.

Four months later it was clear that O'Donovan's problems were not simply a difference with his bishop. In the new influential *English Review*, published by Unwin, he made a scathing attack on the Roman Catholic church's education policy. How untenable his position as a priest had become was clear from his conclusion that it had "no foundation either in reason or religion" and that in a modern democratic industrial society the state should not delegate its power over secular education.

After some four years dividing his time between London and Dublin, May 1908 saw O'Donovan bankrupt and "out of sorts", and he decided to unfrock himself and look around for work.[5] He wrote of having had to shed many an illusion and of having had many bitter experiences. In October 1909 he went to America to work for the co-operative movement and as Plunkett's literary agent on a publishing project. The American venture collapsed and in March 1910 O'Donovan was sub-warden of Toynbee Hall, a workers' education settlement in east London. On a visit that August to

Hugh Law, nationalist MP for Donegal, he fell in love with Beryl Verschoyle, who at twenty-four was fifteen years younger than he. A member of a northern Protestant gentry family, her father was colonel of the Duke of Cornwall's Light Infantry Regiment and her mother was of an upper middle-class English family living in Rome. They were married at Whitechapel Registry Office, London, on 15 October 1910. Because of the unsuitability of Toynbee as a residence for her, he reluctantly refused the wardenship and left the settlement in June 1911. Their first child, Brigid, was born in the following December.

Still preoccupied with the events surrounding his departure from the priesthood, O'Donovan now turned from the idyllic and mythical themes which had occupied him as a writer to undertake his first realist and autobiographical novel, *Father Ralph*. Dealing with the theme of rebellion and exile from family, church and country, and predating Joyce's *Portrait of an Artist* by three years, it is of crucial importance in the history of its genre in Ireland. It provides an inside view of the Irish Church of the period, when its dominance of Irish life could scarcely be challenged. Reform and renewal of the church, already underway in the early 19th century, had been accelerated during the later decades when it gained political and economic power with the transfer of landed estates into Catholic hands and the emergence, in the aftermath of the Famine, of the prosperous tenant farmers who became its mainstay. The political power was manifest in the church's relations with the nation and in its almost unfettered control over education, while the extensive building programme bore witness to its wealth. The church portrayed in the novel had also been moulded by the reforming zeal of Cardinal Paul Cullen who, from 1849, had worked for thirty years to consolidate the reforms already underway and bring it into line with Canon Law. The result was a disciplined institution in which the authority of the bishops had increased and a growing number of religious was ministering to a population in decline. The more communal religious practices of the laity were discouraged, and there was a dramatic increase in Mass attendance and in formal devotions in the church under the supervision of the clergy.

The novel received wide acclaim in the literary pages. A review in the *Times Literary Supplement* cited it as evidence of a revolt by a small minority of educated Catholic laity against the autocracy of their church. But it received a hostile reception in Roman Catholic publications. In the controversy which ensued in Ireland the *Church of Ireland Gazette* saw it as a great Irish novel and one of the most important of the generation, which vividly and powerfully depicted the life of the Irish countryside. In the nationalist *Freeman's Journal* it was described as a gross libel on the Irish priesthood and people.

O'Donovan claimed that the book was "sincere and fair in intention". Instead of making it "a vehicle for attack on the church", he had "toned it down" as much as was consistent with a true picture. To the best of his knowledge it did not contain a "single untruthful, dishonest or overcoloured sentence".[6] While a few of the characters representing movements or opinions were "mere lay figures and were drawn direct from life", the "living characters", though fictitious, "were in all cases true to type". The novel was autobiographical in feeling and experience and the descriptions of such as the seminary and Maynooth were as accurate as he could make them.

With the birth of their second child, Dermod, in June 1913 the O'Donovans moved to the Norfolk coast. His second novel, *Waiting*, dealing with the oppressive effects of the *Ne Temere* decree and reflecting his marriage outside of the church, was published by Macmillan in 1914.

On 24 May 1915 O'Donovan joined the British Army with a temporary commission as 1st Lieutenant in the Service Corps in the Humber Garrison at Hull. Four months later he was invalided out and joined the Ministry of Munitions, from which he resigned in October 1916. Early in 1917, when Geoffrey Collins of the Glasgow publishing company set up the firm's first London office, he became manager and first reader. After a disagreement over publishing policy he resigned and returned to Norfolk where their third child, Mary, was born in April 1918. Within weeks he was back in London having been appointed Head of British Propaganda in Italy, under the Ministry of Information.

The novelist, Rose Macaulay, a fluent Italian speaker, was employed as O'Donovan's secretary, and a secret intimate relationship developed. As her biographer puts it, within months of their meeting "to her astonishment and against her reason" she was "overwhelmed by her responses to his searching mind, his power of sympathy and his sardonic wit". She had fallen "excitingly and painfully in love".[7] He became the most important person in her life and most of her subsequent novels were influenced by him.

With the signing of the Armistice in November 1918 O'Donovan's job was discontinued. His third novel, *How They Did It*, was published by Methuen in February 1920. It deals with his war-time experience as, under a thin veil of fiction, he indicts the muddling incompetence of the politicians and civil servants on the "Home Front". *Conquest*, published by Constable later that year, is an attempt to interpret the Irish question. The critic Norreys Jephson O'Conor believed that it might become the *Uncle Tom's Cabin* of Ireland. Though a plea for tolerance and love against hatred and prejudice, its political point of view was seen by the English reviewers as putting the case for Sinn Féin.

Back in London in 1921 after a period in Italy, O'Donovan broke new ground when Martin Secker published *Vocations*, a novel which focuses significantly on aspects of the "woman question". A realistic work set in a provincial Irish town, it deals with questions of free will and conscience. It is the story of two daughters of a prosperous publican who are forced by their mother to enter a convent. Published also in America by Boni and Liveright, the reviewers there saw it as coming under the aegis of George Moore, whose endorsement was printed on the jacket.

O'Donovan's last novel, *The Holy Tree*, published by William Heinemann in 1922, was written for Rose Macaulay. In it, she recorded, he put "his whole philosophy of love, through the medium of Irish peasants".[8] Treating of the emotional experiences of an Irish Catholic peasant girl torn between love and duty, it is written in an Anglo-Irish idiom reminiscent of Synge.

The early '20s marked a turning point in O'Donovan's career. He now lived a life of relative isolation, as his adopted country failed to fuel the enthusiasm which had so distinguished his early years. Moreover, his continued absence from Ireland, the source of his inspiration, contributed to the ending of his career as a novelist. A number of attempts to involve him in literary projects failed. During the next two decades he was a reader for American publishers and also at Collins with special responsibility for Macaulay's novels. In 1928 he worked for a period as private secretary to Plunkett.

In the mid-'20s O'Donovan's role as a breadwinner diminished when Beryl inherited payments from a family trust fund. Always a family man, he made all decisions about the childrens' education and, though he could ill afford it, sent them to public schools and Oxford and Cambridge. His daughter, Brigid, recalls him spending much of his time in his study reading history, in which he had an avid interest. The afternoons were usually spent reading a detective story and doing the crossword over the telephone with Rose Macaulay. She was now a regular guest and came to lunch almost every Sunday. Beryl sensed from an early stage that something was amiss with her marriage but, in the interest of family unity, clearly chose to ignore it.

In 1937 O'Donovan, who was in failing health, had to abandon work undertaken on behalf of the Royal Society for the Deaf. Early in 1939 he became involved with the Committee for Czech Refugees. This, too, had to be abandoned when he suffered serious head injuries in a motoring accident while holidaying with Rose Macaulay in the Lake District. He never fully recovered, and the family moved to Albury, Surrey. The tragic death of their youngest child, Mary, following an accident in 1941 was a bitter blow. In February 1942 he underwent surgery for cancer and returned to die at Albury. Even now, unable to forget his Irish past, he liked to be read to from the works of George Moore or *The Irish RM*. The local Church of England rector, Philip Gray, who had become a close friend, was a daily visitor. Beryl's diary for 26 July records his death in these stark words: "Gerald left me in the morning".

Two weeks later a short anonymous tribute "From a Friend" was published in *The Times*. It concluded that as a friend he never failed and that his wise judgement and unstinting interest were always on tap behind his reserve and the sometimes sardonic wit that was his Irish heritage. The writer was Rose Macaulay, and she concluded on a personal note with these words: "To know him was to love him".

Though O'Donovan's obituary in the *Times Literary Supplement*[9] compared his work to "a flaming brand in Ireland", there was no report of his death in any Irish newspaper. But Séan Ó Faoláin, writing six months later in *The Irish Times* [10] on the Modernist Jesuit, George Tyrrell, noted his passing. Recalling the schism which had rocked the Catholic church over forty years earlier, he saw the author of *Father Ralph* as the only other Irishman who seemed to be keenly responsive to that "subtle and penetrating and attractive idea" of reconciling science and Catholic dogma. Ó Faoláin, who was first interested in him "solely as a novelist, then as a Modernist" and considered him "a romantic sport - out of the boglands defying Rome, writing so well", was deeply disappointed when Rose Macaulay refused to write on him for *The Bell.*[11] Doubtless he hoped that O'Donovan's memory could still inspire in the battle being waged for a more liberal, tolerant, and pluralist Ireland.

References

Sources unattributed are in the O'Donovan papers.

1. He was christened Jeremiah but as a writer adopted the name Gerald.
2. Horace Plunkett's unpublished diary, 1 February 1899, Plunkett Reference Library, St Giles, Oxford.
3. Ibid. 30 October 1904.
4. *George Moore in Transition: Letters to T. Fisher Unwin and Lena Milman,* 1894-1910, edited with a commentary by Helmut G. Gebler (Detroit, 1968). Letter No 274.
5. Horace Plunkett's unpublished diary, 7 May 1908.
6. O'Donovan, letter to John Quinn, 11 August 1913. Quinn Papers, New York Public Library.
7. Jane Emery, *Rose Macaulay: A Writer's life* (London 1991), pp. 159-60.
8. Emery, pp. 186-87.
9. *Times Literary Supplement*, 15 August 1942.
10. *The Irish Times,* 3 April 1943.
11. Seán Ó Faoláin, letter to the author, 11 June 1976.

Chapter 1

IT WAS HIS mother's idea that Ralph O'Brien should be a priest. She had brooded happily on the thought for months before his birth. She had prayed that her first-born should be a son and never doubted that it would be. He was to grow up unspotted from the world, holy as a priest of God should be. Day after day at mass in Clarendon Street Church she dedicated him to God. One day, during consecration of the mass, when the child in her womb quickened as if in response to a question as to whether he would wish to serve God at the altar, she took it as a sign from heaven. When the child was born, she looked on him as the child of miracle. She had prayed for a son and a son had been given to her. She had promised that he should be a priest; it was because of the promise her son had been given.

The nursery of her house in Harcourt Terrace was hung with religious prints: St Francis Xavier preaching to the Japanese, St Stanislaus Kotska, St Aloysius Gonzaga, the Sacred Heart. Mrs O'Brien kept on her monthly nurse in charge of Ralph while she sought for a suitable permanent nurse. It was, of course, essential that the nurse should be skilled, but it was even more necessary that she should be religious. After many interviews and much disappointment, on the advice of her confessor, Father Eusebius, a Carmelite friar, Mrs O'Brien decided to engage Ann Carty. She was a competent nurse but found it difficult to get or keep a place. A member of the third order of Mount Carmel, she made it a condition of service that she was allowed to attend mass daily and a number of sodalities several times a week. For years she had been in no situation longer than two months. Either she gave notice on the ground that her spiritual life was being interfered with or, more frequently, the mistress insisted that she had hired a nurse and not a nun. Mrs O'Brien, however, was delighted with Ann. Her absences gave the mother frequent opportunities of having Ralph all to herself. She gave him a bath every morning while Ann was at mass and watched him splashing in the water with hungry interest. She persuaded herself that he liked the humming of hymn tunes. As he lay cuddled in her arms she crooned in his ear "Ave Marias", and "Salve Reginas". His eyes were early attracted to the coloured prints on the walls and he crowed as he touched them. His mother read into this a certain sign of his future vocation. In the lives of the saints, of which she was a diligent reader, there were numerous tales of predestined vocations. They were usually manifested in some simple way, somewhat similar to Ralph's predilection in the nursery. He had a special liking for a coloured print of St Stanislaus Kotska. This was a sign that he was to be a Jesuit, endowed with all the virtues of St Stanislaus.

Every day Ralph was taken in his pram to Stephen's Green Park, where he slept or lay silently watching the ducks while Ann Carty told her beads. When eleven o'clock mass was over at Clarendon Street, he was taken to the Carmelite church. Ann took him out of his pram and bore him in her arms to the rails of the high altar, where she knelt and prayed. She entered wholeheartedly into his mother's schemes for his future and always said a special round of the beads that he should be a good priest. Very soon he began to notice the dead Christ in its glass case under the table of the high altar. When his eyes caught it, he stretched out his arms and gurgled. The first day it happened Ann hurried home with the wonderful story to Mrs O'Brien, who came herself next day to see the miraculous happening.

As he grew older, even before he was able to walk, Ann took him to eleven o'clock mass. The heavy incense-laden atmosphere kept Ralph quiet and sleepy. Ann told his mother, "He had that reverence for the house of God that he never let a cry out of him." When awake his eyes were fixed on the high altar at which the priest was celebrating mass. An ordinary observer would perhaps attribute this to the attraction of the light, but to Ann, "He was taking it all in, and learning how to say the mass one day himself."

When these stories were told to his father, Major O'Brien grunted and muttered, "The child will be spoiled by women. A priest indeed! The boy will go into the army like his father and his grandfather before him." The major's great regret was that he himself had to leave the army at the opening of what promised to be a brilliant career. Some years before his marriage an obscure injury to one of the tendons of his right leg had unfitted him for service and he was forced to resign. He had settled in Dublin, where he had fallen in love with Hilda Bermingham during her first season. She was shy and gentle, had little general conversation, rather repelled men by her prudishness and convent ways. An orphan, brought up in a convent, she was taught to distrust the world as a wicked place. She saw something doubtful in the most ordinary conversation, followed a nun's advice and "changed the subject" so often that she soon got the reputation of being "a prude", "a stock", "a saint" or "impossible". From the first O'Brien impressed her. He had the gravity of a disappointed man. He was not "smart" in conversation, and she distrusted "smartness" more than anything else. She saw him regularly at eleven o'clock mass at Clarendon Street, so he must be religious. His slight lameness gave an added attraction to his distinguished bearing and handsome face, especially when she heard that it was due to a wound received in action in Basutoland. He was brave and she liked brave men. She disliked fighting and soldiers, but then he was no longer a soldier. St Ignatius himself had been a soldier, she remembered, and was none the worse saint for it. When he proposed she accepted him at once and shyly confessed her own love.

Inniscar, his family place, being let on a long lease, they settled down in Harcourt Terrace after a short honeymoon. He had got back his youth, which at thirty he thought he had lost for ever. There were happy days in hunting the quays and back streets for odd bits of furniture; in walks up the Dublin mountains and long talks in the evenings. They were happier still when their child was expected, while she worked at bundles of filmy material, fashioning them into the numberless garments every mother thinks every child needs. He read to her, sometimes books of her choosing, sometimes of his. Hers were always religious in tone, his poetry of all kinds. She soon found that his views of life were different from hers. His broader outlook which made him tolerant of the views of others influenced her very little. He did not always accept the stories of the saints. This she attributed to some defect in him which time would heal. He was so good that God would surely enlighten him in His own good time. She did not confide to him all her dreams and hopes for the future of the child she carried in her womb. Once she attempted it, but he laughingly pooh-poohed her and called her a silly little girl. She felt angry for a moment, but, on reflection, was glad that he differed from her in some things. This is a vale of tears and unclouded happiness is impossible. Besides, she could "offer up" any pain his derision caused her as an atonement for her own defects.

At three years old Ralph was a sturdy boy with great brown eyes that looked solemnly out on the world. He played in Stephen's Green and fed the ducks, with whom he carried on long conversations. He told them eagerly that his mamma had sent them their breakfast and, with infinite pains that all should have some, threw them pieces of bread that he had brought carefully tied up in a paper bag. He was now taken every morning to eleven o'clock mass at Clarendon Street. He knelt in the front bench, his little hands clasped, and took a lively interest in the movements of the priest. The server who lighted and quenched the candles, however, engaged his keenest attention. He hurried Ann away from the feeding of the ducks, lest he should be late for the lighting of the candles. It was a special pleasure if benediction followed the mass. Then rows and rows of candles were lighted until the whole altar was ablaze, to his infinite delight.

In his nursery was an altar with a statue of the Blessed Virgin, in front of which a little red lamp always burned dimly. Candles were lighted on feast days, but there were only a few and Ann did not light them well. She fumbled with a match over each candle, while the "man" in Clarendon Street barely touched candle after candle with a lighted taper and, as if by magic, a bright flame shot up. Now that he was grown up Ralph no longer said his prayers in bed, except a morning offering all his thoughts, words and actions to God when he awoke, and a little prayer at night. For his longer morning and evening prayers he knelt on a little prie-dieu in front of the altar of the Blessed Virgin and said the Our Father, Hail Mary, the Creed and the Confiteor and a prayer for a vocation. He stumbled over the big words which he had learned with patience, after many repetitions by Ann and his mother. He always prayed with his eyes closed, for he found by experience that if he kept them open he left out parts of the prayers and had to say them all over again.

He often asked Ann the meaning of words and was especially interested in heaven and hell. This was fortunate as Ann's knowledge of general theology was confused and disjointed, but she seemed to know all about hell and heaven.

"What is heaven like, Ann?" he asked, as he ate his porridge.

"Oh, it's a grand place entirely. There's God sitting on a throne of gold, and the Blessed Mother near Him on another throne, and all the angels playing on harps and fiddles."

"Is it as fine as the altar in Clarendon Street when the candles are lit?"

"Oh! it's more beautiful than anything you could think of."

"Will we go there, Ann?"

"If we're good, dear."

"And why don't we go now, this very day?"

Ann busied herself for a minute buttering some bread, while he waited, spoon poised in the air, eagerly watching her.

"Why, we'd be only paving-stones in heaven if we went now, but when you are a priest and have done a lot of good things, you'll be high up in heaven, with maybe a harp of your own."

He sighed, ate his porridge in silence, and then said, "I suppose we couldn't go to hell either?"

"What put that into your head?" Ann said, startled. "Of course we won't go to hell. Hell is a bad place and no one that says their prayers regularly, and does what they are told, will go there."

"But there are lots and lots of people there."

"Only the wicked, darling."

"Tell me some."

"Oh, there's Cromwell, and Henry the Eighth, and millions more."

"Were they wicked?"

"You'll learn all about them when you grow up. Besides," she added, looking at him severely, "you mustn't ask too many questions. Little boys will be told things, but they mustn't ask questions."

He sighed again and went on with his breakfast.

He was "a fair nuisance" for asking questions, Ann complained to his mother, who consoled her, saying he would understand better when he grew up.

At eight years of age he had learned the whole catechism by heart, and was being prepared for his first confession. He was much exercised by this preparation. He read over the table of sins in his prayer-book and decided that he had committed most of them. He had a lively sense of hell and of its torments. He thought of it at nights in bed and a cold fear crept down his back, seeming to clutch his heart. Ann had long since given him vivid descriptions of hell and he had read with avidity *Hell Opened to Christians*. He shut his eyes tight to keep out the visions that crowded on him, but he still saw "the devil like a roaring lion seeking whom he might devour", whom he had read of so often and had heard so much of from Ann and his mother and Father Eusebius. Ann's descriptions were the most vivid and real. She knew where hell was, while Father Eusebius seemed doubtful on the point. It was in the centre of the earth. At first he felt that it was very far off and difficult to get at, but he now knew that souls could pass easily through solid earth; that the devil seized them the moment they left the body; that almost at once they were cast into hell if they died in mortal sin. It was a roaring sea of fire, Ann said, pitch, brimstone, molten iron and all the hot and burning things that were ever known in the world, all mixed up together. Once you were in, there was no getting out. For a year or more, when he was about five, he was consoled by the thought that it was possible to get out, for Christ had been three days in hell and had got away easily. But when he mentioned this to Ann, she dashed his hopes to the ground. Christ was God and could go where He willed and the devil had no power over Him, but it was different with little boys and men and women too. Once they got in the door was closed for ever. Then the devils were always adding new tortures, pulling at the tongues of the damned with red-hot pincers, scraping their backs with rakes of red-hot iron. Ann knew all this for certain, for she had read of it in the writings of Scaramelli and Father Rodriguez which were in the small nursery bookshelf. These holy men could not be deceived.

The great day of his first confession at last arrived. He examined his conscience carefully, and said act after act of contrition as he knelt before the high altar at Clarendon Street. He put his whole heart into the words and said them as loudly as he could without attracting the attention of those who knelt near him. The words were words of love, but his feelings were of fear of the dreadful hell awaiting such a great sinner. He recalled for the hundredth time how one day when his mother called him he had pretended not to hear; and disobedience to parents was one of the great sins. He had often been inattentive at his prayers; he had been angry sometimes with Ann. He recalled stories from the lives of the saints as to how sins similar to his had been punished. As he was about to rise from his knees to enter the confessional he remembered, with a shudder, how lost souls were placed between the red-hot spikes of harrows eternally drawn in opposite directions. He said one more act of sorrow and went tremblingly to the confessional.

He had chosen Father David for his confessor. He was ashamed to go to Father Eusebius who knew him and who, he felt, would be shocked by the enormity of his sins. Father David had kind blue eyes and sometimes patted Ralph's head as he stood on wet days at the door of the church with Ann, waiting for a shower to pass.

His mother had taught him the method of making confession, but when the priest opened the slide of the confession box and muttered a blessing, Ralph was confused and was unable to speak.

"Well!" said the priest, sharply, after waiting a moment. "'Bless me, father, for I have sinned,'" he continued, without waiting for a reply.

Ralph took the cue, repeated "Bless me, father, for I have sinned" and then said the Confiteor.

He went through his tale of sins. The priest did not seem either surprised or shocked. Ralph stole a look at his face. Instead of the look of horror which Ralph anticipated the priest was smiling and seemed to be peering through a slit in the curtain of his box at something going on in the church.

"Is that all?" he said, when Ralph finished.

"I'm very sorry and I'll never do them again," Ralph said eagerly.

"Say three 'Hail Marys' for your penance and come again in a month. Say an act of contrition now while I give you absolution," the priest said dreamily.

A burden was lifted off Ralph's mind. In his joy he forgot to say the act of contrition and listened vaguely to the Latin words the priest mumbled hastily. He had read pious stories in which penances of several years and long pilgrimages were imposed on sinners who seemed saints in comparison with himself. He had made up his mind that he should at least have to walk several miles with pebbles in his shoes. He had once tried this for the short distance between Harcourt Terrace and Stephen's Green and his feet were terribly blistered. But three "Hail Marys", why, he could say them at once – he would say them now.

The priest closed the slide of the box with a jerk and Ralph was startled to wakefulness. He left the box cheerfully, knelt again before the high altar and said three "Hail Marys". He found himself after a few moments thinking of the ducks in Stephen's Green, and at once opened his prayer-book and read the thanksgiving after confession. It was very easy, he thought, to get forgiveness of sin; but then, between confessions hell was always open to receive him. He felt the fear of it come over him again and he tried to put the thought away. He had confessed and had said his penance and his soul was as white as snow. If he died now he should go straight to heaven. He would never sin again, so there would be no danger of hell for him.

He was a generous boy and liked to share his gifts. There was a little boy, of about his own age, who sold newspapers at the corner of Clarendon Street, who should, Ann often said, "go down to the depths" for his cursing. Ralph determined to tell him to avoid the hell with which Ann threatened him.

When Ann, who herself had been to confession to Father Eusebius, was escorting him home, Ralph stopped behind to talk to the newspaper boy.

"I've been to confession," he said insinuatingly.

"Garn!" the boy said, making a face.

"If you go, you won't to hell," Ralph said.

"Calling me names, are you?" said the boy, flushing fiercely. "Me go to hell, is it? Damme, I'll send you there quick!"

He hit out with his fists and Ralph was soon sprawling in the muddy street. The small boy laughed jeeringly.

Ralph struggled to his feet and hit out wildly. A well-directed blow on the left eye from the small boy again laid him in the mud.

Ann ran back to his help, slapped the small boy soundly on the cheeks and helped Ralph to his feet.

"Yah, yah, yah!" shrieked the boy, his hands stretched out from his face, thumb to nose. "Put a penny or a piece of raw beef to his eye, you old devil. It'll swell out in a minute," he shouted at Ann.

Ralph, white with pain and anger, tried to get at the boy, but Ann held him tight. His eye had already begun to swell and his right hand was badly cut by the fall.

"Keep quiet, you bad boy!" Ann said, wiping the mud off his hands. "This is a nice finish to your confession – falling into mortal sin the moment you come out."

Ralph flushed and stood still. A great fear came over him. He felt he was in sin again. On the way home Ann spoke all the time of his wickedness. Fighting was a sin at any time, but "just after coming out of confession is a black sin entirely". He heard her vaguely. He was running over in his mind the heads of the table of sins. "Quarrelling, fighting, hatred, anger and revenge" were all linked together in the table. He had committed them all. Five mortal sins all at once – enough to send five people to hell. If he died now he would undergo all the tortures. He tried to make an act of contrition, but his tongue was dry and he could not form the words. There was some sin that would never be forgiven – some sin against the Holy Ghost. It must be fighting just after confession. He should never be forgiven. He had read of sinners with hard hearts who could not pray. He could not pray and he felt his heart hard within him. No wonder Ann was angry with him. God was angry. His mother would be angry too, and his father. His father was not always angry when God was angry. It was all very queer. He could understand Ann and his mother; they never fought battles. But God often fought battles. In Old Testament stories he had read that God smote His enemies. Why was He angry with him now? He worked his brain with this thought and could find no answer. Ann said He was angry. Ann knew, and was always right.

When they got home Ann took him straight to the drawing-room, where tea was laid. There was special chocolate cake that Ralph liked, in honour of his first confession. His mother was shocked at his appearance. His hair was touzled, his clothes muddy, the blood from his cut had smeared his face, his eye was inflamed, swollen and discoloured purple and black. She clutched him to her and kissed him.

"What has happened? Was he run over?" she said anxiously to Ann.

"Fighting," said Ann, grimly.

His mother went pale. "And on his first confession day, too," she said sadly.

His father, who was reading in an armchair, looked up with a gleam in his eye.

"With low company, too," said Ann. "That bold little boy that sells newspapers at the corner of Clarendon Street."

"I hope you hit him back," said his father.

"I'm sorry I did," Ralph said, trembling.

"Sorry!" his father said sharply; "don't be a milksop."

"Oh, John!" Hilda said reproachfully. "Take him up and change his clothes," she said hastily to Ann.

Ralph tried to puzzle it out as he lay in bed that night. His mother said she was not angry, but she did not give him any chocolate cake. She was very sad and had cried silently by his bedside for a long time. Ann was angry and had threatened him with special torments in hell if he ever fought again. His father had come up when he was alone in the nursery and got him to tell the whole story of the fight. He was not angry. He merely smiled and felt Ralph's muscles, muttered, "Too much apron-strings," and said aloud, "I must get you boxing-gloves to develop your muscles." Yet God, who had fought more battles than his father, was angry, and Ralph was afraid. He cowered under the bedclothes when the lights were put out and said many acts of contrition. All at once he felt he was in hell and a devil like the newspaper boy, but more fierce, was raising his arm to strike him with a red-hot hatchet. He dodged the hatchet and struck the devil in the eye with his boxing-glove. The devil fell with a thud and Ralph felt a glow of satisfaction. A crowd of devils were rushing at him with raised pitchforks when he woke with a cry, a cold sweat oozing all over his body.

Chapter 2

NEXT MORNING ANN kept Ralph close to her side as they approached Clarendon Street. The newspaper boy was on the look-out and jeered when they came within earshot. Ann glared at him; Ralph walked by with eyes cast down. He flushed when the boy called out "coward", but did not lift his eyes.

"Don't look at them riff-raff," Ann said.

"Why, Ann?" he asked meekly.

"They lead you to ruin," said Ann; "besides, it's not for gentry to have dealings with common boys like him."

"Mayn't I tell him I'm sorry?"

"Cock him up indeed," Ann said angrily. "Say you're sorry to the likes of him! What's the world coming to at all?"

"But I must pray for him?"

"Aye," said Ann, gloomily. "You can pray for him if that'll do impudent scum like him any good."

On his way back from church, after a prolonged silence, he asked Ann, suddenly,

"Was St Joseph gentry, Ann?"

"He was and he wasn't," replied Ann, cautiously. "He was a carpenter by trade, and we all know that's not gentry, but I seen in a book once that he came of good stock, King David, no less. Not that I take much heed of them that claim to be descended from kings. Every O and Mac in Ireland says his ancestor was a king. Sure it's robbers half of them were. Maybe it was different with St Joseph. He might be like the O'Briens and have come of real kings."

"But there were saints who weren't gentry and we have dealings with them. There was one a beggerman."

"Aye, but then they were saints," said Ann, conclusively, "and not impudent young ragamuffins."

"Are you gentry, Ann?"

"There are many that say we were once, but long ago Cromwell took all our lands and castles and we're only poor labouring people now," Ann said with a sigh. "Don't be moidering me with any more questions now. You'll learn when you grow up that gentry is gentry and common people is common people."

"But things puzzle me so, Ann, and you know most things, not about boats and engines and French and things, but about most other things. There is Father Eusebius now. We have dealings with him. He is gentry?"

"Of course he is."

"But his father, old Donlon the tailor in Pembroke Street, is he gentry too?"

"Old Donlon, gentry!" said Ann, laughing heartily, "the old schemer! Why, he never even measured a gentleman in his life."

"Then, how is Father Eusebius a gentleman?" asked Ralph, triumphantly.

"That's as easy as easy," replied Ann, complacently. "He's a priest and every priest has a spiritual mark on him that makes him higher than the angels. And the whole world knows the angels is higher than gentry. Why, popes is higher than kings and queens, and they were only priests to begin with, and many of them came of the lowest of the low."

Ralph sighed. What was so clear to Ann was not always clear to him. However, he should know everything when he had grown up and become a priest.

He now looked forward eagerly to being a priest. His mother often told him he had a special vocation and that he should have a miserable life if he did not become a priest. He liked the idea of being a priest. Nearly all the saints of whom he had read were priests. They always had special graces and were on terms of easy familiarity with God; hell had no terrors for them. They were always triumphant in any attacks by the devil and saw beautiful visions. It was not quite the same now, of course, as in old times. One day Ralph had wished to give his coat to a badly clad boy who sat shivering on a doorstep. He remembered that St Martin of Tours had done that. Ann prevented him. "It was only in the old times saints did the like of that," she said. But they still saw visions. He read all about the appearance of the Blessed Virgin at Lourdes and hoped that one day she would appear to him. He couldn't understand why Ann did not wish to see visions. She had once seen a ghost, but said she was "fair frightened of it". Besides, one never knew, unless one was a saint, "whether it mightn't be a devil that would appear". When Ralph was a priest, of course, he would know how to discern a heavenly vision from an evil one. Ralph easily proved to Ann from the lives of the saints that quite young people, long before they were priests, had visions, but Ann said that the old times were different in that, too. There weren't as many bad people, heretics and Protestants in the world then as now. Ann didn't know why Protestants should have that effect, but it was so; she hadn't a doubt on the point.

Ralph had read all about Protestants in the history books his mother gave him, books written by good old priests specially for the young. He found it hard not to hate Protestants, they were so bad, always fighting and killing Catholics or persecuting them or telling lies about them. Martin Luther was a dreadful person, of evil life, who broke his solemn vows made to God and who lived in sin. Catholics were such a contrast; all were good and holy, and if they fought, it was always for the glory of God; if they killed anyone it was because of his wickedness. Catholics, especially priests, nuns, bishops and popes, were the children of pious parents and lived godly lives, while Protestants were all worldly, when not positively wicked. The worst of all were Catholics who rebelled against the Church. Protestants might be ignorant of the truth, but there was no excuse for Catholics who acted against the wishes of the Pope or the bishops. His special aversions were Henry VIII and Garibaldi: of the two Garibaldi was the worse. He dressed in a red shirt, "the devil's colour," Ann said, "and shut the Pope up in the Vatican, a poor prisoner, taking away his possessions." He had been given a novel by Sir Walter Scott in which the Protestants did not all seem to be bad, nor all the Catholics good. His mother told him that this was because Sir Walter Scott was a Protestant and, of course, Protestant writers could not be trusted. She warned him that this was so with most literature and that a good Catholic should always be on his guard against the prejudices and misrepresentations of Protestant writers.

Ralph thought it was a pity that so many of the writers of books that he liked were Protestants. He prayed often that they might become Catholics or that Catholics might write books like *Treasure Island*, and *Quentin Durward*, and *David Copperfield*. He asked Ann why there were no Catholic books so good as these. She was horrified. "Why, they're nothing but a pack of lies. None of them things ever happened," she said. "Catholics write true stories about Lourdes and St Aloysius and the like. I misdoubt me but a lot of them Protestant stories were invented by the devil."

"But my father reads a lot of them," Ralph said.

"There's no accounting for what men'll do," Ann said. "Anyway, your father knows all the Protestant lies. You're only an innocent child and don't know much, but he's grown up and has the sense not to heed what's wrong, it's to be hoped."

Ralph longed to be grown up. There were so many things which "grown-ups" might do that were forbidden to him. He would then read all the books in his father's study. He would walk through the streets without Ann's vigilant companionship. He was not now allowed to look into shop windows or paddle in the sands at Merrion when he walked there with Ann. Other boys, not older than he, were allowed to walk to and from their homes to the Jesuit school without a nurse. They were sometimes rude to him and called him "suck baby" and "apron-strings". If Ann were relieved of her duty of accompanying him on his walks there would be more chance of walks with his father. One could not speak to Ann of the colour of the sea, but his father was different and saw it sometimes pink as he did. Ann had ridiculed the idea. She said, "Everyone knew the sea was green and how could the colour of it change?" Then his father knew all about boats and could recognise them by their funnels, while Ann disliked talking of boats. "The mere mention of them makes me that sick," she said, "and reminds me of the time I crossed over to Holyhead, lying flat on my back all the time and almost wishing I was dead every minute." She was very disappointing, too, about telegraph poles and tramcars. She knew more about the saints than his father, but then there would be opportunities of hearing about these in the evenings when his father was having the mysterious meal which Ann called "a late dinner".

About three months after his first confession, on a beautiful afternoon in early July, Ralph and his father went by train to Dalkey and walked up Killiney Hill to the park. They sat on the grass near the monument. At their feet the bay stretched, bordered on golden sands, to Bray Head. The sea shimmered in the sunlight and small boats with spotless sails glided lazily over its surface. Near the sea at Ballybrack was a field of ripening oats, golden and red with poppies.

"And God made it all," Ralph said suddenly, his eyes fixed dreamily on the cornfield.

His father looked at him curiously.

"Father," he said, after a few moments' silence, "I shall be a priest."

"Rather young to make up your mind."

"I'm quite grown up now. I'm going on nine."

"Quite a man," said his father, gravely.

Ralph nodded. "You're not disappointed that I shan't be a soldier?"

"The little mother will be very pleased, anyway."

"But I want you to be pleased too, Father. You see, it's this way. I'm called. I feel that I should burn in hell if I didn't become a priest. It's a dreadful sin to resist a vocation. Besides, I want to keep others from hell, especially Jack Brady. The collector at Clarendon Street told me that is the name of the boy who knocked me down. I want to learn, too, all about God and how He made all these beautiful things. People don't see all the beautiful things because they are in sin. When I was in sin everything looked gloomy and grey and horrid. When I know all about God I'll tell it to Jack Brady and the rest and they'll go to confession and see all the beautiful things."

John O'Brien looked at Ralph wonderingly. "Where did you pick up all that? Does Ann see all these beautiful things?"

"Ah, that was a puzzle," said Ralph. "Of course, Ann is good, but the reason she doesn't see them is because she thinks too much of hell and of God as the just judge. I'm sure He is the best Father in the world and we know fathers are kind. If she loved without being afraid, then Ann would see the beautiful things. I'm often afraid, very much afraid myself, and I know."

"It is all very complex," said his father, gravely.

"Com... Yes, it does bother my head so," Ralph said, looking wistfully at the sea; "that's why I must be a priest. Then I'll know all about it."

"Perhaps," said his father, looking at him tenderly.

"Not perhaps, Father, of course I shall know then."

"You shall certainly know more than you do now," John O'Brien said, rising hastily and drawing Ralph's attention to a small yacht which was approaching the shore.

Ralph continued to attend the Jesuit school. He won an exhibition and a gold medal for Latin at the preparatory grade intermediate examinations. He worked hard, never thinking of prizes, especially in Latin, which he loved because it was the language of the Church. At first he was disappointed, on reading the Latin texts, that there was no mention of Christ or the saints or the Catholic Church. He was shocked by the tales of gods and goddesses. Father David, to whom he still went to confession, told him that these stories were not of real gods, only pagan myths. They were written before the light of Christianity shone on the world, but they often prefigured in a wonderful way the deepest Christian truths. Thenceforth he always read an allegorical Christian meaning into the pagan stories. Father Best, his Latin master, a lean stern Jesuit, ridiculed these ideas. "One reads these books," he said, "not for any light they cast on the Christian ideal, but because the stories were written in exquisite language. It is a waste of time," he said, "to worry one's head over foolish allegorical meanings." Ralph was deeply pained and produced a book written by a French Jesuit in which these allegorical meanings were traced out. Father Best became very angry.

"Drivel," he said. "That poor old man was past his work; and to think," he added meditatively, "that he was once a scholar."

Ralph was disturbed by this. Priests then could be mistaken in things. With much anxiety he consulted his mother on the point. She said that there was nothing to worry about. It was not a matter of faith and both views were tenable.

But Ralph found there was something to worry about, for the next time he ventured to give an allegorical explanation of Bacchus he got six strokes of Father Best's heavy flat ruler on each hand.

Ralph bore the punishment stoically and tried hard to keep back his tears.

"But," he said, with a break in his voice, "Father David, my confessor, says Father Dampier's is the right view."

"*Ne sutor ultra crepidam*," said Father Best, angrily. "Let Father David stick to his moral theology ... he may know something of that, but a Carmelite on the classics!" he laughed derisively. "The sooner you make up your mind, O'Brien, to study according to my method, the better for you." He shook his ruler menacingly. "I believe that Jupiter and Bacchus and the rest were demons, but I leave that outside the classroom door. You have to keep that preparatory medal, and get medals through all the grades. Virgil was a poet, not a writer of books of devotion for foolish old women. We must see Jupiter and Juno with his eyes when we read the Æneid, not with Father David's. Besides," he added dryly, "the examiners happen to be more pagan than Christian and we must keep up the reputation of the school."

The day nursery was now turned into a study and Ann's work had become nominal. She kept Ralph's clothes and looked after his room. Occasionally she read his schoolbooks. She shook her head over translations of the classics. "No good ever came of reading such wickedness," she said to Mrs O'Brien, with a sigh; "but then, I suppose, the clergy must know everything." She kept Ralph supplied with religious books from the Carmelite library, "to keep his thought away from the bad books he has to read at that Jesuit school." She consulted Father Eusebius on the subject. He shook his head and looked grave.

"Personally, I think the Jesuits go too far," he said. "A good Catholic has no need of pagan learning. All a priest really wants to know of the classics is to be able to read the missal and the breviary. The Jesuits, no doubt, are very good men, very good indeed. A very old order, that is, as years go. Four hundred years or so. Quite young, of course, in comparison with our own order, Ann. Blessed Elias founded the Carmelites thousands of years ago. Like all young people the Jesuits are – shall I say it? – a little vain and ape the ways of the world. In a few hundred years they will have settled down to steady ways. Bring Ralph to me and I will invest him with the scapular. It will be a safeguard against the wiles of the enemy – not that the Jesuits are the enemy; very good priests indeed there are among them – I mean against the wiles of the world. As you know, Ann, no one who wears the scapular is ever lost – it was a promise from heaven to our revered St Simon Stock."

Ralph's first communion coincided with an important school examination. He went to confession to Father David daily for some days before and gave much time to a course of reading he prescribed. It interfered with his studies and he did badly at his examination.

Father Best's eyes gleamed angrily. "What have you been doing, O'Brien? You cannot have studied hard," he said, fingering his ruler nervously.

"I'm to receive first communion in a few days," Ralph replied, "and I've had to go for instruction to Father David and read several religious books."

"Those friars again," Father Best said, pursing his lips. He shook his head hopelessly. "Having no learning they cannot appreciate its importance. Of course, first communion is important," he added hastily, "more important than the examination, but there ought to be a sense of order about things. He should have fixed your first communion for January – a slack time in class, when your mind would be more free. What did he recommend you to read?" he added curiously.

"Father Faber's *Precious Blood.*"

"Tawdry tinsel and sloppy sentimentality. His religion is as flabby as – however, it's no business of mine. I'd advise you, O'Brien, to choose a Jesuit confessor."

Ralph went back to his seat feeling rather depressed. It was so hard to please everybody. Only that morning his mother had said that Father Faber was a saint and *The Precious Blood* the most beautiful book that had ever been written. His mother was surely right. She was very holy and spent several hours each day in prayer and never got angry. Father Best was angry nearly half the day and, as far as Ralph knew, he never prayed. Father David too was holy. Ralph had often seen him say mass devoutly and kneel afterwards at the altar steps rapt in prayer. Besides, Ralph himself liked the book.

When he first began his preparation for communion he had asked Father David to explain "transubstantiation". Father David repeated the words of the catechism. Ralph asked how bread and wine were changed into the body and blood of Christ. The priest said that was a snare of the intellect and that he must accept the fact on authority; when he learned his theology he should know how. He had just begun to learn chemistry and he afterwards asked the Jesuit professor of chemistry if he know how is was done. Father Barton hemmed and hawed and told him to consult his confessor. Ralph said he had done so and repeated what he had said.

"Wise man," said Father Barton, laconically.

Father Faber did not explain it either, but then he wrote beautifully and was so certain that no doubt remained in Ralph's mind.

During the days preceding his communion he felt exalted. Ann and his mother impressed on him the greatness of the gift God was about to bestow on him – the gift of Himself.

As he walked back from the altar rails, with the particle still in his mouth, his soul seemed to be united with God. For a moment he had been conscious of the acrid taste of the somewhat stale particle, but he pressed his hands firmly together and repeated: "God in me and I in Him." He almost swooned when he knelt in his place. It was his first long fast. Yet he was not conscious of hunger. An ineffable sweetness filled his brain. He felt God permeate his whole being. Though his eyes were closed a bright light surrounded him. He felt passive and, like a wave of light, whole sentences of Father Faber's book passed through his mind. These were succeeded by the most tender words of the Song of Solomon. He was aroused from his ecstasy by the noise of the congregation standing up for the last gospel. He shut his eyes again, but he could not recall the vision. For the first time he felt hungry and weak. He opened his prayer-book and read feverishly the thanksgiving after communion. The words swam before his eyes and his thoughts wandered. He caught himself repeating an ode of Horace, that day's lesson for Father Best. At once he said an act of contrition and asked God to forgive him for forgetting His presence in his soul.

His mother, who knelt beside him, touched him on the shoulder, saying, "Come home now; you can finish your thanksgiving later."

In the church porch Ann gave him a flask of milk. He felt he ought not to take it so soon after communion, but his mother insisted on his drinking it. His mother kissed him and he burst into tears.

"I'm not good enough, Mother," he said, sobbing. "God has left me already."

Hilda soothed him and told him that it was not so, that He would dwell with him until He was driven out by sin.

At breakfast his father presented him with a new engine, in which he became absorbed. He arrived late at school in the middle of Father Best's lecture. When his turn came to construe he made several mistakes and was severely punished. At the first stroke of the ruler he remembered his communion for the first time since breakfast. Surely Father Best had forgotten?

"The other hand, O'Brien," he said. "Order and proportion," he went on, "are the great secret of life. The right hand again. *Age quod agis*. Even Father Faber ought to have known that the mind – although I doubt if he knew anything so sensible – that the mind must not be neglected. Lessons must be done, no matter what spiritual duty one has to perform."

Ralph felt indignant. "What a beast," he thought, the priest was to punish him the first day God took up His abode with him. He prayed silently that he might be a priest like Father Faber and Father David and not like Father Best. He recalled the scourging of Christ at the pillar and felt a glow of satisfaction at the thought that he was punished because he gave up the evening preceding his communion to prayer. He felt on familiar terms with God as he said in his mind, "Father, forgive him, for he knows not what he does."

Chapter 3

FOR MONTHS AFTER his first communion Ralph was harassed by the feeling that he had received unworthily. He had called Father Best a beast in his mind while yet the body of the Lord was physically within him. This was, he persuaded himself, a sure sign that he had been in sin at the moment of communion, else how could he have fallen so soon after? He had defiled the Lord and, in the words of Scripture, which he read over and over again in his catechism, had "eaten damnation to himself". He lay awake at night thinking of the terrible punishment that awaited him if he died, as so many people died, suddenly in bed. He worked feverishly during the day in a vain effort to forget his fears. Never had Father Best been so pleased with him. When it came to Ralph's turn to construe, the ruler was laid on the desk and the stern face of the Jesuit relaxed at some happy phrase.

"We must get O'Brien into the order," he said to the rector. "He's the best pupil I've had for many years and his other masters say the same. A bit sentimentally religious, but the noviceship would knock that out of him."

"His people are some of the Clarendon Street lot, I'm afraid," the rector said.

"Yes; and the boy goes to confession there, too. I believe he intends to be a priest. The Carmelites will do their best to get him. He would be wasted with them – the boy ought to be a scholar, not a pulpit wind-bag."

The more successful Ralph was in class the more miserable he felt out of it. He shirked going to confession. His mother wished him to go every month, and on the first Saturday he was taken by Ann to Clarendon Street. He made his preparation but was afraid to enter the confessional. How could he confess that he had called a priest a beast? He lingered in his seat, his head burning with a racking pain. He begged Ann to let him go home as he felt ill. No, he wouldn't go to confession first, he wanted to go home.

"I did my best with him," she said to his mother afterwards, "but he was that obstinate I could make no hand of him."

Hilda spent an anxious night. She prayed that Ralph should not fall into sin. She was at his bedside next morning before he got up. He had dreaded this interview. His mother had often told him of the heinousness of a bad communion. She would be horrified if she thought that he had made one. She questioned him closely. He would admit nothing, but that he felt ill. He would go to confession next month.

On the eve of the first Sunday of the next month Hilda accompanied him to the church. He tried to pray but could not. His lips were dry and his tongue clung to the roof of his mouth. He could not remember the words of the act of contrition. When he read it mechanically in his prayer-book, he had none of the inward glow he had so often felt in prayer. His mother had long since made her confession to Father Eusebius and was patiently waiting for him, fingering her beads in the pew beside him. Reluctantly he took his place in the queue by Father David's box. When it came to his turn to go in he was strongly tempted to run away, but he felt his mother's eyes fixed on him and he went in. As he knelt in the confessional he heard the muffled sound of Father David's voice talking to the penitent on the opposite side of the box. Five minutes passed by; ten – it seemed an eternity to Ralph. His forehead was wet with sweat, his shirt clung to his back, his hands were clammy. At last he heard Father David's voice raised, saying the words of absolution. Ralph's heart seemed to cease to beat as he heard the priest shut the slide on the other penitent. In a moment it would be his turn. He rose unsteadily to his feet. The tension was broken by the priest blowing his nose loudly. Ralph felt relieved, as if he had escaped some pending calamity. He opened the door quietly and walked out of the box as Father David opened the slide on his side.

His mother smiled at him as he approached her and murmured "good boy" as he knelt beside her. Would she smile if she knew that he was a lost soul? He longed to put his arms around her neck and kiss her, but he felt that if he looked at her she would see his sin in his eyes. She hated sin so much that she must hate him. He felt alone in the world. No one would know him or speak to him, not his mother, nor Ann, if they knew that he was damned.

He walked home in silence beside his mother. "Very good and recollected like a young saint," she told Ann.

When Ann called him on Sunday morning he was feverish and he had an attack of nausea as he dressed. He was so relieved when his mother decided that he was to go back to bed that immediately he felt quite well. He had been in an agony trying to devise some means of avoiding going to communion without arousing his mother's suspicions. When he had broken his fast and there was no longer any danger of his being asked to go to communion, he insisted on getting up for twelve o'clock mass.

"Sure he's that good he wouldn't miss mass for the world," Ann said to his mother.

At luncheon he was in high spirits and was delighted when his father suggested a walk round Howth Head. They took the tram at the end of Harcourt Street. From his seat on the top he saw Jack Brady playing leap-frog in Stephen's Green with other boys, ragged but seemingly happy. Ralph felt envious and wished that he was allowed to play with them. He looked longingly over the railings of Trinity College playing fields, their green undimmed by winter and now bright in a soft February sun. Ann had often told him Trinity College was a Protestant hole. It did not look in the least like a hole, he thought, and admired the graceful lines of the library and the engineering school. The gloomy Provost's House with its spiked gate had always fascinated him and today it looked less gloomy and dingy. As the tram passed the front of the College in College Green, his father, pointing to the statues of Burke and Goldsmith, said, "Trinity has something to be proud of, and Ireland also, in those two."

"But they were Protestants, Father. Ireland couldn't be proud of Protestants; and Ann says Trinity is the road to hell."

John O'Brien laughed. "Ann is a very narrow theologian," he said. "Poor Goldsmith in hell! One of the gentlest men that ever lived; and Burke, one of the noblest and most chivalrous."

"But Ann knows," said Ralph, looking at his father inquiringly, half startled at hearing Ann's authority questioned and half pityingly because of his father's ignorance. "She says all people but Catholics go to hell, and a great many Catholics too, if they don't go to mass and say their prayers regularly and receive the sacraments and live devout lives."

"Astonishing," said John O'Brien, musingly, "and Ann is a good woman who wouldn't hurt a fly herself. I shouldn't believe all Ann says about hell, if I were you. You'll find God is not so truculent as she thinks."

"Oh, I'm so glad," Ralph said, heaving a sigh of relief. "I was very sorry for Goldsmith since I read the 'Deserted Village'. You think he's not in hell?"

"Nonsense," said his father, with a smile.

As they changed trams at Nelson's Pillar Ralph looked with a newly awakened interest at the loungers on the steps, and especially at the old women and girls who sold flowers and apples. Perhaps Ann was wrong about them too. "Hussies" she called them. Ralph had looked it up in his dictionary but could not find the word. Ann, after much hesitation, explained it as "bold, bad women who were walking the straight road down to perdition". The more he thought on the subject the more it seemed possible that his father knew more about hell than Ann. He was always finding out new things about his father. He remembered that once he believed he did not know Latin, but one night when Ralph was in despair over a phrase in Virgil his father had at once solved the difficulty. He could repair a bicycle, too, and set right a broken-down engine. Of course he knew about hell. After all, what could Ann know about it? She didn't know how gas was made and his father knew all about it. His thoughts wandered back to his difficulty in regard to confession. As he mounted the steps of the Howth tram he made up his mind to consult his father about his first communion and his sinful thought about Father Best.

"How bright and gay everything is!" he said, laughing, as they passed through dingy Earl Street.

"It will be when we get out of these squalid streets."

"Oh, but it's glorious. It feels so good!" The mean streets to Fairview seemed to him to rejoice in the sun, even the mud flat at Marino seemed to reflect his joy, while beyond the sands at Dollymount the sea glittered.

As they walked by the cliff to the summit of Howth Head from the village he begged his father to tell him the story of the Castle, a gray

Norman keep which they had passed on entering the village. Grace O'Malley, the sea-roving queen of the west, had been refused hospitality in Howth. She plundered the Castle and carried off the heir captive, and ever since the Castle gates were open at mealtime and a place was always laid for any passing stranger who claimed a meal.

"She was a very sinful woman," said Ralph, sententiously.

"A very brave woman, too," his father said, smiling.

"But surely God punished her."

"We never know these things. There is a lot of give and take in God's dealings with people."

"Is it a great sin to call a priest a beast in your own mind?" asked Ralph, suddenly. It had been on his mind ever since they had begun to walk, but he had felt some difficulty in approaching it.

John O'Brien laughed. "I dare say many of 'em are." He saw that Ralph looked surprised. "What I mean is ...," he said hesitatingly, "that many of them do things that might make one, hastily and thoughtlessly of course, call them beasts. I shouldn't think it a sin in any case. Why do you ask?"

Feeling very much ashamed, with many blushes, Ralph told him what happened in class on the morning of his first communion and of his agony of mind since.

"Father Best was rather a beast, you know," his father said, frowning. "Not a bad sort in many ways, but rather a cold-blooded pig. That Jesuit training knocks the humanity out of most men. Don't worry, old man. You go to confession to Father David and you'll find he agrees with me. Father Best may know the classics, but Father David knows more about boys."

The sun was sinking on the short February day as they reached the summit. The Bailey Light twinkled faintly above a purple sea. A slight mist hid Dublin, but lights began to appear across the bay in Kingstown and Blackrock. John O'Brien walked rapidly in silence, a frown on his face, down the steep descent to Sutton, whence they were to take the tram for Dublin. Ralph had some difficulty in keeping up with him.

"Don't go so fast, Father," he said, panting, "your leg will get bad again."

John O'Brien slackened his pace. Ralph glanced at his face, which was lost in thought.

Ralph himself was busy readjusting values. He felt pleasantly tired, but his brain was active. The feeling of terror which had gripped his heart for two months had gone since this morning, but he was puzzled by his father's opinions. Father Best was a priest and therefore higher than the angels. Not Ann only had told him this, his mother had often said so and he had read it in many spiritual books. All priests were higher than the angels, yet Father Best spoke slightingly of the Carmelites and his father saw defects in Father Best. Father Best brought God down on the altar every morning, held Him in his hands and received Him into his body. Surely his father had forgotten this. But Father Best had forgotten it, too. What matter if the Carmelites didn't know the classics? Anyone could know Virgil who studied him. He was merely a poet, a very great poet, of course, but a pagan, one who didn't know God even. The Carmelites may not be classical scholars, but they too performed the wonderful mystery of the mass every day. Father Best should not have forgotten that....

"Your Aunt Mary lived there before she went to Canada," said his father, pointing to the convent of the Sisters of Charity which they passed on their way.

"That was a jolly fine thing she did on the Fraser river, risking her life to save the Indian at the breaking up of the ice. I read all about it in the annals of the Propagation of the Faith," Ralph said proudly.

"Yes, Mary is a good woman."

"A saint, Mother says," Ralph said eagerly.

"She wouldn't like to be called a saint. Do you know, Ralph," John O'Brien said, taking his son's arm and walking on, "that things have changed a good deal since Mary and I were children. There was not as much talk then as now among Catholics of saints and sinners. We never heard of the devotion of the nine Fridays, nor of St Anthony. I think it's all the convents that have sprung up since then that have worried the lives out of children. I never saw a nun until I was grown up, nor did Mary until she entered her novitiate. She never took to the small devotions of the convent. As soon as she got a chance, after she became a nun, she went off as a missionary. Father Duff and my mother taught us our catechism. My mother told us how our branch of the O'Briens had always been Catholic and had suffered bitter persecution in the penal times. It was in our blood to be Catholics, she said, and it would disgrace our name to give up the old faith. We went to confession and communion four times a year, to mass on Sundays and holidays and said our prayers night and morning. Mary once got hold of a life of St Aloysius Gonzaga and told Father Duff she was going to model her life on him. He told her not to be a fool, and when he looked through the book, called St Aloysius a little prig. I don't know how Mary got the idea of being a missionary. We used to play a good deal at being Red Indians; it was partly from that, I think, and partly from reading about missionaries in Parkman's books. He was a Protestant, by the way, so some good comes of reading Protestant books. But chiefly, I think, because she loved adventure. There was not much chance of any at Inniscar and she saw no other opening. When I joined the army she entered the convent. She said she moped almost to death while I was at Downside at school, that she couldn't stand home any longer. She has spent her life since doing good to others. She doesn't worry about the trifles that occupy the minds of most nuns and wouldn't think twice of calling Father Best a beast if she thought he deserved it," he added, with a smile.

"And she is a good Catholic?" asked Ralph, anxiously.

"She would die for her faith."

"Are you never afraid of hell, Father?"

"Never! I try to do my best, not that I always succeed. But I know that God will never take a mean advantage of me."

"I wish I could feel that."

"You'll grow out of Ann's fancies in time," said his father, laughing. "Come to me when you are in trouble – I'm a better theologian than Ann."

"But mother does not think as you do, Father," said Ralph, doubtfully.

"Your mother is the best woman in the world," his father replied gently. "You will always love her, I know, and serve her, but, except your Aunt Mary and a few others, women are timid. Your mother, now, could never stand the sound of a gun without putting her fingers in her ears. She is spiritually timid, too, and I am afraid she grows worse. It was nuns who were the cause of it," he said angrily. "She was brought up by them to live in terror of hell and model her life on St Aloysius and St Stanislaus. But you are a man and you mustn't be afraid of things. You will never be as good as your mother – still you must try to be good in a man's way. I've talked too much," he added, as they stood at Sutton corner waiting for the tram. "When you are older you will understand things better."

On their way home inside a crowded tram, Ralph reflected on his father's conversation. He closed his eyes tightly and did his best to imagine all the terrors of hell. The bright light and loud voices prevented any very vivid picture, but such even as he succeeded in imagining he was afraid of. He felt that he should be more afraid when the light was off in his bedroom at night. But then his father was a big strong man and he was only a boy. He had felt hurt at hearing the saints spoken of lightly by his father. He was sure that his mother would not like to hear St Aloysius called a prig. That was all very strange, too, about his Aunt Mary. His mother had painted such a different picture of her: called to the service of the Indians from her childhood, always listening for and obedient to the voice of God. It was all very confusing. No doubt he would understand when he grew older. It was a jolly walk anyway and his father was a good sort. He would try not to be afraid. He would be brave for his mother's sake and help her to be brave if she was timid. Yes, he would be brave like his father and his Aunt Mary.

On the following Saturday Ralph went to confession to Father David. After the preliminary prayer he said, "I called Father Best a beast in my own mind."

Father David guffawed loudly and then tried to pretend he had sneezed. "Excuse me, my child, it is the snuff," he said. "Anything else?"

"I called it him the day I received my first communion and I was afraid my communion must have been bad," Ralph said hesitatingly.

"Nonsense," said Father David, sharply. "Anything else?"

"No."

"Tell me some sin of your past life as matter for absolution. Don't let this trouble you any more. By the way, what happened that made you so bold ... so very bold?" He smiled broadly as he took a pinch of snuff.

Ralph told him.

"Ah, these Jesuits," he said, shaking his head sadly. "Of course they are an ornament to the Church, no doubt of that ... in the eyes of heretics and infidels at least. They have learning – pagan learning mostly, I'm afraid. One cannot handle pitch too much and not be defiled. I did some classics myself, but, thank God, I've forgotten them, '*Arma virumque cano*,' I'm afraid I remember very little now. But some of these Jesuits meditate on Virgil and Horace all through their lives. Poor St Ignatius never intended it. He must have many a sad hour in heaven. Fighting the world with the weapons of the world sounds well, but believe me, Ralph, it makes men worldly too. Twelve strokes of a heavy ruler on the morning of your first communion! For neglecting the pagan gods for a few hours when all your thoughts should be given to your soul! My dear Ralph, what we went in the Church is *sancta simplicitas*. It is disappearing fast, but we shall try to keep it at Mount Carmel, that is, with the Discalced Carmelites – unfortunately the Calced are a little touched by the vanity of the times. But the Jesuits! I pray for them, Ralph. No one is past praying for – Mary Magdalen and the penitent thief are saints in heaven today.... I should think he was a beast! By any chance you didn't say it out loud?"

"No, I just thought it."

"'Twas better perhaps. Discipline must be preserved, 'Render unto Cæsar, etc.' We must be obedient in class no matter how our teachers forget themselves ... within limits, within limits. To think it, however, in the circumstances, was, I should say St Teresa herself, I'm sure, would say it – a natural and holy resentment against impiety."

"You think then it wasn't a sin?"

"A sin! A sign of virtue rather, springing from an understanding of, and an appreciation of, holy things. It was a sign of your vocation, Ralph, a clear sign, I should say.... Have you yet made up your mind what order you'll join?"

"My father says that I mustn't decide until I'm through the senior grade examination."

Father David shook his head and took another pinch of snuff.

"There were none of these examinations in my time," he said, "and though I say it, we were none the worse priests for it. Putting ideas of the world into young people's heads, I call it. Signs by, there aren't near the number of vocations there used to be. The best priest we have, Father Tertullian, couldn't translate the mass, yet he can heal the body as well as the soul. Well, well, we must do our best to keep your vocation in spite of Father Best's antics. Have you any leaning now to the Jesuits, Ralph?" he said anxiously.

"No," said Ralph, gravely. "I want to be a priest and not a schoolmaster."

"Well said, my boy." Father David moved his head several times, smiling and rubbing his hands vigorously. "There speaks the true rearing of Clarendon Street."

"My mother used to say I was to be a Jesuit, but I think that now she prefers the Carmelites; my father is not very keen that I should be a priest. If I must be a priest he would prefer me to be secular, but he says he won't interfere – I want to be a Carmelite myself."

"Better and better," said the priest, beaming. "Sure I knew the grace of God and St Teresa would work in you. I often said to Father Eusebius, 'Let the boy alone. Father Best'll beat any liking for the Jesuits out of him.' And, now what do you like about the Carmelites, my son?"

"The habit," Ralph said, after a moment's thought, "and the sandals and the singing of the office; and Brother Giles who lights the candles is an old friend of mine. I knew him since I was quite small. All the priests are so kind, too. I don't know how to explain it," he added helplessly. "I always felt when at mass here that I should like to be the priest saying mass at the altar. Ann says that's a sure sign that God intended me to be a Carmelite."

"The ways of God are wonderful," said Father David, raising his eyes to the roof of the confessional. "But sure it would be queerer if all the saints of Mount Carmel didn't get hold of you, all the years you've been coming here. I often saw you when you were a baby with your eyes fixed on the altar. I'm sure the blessed saints were talking to you, you looked that happy. You must let me tell Father Prior – a secret of the confessional, you know – he won't speak about it. Don't tell the Jesuits either. You see nothing is decided until your father gives permission – I'll talk him round, you'll see. Won't it be a sell for the Jesuits, though?" he added, chuckling. "Say a special prayer every day to St Teresa to strengthen your vocation to be a Carmelite," he said as he was about the shut the slide.

"You forgot to give me absolution, Father," said Ralph anxiously.

"Well, well, to be sure and so I did. You told me a sin of your past life? Say three Hail Marys for your penance. I was that excited I forgot. Say an act of contrition now while I give you absolution."

Ralph felt happy as he knelt in front of the high altar making his thanksgiving. One day he should be a priest saying mass at that altar. He saw himself kneeling on the altar steps after mass in his brown habit and sandals. He would be very kind to penitents at confession. He had been foolish to be so much afraid of hell, which was intended only for bad sinners, and he should never be a bad sinner. St Teresa would be his friend. How was it that he did not think of her when he was in so much trouble during the last few months? All the saints of Mount Carmel would now be his friends. He thanked God for the special favour of giving him so unmistakable a vocation to be a Carmelite. It was wise of Ann to recognise it. What a holy woman she must be. She knew it even before Father David, who was a great reader of souls, Ann said.

Chapter 4

HILDA O'BRIEN SAT alone in her drawing-room. The faint brown wallpaper and faded Persian rugs made a becoming setting for her slender figure, clad in a clinging fawn-coloured tea-gown. The *Imitation of Christ* lay open in her lap. Her soft brown eyes, browner by contrast with the delicate paleness of her long thin face, were fixed dreamily on a tryptich hanging over the mantelpiece. It represented the gathering in of the wheat harvest on the left; on the right, a father in the midst of his family blessing bread for the evening meal; and in the centre, a priest breaking bread for communion according to the Greek rite. The hard lines of her firm mouth and chin relaxed as her thoughts wandered to Ralph. God often chose the common things of earth and made them instruments of His power and of His love. He had chosen Ralph, whom she had tended as a precious flower for the altar from his birth. God would accept, too, this offering of her son as an atonement for all the sins and imperfections of herself and of her husband. Tears welled in her eyes as she thought of him breaking bread – the day she received communion at her son's hands God would have given her the great joy on which her whole life centred.

In her absorption she did not hear her husband enter the room. He stood for a moment by the door and gazed at her tenderly.

"Praying, madonna mia," he said, with a smile.

"No, just thinking of Ralph," she said, smiling.

He laughed and stroked her hair. "Quite a new subject," he said, smiling with gentle irony.

"Don't laugh at me, John. It is quite serious this time."

He drew a chair towards the fire, sat down, and lighted a cigarette.

"What's the paragon up to now? More gold medals?"

"That too," said Hilda, smiling proudly. "Remember he finishes with the Jesuits today. We must decide what he is to do."

He looked thoughtfully at the fire. "There is another thing we must decide first, dear," he said, rising and taking a seat beside her. "Harvey's lease expires at Christmas. He doesn't intend to renew it. Inniscar will be on our hands. Shall we let it again or live there ourselves?"

"Let it, of course." Her eyes wandered lovingly around the room. "It would mean our leaving all this," she added with a sigh.

"We could brighten up Inniscar," he said, smiling. "I think, Hilda, we ought to live at Inniscar. I've been the worst sort of landlord, an absentee. Harvey cared only for hunting and took no interest in the people around. Since I was in Denmark last year my conscience has been pricking me. I saw what a lot of farmers could do for themselves if they were encouraged."

"But you are always helping the tenants."

"Yes, in the worst way, with money! I haven't seen them for years and don't know their circumstances. I probably have done more harm than good."

Hilda gazed at the crucifix beside her on the table.

"If it's a matter of conscience, I suppose we must," she said plaintively. "How I shall miss daily mass at Clarendon Street and the direction of dear Father Eusebius," she sighed deeply.

"I've no doubt Father Duff says mass and I'm sure he'll direct you all right."

Hilda smiled. She and her husband had been lovers all through their eighteen years of marriage, but she had long since made up her mind that he lacked spiritual feeling. It was a cross which she tried heroically to bear.

"Father Duff is, I am sure, a good priest," she said, "but no one could call him spiritual. Don't worry, however, John; if it is our duty we must do it." She clasped the *Imitation of Christ* tightly in her hands and said in her mind, "Accept this cross, O Lord, as an atonement for my many sins."

John O'Brien looked relieved. "Now about Ralph," he said. "I've been talking to him. He is still determined to be a priest."

"As if there could be any doubt on the point!" said Hilda, looking towards the tryptich.

Her husband's eyes followed hers and frowned. "The boy has been influenced too much, Hilda. Some day, when too late, he may find it out – then there'll be the devil to pay."

"John!" she interrupted him abruptly. Tears filled her eyes, her lips hardened and she moved the book nervously to and fro in her lap.

He winced. "Don't worry, little mother," he said, stroking her hair. "I'm a brute to say these things to you."

She smiled at him through her tears. "I know you don't mean them," she said, with a catch in her voice. "I can't bear," she continued in an excusing tone, "to hear holy things spoken of lightly. I wasn't really angry," smiling pitifully. "But Ralph's vocation is so clear to me; it is almost a matter of faith." With clasped hands she gazed abstractedly at the crucifix.

"I'm only an old blunderer," he said, rising and standing in front of the fire with his hands in his pockets, looking ruefully at the flame.

"Are you still keen on the Carmelites?" he asked after a minute's silence.

She stood up and leant her head against his shoulder.

"John, I'm very weak. You must be very gentle with me."

He put his arm around her and looked at her enquiringly.

"My life seems bound up with his being a priest," she said dreamily. "I think I should die if he hadn't a vocation. Thank God he has. But the thought of being separated from him is almost breaking my heart. It was charming to look forward to when he was young, but now that the time has come it is more than I can bear," she sobbed bitterly.

"Don't – don't, little woman!" he said brokenly. "Don't make me break down, too."

She removed her arm gently, leant with her hand against the mantelpiece and moved her lips in prayer. Her lips and face slowly hardened. "Forgive me, dear God, for these unworthy feelings," she said, turning again towards the crucifix. "This is the last time I shall give way to this weakness of the flesh. He is yours, to do with what you will."

John O'Brien gazed moodily at the fire. Suddenly his eyes brightened.

"Going to Inniscar may be a special providence after all!" he said slowly.

Hilda started and looked at him anxiously.

"Why shouldn't he be a secular priest in the Bunnahone diocese? He might be within a few miles of Inniscar. In any case he shouldn't be far off and you could see him often."

A dawning expression of hopefulness on Hilda's face was succeeded quickly by one of disappointment. She leant listlessly against the mantelpiece.

"No, John, I mustn't be selfish. It would be unfair to Ralph. Life on the secular mission is so difficult spiritually – so full of temptations."

"For that matter even the hermits were tempted," O'Brien said, laughing.

"Then – secular priests are – I'm sure they are all good holy men. But don't you think, John, that they are a little rough, a little wanting in manners?"

He laughed heartily. "Then Ralph can teach them. For that matter some of the Carmelites are a rough lot, too. Do you know, Hilda, the more I think of it the better I like the idea. It has always been my idea, too, by the way. Never mind the temptations – he will be all the greater saint for overcoming them – nor the lack of manners among the priests. St Peter himself was a fisherman. St Vincent de Paul was a secular priest and so was your favourite, St Charles Borromeo. If he must be a priest," he added, with a sigh, "I can see a very useful life for Ralph in the Bunnahone diocese. You are always looking for signs and miracles. Can't you see the meaning of having Inniscar thrown on our hands at this moment?"

"I must pray for more light," she said hesitatingly. "I cannot ..."

The entrance of Ralph interrupted her.

"That's the last of the intermediate exams over," he said, kissing his mother. "Father Best walked home with me. He's not a bad chap after all. He's gone in to see the Delahunts, but he'll come in for tea here later."

"Brought the medals home with you?" asked his father, dryly.

Ralph blushed. He had his mother's brown eyes, more deeply set, but with his father's ironic twinkle. He succeeded in conquering his shyness and had a flippant reply on the tip of his tongue, when his mother said, "Don't mind your father, Ralph, he's as proud of your medals as I am, not that one should be too proud of worldly distinctions. They are only dross."

"At four pounds an ounce," John O'Brien said. "We were just discussing you, Ralph," he continued seriously, "but I must tell you first that we are going to take over Inniscar and live there."

Ralph's eyes flashed. "That will be jolly," he said excitedly. "I can ride at last. Father Duff said he would give me the loan of his cob if I went to Inniscar."

"I'm afraid the riding will have to wait. You must begin your studies for the priesthood," his father said, looking at him keenly.

"That will be a still greater pleasure; won't it, Ralph?" said Hilda, taking his hand.

At his father's words he looked dejected, but his face set gravely when his mother spoke:

"I forgot, Mother, for a moment. Of course I shall be glad. I'm ready to begin at once."

Hilda patted his hand. "Would you be very disappointed if you did not become a Carmelite?"

"You would, Mother?"

"You must choose for yourself. Your father wishes you to be a secular priest."

Ralph thought for a while. "Years ago," he said, "I gave Father David to understand that I should become a Carmelite. Latterly I am not quite so sure. It is not so easy as Ann and Father David think to make out what God wishes one to do. I want to do it, if only I could find it out. I don't know much about secular priests. Neither the Carmelites nor the Jesuits think much of them."

"All the more reason why a zealous man should become a secular, then," his father said ironically. "He might win them some reputation."

"Oh, I'm not zealous," said Ralph, gravely, "but I want to do what's right."

Tea was brought in. "Chocolate cake!" said Ralph, "jolly good too! From the little shop in Grafton Street, I know by the look of it!"

"There would be no chocolate cake with the Carmelites!" John O'Brien said, munching a huge mouthful appreciatively.

"There would be a much better thing - prayer, and -" Hilda said, looking reproachfully at her husband.

"Yes, greasy fish. I lunched once at one of their houses. It was nearly a year before I ate fish again. I remember it still," he said, grimacing.

Ralph's face fell.

"You are not an ascetic," said Hilda.

"No, I'm not as fat as Father David."

"John, you are incorrigible. Speaking so to Ralph, too! You know it is due to their sedentary life."

"Too much oil," said John O'Brien, maliciously.

Father Best was announced. "Feasting the hero!" he said grimly, as he shook hands with Hilda.

"Sacrificing him to the Carmelites," said John O'Brien tragically, holding up the cake.

Ralph felt very uncomfortable and left the room with a muttered excuse.

"Surely not a Carmelite?" said Father Best, as he chose carefully a crisp scone.

"They are very holy men," said Hilda.

"Very," said the Jesuit, pursing his lips. "I admit it, my dear Mrs O'Brien. But is that all! These scones are very good – just rightly browned. A scone may be either a mass of hot dough or delicious. This is delicious. Have the Carmelites a monopoly of holiness? We have had a Jesuit saint or two," he said dryly, as he munched the scone.

Hilda blushed. "Ralph doesn't like teaching," she said hesitatingly.

"A horrid profession! I don't know why I like it. So many of our men don't," Father Best said, taking another scone. "But the Society of Jesus spreads its nets very wide – teachers, preachers, students, administrators, social workers, contemplatives, we have them all. Whatever a man has a special aptitude or taste for – there lies his work with us, provided, of course, it is good for him. It is a great resource, Mrs O'Brien, even in the spiritual life, to have many strings to one's bow. It's a restless age and men get tired of harping on the one theme, or get worried over their work. That chocolate cake is very tempting. May I have some? Thanks. Variety has its advantages in the spiritual life just as in food. The Carmelites now! Preaching, the confessional, the singing of the office sum up their energies. Their round of spiritual duties is almost as monotonous as their meals. The order suits many men undoubtedly. Many Carmelites are holy men, as you say. A certain type of man likes the food and the life. Now Ralph is what I call a prober. He worries a difficulty to death. He'd get on the nerves of the whole Carmelite order in a month and would himself be miserable in three. Let him come to us, Major. He'll find his metier in a short time, or we shall find it for him."

Mrs O'Brien's lips hardened. She disliked Father Best's reflections on the Carmelites and wished to close the discussion.

"I fear my husband has other views for Ralph," she said dryly. "It would suit us best if he became a secular - if it suits him." She made the plunge hesitatingly, more from the desire to counter Father Best than from conviction.

Father Best flicked some crumbs off his trousers with much care.

"A secular," he said. "I shouldn't have dreamt it! Why this change of front?"

John O'Brien explained. "And in the Bunnahone diocese!" the Jesuit said regretfully, his set, machine-like face becoming almost human. "I am very fond of the boy. Perhaps, because I slapped him so much," he said awkwardly.

Hilda was moved by the priest's evident emotion. He might be a good chap, as Ralph called him. She smiled at the incongruity of applying the term to Father Best, who had regained control of his features and was looking at John O'Brien cynically.

"You want to make a bishop of him, I suppose?" he said, snapping his lips.

Hilda blushed. The thought had occurred to her within the last few minutes. She had imagined Ralph in episcopal dress. His tall well-knit figure and finely cut features would look well in a *cappa magna* - much more striking than in the brown habit of the Carmelites.

John O'Brien laughed heartily. "I don't think Ralph is made of that timber. Besides, he's not even a curate yet. His mother hasn't quite taken to the idea."

"If Ralph agrees," Hilda said decisively. "I shall see more of him, and ... there will be the variety Father Best values so highly."

"With a difference, an important difference," the priest said grimly. "With us the variety would be made for him; on the secular mission he makes it largely for himself."

"Ralph may be trusted to use his discretion wisely," Hilda said primly.

Father Best shrugged his shoulders. "We believe in a leading rein and curb. However, I prefer Bunnahone to the Carmelites. If Bishop Devoy is still there when Ralph is a priest he'll get enough of the curb. He may come to us yet," he said meditatively, "if we can catch him at the right moment."

"He is not a young tiger," said Hilda, bridling.

"No," Father Best replied, smiling. "He is only a boy with brains, a logical mind, a minimum of experience of the world and a singularly winning disposition – a doubtful equipment for a priest, except in the Society of Jesus."

"Oh, he'll muddle through all right," said John O'Brien, uneasily. "He's straight anyway."

"He might break under the curb...." The priest stopped short. "But you know what you are doing; you know Bunnahone well," he added hastily to John O'Brien.

"Very little, since I was a boy. The bishop I've met. And, of course, Father Duff is an old friend. We see him here often."

"A fine old farmer, a shrewd man of the world, too. Do you know Sheldon?"

"Have only heard of him."

"Get him to take an interest in Ralph. Some of the others are a queer lot. I mustn't let my tongue run away with me. Imagine Ralph curate to Molloy! The Holy Ghost does work through some strange instruments. Forgive me, Mrs O'Brien," he said, turning to Hilda and speaking with unwonted gentleness, "I'm only an old bear, and a disappointed one at that. It makes me grumpy and gloomy. I hoped Ralph would come to us. But one never knows. It may be all the better in the end. There's plenty of work for a good priest in Bunnahone, God knows."

Meanwhile Ralph sat at the desk in his study, Cardinal Manning's *Eternal Priesthood* open in front of him. His eyes were on the book but he had ceased to read. It's the priesthood that matters, he thought, not whether one is a Jesuit or a Carmelite or a secular. Father David would be disappointed if he became a secular priest. But his father would be pleased. It was hard to please everybody. Impossible, indeed, he thought with a puzzled frown. He would rather please his father. Since his talk with him on that walk to Howth Head many years ago his father had been a great help. He understood boys so well, better than his mother or Father David, better even than Father Best, and he was pretty good. St Teresa would understand. There were so many things he could do to promote God's honour and glory on the secular mission. The children in the schools! To help them would be holy work. Then, too, his father had spoken so much lately on the backwardness of the farmers. Priests often took an interest in people's temporal affairs as well as in their spiritual. He had read of what some Belgian priests had done to further the co-operative movement. He would be able to help in working out his father's ideas. They were religious ideas really, springing from brotherhood and mutual help. As a Carmelite he could not help in this work. He would always be attached to the Carmelites and reverence them. Father David would be sure to pray for him.

His thoughts wandered back over the years since his first communion. He would be seventeen in a few days and he had as yet done very little for God. It was disappointing that he had advanced so little spiritually. Spiritual dryness was a trial of the saints, Father David had so often told him when he complained of aridity of soul. But he was not a saint. His difficulties, too, in regard to temptations and doctrine were all unsolved. Father Best and his other teachers were definite in their solution of knotty points in his secular studies. But Father David was vague and unintelligible when questioned in regard to spiritual difficulties, or put him off to the future, until he should have read theology, or had become a priest, when he should understand everything.

It must be wonderful to read theology, the science of God. Then he should know why God had to be so often just and had to punish people, why He could not be always merciful. It was all very mysterious. Yet God wished to save all, and he, Ralph, was to be one of His special instruments in the salvation of souls. It was a high vocation and he must try to be worthy of it.

No, it was not possible so many were lost as Ann thought. She did not understand about invincible ignorance, which saved many outside the visible Church, provided they did not die in actual mortal sin. What a pity so many learned men were carried away by pride of intellect and would not submit to the teaching of the Church. There was an office in Rome, Father David had told him, called the Curia, where every doubt could be solved. Learning was always a snare. Yet it was rather surprising that learned men could be so foolish. They did not shirk hard work. They devoted so much time to an edition of Sophocles or to the finding out of a star or to some wonderful invention, all difficult, and God was so easy to find. He was in every flower and in a night of stars. Heaven was so beautiful a thought and hell so certain. He smiled as he thought of Ann's hell with its pitchforks and harrows. It was real fire for all that, and lasted for ever. But the pain of loss was worse even than the torment of fire. To be shut out for ever from the glory of God and the infinite happiness of heaven was a dreadful thought ... though it was so easy to know of God and heaven and hell, yet it was not so easy to save one's soul. Salvation must be worked out with fear and trembling. A priest had many special helps and it would be glorious to save even one soul besides one's own. It was a wonderful thought; he might be the means of saving ten, or a hundred or more. Nothing was comparable to a soul, the image and likeness of God. The whole world he knew was as nothing compared with it; the inspired writings said so, but that he could easily have known for himself.

He must make up for all his wasted years. He would do his best to be everything that Cardinal Manning demanded of the good priest....

"Is it asleep you are, Master Ralph?"

He rubbed his eyes and looked round. Ann was standing beside him.

"Them examinations," she said fiercely. "It's little good they do anyone. Tired to death you are and worn to skin and bone." She wiped some dust off the mantelpiece with the corner of her apron.

He shut *The Eternal Priesthood* and put it back on a shelf. Ann faced him, her arms akimbo.

"Your mother has just been telling me that it's a country priest they're going to make of you."

"It's not quite settled yet."

"Isn't it though. She's given in. She was the only one that was true to the Carmelites, not that she was very true to them either. I wash my hands of the whole of it – it's enough to make the blessed St Teresa turn in her grave."

"We all love the Carmelites, Ann."

"A nice way to love them, indeed! To turn your backs on them! What'll Father Eusebius say? and Father David? The hearts will be broken in them."

"They will understand."

"A saint out of heaven, with all his knowledge, couldn't understand it. It's that lean Jesuit, I doubt, that done it all. I never could bear the look of him – may the Lord forgive me for saying it of a priest. Jealous of the Carmelites they are."

"He had nothing whatever to do with it. My father –"

"Your father, is it? I must say I thought better of him. Led away by his mocking ways, he was; may the Lord forgive him!" She rubbed her eyes with her apron.

"To think of living down in the country! Nothing but muddy roads and green fields and trees that would frighten you in the night with their wailing, and leave the grand streets of the town, and nothing but a candle or two in a bare country chapel, instead of all the light and grand music of Clarendon Street!" she said, sobbing.

"Don't cry, Ann," he said gently. "You were born in the country, and you often told me such nice stories about it and said what a beautiful place it was."

"That was when I wasn't thinking of going back," she said, drying her eyes. "I thought I'd never leave Clarendon Street, but I know my duty. 'We would be glad to pension you off,' said your mother. 'And who'd look after your house, ma'am,' said I, 'and keep them other hussies of servants from misbehaving themselves, and keep the whole country from robbing ye? Sorra foot I'll leave you, ma'am,' I said, 'until Master Ralph is a priest and have a house of his own. Then he'll want me more than you do, and that's saying a good deal. It's play away entirely with him, the country people would; they're so cute and scheming, and he that innocent, unless he had me near him to tell him a thing or two.' Sorra word she had to answer, but she pressed my hand. 'Though I'm against the whole plan, ma'am,' I said, 'it's some consolation to me, and it must be to you too, ma'am, that when he has to leave you and set up for himself, that he'll have me to look after him.' 'You're very good, Ann,' she said, and we left it there. Run away now and make yourself decent for dinner – it'll be on the table in a few minutes – and leave me to settle up the room."

Chapter 5

IT WAS SETTLED that Ralph was to have a long holiday until the family moved to Inniscar, when he should go to the Bunnahone Seminary preparatory to going to Maynooth for his final training for the priesthood.

It was practically the first time for nine years that he had been free from the restraint of lessons. His Jesuit masters had been exacting and had kept him hard at work even during holidays. He now put his school books on their shelf and solemnly resolved not to open one of them until after Christmas.

He worried himself out of a night's sleep over his promise to Father David to enter the Carmelites. He mentioned the matter next day to his father, who looked at him quizzically.

"Look here, Ralph!" he said. "Let your soul rest for the next six months - put it on the shelf with your schoolbooks. Try to remember that a few hundred millions of us in the world have souls, too. If we all worried over them as you do nothing would get done."

It was a glorious summer with hardly a drop of rain in July or August. Every day there was something to do: golf at Dollymount, where he got a fresh breeze off the sea even on sultry days; long walks up the Dublin mountains, with delightful lolls, flat on his back in the heather. Once, on the Three Rock mountain, he thought he heard the fairy music he had read of in some old tale. He read aloud to his father old Irish ballads or O'Grady's *Flight of the Eagle*. For weeks they tracked Red Hugh's flight through the Wicklow mountains and northward to the Boyne. One day they got lost in Glenmalure, finding their way after midnight to a lonely farmhouse where they got shelter for the night.

"The boy has changed for the better so. A little roughing has done him good. He has become a boy at last and is no longer the old man he used to be. He is making a boy of me again," his father confided to Hilda when they arrived home.

After that they did not go so far afield, but there were rambles to Poul-a-phooca and never-to-be-forgotten explorations of Dowth and New Grange.

Ralph was fascinated by these underground temples and traced the circles and the spiral ornament in the gloomy caverns, candle in hand. He insisted on going next day to the museum to see the Celtic ornaments. "All the work of Irish speakers," an enthusiastic attendant said.

"Why don't we speak Irish, Father?" Ralph asked on his way home.

"Rather a useless language, I should think. No one speaks it now but a few of the peasantry in the west."

"But the O'Briens must have spoken it once?"

"And were glad to give it up," said John, carelessly. "Ask Ann about it; she speaks it, I believe."

Ann reluctantly admitted that she knew it once. "It's a language only fit for spalpeens, it's that coarse and rough," she said. "No respectable person would be heard talking it."

"Then how do you come to know it?" Ralph asked gravely.

"My father and mother never spoke anything else, God rest their souls," said Ann, uneasily; "they didn't know any better, poor people! It's proud they were when I learnt the English at the national school. Since I went into service I never spoke a word of Irish, thank God, nor never heard a word of it these twenty years past. A hard job it was, too, to get me out of it at first. The schoolmaster put a tally stick round me neck and put a notch in it every time I spoke a word of the Irish. On Friday I got a hard slap of a sally rod on the hand for every notch. I cried enough over it at the time, but it's glad I am since."

Ralph wasn't convinced. It was hard to believe that people who made the beautiful things in the museum spoke such a barbarous tongue. He hinted this to Ann.

"Most likely them things were made in Johnson's in Grafton Street. No person I ever knew that spoke the Irish could make the like of them; hard set they'd be to mend an old gate, let alone make them grand things. It's joking you the man was, Master Ralph."

One evening his father took him to a language meeting in the

Rotunda. "A cousin of ours is to speak – a clever fellow, but wasting his time in trying to get the Irish language spoken again. The whole thing will bore me, but Dillon wrote asking me to go."

The immense round hall was packed. Ralph had never been at such a big meeting before. "Three or four thousand people," his father said. On all sides men and women spoke in a strange tongue, excitedly and with many gesticulations. At the few meetings Ralph had hitherto attended the audience sat solemnly silent, but here all was movement. Ralph listened eagerly to their speech and thought it wonderfully soft and beautiful.

Loud applause broke out as a few people emerged from a side door leading to the platform. The audience rose to its feet and shouted vociferously. A white-haired old priest was moved to the chair. When he rose to speak applause broke out again.

"It's a great night for Father Dan entirely," said a man near Ralph. The priest stretched out his hand for silence. There was an expectant hush throughout the hall, as at the consecration of the mass in Clarendon Street.

"Thank God I have lived to see this day," said the priest, in a low, broken voice, which, however, seemed to penetrate to every part of the hall.

"Who paved the way for it but Father Dan?" shouted a voice from the gallery.

Loud cheers again broke forth.

The old priest's eyes gleamed, and with an effort he conquered his emotion. His voice rang out clear and resonant in an eloquent defence of the Irish language.

Ralph rose to his feet with the crowd when the priest sat down and shouted until he was hoarse. The priest held up his hand in vain for silence. Men stood on seats and waved hats and sticks. Several women wept aloud. Ralph brushed away the tears from his eyes and looked at his father shamefacedly.

John O'Brien was smiling. "Taken the fever, Ralph?" he said in a low voice.

"It is a beautiful language," Ralph said, blushing, "and I am an Irishman."

"Well, so am I. I even remember one Irish word, '*ráméis*'. I believe it means nonsense. That's what Father Dan's speech would be called by most Irishmen."

Ralph shook his head incredulously.

The priest still motioned for silence. The audience settled down slowly.

It was some minutes before the next speaker, Ralph's cousin, Charles Dillon, could begin. He was greeted with deafening applause. He was short and broad-shouldered. His face had a delicate pallor, intensified by shining black hair worn rather long. A long moustache concealed his mouth. Men would call him ugly. His nose was broad and flat and his forehead bulged. Even in repose, as he waited for the cheers to cease, his eyes glowed and sparkled and one forgot the ugliness of his features.

In a hoarse, even tone he began, "Cheering is unseemly tonight. We must respect the dead. This is the wake of the English language in Ireland."

"It is speaking at its own funeral," said John O'Brien, joining in the general laugh. "A born actor like his father," he added grimly.

Dillon sketched briefly the history of the Irish language and then launched into a fervid appeal for its preservation. By nature and tradition it was the only fit vehicle of expression of the Irish mind. It was their duty tonight to help on the movement that would make it the living tongue of every man, woman, and child in Ireland. With eyes that burned like coals and an eloquence torrential in its swiftness, glowing with vivid metaphor, biblical in the force and strength of its denunciation, he attacked the various influences now at work to kill the language: the government, the educational system, the Church, the ignorance and apathy of the people.

The audience was spellbound. Ralph thought of the Hebrew prophets. Surely Dillon was a prophet. The large white teeth of the speaker gleamed through his black moustache as they seemed to grind out the harsh staccato sentences that seared as they fell.

He sat down exhausted. All eyes in the vast audience were fixed on him as he sat, his elbows on his knees, his hands pressed against his eyes. There was the long sigh of a multitude drawing a deep breath in unison and the crowd woke as if from a trance. There was an indescribable scene of cheering and shouting and weeping. Ralph was almost dazed. A sharp knock on the head from a chair which his neighbour waved aloft frenziedly awakened him. His eyes at once sought Dillon, who was chatting easily with Father Dan Murray, seemingly indifferent to the excitement in front.

"Let us get out of this or you'll be waving a chair, too," said John O'Brien, dryly.

"But it was a wonderful speech, Father."

"Undoubtedly. He pulled out all the stops."

They threaded their way with difficulty out of the hall. A group of young men in the courtyard were lustily singing, "A Nation Once Again." The O'Briens were among the first to leave the meeting. As they walked down O'Connell Street the wide pavements were thronged. Under the portico of the Post Office a number of young men and girls were singing a low music-hall song.

"They will soon sing nothing but Irish songs," said Ralph.

John O'Brien laughed. "Dillon has a harder row to hoe than you think. All these people," indicating the passers-by, "are either indifferent or hostile. Even the crowd at the Rotunda will be less enthusiastic tomorrow. Emotion is a skittish thing and shirks sustained work. Irish people love an eloquent speech. I confess that Dillon moved me a little for a moment. The more impracticable the idea the more we cling to it. We talk and talk of great plans, and go to bed and dream that we have carried them out. Nothing will convince us that we haven't done them when we awake. The great majority of these people at the Rotunda will believe that they have done their duty by the language in a riot of emotional shouting and the breaking of a few chairs. Tomorrow they'll feel the pride of a great achievement. In a week they'll have forgotten all about Dillon and his language movement and will be applauding Little Tich equally vehemently at Dan Lowry's music-hall. I have been at so many enthusiastic meetings in my day."

"But this is different," said Ralph, eagerly. "I feel it is different. I feel it all through me somehow. How earnest all the people were!"

"Well, we can only be young once," his father said, taking his arm. "I'm glad in a way that you are interested. It will take you out of yourself. You'll have some other preoccupation besides your soul. That's a good thing."

"I shall get some Irish books tomorrow and make a beginning. I am certain that most of the people at the meeting who don't know Irish will do the same."

"Hum, your old father won't, anyway," his father said, making a wry face.

"Oh, I'll convert you, when I find out all the beauties of the language," Ralph said gaily.

On the following day, on their way to Dollymount to play golf, Ralph and his father met Charles Dillon in the tram, golf clubs between his knees.

"I am shocked, Charlie, at your playing such a Saxon game," said John O'Brien, making a grimace.

"One cannot play hurley always. Besides golf's not Saxon, it's Scotch, and that is Irish a few generations removed," Dillon said, with a humorous twinkle.

"How far do you believe in it all?"

Dillon became serious. "Absolutely," shutting his teeth with a click. "I saw you at the Rotunda last night – that meeting was the basis of a strong movement."

"Froth," said John O'Brien, sententiously.

"On top, no doubt, but there is something beneath this time."

"There always is – in the enthusiast's imagination," John O'Brien said dryly.

"I shall learn Irish," Ralph said, blushing; "the meeting was splendid."

"A convert from the house of the scoffers!" Dillon said, looking at John O'Brien triumphantly. "Of course," he continued gravely, "one talks a lot of nonsense at meetings. I don't mean to, but I get carried away. I feel a sorry mountebank for some hours after a big speech; yet, apart from the accidental emotional trimmings, I mean all I say." His eyes glowed as he turned to Ralph.

"What moved you to become one of us?" he asked eagerly.

"The meeting last night," Ralph said timidly. "I finally decided then – I had been thinking of learning Irish for some time."

"A fit of sentimental emotion – you'll find it will pass away," said John O'Brien, laughing.

"Don't mind your father's cynicism, Ralph – I may call you Ralph? – it's not even skin deep. Why," he continued musingly, "every great movement in history was founded on emotion. Men's minds lead them astray, but their hearts bring them right."

"Seriously. You don't think anything will come of last night's meeting?" asked John O'Brien.

"There's a first fruit," said Dillon, nodding at Ralph. "This country is just ripe for such a movement. People, the thinking ones, are growing sick of merely destructive politics. We've got to construct...."

"Ah, there I agree with you," John O'Brien interrupted. "That is why I'm so interested in Randal Clayton's ideas."

Dillon's eyes again gleamed humorously. "I was right in saying your cynicism was only skin deep. You are infected with Claytonism. Why he is an idealist if ever there was one."

"A practical man," said John O'Brien, decisively.

Dillon laughed. "I agree. But all really practical men are idealists. No one ever did anything worth doing without vision. Clayton has his feet on solid earth, but his head is among the stars for all that. I'm staying with him. He may possibly come for a round to Dollymount today. He is deeply interested in the language movement."

"I can't imagine Clayton with a primer in his hand."

"No. But he caught hold of the idea at once. At the back of all his preaching of better farming, better business, better living, is his desire that the people should have some *morale*, some backbone. He doesn't want an Ireland with a well-filled belly merely. He wants an Ireland with an imagination, a mind and a will."

"I shouldn't count on Clayton," John O'Brien said; "he's up to his neck in his own industrial work. Stick to Ralph. When he is a priest he may help you, if he hasn't given up the fad by then, or they haven't knock it out of him at Maynooth."

"A priest!" Dillon said, laying down his club as he was about to strike his ball and addressing Ralph. "What put that idea into your head?"

Ralph considered the question gravely.

"He has been reared on the idea by his mother and Ann Carty," John O'Brien said, laughing. "I hadn't a look in. Nor, I think, had he."

"Ever since I was a child I have wanted it," Ralph said, looking at his father reproachfully.

"Very interesting," Dillon said, gazing out at the sea beyond the sandhills; "if only we had all the priests in favour of the language we'd sweep the country into our net. I had a notion of becoming a priest myself once – I didn't. My mother was dead against it. You know her, Major. She'd cut off her right hand rather than eat meat on Fridays or miss mass, but the idea of a son of her becoming a priest was unthinkable. She had a theory, or she developed it at the time, that the priesthood was a special privilege conferred on the lower classes to make them contented with their lot. We had just had the parish priest to dinner, an awfully jolly chap, who sopped up gravy with a knife. She drew a lurid picture of the certain degeneration of my manners in Maynooth. She said she respected priests on the altar, of course, but one could not have them to dinner except once a year or so, and then only by screwing up one's courage."

He laughed boyishly, stopped abruptly, frowned, and said gravely, "I'm glad Mrs O'Brien has broken away from that tradition. It doesn't do much credit to Catholics of our class. It's splendid of Ralph to wish to become a priest. He might preach in Irish yet, and who knows what he may do in Maynooth to help on the movement?"

"I shall do my best," Ralph said eagerly.

"You'll find that a much harder nut to crack than converting me," said John O'Brien. "It would take a miracle to get the priests to take up Irish. All the priests that I know scoff at it."

"That is true, unfortunately," said Dillon, moodily. "A few, like Father Dan Murray, are enthusiastic, but the majority are against us or indifferent. You have a great work before you, Ralph. Put your back into it."

Ralph felt elated. Here was work worthy of a priest, he thought, as he walked along in silence, the fresh sea breeze blowing in his face. He built castle after castle in the air of a glorious future for Ireland, when every one would speak Irish and be peaceful, happy and religious.

As they sat down to lunch in the club-house, Dillon said to a man who had just entered, "Hallow, Clayton! You're late. Fortunately I met the Major and we had a round."

"I'm so sorry," Clayton said shyly, taking a seat beside Ralph. "I was delayed at the last moment."

"My son," said John O'Brien.

"Has Dillon been enrolling you in his language movement?"

Clayton asked, smiling.

"How are things going? Have you started a society yet?" asked John O'Brien.

"Not one. I have held a great number of meetings. The people are suspicious. At one meeting I was asked what I was making out of it. With a temper that gave me the lie I said 'patience'. I got a laugh but that was all."

"I can't make any promise," John O'Brien said, "as I don't know how the people may take it, but we may possibly make a start at Inniscar. I have a dairy farm of my own there, a hundred cows or so, that might be a nucleus. I have been in correspondence with Father Duff, the parish priest, and he is sympathetic – he's a shrewd farmer, too, and has a good deal of influence."

"Splendid," said Clayton, his eyes lighting up. "The co-operative commonwealth may come true yet, after all." His eyes took on a far-away expression. "Increased wealth is but a small part of what co-operation may do for Ireland," he said, "though that in itself is much. A comfortable hearthstone offers some scope for the growth of a soul."

He chatted pleasantly with Ralph of golf, of his school. When he heard that Ralph intended to become a priest, he said, "This is splendid news. No one has such influence in Ireland as a priest.

"I'm afraid I was letting my mind dwell on the priest as a possible co-operator," he added, laughingly, to John O'Brien.

"Poor Ralph!" John O'Brien said. "You have chosen a burdensome life. What with the Church ordering your life, Clayton pulling you on one side and Dillon on the other, you will have a sorry time."

Chapter 6

JOHN O'BRIEN'S TENANT gave up Inniscar some time before the termination of his lease, and by the first week in December it was ready for occupation again.

Hilda had never seen the place, which had been let before her marriage, and had visions of some pokey, damp, uncomfortable house which, however, she was prepared to put up with from a sense of duty. She had offered to go down and superintend the fitting up, but her husband said that it was unnecessary. The house was fully furnished; any small things she needed could be got when they lived there. The Harveys, if they neglected the people, had been lavish on the house and grounds, which they had maintained in a style that he could not attempt.

The home coming was fixed for the first Monday in December. There was much excitement among the Inniscar tenantry. No O'Brien had lived at the "big" house for twenty-five years, and speculation was rife as to what the new people would be like. The older tenants remembered John O'Brien as a "fine strappin' lad before he went soldiering". "With that kind of pride in him," Larry Gallagher, an old dependant, said to a sympathetic audience in the bar of Darcy's public-house at Bunnahone, "that all the O'Briens had; sorra sign of it one could see, only you know well 'twas there."

"Sure there's no wonder in that," said Mrs Darcy, leaning her ponderous body over the counter, "and the whole world knowing that they came down from the flood."

"Aye, and before it," said Larry, importantly. "I often heard my father say that there's a pedigree of their descent from Adam himself."

"Do ye think now, Larry, they'll be dealing in them stores in Dublin or London or the like?" asked Mrs Darcy, anxiously.

"Indeed, and I'm sure they won't," said Larry, emphatically. "Sure I remember in the old mistress's time when anything was wanted in the house she'd come to me with a long list and she'd say, 'Put the grey horse to the car, Larry, and go into Darcy's for them things.' Your father-in-law was alive then, ma'am, God rest his soul, and you were only a slip of a girl, not thinking of being married to Mr Darcy. I don't doubt Master John'll remember all about it and get the new mistress to do the same. I don't know much about her, never having set eyes on her, but Father Duff says she comes of decent stock and is a very holy woman."

Mrs Darcy sighed hopefully. "It's great doings entirely ye are having at Inniscar tonight, I believe," she said, pouring out a glass of whiskey for Larry.

"The best of health to you, ma'am," he said, bowing to her as he raised the glass to his lips. "The likes wasn't seen for many a long day. A big bonefire right fornint the gate, twenty loads of turf and a couple of gallons of paraffin went in the making of it. The whole country from far and wide'll be gathered round the gate. Mr Cassidy, the schoolmaster, has written out a grand welcome home, in the finest of copper-plate hand. The night'll be dark when the carriage'll get to the gate, but with the light of the bonefire and some sticks of bogwood dipped in paraffin that a score of the boys'll hold lighted up in their hands, sure it'll be as bright as day and Mr Cassidy'll be able to read easily."

"Troth, Bunnahone must do something!" said Mrs Darcy, looking at the clock. "It's little time there is to prepare before the four o'clock train. It won't be dark enough then either for illuminations; besides, the League – my bad cess to it, although Pat is chairman of it – might make trouble because Mr O'Brien is a landlord. I often say to Pat I like the good old times, when there were no leagues, better myself. We might get the band out! I wouldn't mind standing them plenty of drink afterwards. Pat'll meet the train as chairman of the Town Commissioners and give 'em a welcome on the part of the town, no matter what the League says. I'll see to that. And I'll go down myself and get the stationmaster, a real decent man, to put a few fog-signals on the line."

Hilda was frightened by the fog-signals, which she thought were shots. She had heard that Bunnahone once had a reputation for shooting landlords. She was reassured by Pat Darcy's pompous welcome as they stepped out of the railway carriage. The platform was crowded, Mrs Darcy having taken the precaution of having the arrival cried by the bellman.

"Sure it's nothing to what the Inniscar people'll do," Larry Gallagher said, as he clasped John O'Brien's hand; "only keep it a secret from the mistress until she sees it."

John O'Brien groaned, but Ralph was frankly delighted. It reminded him in a small way of the Rotunda meeting. He was disappointed when the band struck up "Pop goes the weazel" – one of the two tunes they knew – but he had to laugh when Larry Gallagher said reverently, "Thank God we have such fine music to welcome ye. Sure it's a great day for Ireland entirely."

Cassidy's grandiloquent address on their arrival at Inniscar gate was trying. He mispronounced half of the longer words on which he dwelt with special zest. There was a reference to Brian Boru, at which the mob of tenants shouted and waved their torches wildly in the air.

Hilda was excited and nervous. Order had been the keynote of her life and this weird scene unnerved her. The lurid glare of the bonfire and of the waving torches gave a barbaric look to the crowd of faces hemming in the carriage on all sides. She had almost fainted from terror when Father Duff elbowed his way to the carriage as Cassidy finished the address.

"I'm sorry I'm late," he said, shaking hands with Hilda, "but I had a sick call." Seeing that she was pale and frightened, he called out, "Now, boys, the lady is tired after her long journey. Let go of the horses' heads. But first give three cheers to welcome Mrs O'Brien to the old place."

Hilda smiled faintly and bowed in response, half dead with terror, which increased when the horses were taken from the carriage, which was drawn along the avenue to the house by wild-looking figures at a running pace.

Ann Carty, who had arrived a few days before with the other servants, was on the steps to receive them.

"They mean well," Ann said, supporting Hilda up the steps, "but sure 'tis easy known they've never seen a procession in Clarendon Street, or a Lord Mayor's Show for that matter."

John O'Brien, who was much moved, thanked the people simply for their welcome. "You were friends of mine as a boy," he said;

"nothing, I hope, has happened to change that. You will, I hope, be friends now of my wife and son."

When the cheers subsided, Father Duff said: "Run away home now, boys, and if I hear of any drinking or trouble of any kind after tonight, ye'll hear of it on Sunday."

"Oughtn't they to have a drink or something first?" asked O'Brien.

"Not a drop. I'm determined to put down drinking in the parish. They don't expect it either when they see me here."

The crowd dispersed slowly and reluctantly. There were murmurs against Father Duff.

"Troth it's a hard man he is on the drop o' drink, and no doubt he will have his own glass of punch in ease and comfort within," said an old man to Larry Gallagher.

"True for you, Thady Lynn," said Larry, dolefully. "I must say I'm a bit disappointed with Master John. Up to this day there never was a funeral or a wedding or a christening or a home-coming of an O'Brien of Inniscar without lashings of drink. I mind me when Master John himself was christened. I was a grown lad then and able to take my glass with any man, and a couple if I was pressed. There was a big barrel on tap in the barn and handed round in jugs the whiskey was; my father himself, God rest his soul, stood by the tap to see fair play. Not that there wasn't enough for every man unless he had the drought of a limekiln on him, but to keep order like."

"I mind it well," said Lynn, sadly, "and the same at the funeral of th'ould master. I doubt it's changed times is in it."

"The master had the good thought, anyway," said Larry, brightening. "I heard him mention the matter of drink, but Father Duff put a stop to it. Sorra priest in the world could ride roughshod long over an O'Brien! Wait till he knows the customs of the country. He's lived so long in foreign parts and Dublin that he don't know rightly what's expected of him. I'll drop him a word of advice in season."

Hilda went straight to her room. "I don't doubt that your head is moidered, ma'am," said Ann Carty. "I've put a hot bottle in the bed and you can have a bite of dinner there in comfort. It's a grand house entirely," she went on, as she helped Hilda to undress. "The furniture is a bit old and dowdy; the lad from Dublin who was doing it up seemed to think a lot of it and said it came down from Queen Anne. I thought she must have queer taste, but I said nothing, as he was rather uppish. But I said to myself all the same that the mistress'll be sure to brighten up the rooms with some of them spindly things that look so nice in Oetzman's window in Grafton Street. I doubt if he knew much, for he said that press there was chipping deal, when the whole world could see it was mahogany."

Father Duff stayed to dinner. "I've had dinner already," he said, "but I think I can manage another bite or two." He had second helpings of all the dishes.

"No coffee for me. I can't do without my night's rest; but if there is any hot water handy, and a squeeze of a lemon, and a drain of whiskey I think I'd take a glass of punch to round off the meal.

"You wouldn't take me to be seventy?" he said, as he poured two wine-glassfuls of whiskey into a tumbler already half-full of hot water. "A regular life does it, one stiff glass of punch a day after dinner; on occasions like this, two - never more. God didn't mean us to drink wine in this climate, else He'd have given us grapes - I never take it. You don't take punch? No. People have these new-fangled ideas. Your poor father, God be good to him, had a head for it. Six tumblers was his limit." He ladled the punch from the tumbler to a wine-glass and sipped it appreciatively. "Ralph is a water drinker, I see - well, he might be worse. So you're the makings of a priest, young man," he said, looking Ralph all over critically. "Well, well," shaking his head meditatively, "I never thought I'd see the day when an O'Brien of Inniscar would be in the Bunnahone Seminary. I hope you'll like it," he added dryly, stirring his punch.

"He's making his own bed at all events; he must learn to lie in it," said John O'Brien, firmly.

"Hum," said Father Duff.

"Of course I shall like it," Ralph said.

"You won't have ... however, it's time enough to bid the devil good-morrow when you meet him. Besides, the O'Briens were always able to take the rough things with the smooth," Father Duff said, holding his glass between him and the light.

Ralph looked at the priest enquiringly and was about to speak when Ann came in and said that his mother wished to see him.

"It's his mother's doing, I suppose," said the priest, when Ralph had gone.

John O'Brien hesitated.

"Ah! I thought so," Father Duff said. "It won't be all a bed of roses for him, you know that, John?"

O'Brien moved uncomfortably in his seat. "It isn't as if he were to be ordained right off," he said. "He will have plenty of time to make up his own mind in the Seminary and in Maynooth."

"And so there'll be an end to the O'Briens of Inniscar."

O'Brien looked moodily at his cup.

"Don't worry, John! Sure I oughtn't to have said that, but then you were always like a son to me. It's all God's will, no doubt," shaking his head sadly. "But what'll become of the place?"

"It will go to Ralph. The entail was broken in my father's time, but that doesn't matter. I've willed it to Ralph."

"It's a blessing anyway that I won't be alive when the house'll be turned into a convent or the like. It would be the death of me to have friars or nuns prying round my parish. I'm old-fashioned, I suppose," he said, as he drank the last of the punch and turned his chair towards the fire, "and it was the old fashion that an O'Brien should marry and settle down at Inniscar. It's a pity that you didn't settle here before this. If I had the bringing up of Ralph things might be different. There's too much talk of calls and vocations in these days. The invention, half of them, of a lot of friars and nuns who have nothing else to occupy their minds. Most of them would be better employed helping their fathers to weed a turnip field or their mothers to hang out the washing. I'm sure the friars expected Ralph to enter their own order?"

O'Brien nodded.

"What a sell they must have got!" Father Duff said, smiling and rubbing his chin softly. "Inniscar would have been a nice haul for them. Poor people! I suppose they must live too."

"But you had a vocation yourself?" said O'Brien.

"I never could rightly make out. It was this way, you see. The farm was to go to my eldest brother. There was some dry money in the house and my mother was jealous of the Roches, who lived next door and had a son in Maynooth. To be even with them I was sent to Maynooth. Now if I was the eldest son I'd be a farmer today if I was alive; and if Jim Roche wasn't in Maynooth, I'd likely be dead from hard work in America. I liked the life in Maynooth and I managed to scrape through. That's how I became a priest and I can't say I'm any the worse for it. It's a nice life enough for the likes of me. I've a tidy farm to fill my time. I know the people in and out, and we get on fairly well together."

O'Brien laughed. "But Ralph is certain he has a vocation and is always worrying about his soul," he said.

Father Duff scratched his head. "That's beyond me," he murmured. "You see I was never very clever at the books; to tell you the truth, I never could make out to this day why on earth all the books on theology were ever written. Heaven is there, and hell is there, and if you live a good life you go to one; if you live a bad life you go to the other. The catechism and common-sense will tell you what's a sin and what isn't. I try not to be too hard on the people, except in the matter of porter sprees; I say my office and mass and administer the sacraments. I never gave ten minutes to thinking about my soul in my whole life and if the catechism didn't tell me I had one I wouldn't know it. But since it does tell me I know it's there and that's enough. I never knew any good come of worrying about it. I hope I'll be able to put some common-sense on the matter into Ralph before it's too late. But I must be off," he said, looking at his watch and rising hastily; "I promised to look in again on old Joe Burke that I anointed this evening. He once made a lot of money out of a field I persuaded him to drain; he has great faith in me ever since and he believes he cannot get to heaven unless I'm beside him at the end."

After breakfast next morning, John showed Hilda and Ralph the house and grounds. Hilda was somewhat reconciled to the change from Dublin on seeing the small chapel on the ground floor, where mass was formerly said once a week. The bishop, John thought, had power to renew the privilege if Hilda wished it. The house, too, pleased her. It was an eighteenth-century house, after Palladius, a long way after, some of its critics said, but it was comfortable, with large lofty rooms. Several bedrooms were unfurnished, as was also the finest room in the house, the salon, finely proportioned and still beautiful in its original decoration of green and gold, tarnished by age to an exquisite bronze.

"The Inniscar O'Briens," John said, "were never rich; the O'Brien who built this house was a comparatively poor man. 'O'Brien's Folly' it was called for many years. It impoverished him and his son after him and no O'Brien since has been rich enough to finish it. Each generation has shut up a few more rooms. It will be a tight pinch for us to be able to live here at all. You must economise, Hilda!"

Ralph laughed. Hilda blushed. Her want of knowledge in money matters was a family joke. Ann Carty had gradually taken over the housekeeping and Hilda dealt only with her own personal expenditure, most of which was spent on masses and Church charities.

"Of course, John, I shall be most careful," she said.

"We'll need every penny. Fortunately, we saved something by having the house let and living quietly in Dublin, otherwise we shouldn't be able to manage. We must let this Italian garden go."

"Oh, John, what a pity! Surely not; we shall need a lot of flowers for the altar," said Hilda.

"The beginning of economy!" John said genially. "Well, perhaps, I shall be able to make the farm pay. I have been losing on it for some years."

Beyond the garden, a few feet lower, was a terrace for tennis-courts, green in midwinter as in summer. A thick belt of trees shut off the sea, a glimpse of which could be seen at a corner of the tennis ground through an opening in the trees. Sky and sea were of a deep blue save where a thin line of white waves broke on the sandy beach. At the opposite side of the bay lofty mountains, of a darker blue than the sea, rose clear cut and sheer from the edge of the water.

They stood for a few minutes listening to the solemn drone of the breakers on the beach. Hilda turned round and gazed in silence at the house standing solid and grim in the background. It seemed to smile in the sunlight, the grave smile of massive cut stone willing enough to enjoy a moment of solemn gaiety, yet brooding ever on its stern duty of buffeting many a winter storm. How secure it looked! She glanced at her husband and son, who were watching the play of the waves on the shore. How much more at home they seemed here than in Harcourt Terrace. Last night, as she lay in the huge canopied bed, turning over the pages of "à Kempis", she found it hard to keep her attention fixed on what she read. The candles by her bedside only feebly lit the large room. The massive furniture seemed still more massive in the gloom. She read that the things of this world were fleeting as a dream and her eyes sought the huge press which stood over against the bed, solid and dark.

She shivered as she looked again at the house. Outside and in it seemed to assert itself.

She took Ralph's arm as they walked towards the stables, and pressed him to her side. He smiled, saying, "It's all jolly fine, Mother, isn't it?"

She said an ejaculatory prayer to St Teresa to give her strength. Her lips hardened and she felt a load fall from her heart. God had given Ralph as a pledge of His intentions. She looked scornfully at the house and smiled at her foolishness in allowing it to depress her.

"His lordship the bishop is within," said Larry Gallagher, excitedly, as they reached the stables.

"What a time to call – before we have had time even to look around," said John, frowning.

"Oh, John, the bishop! I am very glad. We can arrange about Ralph's going to the Seminary."

"Humph," said John, with some vexation, "there's time enough for that."

She thought he looked very like the house in his present mood. She hurried round to the front entrance. A smart victoria, with a liveried coachman on the box, stood in front of the steps.

"He does himself well," said John, "though I must admit he has good taste in horseflesh," looking admiringly at the chestnut horse between the shafts.

The bishop had been shown into the library and stood in front of the fire, with his head slightly thrown back. His tall figure showed to advantage standing. His shining black hair, worn rather long, fell in loose curled waves across his somewhat narrow forehead.

He advanced to meet Hilda, holding out his hand. She knelt to kiss his ring.

"Please don't kneel," he said, helping her to rise with both hands. "I owe you all an apology," he went on, as he shook hands with John and Ralph, who both kissed his ring. "I said early mass at the convent and wished to see Father Duff. I did the eight miles in fifty minutes. Not bad for a victoria. I knew you had arrived and could not pass the gate without paying my respects and welcoming you home."

"We are highly honoured, my lord," said Hilda.

He bowed gravely, saying, "It is reciprocal. What a charming room. I've been ten years in the diocese and have never been in Inniscar before. Your tenants were Protestants! Only too few of our larger places are Catholic. I am glad Inniscar has resumed its Catholic tradition." He laid bare his regular white teeth as he smiled faintly.

Hilda was confused and said, timidly, "Ralph and I were seeing the place for the first time when we heard your lordship was here. Won't you walk round with us and stay to luncheon?"

"Not today, thanks. I fact, I don't lunch. I dine at four and take a mere snack in the middle of the day. Some day, if you wish, I shall breakfast with you. You will like to have mass in your oratory? I shall be pleased to say mass for you, and breakfast afterwards."

"And dine and sleep the night before?" John said, "Dr Boland always did. I will give us all much pleasure."

"It would be a pity indeed to break with such an excellent custom of my predecessor," Dr Devoy said dryly, with the same faint smile. "A saint, if ever there was one! Lived a little too much in the clouds, perhaps," he fingered the heavy gold cross on his breast meditatively for a few seconds. "By the way," he said abruptly, "Father Duff tells me that your son," smiling at Ralph, "has a vocation and is coming to us. We must make it easy for him. He must go to the Seminary, of course, though I did think of letting him go to Maynooth direct. My sainted predecessor, I say it with the greatest reverence, rather neglected our Seminary and it has fallen on me to make it a credit to our ancient diocese. I had to make it a rule that only from the Seminary could students for this diocese pass into Maynooth. The temptation to break the rule in your son's case was strong, but rules cannot be lightly broken. Moreover, it will be good for him. The example, too," frowning, "will be good for some other Catholics in the diocese. Not every one, Mrs O'Brien, has your devotion to Holy Church – you see," smiling, "your reputation has preceded you."

John O'Brien fidgeted in his chair. "Shall we say six months or so at the Seminary?" Dr Devoy continued, smiling. "In September I shall have a vacancy in Maynooth. He will be about the right age then. He can enter the Seminary after the Christmas holidays."

Hilda smiled assent. She liked the bishop's ascetic appearance and decided that he must be a very holy man. He was the antithesis of the rough men she had pictured all country priests to be.

"Ah, reading 'à Kempis,' I see," he said, taking the book off the small table beside him. "I dip into him every day to shake the dust of the world off me."

John O'Brien smiled as he glanced at the bishop's well-cut clothes and well-groomed figure.

The bishop caught the glance, shut his thin lips and said, smiling to Ralph, "Don't ever ambition being a bishop. We are forced to be too much of the world. My desire - unfortunately," sighing, "it was never accomplished - was a quiet country parish with time for meditation and prayer. God willed otherwise. Perhaps I said '*Nolo Episcopari*' too often and to punish me this burden was placed on me. One has to keep up the dignity of the office, distasteful as it may be to the spirit," he added, turning to Mrs O'Brien. He stood up, smiling. "You must come and see our beautiful Cathedral," he said to Hilda. "You must not devote all your energies to Inniscar; we shall need your help at Bunnahone."

Hilda again knelt for the episcopal blessing. "What a charming man!" she said to John, when he returned after seeing the bishop to his carriage.

"He has a mouth like a vice," said John grumpily. "I hear he has an eye on a cardinal's hat. I shouldn't wonder if he got it, too."

Hilda looked distressed. "I'm sure he would hate it," she said gently. "Your father is only jesting," she said to Ralph. "You liked him, dear?"

"Oh, right enough. He does jaw, though, just like the Jesuit rector," said Ralph, smiling.

Hilda wandered in the old-fashioned walled garden until luncheon.

"Sorry I am that it's in December you came home, my lady," said Mick Walsh, the gardener, "without a show of flowers to give you welcome. Barring what's under glass there's hardly a thing worthy of you. If it was in the spring it would be a blaze of glory fornint you.

Man and boy I've been here this fifty years come Lady Day, sure I remember the master when he wasn't higher than my knee, and to think you should come at such a forlorn time." What flowers there were he showed with much pride, handling them tenderly. "The best garden in the county it is, my lady, though it's myself that says it," he said, as he led the way to a small greenhouse full of rich blooms.

"How exquisite!" said Hilda.

The old man's face glowed. "'Twas the old mistress made it, God rest her soul," he said, taking off his hat reverently. "The oratory greenhouse, we call it. Not a flower used to go anywhere but to the little chapel in the house. It near broke my heart when Protestants came to live in Inniscar, not that they were bad neither, one of the kindest of ladies Mrs Harvey was, but even so, sorra flower from here ever went into the big house in their time. I told her they were chapel flowers. 'Then send them to Father Duff,' she said. Not but it would break your heart to see how Father Duff would pack them into an old jug, anyway. A fine man for the people he is, but clover is the only flower he cares a pin for, and 'twould be hard to beat him at that. Sure it'll put the heart in me again to be able to grow them for our own chapel."

The house looked gentler to Hilda as she went in to luncheon. She felt glad that she had come. She dwelt on the bishop's kindness, on Mick Walsh's piety. Perhaps God had inspired her husband to this change. She reproached herself for having doubted God's providence. She had been rebellious when He was preparing a great gift for her, the infinite happiness of having her son celebrate mass in their own house among their own people.

Chapter 7

THE MONTH AT Inniscar, previous to his entering the Seminary, Ralph, in after years, thought the happiest in his life. There were hours exploring the garden with Mick Walsh, who loved each plant as a child; wandering about the fields with Teig Moriarty, who had charge of the home farm, a spare, cleanshaven, elderly man, taciturn on all subjects except cattle, of which Larry Gallagher said, "barring Father Duff himself, Teig was the best judge in the parish, or maybe in the county, or all Ireland"; or, with Larry in the stable-yard, hearing all the lore of the country-side, in intervals of regret that there were not more horses in the stables "like there were in the old master's time". With difficulty he got Larry to speak Irish to him. "Sorra one of me speaks it once in a blue moon," Larry said contemptuously, "unless it be to an odd spalpeen out of Connemara that wanders down into these parts now and again. Not but what I'd not deny that it's a beautiful language entirely to pray in, especially when one is the least taste elevated with the drink. There's a kind of poetry in it then that lifts a man out of himself. Leave it alone, though, Master Ralph, it would only spoil your mouth. It comes easy enough on the tongue of the likes of me that was born to it, but them that was reared on the English speak the Irish with that twisting and turning of their jaws that you'd think a big bit of a turnip had stuck in their throats. There's Mr Charles Dillon, now, with all his talk about it, sure he speaks it like I used to read the readamadaisy when I was a gossoon. Sorra taste of the *blas* he has, and he turns it the same as the gentry turns the English."

"But he is a great Irish scholar," said Ralph.

Larry scratched his head. "That may be as may be," he said doubtfully. "All I know is, that I'm no scholar, but troth he'll be an old man with one foot in the grave before he'll speak the Irish half as well as I do. It bangs Banagher to know what a man like him bothers about it all for. Only that he knows the points of a horse nearly as well as myself, I'd say he was touched there," tapping his head significantly.

"Not in the least," said Ralph, laughing.

Larry shook his head thoughtfully. "Then I suppose it's only a vagary of the gentry. Saving your presence, they've so little to do that one doesn't know what they'll be up to from one minute to the next."

"Still wasting your time on the Irish?" Larry said one day, as Ralph was discussing the relative merits of Shorthorns and Herefords with Teig Moriarty.

Teig's eyes gleamed wrathfully and he said, contemptuously, as he hurried Ralph away: "It's on little that's any good, that you either spend or waste your time, Larry Gallagher."

"Do you mean to tell me it's learning the Irish you are?" he asked Ralph eagerly.

"Yes," said Ralph, smiling, expecting another attack on his hobby.

Teig took off his hat, and lifting his eyes, said reverently, "Thanks be to God for that same. Sure it's a happy man I am to see this day. Your grandfather, God be good to him, often walked this very field with me and not a word of English did we speak from one end of it to the other." His stern face grew soft. "Silent Teig, they call me," he said, "but sure if they only talked about the Irish to me, I'd talk until the sun went down. Aye, and till the stars followed it."

"You love it?" asked Ralph. "I had begun to think that every one at Inniscar despised it."

"Love it! Why it's eating and drinking to me. There's a music in the sound of it, like what the angels play before the throne of God. Sure it's a madness must have come over the people to give it up. True for you," he added sadly, "it's few here now that cares anything for it. It's enough to break a man's heart to see how it's looked down on. I wouldn't mind the master, for he never, more's the pity, knew the Irish and the likes of Larry Gallagher that don't know any better; but there's Father Duff, now, the most knowledgeable man in the county in regard to a beast, and it's no disgrace to admit it. He knows the Irish well, but if you speak to him in it he answers you in English. And the grand stories and poetry that are in it! I said to him one day. 'Do they tell you anything,' he said, 'of clover or turnips or silos,' he said mighty sharp; 'it's poor farmers we'd be,' he said, 'if we were depending on them old tales with nothing in them that's any use to a man either in this world or the next,' he said. Good man that he is, I doubt it's many a long day he'll spend in purgatory to wipe out his sins in regard to the Irish."

"It is a wonder to me that any priest is against the movement," said Ralph, thoughtfully.

"It passes the wit of man to tell," said Teig sadly, "but," brightening, "except at the farming, sorra much good the clergy are outside their own business and many of 'em aren't much good at that itself, and to have 'em agin a movement at times isn't the worst thing either. They were agin the land movement and a bad fall they got over the same. They were agin Parnell, but sure when he got into high power they ran after him and you'd think from the way they talked that they made him. They have their revenge on him now, since he got into the divorce court, but sorra much good that'll do them in the end either. They did a lot to kill the Irish, but if this move of Mr Charles's and his friends comes to anything, you'll have plenty of the clergy going round spouting in its favour. It's a way they have of backing the winning horse when it's well up to the post. Not Father Duff, for he'd scorn the like. Sorra much of the trimmer is about him."

Ralph had grown accustomed to hearing priests criticised. Even Mick Walsh, whom Larry Gallagher called a voteen, spoke freely of the faults of priests. He spoke to his mother on the subject. She sighed, saying it was very regrettable and advised him to change the conversation if possible. John O'Brien said this was nonsense. Why shouldn't priests be criticised like any other men, not in matters affecting their office perhaps, but in affairs of the world?

"But the priest at Mr Dillon's great meeting in Dublin ..." Ralph said.

"Oh, I read of that," said Teig. "Father Dan is all right. But one swallow doesn't make a summer, nor a score here and there for all that."

Ralph felt more at ease when Teig spoke of the glories of the Irish tongue. It was the only language in the world a man could rightly pray in or make love in. Not that he did much lovemaking now, but there was a time when it came in mighty useful. He felt that mean in speaking the English which hadn't the words, at least he didn't know them, for giving out the thoughts that were bursting in his head. He recited a long poem with glowing eyes.

"I can't do it. It's unfair to the beautiful words," he said, after making an effort to translate a love-poem into English. "Mr Charles could do it, for, of course, he has the English as well as the Irish. Not but that there's a lot lost in any case; the English is so cold-like. That's a great man is Mr Charles," he added thoughtfully, "and to think that he learned the Irish only when he was a gossoon not much younger than you!"

Teig transformed the mountains beyond the bay into pages of romance. There Ossian and St Patrick had wrestled in song, "and I have my doubts," said Teig, musingly, "if St Patrick had entirely the best of it"; there Diarmuid and Grania had rested in their flight; while every purple hill-top had some legend of Fionn.

"Don't talk to me of the heroes of Greece. I read of 'em once in a book written by a blind man by the name of Homer. Helen of Troy, though Raftery himself put her in a poem, couldn't hold a candle to Maeve of the Red Hair, who had such beauty that she made hundreds sick with longing for her. Helen may have done that same, but over and above her looks, Maeve was a mighty fighter that could knock down men with a sword like you'd blow the fluff off a clock. And it's poor creatures the men were compared with Cúchulain and many of the old ancient heroes that maybe tramped the very ground we're walking on."

Ralph toiled through the primers of the Society for the Preservation of the Irish Language. Mindful of Larry's criticism, he apologised to Teig for not having the *blas*. "It's the spirit and not the *blas* that's wanting in most men. Thanks be to God you have that. Sure the *blas*'ll come in time, and if it doesn't itself it won't matter a thraneen," Teig said cheerfully.

Ralph made rapid progress. During the long winter nights he worked even harder than in the strenuous times preceding examinations, when Father Best put on extra pressure. Larry, at first under protest, but afterwards with a good-humoured tolerance of what he called the foolishness of the gentry, was a ready reference book always at hand in the stable-yard. He had no interest in heroic tales or poetry and spoke of Cúchulain as "a foolish old man who went out on the strand below, lashing the waves, and he up to his waist in them. Sorra one of us remembers when he was drowned or taken to the lunatic asylum, for it was long before my time." But he was rich in tales of the "good people", who could be seen at the right time of night in any thorn bush or hazel tree, or wandering about "up to their tricks". He had often seen them, and ghosts too, mostly late at night when coming home from the Bunnahone market, "and as sober as a judge, too, with no more drink taken than to feel comfortable like".

About a week before Christmas, Ralph was invited to dinner by Father Duff. The hour was three o'clock. It was his first invitation to a meal at a priest's house and he was full of curiosity.

"It's rather an odd hour," he said to his father. "I can't well have luncheon before; yet I shall be dreadfully hungry."

John O'Brien laughed. "You may as well begin to practice the customs of the clergy," he said. "Eat a good breakfast; that will carry you on to three o'clock."

"Why don't they eat at more reasonable hours?"

"Father Duff, no doubt, thinks our hours foolish, and his own quite reasonable. Perhaps he's right. I rather like these conservative old customs. The social customs of the priests take a jump every century or so. Our great grandfathers dined early, wore silk hats in the country, drank punch and made speeches after dinner. The priests are still in that period. You'll soon get used to it."

At three o'clock, Ralph arrived at the parochial house, a hideous two-storeyed building, square and stuccoed, with red-brick mouldings around the door and windows. A small garden separated the house from the road. Several dogs barked loudly as Ralph opened the gate. He was trying to make friends with the dogs when the door was opened by Father Duff, who called them off.

"Not that they'd hurt a fly," he said, patting a fierce-looking Irish terrier on the head. "Come along in and take off your coat. You're heartily welcome. Jane is busy preparing the dinner."

Through the open door came the strong odour of cooking food. "I hope you don't mind if it'll be a bit late. I put it back half an hour. Father Sheldon is coming and he couldn't get here before ha'-past three."

Ralph's heart sank, but he managed to muster a smile. His nose told him they were to have apple tart. He hoped Jane would not allow the paste to get too burnt; that it was burning he felt convinced as he sniffed the delicious smell.

"Take that chair and get a heat of the fire," the priest said, pointing to an armchair. A huge turf fire burnt brightly in a large open grate, giving an air of comfort to the otherwise cheerless room, with its grey plastered walls and stiff mahogany chairs, covered with black hair cloth. A framed chromolithograph of Leo XIII hung over the mantelpiece: the curiously ugly mouth and piercing eyes dominating the room with their subtle expression at once understanding, cynical, sneering and tolerant. Beneath it, at the side of the fireplace, was a gaudy hunting calendar, advertising Darcy and Sons' teas and whiskies: a sideboard, a glass-fronted bookcase, a centre table covered with a course white cloth, roughly laid for three with black-handled steel knives and forks, and a huge box filled with turf, standing by the fireside, completed the furniture. The floor of unpolished deal was carpetless: not even the gathering gloom of the short December day hid the muddy footmarks.

Ralph looked around with interest, his eyes resting on the calendar. The priest laughed. "That picture gives me many a laugh," he said. "Sheldon says it's atrocious, but I like the bright colours of it. I'd give anything to see the look on the fellow's face that's riding the front horse after he takes the first fence. With them legs the horse is sure to come down. How do you like the cob I sent over to you?"

"He's ripping," Ralph said gratefully. "It was very good of you. I ..."

"Oh, don't mention it. Aye, he has breeding and substance both. You'll miss him when you go to the Seminary."

"I've been idle so long I shall be glad to get to work again," Ralph said gloomily.

"Finding the time hang heavy?" the priest said dryly.

"Well - no." Ralph hesitated and blushed. "I can't say I do. There are so many interesting things to see and do. I've never really lived in the country before."

"It's the greatest pity in the world that you won't stay where you are ... until you go to Maynooth next September," he finished lamely. "With the learning Father Best tells me you have it's only a waste of time to spend six months at the Bunnahone Seminary."

"I'm sure I shall learn a great deal there. I've had no spiritual training, you know. Cardinal Manning in his book lays great stress on the value of Seminary experience."

The priest looked at him with astonishment, his mouth hanging open.

"Spiritual training!" he muttered, his forehead puckering in an apparently vain effort to follow some elusive thought.

"I mean meditation and examination of conscience and the observance of the regular life," Ralph said, feeling vaguely troubled and priggish.

"Huh," said Father Duff, lifting a sod of turf with the tongs and laying it carefully, end up, on the fire. "Do you tell me that now? And at the Bunnahone Seminary, too! Well, well now! Wonders'll never cease. And it's Father Phil Doyle'll teach you all that," chuckling, as he rubbed his hands together in front of the blaze.

Ralph looked at him blankly.

"You don't know Father Phil? No. He's president of the Seminary. A great man entirely. You'll find it out soon, I don't doubt."

He took out a huge snuff-box, tapped the lid, and taking a pinch in each nostril, blew his nose vigorously in a big red handkerchief.

"Nothing like snuff for clearing the brain," he said, smiling, as if at some thought that passed through his mind. "In my time every priest snuffed. Now most of them have taken to smoking. A queer habit, but it's hard to understand the new ways. I don't know much of the Bunnahone Seminary, but if I were you, I wouldn't expect too much of it. You've been accustomed to a grand school in Dublin, great doctors' sons from Merrion Square and Rathgar. Where would we find the like down here? And there's the least taste of diffference, too, between Father Phil and the Jesuits. Sure, Father Best knows him well. What in the world did he say when he heard you were going to the Seminary?"

"Very little. He wasn't enthusiastic."

"No; he wouldn't be," the priest said dryly. "They're mighty cute, the Jesuits," he added with a smile. "They come down to the country to give retreats and missions and sorra much escapes them. Father Best stayed at the Seminary a few times. No doubt he and Father Phil had a pleasant time on the classics. I wouldn't wonder if Phil didn't give him a point or two. I'm sure –"

He was interrupted by the entrance of a priest, white haired like himself, spare, with delicate features, about ten years younger.

"Ha, Sheldon," Father Duff said, rising from his chair, "you're welcome. Now we can have the dinner up. The young Levite I told you of, young Mr O'Brien."

Father Sheldon shook Ralph's hand warmly, and gave him a keen glancc as he said, "I intended to call before this; I fear I'm negligent. Father Best wrote to me about you. What a good fellow he is and a great friend of yours."

Father Duff went to the door, and shouted, "Now, Jane, you can dish the dinner. I'm starving. As for young Mr O'Brien he's that hungry he could eat a piece of old leather."

"I don't doubt but it's leather ye'll get too," came in angry tones from the kitchen. "Keeping the dinner half an hour late."

"I feared as much," said Father Duff, winking at his guests. "Jane is in one of her tantrums."

Jane, a stout, elderly woman, her scant grey hair gathered in a knot behind, stalked into the room and laid a dish on the table with a bang. The noise of her heavy boots on the bare boards as she went out and in several times was getting on Ralph's nerves, when she said, "There's the dinner for ye now. If it's spoiled don't blame me."

The food, however, was excellent. Boiled turkey with celery sauce, boiled ham flanked by piles of white cabbage and floury potatoes in their jackets.

Father Duff and Ralph had vigorous appetites, but Father Sheldon ate sparingly. In a low musical voice he told them of a sick call from which he had just come – a rather touching story of the reconciliation of a stern father and an erring daughter on his death-bed. "They have a wonderful faith," he wound up, seemingly lost in abstraction.

"A good trouncing with a stock I'd give her," said Father Duff, fiercely. "You're too easy entirely with that sort of person. They come round you with any kind of soft story."

"I read somewhere of refraining from casting the first stone!"

"I wouldn't go as far as stones," said Father Duff, "but a few tin cans now to rattle her out of the parish! I've known that to work well. Molloy got that done once and the bishop approved of it," he added slyly.

"Poor thing!" said Father Sheldon, sadly. "I heard of that. She died shortly afterwards; the effect of fright, the doctor told me."

Father Duff looked grave. "I shouldn't have made a joke of it," he said. "Maybe I don't approve of these new methods myself. Molloy boasts that Bunnahone is the most moral town in Ireland. He's always around with a whitewash brush, anyway."

Father Sheldon sighed. "I wish the Molloys of Ireland would face their own responsibilities, instead of shifting them to the slums of English and American cities," he said, as Father Duff rang a small handbell.

Ralph had taken no part in this conversation, which he but vaguely understood. There was some explanation, no doubt, of Father Molloy's action, as no priest could possibly act in such a manner. He wished to ask Father Sheldon, but was too timid.

Jane came in to remove the plates, looking rather shy, as if ashamed of her previous temper.

"That was delicious turkey, Jane," said Father Sheldon, "and so well cooked."

"I'm glad you liked it, Father; but sure you didn't ate enough of it to fill a sparrow. No wonder it's only skin and bones you are. There's Father Duff now, though he doesn't show his food, it's a fine appetite he has, thanks be to God."

"Bring in the apple tart now, Jane, there's a good woman," said Father Duff, hurriedly.

"Sure it's a tongue like one of them gramophones I once heard in Dublin, she has," he added, when Jane, somewhat offended, had flounced out of the room, "if only it gets rightly turned on."

They sat round the fire after dinner, Father Duff sipping a glass of punch, Father Sheldon smoking. "I doubt but you'll take to smoking yet," said Father Duff, looking at Ralph meditatively. "I can't abide a man that mixes smoke with good drink. It's unnatural. Any man can afford one vice, but more than that is trying. What do you think of him as timber for a priest?" he said, turning suddenly to Father Sheldon.

Father Sheldon laughed. "I can hardly appraise him to his face," he said. "I can say, however, that I'm glad he's coming to us."

"Are you, then?" asked Father Duff, doubtingly.

"Yes," said Father Sheldon, firmly. "It's not going to be an easy time in the Church," he added to Ralph. "You must prepare for rough times."

"I know so little. Everything is so strange. I daresay I shall learn in time," said Ralph, shyly.

"It's kind ancestry for him to have grit, anyway," said Father Duff, "not that I believe a bit in them fears of yours. It's moidering your head with books and reading that's the cause of it all. The Church is the same as ever she was. Except a few returned Yanks and the like, the people come to mass as they always did; and Yanks and all they send for me when they're dying. I keep a firm hand without interfering too much. I don't trouble them with theology and I amn't too hard on the dues, and I give a leg up to a man that's down whenever I can."

"No, you wouldn't have any trouble," said Father Sheldon, looking at the fire.

"Of course," Father Duff continued, "I admit there's feeling against some of the clergy since the Parnell split, but they brought that on themselves. Besides, it'll blow over in a couple of years."

"The Church has always had her enemies," said Ralph, sententiously.

Father Sheldon checked an obvious smile and said, gravely, "Yes! within and without; though often her enemies have been her best friends, and her defenders her worst enemies."

"Sheer nonsense, I call that," said Father Duff.

"Perhaps so," said Father Sheldon, gently. "Don't be disheartened by appearances," he said to Ralph. "The spirit of Christ is still in the Church."

"Don't preach a sermon to the boy," said Father Duff. "He'll have more than enough of that before he's done."

Father Sheldon's thin face flushed. "Quite right," he said humbly. "I was only going to tell him that the Holy Ghost works through queer priests sometimes, that he may get many a shock."

"There's very little of the Holy Ghost in many of 'em," said Father Duff, dryly.

"If one only looked deep enough one could find Him in everyone," Father Sheldon said.

"Oh, I'm only an ordinary old man, and short-sighted at that, and I must take people as I find 'em."

Jane brought in tea.

"Put it beside Father Sheldon, Jane," Father Duff said, drinking off the last of his punch. "How anyone could prefer it to a stiff glass of Pat Darcy's best, hot, is always a puzzle to me."

After tea Father Sheldon rose to go. "I hope I shall see something of you," he said to Ralph. "It's only a short walk to my house from Inniscar. Do come."

"See as much of Father Sheldon as you can," said Father Duff, as he drove Ralph home on his way to a sick call. "He's the salt of the earth. I'm only a hard old man, with a little edge to my tongue sometimes. Sheldon is about the only man I've known for forty years on a stretch that has escaped the lash of it. I don't count a little dig I give him to his face by way of a joke. I don't know much about learning, but once when Father Best was giving a mission here for me, he told me that Sheldon could put him to shame in his own subject; and I believe Sheldon knows a power of theology and other learning besides. And there he is, in the poorest parish in the diocese, at the beck and call of the simplest, late and early. I'm prouder of having him for a friend than if I was the Pope of Rome himself. Do you know what," he continued, with a feeling Ralph had not known him to show hitherto, "if I ever had a doubt of the goodness of God, which, thank God, I never had, the recollection of what I know Sheldon to be would be the best proof to me of what an ass I was for being so foolish."

Chapter 8

As the day of Ralph's entrance to the Seminary approached, Hilda became moody and fitful. Prayer and spiritual reading, her usual resources, were no consolation. She read pages of "à Kempis" with no memory of having seen a word. She tried to convince herself that his few months at the Seminary would be no separation, that his training for the priesthood would draw him closer to her in aspiration and ideal, but no thinking would still the aching pain in her heart. She moaned aloud on her knees in the little chapel, "My son, my son," over and over again. Her husband, when she spoke of her trouble, was grumpy and snappy.

"It's really your doing, Hilda," he said with a frown. "You must grin and bear it now."

Ann Carty shook her head, saying, "I doubt, ma'am, but you must put up with it. I often heard my mother tell that mothers had them sort of feelings about their sons. 'Nature must have the upper hand at times,' she said. She wasn't, so to say, a religious woman, but she was wise enough in her own way."

Hilda clasped Ralph to her heart as he set out to drive on an outside car for the Seminary. It was a cold January day and she shivered. She had asked John to send a closed carriage with Ralph, but he had refused.

"Don't make a laughing-stock of the boy to start with," he said; "he is bad enough as he is."

She clung to Ralph, her strained face fixed on the trunk strapped to one side of the car. "Are you sure I put in all his warm things?" she said, appealingly, to John. He smiled and said gently, "Come away now, darling. 'Twill only make him cry, too." She kissed Ralph again and allowed her husband to lead her away.

"It's only for a short time," he said cheerfully.

"No," she said, weeping hysterically. "I feel it in my heart - he's gone from me for ever."

Ralph soon grew cheerful as Larry Gallagher drove briskly along the road to Bunnahone, a thin coating of ice on the frequent ruts crackling beneath the wheels.

"Bad cess to that same grand jury," Larry said crossly, as the car jolted out of a deep rut, "to give the people such roads after all the rates they must pay."

Ralph remonstrated with him for beating the horse.

"It's as cross as two sticks I feel," Larry said, half turning his head, from his seemingly unstable seat on the dicky. "What in the world made you do it, Master Ralph? You could knock me down with a feather when the master sprung it on me last night. 'Put the bay horse under the car tomorrow,' he said, 'and drive Mr Ralph to the Bunnahone Seminary. He's going to be a student there,' he said. 'Is it a priest you're going to make of him?' I said, my mouth wide open. I often heard Ann Carty give a hint of it, but knowing her to be a voteen, sure I paid no attention to her. 'It is that same,' he said. And mighty dark he looked as he walked away, like as if he wasn't too well pleased himself. Go on straight, will you, you old thief of the night," jerking the reins sharply. "That old fool of a Teig was that put out when I told him that I nearly felt sorry for him. 'They'll wean him off the Irish,' he said, heartbroken like. To hearten him, I said that they'd find it hard to wean one of your stock off anything. 'That's true,' he said, brightening up; though in my heart I felt that it might be no great loss. To think of your being a common priest now! It clean passes my understanding. If it was a bishop now, with the purple in front of you and a grand bellyband round your middle and a big gold cross, or one of them orders that come down from Dublin to give missions that'd frighten a man into the middle of next week about his soul, it'd be different. But a priest like my own second cousin beyond in Lisslea; it fair takes my breath away."

Ralph smiled, but Larry did not lose his breath, for he talked all the way to Bunnahone. As they drove through the little town, feeble lights glimmered in the shop windows, although it was not yet dark. Mean thatched hovels gave way to more substantial two-storied slated houses, washed in different hues of drab colour. The dark, grim workhouse shut out the skyline. A huge cut-stone building, shut off from the streets by a wall, the top stories visible from the car, attracted Ralph's attention by its brilliant lighting.

"Oh, that's the convent," Larry explained. "Sure the whole town is jealous of 'em for the gas that you see shining. It's of their own making in a little house at the back. A power of money it costs, and the town wants the Commissioners to get it, but they're afeard of the expense. Not but I think myself that a paraffin lamp gives light enough to find your way to your mouth with a glass, even in Pat Darcy's big shop. The whole money of the country the same nuns have gathered into them. Sorra likely girl in the county with a bit of money in these times but it's a nun she must be. Only last week they got a daughter of Pat Darcy's with two thousand pounds, no less, and more to follow when Pat dies," he added with awed tones.

"There seems to be a great number of public houses," said Ralph.

"Seventy-one, I heard Teig say once; he counted them, as he's rather agin them."

"To three or four thousand people," said Ralph in surprise.

"It's very convenient," said Larry, thoughtfully, "if you're at a fair or market to be able to drop in without having far to walk."

Larry drew up before a long, gaunt three-storied house. "There's the Seminary," he said, pointing with his whip, "and may bad luck go with it. May the Lord save us from all harm for speaking that way of a holy place," he added piously.

"Father Phil told me to show you into his own room," said the maid who opened the door. "He's beyond in the class room, but he'll be here in a minute."

Ralph walked around the room while he waited, enjoying the warmth of a fire after his cold drive. He vaguely felt the vulgarity of the room, which had a cheap feminine air in comparison with the severe simplicity of Father Duff's: wicker chairs in bright chintz covers, an elaborate bamboo over-mantel, several bamboo whatnots, little china ornaments everywhere, an open piano in a light walnut case with a copy of Tosti's "Goodbye" on the music-rest, a *Strand Magazine* on the imitation chenille table cover. Photographs in silver frames, in plush frames, in wood or unmounted stood on the piano, on the whatnots, on the mantelpiece or hung from the walls. The subjects were all either priests or ladies. A number of sentimental German coloured prints of religious or love scenes, in heavy gilt frames, covered the walls.

"Admiring my pictures? They are considered very good." Ralph was startled by the harsh throaty voice and still more by the loud guffaw which followed the words. Father Phil Doyle was what was once called a fine figure of a man. Tall and well-proportioned, his head held well back, he would have been handsome were it not for his receding chin and a curious pursing of his lips in a circle when he spoke. His abundant black hair was well oiled and brushed.

"Sit down," he said, pointing to one of the wicker chairs.

Father Doyle sat, too, first carefully pulling up the legs of his trousers beneath his long soutane. Placing his feet on the fender, he drew his white cuffs well down over his hands and gazed into the fire thoughtfully.

"Of course, I know your intermediate record. You're a great gun," he said, and again laughed harshly. "This is most unusual, you coming here in this way. You'll have an easy time, anyway. Let me see now. It's not quite regular, but I could make a monitor of you," looking at Ralph gravely, with one eye screwed up.

"There are older boys here, of course, but none that has passed the senior grade. You might take a class for me if I'm called away. There are so many calls on one's time in a big town like this. I take the important subjects myself when I have time, Latin and Greek, of course," he said pompously. "For the minor things, English, mathematics and a little French, there are lay teachers. Run away now and fix up your cubicle."

Ralph had not opened his lips, but Father Phil seemed not to expect it. Ralph wandered along a winding passage. A maid told him to continue "till you get to the back door, and then fornint you you'll see the school". The school had been an old warehouse of two stories that had been simply transformed. The whole upper floor was a dormitory, the lower floor classrooms - one large room called the hall, three smaller ones - and an oratory.

As Ralph reached the door Larry Gallagher was taking his trunk up the stairs. He followed Larry. A number of boys of varying ages from twelve to eighteen lounging by the door, their hands deep in their trousers pockets, stared at him without speaking. When he had passed there was a loud buzz of conversation and he heard, "He's mighty stuck-up with his overcoat." The staircase was lit by a single oil lamp which barely showed the dirty plastered walls and greasy, unpainted deal balustrade. Through the open door of the dormitory at the top of the stairs he heard shrieks and laughter. There was dead silence, however, when he entered. He underwent another scrutiny from a number of boys who had evidently been arranging their cubicles, but who all turned and stared at him frankly.

On each side of the long, lofty room were rows of narrow, curtained cubicles, the curtains drawn back to plain deal poles.

"It's a mighty queer place entirely," said Larry, on seeing Ralph. "Like a lot of loose horse-boxes they are, only it's many a horse has better quarters. Where am I to put your box, Master Ralph?"

A florid-faced youth of about twenty, with weak staring eyes and light hair, said nervously, "Mr O'Brien is number seventeen."

"Catch Ginger not to interfere," said a smaller boy in a disgusted tone. "It'd be fun to see the old lad poke round with the box."

"Unmannerly brats!" said Larry, wrathfully, as he laid the trunk at the foot of the narrow bed.

There was just room for the trunk. The only vacant space left was a tiny strip along the side of the bed, enough to walk along but hardly enough to turn in. When Larry had gone, Ralph sat on his bed with a sinking heart. He looked helplessly at his trunk. Save a wooden ledge on the wall at the head of the bed and a few rough nails in one of the lateral poles of the cubicle, there was no place to put away anything.

"Best leave them all in your trunk," said Ginger, whom Ralph asked what he was to do.

"I'm Mr Magan. I expect to go to Maynooth this year," he said by way of introduction.

"I'm O'Brien," said Ralph, grateful that anyone should speak to him.

"Oh, sure I know that, Mr O'Brien. I heard tell of you, and as you are the only new gentleman expected after this vac, I knew you at once. You can hang up the clothes you'll be using on them nails and put your comb on that shelf. I'd lock my box if I were you when you're going down, in case you have a cake or the like; you might find it gone when you come back if you don't."

Magan took Ralph to the large classroom, which was also used as a study hall.

"We don't settle down to work," he said, "till tomorrow. This is a free night and there's nothing to do till supper."

Magan, who seemed to be somewhat of a butt, was soon engaged with a small group by the fireplace and left Ralph to his own resources. Beyond being stared at, he was left severely alone. He brought down some books and sat at his desk reading. He felt he was the subject of conversation among several groups. He heard "Inniscar", and "Jesuits" – "old sweater, that's how he got his prizes".

There was a hissing sound from the door. Someone whispered "*Tace* – Nibs". There was general silence. The group at the fire dissolved as Father Phil stalked into the room in soutane and biretta, a light cane under his arm. There was a feeble clapping of hands as he stood at a rostrum by the fireplace. He struck the desk sharply a few times with his cane and shouted "silence," glaring around fiercely.

He called the roll and each answered "*adsum*". When he came to Ralph's name he said, "Mr O'Brien is a sub-prefect. When he is in charge of the hall, he will get the same obedience as I get, or you will hear of it."

He glared again. "I see you've taken my warning and are all here in time this term. All I shall say is that it is well for you that you are." He looked at his watch. "It's just five minutes to supper-time. There is no spiritual reading tonight, but go to the oratory for a visit to the Blessed Sacrament and examination of conscience."

Ralph followed Magan to the oratory, where all knelt for a few minutes in front of the Blessed Sacrament. They were silent and recollected for the most part, but behind him a few were whispering and sniggering. His thoughts wandered and he found himself listening. He said an ejaculatory prayer and tried to fix his attention on the Divine Presence in the tabernacle, but his thoughts strayed to home. He felt hungry, and for the first time missed his tea. A tall, good-looking young man with fair hair said the "*Salve Regina*" aloud.

"No one can stand that Devine since he was made a prefect," whispered a voice behind. "Hear how he says the prayer, imitating Nibs himself."

The dining hall in which supper was served was an annex to the priest's house, abutting on the courtyard. Ralph was struck on entering by the odour of stale food. At the end opposite the entrance was a raised table running across the room, "the professors' table," Magan whispered to Ralph. At right angles to it were three long tables for the students. "Since you're sub-prefect you sit at the top of the middle table," said Magan, pushing Ralph forward. There were no chairs at the students' tables, long forms without backs serving instead. The tables were without tablecloths, of deal, and smelled of rotten cabbage. A rough tin urn stood at the head and foot of each table, surrounded by stacks of bowls. Trays of thick slices of unbuttered bread lay on the tables.

Ralph's appetite having completely gone by the time he sat down, he looked idly around, listening to the life of St Aloysius Gonzaga, which a small boy perched in a high pulpit near the door was reading aloud.

"Can't you pour out the tea?" his neighbour said, nudging him. "*Agimus tibi gratias*'ll be said before you know where you be."

He turned the tap and filled bowl after bowl with the strong mixture of tea and milk. He watched the others eat dry bread ravenously and gulp down the tepid tea, but he could not bring himself to eat.

The sole occupant of the professors' table was a pallid, delicate-looking young man, round-shouldered and long haired, with a yellow moustache, who leaned forward and whispered to Ralph, "It's not nice, but eat it. You'll get nothing else. If not, you'll be hungry before half-past eight tomorrow morning."

Ralph nibbled a crust of bread and took a long drink of tea. He could not eat the bread, which was stale, and had a sour smell. Nor could he drink when he discovered that the dirty table was greasy to the touch, as if it had been wiped with a greasy cloth.

There was a growing murmur of conversation at the lower end of the tables.

"How long shall we have to stay here?" Ralph asked Magan, who sat beside him.

"Shi-shi-shi!" Magan said under his breath, his eyes fixed on the table. "Don't talk like that. It's against the rules. The rule of silence binds in the refectory."

"But they are talking down there."

"They might then! but, you see, the professor can't see them. That makes all the diference. He might tell Nibs."

While Ralph pondered this interpretation of a rule, the noise grew louder, drowning the reader's voice; pellets and crusts were thrown from table to table.

The teacher at the high table struck it sharply with a spoon. Rising abruptly, he said grace.

"You see," said Magan, as they left the hall, "the lads know Father Phil don't like Boyle, and so they think Nibs won't pay any heed if Boyle reports them. I think it better to be safe myself. I don't want to run any risks of not going to Maynooth this year."

Devine, the prefect, came up to Ralph at the door.

"We have free time till night prayers," he said shyly "Will you walk round with me?"

Ralph smiled assent.

Magan said eagerly, "I'll come, too, with ye."

As they walked away some one jeered behind, "Bedad, Ginger has got into the swell set at last."

There was a general laugh.

The night was moonless, but bright clusters of stars gave enough light to prevent the small groups of two or three from colliding as they walked briskly around the courtyard.

"There's a field beyond, behind the bishop's house, that we use as a playground, but it's too dark for it tonight," said Devine.

"When does the rule of silence bind?" asked Ralph.

"Always, except during recreations," Devine answered hesitatingly.

Magan laughed. "Troth, it's more like the truth to say when the lads are asleep or Nibs' eyes are on them," he said.

"They are so young here," said Devine, apologetically. "It will be different when we get to Maynooth. There everything is beautiful," he continued enthusiastically. "No one thinks of breaking a rule – they are all so full of spiritual fervour."

"Is Nibs Father Doyle?" Ralph asked.

"Mr Magan shouldn't have used that name. It's not becoming, especially in a senior," said Devine, primly.

Magan muttered something which Ralph did not catch.

"Father Doyle is a fine character," said Devine. "He has to be severe sometimes, but he has the true priestly spirit."

"He's having it now, I don't doubt," said Magan, chuckling.

"I expected to see him at supper," said Ralph.

"It's expecting him you'll be, then," said Magan. "It's down at Father Molloy's he is every night, playing nap, or beyond at the Hinnisseys', singing a song with the young ladies, when he's not having a party of his own in the –"

"That's wicked gossip, Mr Magan," said Devine, angrily. "I'm really surprised at you. I'm sure the President," turning to Ralph, "is attending to his spiritual duties somewhere. He has often told me he was so occupied in giving spiritual advice that it seriously interrupted his other duties."

"Giving spiritual advice to the Miss Hinnisseys, I don't doubt," Magan retorted. "Sure the whole world knows that the reason you're a prefect is because you're such an ownshuck and it's so easy to throw dust in your eyes."

The light of the lamp over the doorway of the school fell on Devine's white, strained face. He bit his lips angrily and endeavoured to calm himself.

"We shall say goodnight, Mr Magan," he said. "I wish to speak to Mr O'Brien."

"Thank you for nothing, Mr Devine," said Magan, angrily, as he turned in at the door, "I can see when my company's not wanted."

Ralph felt inclined to laugh, but the pained look on Devine's face restrained him. He was distressed by the scene and not a little shocked at Magan's way of talking of Father Doyle, but the care which the two young men took to address each other as "Mister" in the height of the anger amused him.

"Why do you 'Mister' each other all the time? It sounds so odd."

"'Mister!' Oh, it's the custom. Don't they do it everywhere? All the spiritual books speak against undue familiarity. 'Mister' must be ecclesiastical. Father Doyle and the bishop use it always in addressing the students.... You weren't scandalised, I hope," he added hesitatingly. "I must apologise to you for giving way to anger. It was very sinful of me, but Mr Magan is very trying. You mustn't pay any attention to the rash judgments of some of the students. It's very sad, but they give way to them sometimes. I do what I can to stop it. But it's my temper. I pray and I pray, but I can't get it under proper control. You'll pray for me sometimes, won't you? And don't feel badly against Mr Magan either," he added wistfully. "He has a kind heart, though he is unjust in his speech. I – I think we ought to pray for him, too."

In a rather depressed but gentle voice he told Ralph the hours of class and other duties; as sub-prefect he would have to keep order in the study hall in Devine's absence and generally use his influence in having the rules of the school observed.

The bell for night prayers sounded as Devine was in the middle of a sentence. He stopped speaking at once, and they walked in silence to the oratory, where Devine recited the prayers. When he finished, the majority of the students hurried away, but a few remained on their knees in prayer before the Blessed Sacrament.

When Ralph got to the dormitory there was a loud murmur of conversation behind many of the drawn curtains. He took off his boots and put them outside his curtain.

"What are your boots doing out there in the gangway? I nearly tripped over them," said Magan, pushing them aside.

"To be cleaned."

"Did one ever hear the like! And who do you think'll polish them for you but yourself? There's a boot room down below at the back; you can black them there after mass of a morning. Some of the lads do it every day, but I find once a week enough myself."

"Oh!" said Ralph, gloomily. "By the way, where can I have a wash?"

"Do you mean now?" asked Magan in astonishment.

"Yes."

"Wanting to wash at night! Sorra one of me knows. I never heard of any one wanting to do it before. You can't use the basins beyond at the end of the dormitory. They can only be used in the morning. There's a wash-basin in the lavatory downstairs; maybe you'd find some water there. There's generally a can left in at night for a few lads who are mighty particular of themselves and have little brushes for their teeth."

Ralph remembered that it was silence time. He put his finger to his lip.

"Oh, there's no fear. Father Phil is out. There's no light in his window, and Devine never leaves the chapel till the last minute."

Ralph shook his head and did not speak.

Magan pursed his lips and whistled. "Oh, are you one of that sort?" he said in a contemptuous tone. "However, you're new to it. I doubt you'll grow out of it soon. They mostly do," he said, more cheerfully, as he shuffled off.

Ralph tried the lavatory, but there was no water left. When he reached the dormitory again Devine was just entering.

"It's within three minutes of half-past nine," he said; "the light is put out then."

Ralph scrambled into bed. A brisk conversation was kept up from cubicle to cubicle for some time, but gradually it died out. A short distance off a boy was snoring stertorously. The faint rumble of a distant cart seemed to keep time with the snorer. Ralph tried in vain to sleep. A curious smell pervaded the room as of clothes worn too long. It got on his nerves, and he twisted and turned restlessly. Thoughts kept crowding on him, but he tried to put them away. It was all so different from his ideal. He felt horribly homesick. What after all if everything was not as he had once pictured it? Yet who was he to judge? A miserable sinner, vain and proud. All the true servants of God had their trials. Ought he not to be glad to have an opportunity of offering little sacrifices? Up to now he had done nothing. The saints made real sacrifices and did not moan under petty trifles....

He was about to sit down to a comfortable meal when the dining-table fell to the floor with a bang. He seemed to hear a fire brigade bell. He rubbed his eyes, jumped out of bed, opened the curtains and looked out. The lights were again on. Devine was walking along the passage, an old waterproof coat over his night things, vigorously ringing a hideously-sounding handbell and saying at intervals in a loud voice, "*Benedicamus Domino*", to which sleepy voices responded, "*Et cum spiritu tuo*".

Ralph did not know where the bathroom was, so he partially dressed and had a prefunctory wash at one of the half-dozen wash-basins in the dormitory, where Devine and one or two others were making their toilettes. There was no movement behind many of the curtains until a warning bell was rung at five minutes to seven. As Ralph was leaving for the oratory, there was a rush on the wash-basins by thirty or forty boys in different stages of undress, but as there were only six basins, the majority had to dispense with washing.

When Devine began to read morning prayers, about half the students were present. A few were completely dressed, but, for the most part, clothes had been put on anyhow; collars and ties were missing, boots were unlaced and hair was guiltless of a brush. Stragglers continued to arrive at intervals. When Devine marked down the names at the conclusion of prayer,s all seemed to be present. Two of the students went to the little sacristy behind the altar and soon appeared in soutanes and surplices and prepared the altar for mass.

The oratory was cold and dimly lit. There was much coughing, yawning and shuffling of feet. When the candles on the altar had been lighted for about ten minutes, the shuffling of feet increased, and there was much muttering in the back benches.

"I doubt he was out late last night," someone said. Two or three sniggered. Devine looked at his watch uneasily two or three times, and at last, when more than half the students seemed to be deliberately scraping the floor with their feet, he went hastily to the sacristy. One of the servers came out at once without his surplice and extinguished the candles.

There was a stampede of the students to the study hall, where Ralph found them gathered round the fire, which had just been lighted.

"What did I tell you?" said Magan, chuckling, his florid face a bright purple with cold. "Didn't I tell you Father Phil was making a night of it?"

Devine came in and said, "I'm sorry that Father Doyle doesn't feel at all well. He was unable to say mass, but he will be down to breakfast, after which business will go on as usual. As this is the opening day, he says you may have a free study now and talk if you wish."

One said, ironically, "Hear, hear."

Ralph asked Magan where was the bathroom.

Magan looked at him suspiciously. "Is't joking me you are?" he said. "You might be the one too many that'd try that game on me."

When he saw that Ralph was serious he burst out laughing. "What'd we be wanting with the like?" he said. "Sure I never heard tell of any grown-up person taking a bath unless he'd be delicate. There's a bath-house down by the sea for the visitors that come in the summer for their health. I heard tell there was one in the bishop's house, but I doubt if it's true. What'd he be wanting with it and he a strong man? You're not delicate, are you?" he said eagerly.

Ralph spent the time before breakfast in writing a cheerful account of the Seminary in four pages to his mother. He dwelled chiefly on Devine.

Father Phil was at breakfast. Beside him sat an old man, his grey hair brushed carefully over a bald top, with shaggy eyebrows and moustache and a purple and enlarged nose. Boyle, looking cold and white, sat at the corner of the high table, as far away as possible from Father Phil.

"That's old Nolan, that teaches French and things, alongside Nibs," whispered Magan, as the students took their seats. "It's not often he feels like taking any breakfast."

There were cloths on the tables. Each student had a knife, plate and butter. Otherwise breakfast was the same as supper, except that the bowls were larger.

Father Phil's keen glance seemed to be on everyone. There was complete silence, save for the reader's voice, the clatter of knives on plates and the gurgling sounds made by many of the boys in drinking tea. Ralph was ravenously hungry and ate huge quantities of bread. He had never cared for eggs and bacon, but he longed for some now; the smell of the dish standing in front of Father Phil, for use at the high table, was so delicious.

Boyle followed Ralph from the refectory and picked him up halfway across the courtyard.

"Hello! O'Brien," he said. "Let us have a walk. I'm Boyle, one of the teachers, God save the mark! in this blessed place. I'm an old Ignatian and I've some of the marks of Father Best about me still." He smiled wanly. "Father Doyle doesn't encourage my mixing with the students, but I think we may risk it for once. I'll take the responsibility, anyway."

He buttoned his thin coat tightly around him.

"This is rather a jolly field," he said, opening the wicket that led to the playing-ground, "with a view of the sea from the top of the hill." They walked briskly over the hard ground, still white with a hoar frost. The sun glittered on the frosted branches of a clump of beech trees.

"Trees look so much better without their leaves," he said abstractedly, "especially in frost and a bright sun."

He asked innumerable questions about Father Best and the old school.

"You got the ruler sometimes!"

"Often," said Ralph, smiling.

"I was miserable enough when I was there. Yet what a paradise it seems now when I look back on it," Boyle said sadly.

They had reached the top of the short hill and stood looking at the sea, which broke over long shelving rocks almost at their feet.

"Where all save the spirit of man, and the work of man's hands, too, is divine," Boyle said bitterly. "We must be off. It is nearly class time. Look here, O'Brien," he said gravely, taking Ralph's arm, "you mustn't allow yourself to be disillusioned here in this opera bouffe of a school. Stick tight to every dream you ever had about the Church and religion. If things jar on you, make yourself believe that they are all right somewhere else." His voice had grown shrill with excitement. "They must be," he said more calmly, "or my old mother wouldn't be the saint she is. I excite myself over everything. Faith ought to be easy for me." He laughed nervously. "There's no fear of the old Church ever petering out! You stick to your ideals, anyway."

The class bell ceased ringing as they crossed the courtyard. They met Father Doyle, who was coming from his house with a bundle of books and papers under his arm, on the school doorstep. He moved aside to let them pass.

"A bad beginning, Mr Boyle," he said dryly, a hard smile on his thin lips. "You should be in your classroom now ... keeping Mr O'Brien late, too."

Boyle's face flushed. "It was my fault," he said stiffly, and passed on.

"You follow me, Mr O'Brien," Father Doyle said, sweeping past him into the large hall.

The priest knelt on one knee on his desk stool and said the "*Veni sancte spiritus*" hurriedly.

He gave a short lecture to the senior grade class on the importance of studying hard until summer.

If those who expected to go to Maynooth showed any slackness he would have no hesitation in keeping them back a year. He appointed lessons for the following day in Latin and Greek. He yawned two or three times.

"The night is telling on him," said Magan, under his breath.

"As we have no lessons today we shall fill in the hour with recitations. Come, Mr Lanigan, give us 'Excelsior'."

"He must be going out to dinner; he's in such good fettle," said Magan.

Lanigan, a sallow-faced shock-headed youth, whose hair had not been brushed for weeks, came forward awkwardly and leant his back against the wall. He put his hands in his trousers' pockets and closed his eyes.

"Take you hands out of your pockets."

He took them out and clasped them across his breast. He began the first verse in a lugubrious voice, stammered and broke down.

"I can't go on," he said miserably.

"Go back to your seat, sir. What a pulpit orator he'll make!" said the priest, sneering. Many of the boys laughed.

"I suppose I must recite something myself," Father Doyle said, smiling.

The class shouted uproariously. The priest waved his hand deprecatingly for silence. He first gave "Lochiel's Warning", and, in response to the loud cheers with which this was greeted, "King Robert of Sicily".

There was applause for several minutes.

Magan yawned. "It's all a rotten bore," he said, "but it's better than work, anyway."

"You can now study your Greek for tomorrow," the priest said, "until it's time for Mr Nolan's class." He took a folded newspaper from between his books and read it at the desk. When the clock struck ten he again knelt on one knee on the seat, said a short prayer and, gathering up his book,s left the room.

"It's the last we'll see of him for the day, I doubt," said Magan.

No sooner was the priest outside the door than a general conversation began. Devine in vain called "silence".

"'Silence' for Mr Devine's sermon on how to be a goody-goody," said a muffled voice from the back.

"I wonder what's keeping old Nolan?" said Lanigan.

"Oh! he's out the town for sure," said Magan.

"There'll likely be some fun then."

"There might then."

There was a sudden hush in the conversation and all eyes were turned towards the door. Ralph looked round to see the cause. Mr Nolan had just come in, hat on head, and was shutting the door with elaborate care with his left hand, balancing himself with a stick in his right. He walked cautiously, but erect, towards the desk, touching the wall with his left hand and leaning heavily on the stick in his other. Half-way he stopped, keeping one hand on the wall and one on the stick, glared at the boys, and said in measured tones, "What are you looking at, you country bumpkins? Have you never seen a gentleman before?"

He reached the desk at last, took off his hat, overcoat and gloves very slowly, and sat down with difficulty.

"I have to apologise, gentlemen, for being so late," he said suavely, "my rheumatism is very bad today."

"He has been oiling it with Pat Darcy's rum," said Magan. "I smelled it the minute he came in the door."

"Did you speak, Mr Magan?" said Nolan, slowly.

Magan's red face grew redder; he stood up and said glibly, "I only said how sorry we all were to hear tell of your rheumatism, sir."

"A very proper remark ... somewhat infelicitous in structure, but very proper."

He opened a book. "I have here the French text for this term, a simple book...."

"I beg pardon, sir," said Lanigan, rising, "but did you do that text at Beaumont?"

"No, sir, we did not do such a trivial book at Beaumont in my time, but these so-called Intermediate Education Commissioners...."

For the remainder of the hour he spoke of the superiority of Beaumont to all other schools in the world and of the incompetence of the Intermediate Education Commissioners.

"That was cute of Lanigan, I must admit; when old Nolan is just at the proper stage any mention of Beaumont sets him off and he forgets all about the lesson. I thought myself he was a bit too far gone. When he is, he's likely to turn rusty. 'Twas mighty cute of Lanigan," said Magan, admiringly.

When Nolan had negotiated the passage out of the room with somewhat more ease than he entered, Devine announced a half free day – the next forenoon class off and no class in the afternoon.

Books were hastily thrown into desks, and all the students looked cheerful. One or two spoke in friendly tones to Ralph. They were to have lunch at once and then a long walk.

Lunch was a simple affair of a hunch of bread taken from a basket in the refectory and put in one's pocket to be eaten on the walk.

Ralph got back tired, after an interesting talk with Lanigan who knew Irish, to hear that his mother had called in his absence "in a carriage and two horses", the maid said impressively. He tried to make up his mind, while he ate his one-course dinner of boiled mutton, turnips and potatoes, whether he was glad or sorry that he had not seen her. On the whole he thought he was glad. She would have been inquisitive about the Seminary, and he should not have known what to say.

Chapter 9

RALPH STUDIED HARD, with little encouragement from any of the teachers except Boyle. Nolan's classes were farcical. He was seldom sober and was kept on, Magan said, because he was a connection by marriage of Father Doyle's. Ralph and Devine alone did their French lessons regularly. In addition to his own work Ralph had to keep abreast of the studies of the junior classes, as every day he was called on by Father Doyle to take some class when the priest was called away on "urgent business". Up to Easter Father Doyle was frequently absent. Even when he took a class, for most of the time he read a newspaper or book, generally a novel of Gaboriau's in the red paper covers of Vizetelly's edition. When Magan jeered at this, Devine said that priests had to read these books to be able to give advice to penitents in the confessional. Father Doyle had himself told him this, he said.

Ralph was struck by the difference of methods between Father Doyle and his Jesuit teachers. Father Best liked to be asked questions, but Father Doyle severely punished Lanigan for asking a question, saying that it was highly improper. It was for the teacher to impart all the information he considered necessary and for the pupil to receive it humbly. The only information Father Doyle though it necessary to give was covered by the notes in the textbooks. One day, Magan was translating a chorus of the Antigone in language that would have made Father Best tear his hair, but Father Doyle took no notice. He even passed over a gross mistranslation.

"Nibs must have lost his own crib," whispered Lanigan.

Magan, who was hesitating and stammering, got suddenly fluent, making a travesty of the text. After a few minutes, Father Doyle stopped him with "Very good indeed, Mr Magan," and appointed the lesson for the next class without asking any questions.

"Poor Father Doyle is so overworked that he was inattentive at class today. He often gets these fits of absent-mindedness," said

Devine to Ralph.

There was much sniggering among the students during recreation, and many small jokes were made about Magan's new translation of the Antigone with an introduction by the learned Father Phil Doyle.

Ralph said to Lanigan that it was very wrong to make these jokes about a priest, all the more as they were untrue.

Lanigan looked at him pityingly. "With all you know, it's little sense you have," he said. "Why, with all I've picked up from Boyle I know ten times more Greek than Nibs, and it's little I know at that. And I could say the same of Latin, for that matter. Didn't I often find the word-for-word translation hid in a book on his desk? Sorra line he could do without it. And I can manage with an ordinary translation myself."

Ralph was worried for a while, but Devin's faith in Father Doyle swept away the slight doubts he had momentarily entertained. It was impossible to believe that the priest could fail to know Greek and Latin well. Of course, he was not a good teacher, like Father Best, but he must be a competent scholar, otherwise he would not have charge of a Seminary.

The bishop confirmed him in this view. Father Doyle told him one morning that his lordship wished to see him and that he was to call at the "palace" at eleven.

The episcopal "palace" was an ugly two-storied house adjoining the Seminary. Ralph was shown into the study, a large square room lined with books. The bishop was seated in an armchair in front of the fire, in soutane and sash, his purple biretta far back on his head, reading the *Freeman's Journal*.

"Sit down, sit down, Mr O'Brien," he said, when Ralph had knelt and kissed his ring. "I have just been staying with your estimable parents. Devoted children of the Church, both of them – in different ways, of course. Your mother is a wonderful woman. The best type that our modern convents turn out. The olden time's St Chantal, a helper of that holy bishop St Francis de Sales, was of that kind – capable of heroic sacrifice for Holy Church, if the occasion arose."

Ralph assented warmly.

"And how are you getting on at the Seminary? Although I don't visit it often it is the apple of my eye. But I have such confidence in

Father Doyle – a wonderful priest, when you come to know him. A man of strong character, but humility itself. He anticipates my wishes before I can express them. An example of obedience, too, that I wish all priests to follow. Notwithstanding his arduous work at the Seminary he is constantly helping me. I don't know what I should do without him."

In the afternoon, during a walk in the playing-field, Ralph repeated this to Boyle, who had heard of the Antigone incident.

"They are both wonderful people. It's a toss up as to which is the more unique specimen," Boyle said, staring at Ralph.

Ralph was distressed that Boyle had not taken the story with more sympathy, but attributed it to his ill-health. Lately, much of Father Phil's work had been thrown on him, and he had become very fretful. Ralph thought it a pity that the parish work was so arranged that so much of it fell to Father Phil. The work of the students suffered, and there were these misunderstandings with Boyle.

"The intermediate exams this year will be a greater mess than usual, and that's saying a good deal," said Boyle, sighing. "I'm doing the best I can, but I can't teach sixty to seventy boys in four grades Latin, Greek, French, mathematics and English." He shrugged his shoulders. "Unless Father Phil gets enough fees to enable him to throw money about at Harrowgate and London during the holidays, I shall probably get fired."

"But everyone knows you overwork yourself," Ralph said.

"You've heard of the scapegoat? It's a biblical animal still religiously preserved in the Church. However, I oughtn't to speak in this way to you. I'm only an old grumbler."

There was a break in class for some days before and after Easter. The Seminary students attended the Cathedral for the ceremonies of Holy Week. Ralph was thurifer and was a good deal in the sacristy. He had been accustomed to attend religious ceremonies in Dublin and could not help contrasting the want of order in Bunnahone with the order of the Dublin churches.

It was the first time that he came in touch with a large body of priests. They had come in for the week from the surrounding country parishes.

Ralph had always associated Holy Week with mourning and gloom. The Church put on her saddest garments to commemorate the sufferings and death of the man God. Both Ann and his mother went to services clad in black and spoke during these days in low tones. Even his father became unusually grave.

The Bunnahone Cathedral was draped in purple, but in the sacristy the priests were in holiday humour. The centre of gaiety was a fat priest, almost bald, with blinking eyes, Father Molloy, whom Ralph had seen at the Seminary a few times and who was, he knew, the administrator of the Cathedral. He carried a snuff-box open in his left hand and poked his right forefinger at the breasts of all the priests to whom he spoke. Everybody called him Father Tom, and he seemed to be popular.

"As fine a bit of salmon as ever was seen! Two whole ones, for that matter – about fifteen pounds each. Came down from Dublin last night and lying snug up at the parochial house now. Catch Tom Molloy for not feeding ye well, boys," he said to a small group of priests.

"I can imagine I was eating it now," said a short, apple-faced priest, licking his lips.

"And a nip of Three Star brandy afterwards," Molloy said, "to prevent the fish upsetting the stomach. Pat Darcy got it down for me special."

"More power to you, Tom. Sure 'tis you think of everything," said the apple-faced man.

"And when all the mugs," nodding towards Father Sheldon, who was reading his breviary at a window, "are gone, we'll have a game of nap – Doyle and five or six more of the lads," said Molloy, confidentially, in a lower tone.

"Fine," said the apple-faced man, rubbing his hands. "There's no fear of the lord getting wind of it?"

"Who cares?" said Molloy, pompously. "Besides," he added, leering, "with all his shaping, 'tis glad enough he'd be to take a hand himself, only he's high and mighty since he got the belly-band on him."

"Does Doyle still pull the strings?"

"Aye, and twists him round his little finger."

"I wouldn't wonder if he was a bishop himself some day. Begorra, he's great."

"All my training," said Molloy, with a gratified smirk. "Did you hear about him and the eldest Miss Hinnissey?"

Ralph coughed loudly. He was hemmed in a corner between the vestment press and the wall by the group of priests. He had grown more and more uneasy as the conversation developed and was now blushing furiously.

"What the dev – what are you listening for?" said Molloy, angrily.

Ralph's face became white, then flushed a dark crimson. His usually soft eyes had a hard look as he said, curtly, "I didn't listen. Please let me pass."

Molloy laughed uneasily. "How very lofty we are! I often say things," he said, winking at his companions, "to take a rise out of these Seminary lads."

Ralph did not believe him. Was it possible that any priest could speak in this way? Then to accuse him of listening – it was intolerable; and to tell a lie! These thoughts ran through his mind during the service that followed. Father Molloy's squeaky voice, singing out of tune, grated on his ears. He looked at the priest and wavered in his judgment. The squat little man seemed grotesque, gripping the vesperale in his podgy hands, his pendulous cheeks distended as he sang – or rather shouted, for he had no sense of pitch – his eyes fixed earnestly on his book. He had heard Father Molloy referred to as a great joker. Perhaps he was only jesting? Out-of-place jests, but who was he to judge? He thought, with a shock, that while Father Molloy was now singing a hymn of praise to God, he himself was indulging in uncharitable thoughts. He fixed his eyes on the thurible, which he was swinging rhythmically, and said an act of contrition.

Ralph confessed in the evening to the old Dominican prior, who was the Seminary confessor, and accused himself of thinking badly of a priest. He told the story of the sacristy incident confusedly.

The old priest listened in silence. "I wouldn't let it come between me and my night's rest, if I were you," he said gently. "There are all sorts of priests, from Francis of Assisi to the other extreme. It is for you to aim at being the best. As to the others, unless you can help them, leave them alone. God is a kinder judge than the best of us; let us always remember that, and try to imitate His patience and mercy. We see only the surface of things and are offended by coarseness or by a slight to our own pride. He sees deeper down. Take the advice of an old man, and dig your own furrow. Don't criticise the make of the other man's spade, or the way he holds it, or puts it into the earth, unless you're pretty certain of helping him to dig deeper and better ... and it's very hard to be certain of anything in this world. Go round the stations of the cross five times for your penance."

At the first class after the Easter recess, Father Doyle made a vigorous speech on the necessity of hard work until the examinations were over. Instead of a red-covered novel he had in his hand a sheaf of dummy examination papers with the answers attached. In some subterranean way he had found out the names of the examiners in the several subjects at the forthcoming examinations in June. He had then looked up all the examination papers previously set by these examiners and picked out what seemed to be their favourite questions. The students were ordered under pain of severe punishment to learn all these questions and their answers by heart.

"Have you been reading over the papers Nibs gave out this morning?" said Magan to Ralph at recreation.

"Yes."

"Do you think they are good answers, now?"

"As far as I can judge they are."

"It beats me to know how he done them then," said Magan, in a puzzled tone.

"He do them!" said Lanigan, contemptuously; "he'd ate them first. For sure it's that clever cousin of his at University College that did 'em for him. I'd bet sixpence to a penny on it."

Magan gave a sigh of relief. "Troth I'll learn every word of 'em then," he said. "I was doubtful whether it'd be worth while as long as I thought they might be his own doing."

Good or bad, Magan would probably have had to learn the sets of answers, as Father Doyle mercilessly punished those who failed to be word perfect.

All available time was now given up to study or to lessons. Half days were stopped; several religious exercises – spiritual reading in the evenings, catechism, religious instruction on Sundays – were dropped; recreation time was shortened. Students who were to be presented for the intermediate examinations were entirely separated from those who, for reasons of age or stupidity, were not allowed to present themselves. These latter were left severely alone, got no instruction whatever and had, as one of them said, "the finest of times". Ralph was given three or four doubtful students "to work up". Boyle worked unceasingly in class and out. Even Nolan kept more or less sober and helped a little. But it was Father Phil who kept up the constant pressure.

"There is no doubt he has driving force," Boyle said to Ralph. "If he had knowledge to back it up he would be one of the most successful teachers under this stupid system." He smiled cynically. "It would be amusing," he said, "if one of those fellows got an exhibition. Anything is possible in those rotten examinations. If a sufficient number of the questions Doyle has picked out are given, and if the fellows are clever enough to hide their general ignorance, Her Majesty's Commissioners for Intermediate Education in Ireland will pay a tidy sum to this great seat of learning."

Hilda, who went to see Ralph about once a fortnight, reported to her husband that it was most edifying how hard the students worked. "They were rather unkempt," she said, "and their linen was not very clean, but it was wonderful to see them studying in the playing-fields during recreation." She complained that Ralph had grown more reserved, less enthusiastic. Yet she was glad to find that he was more keen than ever on being a priest. She was sure that Father Doyle had a good influence on Ralph – he was so holy and so kind. Unlike Father Best, Father Doyle was not entirely absorbed in his secular studies. They had a most interesting conversation on the efficacy of the nine Fridays, in which he disclosed a highly spiritual nature, treading heights of spirituality which she, indeed, could not attempt....

Meanwhile, the days of examination approached. There was a night study up to half-past ten and the hour for rising was six instead of half-past. Father Phil's cane revolved rapidly. Magan said, ruefully, that though he worked like a nigger and had the best memory in the Seminary, he got a hundred and twenty slaps in one week, "and me a grown man, too, you might say," he added. "Only that the whole world knows it's a mortal sin to strike a priest, and besides, it would ruin my chances of getting to Maynooth, I think I'd have a go back at him. Now if I was going to be a doctor or the like, like Delaney there, I think I'd risk the sin of it. Sorra bit of spunk Delaney has in him that doesn't have a go for him."

"And he over six foot!" said Delaney, "and his muscles that hard from using the cane! Troth, I'd rather the cane itself than his fist, and it'd be that surely if his temper was up."

At supper on the evening preceding the examination there was much excitement. There had already been much discussion as to what the superintendent of the examinations would be like. At his examinations Ralph had taken no notice of the superintendent, but at Bunnahone he was evidently a person of importance. Magan said enigmatically, "Some of them is that sharp it's little one could do without their noticing it. On the other hand some of them is that looney that they might just as well be asleep, or not there at all." The superintendent came to supper with Father Phil and was the object of much attention. "I think he'll do," whispered Magan, nodding his head approvingly.

"It's a good sign that he's staying with Father Phil," said Magan to a small group at the playing-field gate after supper. "The particular ones stop at the hotel."

"I found out his name from the maid," said Lanigan, "and I asked Boyle if he ever heard of him. He said he was one of them lads that are always writing books on old ruins that nobody ever reads. It'd be great entirely if he'd only write during the exam."

"It's very likely he will," said Magan. "I watched his eyes when he had done supper and they were fixed on the wall by the door. Sorra one of us he ever saw, and we right fornint him. He was like a man in a dream like."

Ralph was surprised to see Magan wearing white cuffs on the morning of the examination.

"I'm a swell today," Magan said, leering. "They're mighty convenient for writing an odd note or a date on."

"You wouldn't do that!"

"Wouldn't I, then? And where's the harm? Sure it's many a place they do worse. Not but that some of the lads here are fairly spry. Did you ever hear tell of Creddin, who got a junior exhibition and a medal? That time there was a blind sort of superintendent, like the lad in there now. What did Creddin do but pass out the examination papers through the window to an over-age fellow who wasn't standing the exam – a clever enough fellow, too. He passed back the answers to Creddin the same way. Nibs himself couldn't make it out, Creddin was that stupid that no one expected him even to pass. A year after, when the story was let out, Nibs nearly laughed himself to death over it. For in the meantime one of them colleges, that send touts round the country to pick up likely students, nobbled Creddin by the offer of a free place, in the hope of gaining some credit by more exhibitions. But sure sorra even pass an examination he ever did again, and the college lost by his keep and teaching for near three years. He hadn't the cleverness to be able to do the trick again," he added contemptuously.

"Father Doyle must have been very angry," said Ralph. "The whole incident was so dishonourable."

"What! and an exhibition coming to the Seminary! And why would he be vexed? Vexed indeed! If he was, it's a queer way he had of showing it."

At the recess for lunch Devine was rather depressed.

"I suppose it's all right," he said to Ralph, "since Father Doyle did it, but in the Latin paper three of the most difficult questions were exactly as they stood on Father Doyle's paper."

Ralph looked uncomfortable.

"He's worse than yourself, Mr Devine, and that's saying a good deal," said Magan, winking at his companions. "There'd be no living in the world at all if it was made up of the likes of ye, and mighty few would pass an exam, in Bunnahone, anyway. What would you say now to some of the lads working a trans for that long passage from the Georgics?"

"They wouldn't dare to do it," said Devine. "If I knew that any one did that I'd tell Father Doyle."

"You make me laugh, you're that innocent," Magan said. "Are you so sure now he'd thank you for your pains? You can't use your eyes no more than that lad that's superintending the exams. Only I had to write a trifle I could enjoy myself greatly watching him, the way he sat there prodding a stump of a pen agin his teeth, and his eyes looking into nowhere. He must be a half idiot or something like, for sorra line but two he ever got down on the paper the whole time. I have a great conceit of myself that I never looked at a text or a trans or a grammar all the time. If I had them with me I might be tempted! Anyway, if we don't get some prizes this time, anyone might readily say we're that wanting in sense that we're only half there.

Why, I could walk out of the room, do my paper outside and the fellow'd never notice that I stirred."

Ralph was reading under the chestnuts during the afternoon examination when Father Doyle came by and took his arm. The priest was in high spirits.

"It's a great pity you've been through these exams, Mr O'Brien," he said. "You could have done some credit to Bunnahone this year. Not but I think we shall do well in any case. All the gentlemen seem to have answered the questions remarkably well."

Ralph hinted at possible irregularities.

The priest frowned. "Surely not. I should not dream of suspecting it. Besides, of course, the responsibility is entirely with the superintendent. If any student gets caught I shall certainly deal summarily with him. I can't have the Seminary getting a bad name. But unless that happened I could not interfere. It would be a reflection on the superintendent, a most charming gentleman."

There was a lurking smile in his grey eyes but his voice kept its even harsh tone.

"Hallo! there's Mr Boyle," said Ralph, as Boyle came into view over the hilltop from the direction of the shore.

Father Doyle's lips hardened.

"You are a friend of Boyle's?" he said, turning so as to avoid Boyle.

"Oh, rather!" said Ralph. "He's such a good chap."

"Hum," said the priest, pursing his lips.

"He's such a good teacher and so kind," Ralph said assertively.

Father Doyle shook his head sadly. "Purely natural virtues!" he said. "I wish he had a little of the spirit of Mr Nolan."

Ralph looked astonished. "Oh, I admit Mr Nolan has some defects," the priest said hastily. "But then he has the great merit of being one of the few lay teachers I know who has a true spirit of devotion to the Church and a proper reverence for priests."

"But surely Mr Boyle is an excellent Catholic. An old Ignatian, too – he is devoted to Father Best."

"He hasn't been criticising things here to you, then?" the priest said, looking keenly at Ralph.

"He is a most honourable man," Ralph said, looking the priest straight in the face.

"He's a dangerous man for all that," said the priest, dryly. He walked a few steps, striking the nail of his thumb against his teeth thoughtfully.

"You are one of us," he said, genially, to Ralph; "I never looked on you as a mere student here and even your nominal pupilage ends in a day or two. You are now practically a Maynooth student, and therefore well within the circle of the priesthood. Let your friends be clerics as far as possible. There is a growing spirit of antagonism to the Church among men of Boyle's class. I don't wish to prejudice you against him. Far be it from me, but I've watched your growing friendship with him with some anxiety. His greatest friend in the town is a man who is suspected of being a free thinker, who is certainly anti-clerical, having on more than one occasion strongly opposed his lordship the bishop in public matters. Boyle may not be quite as bad, but there is evidently sympathy with dangerous views. Then, I don't like his manner. He has a way of lifting his eyebrows that is, to say the least, disrespectful to a priest. He reads books, too, that are highly dangerous, that no good Catholic ought to read. I have seen nothing wrong in his moral conduct, but it is a sad experience that freedom of mind tends to deterioration of morals."

Ralph flushed angrily. The priest shook his head deprecatingly and went on: "I don't forget you have a feeling of friendship for him. It tells well for your good heart. So have I, for that matter. But it is my duty to advise your inexperience. Young students cannot be too careful."

They had reached the gate. Ralph tried to speak, but the priest stopped him. "Don't say anything now. Reflect on what I have told you. Remember, I don't blame you. Ta-ta, I think I'll have a bathe before dinner. I'd ask you to come, but you must keep up the forms here for a day or two yet."

Ralph felt furiously angry and accused himself bitterly of meanness in not defending Boyle. He lay on his back under a chestnut tree and recalled all the priest had said – it was nothing very definite after all. Boyle had an aggressive manner with those he did not like, and that he thoroughly disliked Father Doyle, Ralph knew. Surely the priest was wrong in suspecting Boyle's faith. He found himself at length pitying Boyle's manner. Father Doyle was no doubt right in his anxiety about faith and the Church. Yet Boyle was a fine character at bottom. He could not do a mean thing. He was not so sure of Father Doyle.... It was all very puzzling. His mind went back over his six months at the Seminary. Right and wrong were not the simple things he had thought them. Characters, too, were more complex. He recalled his old confessor's advice. Things had been disagreeable at the Seminary – things which he could not reconcile with his ideals. Priests and students were not angels, though he had once thought they were. Was his inexperience leading him astray? Even Magan might have some good in him? He ought to aim at being a good priest himself and not to be so free in criticising others. All the same, Boyle was a thoroughly good fellow and he would not give up his friendship.

The examinations dragged on. Father Doyle began to go out again and was rarely present at any meal. Magan had fresh tales every day about the superintendent, whom he now called "the old gom", the Seminary equivalent of a fool. Devine was uneasy. He told Ralph that he had reported his suspicions to Father Doyle, who told him that his duties as prefect were in abeyance while he sat at the examinations, that he might conscientiously leave everything to the superintendent. The students were in hilarious spirits and Magan, who, previous to the examinations, had fears of not passing, speculated as to how he would spend a prize, "if I get one, or maybe an exhibition".

Boyle left for his holidays before the examinations were over.

"You're lucky to be leaving this hole for good," he said to Ralph. "I've got to come back for my sins, unless I'm fired," he said gloomily.

"You ought to be able to get a more congenial post easily."

"I wish I could, but it's not easy. I took no profession, as I thought I could make a living by my pen. But I don't sell. Schoolmastering was all that remained. All the Catholic schools are in the hands of the priests. Forty pounds a year and my keep is the most I can get, and that only so long as I succeed in pleasing Father Doyle and his like. If I get into their black books, every school will be closed against me. It's too exciting at times to be pleasant."

Ralph asked him to stay at Inniscar sometime during the summer. He blushed and said he was afraid he couldn't manage it. He looked ruefully at his shabby clothes, hesitated for a moment and said, as he shook Ralph's hand warmly, "I should like to come very much. In fact, I will come. Your people are not likely to mind my clothes, and I have an ancient evening suit somewhere."

Chapter 10

"IT'S BETTER TO be here, anyway, than poked up in that hole at Bunnahone," Father Duff said, surveying a field of ripening oats with pleased eyes as he strolled around his farm with Ralph.

"That rig out of yours, too, is mighty convenient. You couldn't wear that now at the Seminary," looking critically at Ralph's flannels. "When you're a Maynooth student you'll have to give 'em up. '*Niger vel sub niger*', the statutes say. Not but they say a good many foolish things, and '*sub niger*', as far as I can make out, may be any colour under the sun. The bishop once caught me wearing a white flannel bawneen. 'That's not black,' he said, as cross as two sticks. 'Jane was just saying it was as black as the hob,' I said, as innocent as you like. 'And,' he said, 'it's highly undignified, as well as being contrary to the statutes.' 'Oh,' I said, 'I carry my dignity in my four bones and not in my coat.'"

The old priest laughed heartily and looked complacently at the old battered rush hat he held in his hand, and at his clothes, green with age where they were not browned by snuff.

"For a wonder, he saw the point," he added, chuckling.

They wandered along slowly under the hot July sun, tempered by a refreshing breeze from the sea. Ralph had been home for ten days and the Seminary already seemed a distant memory. The golden haze that hung over the fields coloured his thoughts of Bunnahone.

"It's always a puzzle to me what seminaries are for," said the priest, pulling a weed and throwing it into the ditch. "In my time there weren't any. There was a day school in Bunnahone that we went to and learnt the classics off an old hedge schoolmaster by the name of Dignam. He was a queer old man, but maybe I only thought so because I was young. I'm thinking now sometimes that all old men are queer, myself not the least. Dignam used often to have the asthma bad, and then he heard our lessons in his bedroom, we standing up round the bed and he crouched under a blanket that had two holes in it for his hands to get through and hold a book."

He stood looking at a field of potatoes. "A fine crop, thanks be to God," he said. "Anyone, like me, that remembers the black famine feels a rising in his heart at the sight of a good crop of spuds. Ye have a lot of rules and regulations at the Seminary. Are they all kept now?"

Ralph hesitated, the old man eyeing him keenly.

"I thought as much," he said with a sigh. "Do you know what, young man, but I think old Dignam's school was better after all as a training for the priesthood than the great University at Bunnahone – that's what they call the great seats of high learning, I believe; and sure, to hear the bishop and Phil Doyle speaking, anyone would think Bunnahone was one. A lot of the boys were spree boys, sure enough, but the life weeded them out. They turned to drink, or went off to America, or went home and got married. There was very little pretence about anything, for there was nothing to pretend about. An odd fellow like Sheldon would be holy even if he was reared behind the bar of a pub. If there was never a rule in the world he'd make 'em for himself, and keep 'em, too, though he's not much of a hand at keeping other people's. Myself and some others just plodded on; we mightn't be great on spirituality, but we didn't pretend to be any better than we were. We never did anything very wrong either and we had the faith our mothers taught us. But there's Bunnahone Seminary now! Sure no man in his proper senses would lay a lot of rules like they have on the like of the lads they have there. My own sister's grandson, Charlie Magan, among them, that I wouldn't let inside my door and that she's making a priest of in spite of me. Young hypocrites many of 'em were before they went there, and the Lord only knows what they'll be when they're done with it. And Phil Doyle standing in front of 'em as an example, and Tom Molloy, I don't doubt, coming in an odd time to give his blessing to the holy work. Faugh! it's enough to make one sick," hitting the top off a dandelion viciously with his stick.

"There are a lot of very good fellows," said Ralph.

"Small thanks to the Seminary for that," said the priest, angrily. "Are you sure of yourself now, Ralph? Do you think you'll go on?"

"I'm becoming less certain of many things than I used to be," said Ralph, "but my wish to be a priest seems stronger than ever. It has been so much in my mind all my life that it seems part of me. I suffer all sorts of disappointments in myself and in others, yet the feeling that I have some sort of call to be a priest persists."

"No wonder, since you had it drummed into your ears all your life," Father Duff said dryly. "Are you sure, now, you're thinking for yourself?"

"I think so," said Ralph, thoughfully. "The more difficulties I see, the stronger my determination seems to grow. When I have been most shocked at things – it may be priggish of me to say it, but I have been shocked more than once – the clearer my own ideal seems to become; there is so much that a priest might do. Not that I'm foolish enough to think that I shall realise my ideal, but I can aim at it."

"Don't build too many castles on the sand. They have an awkward way of tumbling down at inconvenient times. I never trust myself above the top of a hayrick, and even then I like to keep a solid ladder beneath my feet. I hope no harm will come of those ideals you speak of. I don't know much about ideals, though it's often enough I've heard Sheldon meandering about them. But here we are talking," he looked up at the sun, "and it's twelve o'clock. I ought to be readying myself if I'm going to drive you over to Inniscar for lunch to meet Gray – that fellow from Dublin about the creamery."

"You have one ideal at least," said Ralph, laughing.

"Lunch! Why, I have to make my dinner of it! and it upsets all my meals for the day, and my old stomach, too. Oh! the creamery you mean," as Ralph shook his head. "That's what I call sound common sense. I understand it from A to Z. 'Tis true that Sheldon sees a lot of frillings in it, too, about brotherly love and the like. I prefer myself to stand on the certainty of making better butter."

When Father Duff and Ralph arrived at Inniscar, they found a large party awaiting luncheon in the drawing-room.

Father Sheldon sat in a corner talking to Lady de Lacey, the wife of a neighbouring landlord, Sir Charles de Lacey, who gazed gloomily out of a window, his hands deep in his pockets. Hilda was on a sofa beside Mrs Dillon, who sat very erect and stiff with a disapproving eye on two young priests: Father Dempsey, a freckled, red-haired, thin man in spectacles, and Father Hardy, a round, chubby-faced man with a snub nose and an awkward, pompous manner, who stood uneasily by the piano. Sitting on the edges of their chairs were a stout, florid-faced man with mutton-chop whiskers, Mr Robinson, under-agent to Lord Dawlish, lieutenant of the county, and his wife, a pale little woman, very ill at ease. In the centre of the room was the only lively group: a local landlord named Bowen, tall, handsome and jovial; John O'Brien, Charles Dillon and John Gray, a tall man, with long brown hair and beard and soft brown eyes.

"Late, are we, Mrs O'Brien?" said Father Duff, genially. "That son of yours led me into talk, and I had to change my duds afterwards," looking complacently at his clothes, which were a little less green and snuff-soiled than his working suit.

Hilda murmured "not at all" while Mrs Dillon raised a lorgnon and looked at the priest critically.

"Mighty convenient them little spectacles must be," said Father Duff, imperturbably, "but troublesome to carry round in your hand I doubt. How are you, ma'am? It's an age since I saw you. Looking brave and hearty. Thanks be to God."

She gave him a frozen smile and a limp hand, which he shook heartily. When Father Duff had joined the group in the centre of the room, she said to Hilda, "These new movements are rather trying, dear." She turned her lorgnon on the young priests by the piano and the Robinsons. "They bring people together who don't mix. Charles fills Dillonsmount with worse even than these. You might assert yourself a little."

"John says it is our duty. You encourage it yourself," Hilda said.

"Encourage it! Barely tolerate it! I hate the whole idea. Charles has become so headstrong. One can be excused for indulging a son a little – besides, he'll grow out of it," she added defensively, "but a husband I should certainly keep on a tight rein."

Hilda was saved a reply by the announcement of luncheon.

"You'll support the creamery, of course," said John O'Brien to Lady de Lacey, when they had taken their seats.

"Charles says he'll see it damned first," she said with a grim smile, "but you may count on us."

"I read somewhere the other day that creameries are a regular plague spot," said Sir Charles gloomily to Hilda, giving an aggressive look at Gray, who sat on her left. "Bring typhoid and diphtheria around a place, reduce the children to skin and bones and ruin the trade in store cattle."

Gray's eyes twinkled humorously, but he went on eating quietly.

"Surely not," said Hilda, with an appealing look at Gray. "John wouldn't be so keen on them if that were the case."

"It's another scheme of those damned Nationalists to nobble the landlords," said Sir Charles.

"For the moment, unfortunately, many Nationalists won't touch us," said Gray, smiling.

"Well, it's some damned scheme, anyway," said Sir Charles, cutting his meat viciously. "Whatever happens, the landlords suffer. Rents have gone down to nothing. Now you'll bring disease among our cows - you'll take the beds from under us next."

"Poor man! you'll have to go into the poorhouse," said Father Duff.

"That's pure bluff," said Father Hardy in a low voice to Father Dempsey, who sat next him. "I have the best information that these creameries are all a landlord dodge. Old de Lacey isn't such a fool as he looks. I strongly suspect," he added mysteriously, "that he's up to his neck in the scheme."

"The best fiddlesticks!" said Father Dempsey, contempuously. "You'd suspect the Pope of robbing a poor-box. What does one eat this thing like a pudding with? It's fish, I know by the smell of it."

"With a spoon, of course," said Father Hardy, pompously.

"These creameries sound well," said Bowen to Robinson. "They ought to bring something into the poor landlords' pockets."

"What did I tell you?" Father Hardy, who heard the remark across the table, whispered triumphantly to Father Dempsey.

Robinson shook his head, saying sadly, "There's little chance of touching anything the tenants make nowadays."

"Well, we'll make a bit on our home farms, anyway," said Bowen, cheerfully.

"That's to throw dust in our eyes," whispered Father Hardy. "He suspected I heard his other remark."

"Oh, let me eat my dinner in peace," said Father Dempsey, fretfully.

"Luncheon, luncheon," said Father Hardy, glancing round anxiously. "I hope no one heard you make that foo pass. We must keep up the credit of the clergy."

"What do you think of the creamery idea?" Lady de Lacey asked Father Sheldon.

"If it were to stop at creameries, I should still be interested – not very deeply, however – but as I feel it will go further, I attach what may seem an undue importance to it."

She lifted her eyebrows enquiringly.

"It will get the farmers out of the grip of the gombeen man, make them more self-reliant, give them habits of business, widen their outlook and help to do away with that curse of a country parish, jealousy and fighting among neighbours."

"Where does the landlord come in?" she asked dryly.

"As a man."

"You can't deny that the tenants have been cruel."

"And the landlords?" he said gently.

"Well! there have been abuses," she said, her pale face flushing slightly. "My husband, even when exasperated, was just. I know you were not personal."

"No. I never mistook his bark for a bite."

"You think this may be a bridge."

"Yes."

Ralph sat between Mrs Dillon and Mrs Robinson. Mrs Robinson was conscious of Mrs Dillon's disapproving eye and ate nervously. Ralph tried to talk to her, but she was confused.

"We have only lately come into the district. It's not as select as Rathmines," she said, in answer to some question.

Mrs Dillon laughed harshly.

"Rathmines is charming, but I prefer the country," Ralph said, smiling.

"But how can you stand the Irish?" She caught her husband's frown and said lamely, "The common people, I mean!"

"We hadn't the advantages of the social life of Rathmines," said Mrs Dillon.

"What's this I hear about you?" she continued in a lecturing tone to Ralph. "It's no wonder strangers should confuse our social position. Charles is bad enough – our house reeks of frieze coats. But you are worse – I won't discuss it – it makes me too angry. I wish I was your mother. I'd soon knock this idea out of your head."

"I haven't been meditating murder," said Ralph, smiling.

"Suicide," she said grimly.

Ralph laughed. Her face relaxed. "Well, there's some hope of a man who can laugh at himself. I'm a cousin and I can say what I think. You'll grow out of this priest foolishness. The O'Briens are always doing freaky things. The strain was in Charles, but I cured him of it - though he's going too far the other way now. People ought to be as moderate in their religion as in their food. They'll have indigestion if they don't. Though you never know when you have an O'Brien! There's your Aunt Mary living in a wigwam somewhere near the North Pole! Religion breaks out in them like a fever. Today they're normal and tomorrow they've a temperature of 106. There was my grand-uncle, your great-grandfather. He never entered a church for thirty years and abused the priests in the vilest terms. A Protestant friend congratulated him on being so open-minded. It rankled in his mind for a few days, and at length he sent his friend a challenge saying that he wouldn't stand such a reflection on his character; that he'd let the world know he was a bigoted Catholic. He was quite happy when he shot the man through the arm. The Lord only knows how you'll turn out," she added, sipping her coffee slowly.

Hilda gave the signal to rise, saying to Gray, "We are all coming to the meeting. I shall be ready in a few minutes."

"I'm not sure that I shall not speak against you," said Sir Charles, frowning at Gray.

"Differences of opinion are always interesting," Gray said, smiling.

The meeting was to be held in the schoolhouse, about a quarter of a mile from the Inniscar gate. It was called in the joint names of Father Duff and John O'Brien, "for the purpose of building and equipping a creamery by the farmers of the district, to be owned and worked by the farmers themselves".

When the Inniscar party arrived, the schoolhouse was already full of farmers, a few of their wives and daughters, and half a dozen shopkeepers from Bunnahone.

Father Duff took the chair, and said. "I beg to introduce Mr Gray, from Dublin, who knows all there's to know about creameries. He'll tell you all about them. I'll say no more now, but I'll have a few words to say at the end."

Gray spoke for half an hour on the method of organising and running a creamery co-operatively and on its economic advantages. His clear business statement interested the farmers, who, however, showed little enthusiasm until he spoke of co-operation as a vivifying national force, when the younger men cheered loudly. He wound up with a few eloquent sentences, his body tense and his brown eyes glowing, describing a new Ireland, freed from dissension, contented, save for that divine discontent which urged men ever to strive for higher ideals.

When Gray sat down, an alert business-like man rose at the back of the room and said, "May I ask the gentleman if this is a nationalist league he's proposing to set up?"

Two or three voices said, "Hear, hear."

"No," said Gray, curtly.

"I knew it was a landlord dodge."

"You're not on a League platform now, Mr Donaghue," said Father Duff, dryly.

"I wish to support my friend Mr Donaghue," said Father Hardy. "This is a most dangerous proposal just when the people are getting some control of their land, to make the landlords a power again. The shopkeepers of Bunnahone, who have been the farmers' best friends, are opposed to the idea. The priests there are not friendly to it. His lordship, though I can't use his name, is, I'm informed on the best authority, against it."

"But his lordship is for it," interrupted Robinson.

"Of course I meant his lordship the bishop, not Lord Dawlish," said Father Hardy, waving his hand impatiently. "In all my experience this is the most insidious attack on the Home-Rule movement, and I hope no farmer will support it."

Father Duff took a huge pinch of snuff and blew his nose vigorously three or four times.

"Father Hardy is a fine speaker entirely," he said; "and we're all glad to hear a young man just out of Maynooth advise us how to run the parish of Inniscar. Now I was a Home-Ruler before he or Mr Donaghue were born, and with all respect to them, we're going to set up a bit of Home Rule of our own and manage our business ourselves, without any dictation from outside. I'm sorry to intrude the matter of filthy lucre after Mr Gray's beautiful speech. The price of butter this minute in London is over a shilling a pound, and you get sevenpence for it from our friend Mr Donaghue in Bunnahone; and it takes about three and a half gallons of your milk to make that pound of butter. With your creamery you can make a pound out of two gallons and get a shilling for it by selling direct to the big markets. Most of you learned to do sums on the desks ye are sitting on. Mr Donaghue is a great patriot, we know well, and it's not the trifle of money he makes out of ye that troubles him. He's only uneasy for fear your national spirit should be destroyed. The people of Inniscar ought to know me by this, and I think they'll be able to tell Mr Donaghue, to ease his mind, that I'm not going to become a landlord's man at my time of life. As far as the creamery is concerned, sorra difference it'll make in the taste of the butter whether the milk comes from a tenant's cow or a landlord's cow. I propose we set up our creamery; and there's a deposit on twenty shares to start with." He laid a crumpled note on the table in front of him. "Perhaps Mr Donaghue will take a few shares?" he added with a chuckle.

"Go up, Donaghue, and pay back some of the money you made out of our butter," said a voice.

"Poor man! he'll want it all now," said another.

"You'll hear from the League about this," said Donaghue, angrily.

"I second Father Duff," said a muscular farmer, rather shyly. "I'm not good at the speech, but we all have the money in our pockets and that's as good as talk for today's business, anyway. We had a chat about the creamery in the chapel-yard on Sunday and we all agreed it was a good thing."

About two-thirds of the farmers gave in their names, the others leaving quietly. Donaghue and his Bunnahone friends remained to the end.

Lady de Lacey whispered to Sir Charles.

"Excellent idea, this creamery," he said afterwards to Gray; "thought so all along."

"Why was Donaghue taking notes?" John O'Brien asked Father Duff, as they walked back to Inniscar after the meeting.

"Oh! he's half publican, half butter buyer, and whole gombeen man. He has all those fellows who slunk away in his books, and not a few of those who joined, too. He'll fire writs at 'em next sessions, very likely. I must do what I can to help them. When Donaghue knows I'm in earnest he may cry off. He won't like to bring his books into court. The swindler! He keeps the League in Bunnahone in his pocket to help on his gombeen business."

"Father Hardy was wrong, I'm sure, about the bishop. He couldn't be against such a movement as this."

Father Duff smiled enigmatically. "Bishops are diplomatists," he said. "That's a fine word, now? All the same, he'll come down on that little Hardy for letting the cat out of the bag. I haven't my mind made up yet whether that fellow is a fool or a rogue. The way he struts about, like a little bantam I have at home. It's many a long day before he opens his mouth at a meeting in my parish again. How on earth did he get to lunch with you?"

"He was staying with Father Dempsey, who asked if he might bring him," John O'Brien said.

"Poor Dempsey! A decent lad. Full of them foolish notions of Charlie Dillon's about the Irish, but too good to be led astray by Hardy. Look here, young man," he went on, turning to Ralph, "Size up fellows like Hardy or you'll get left. You can be as holy as you like and hold out the other cheek for a blow and love all your enemies, provided you know your man. It saves a lot of trouble to be able to give a fair guess as to what's going on at the back of the other fellow's mind. But I'm talking a lot of nonsense! Do you know what, John? I'm a proud man that the meeting went well today. I hope I may live to see the farmers out of the power of gombeen men, and this co-operation seems to offer a way. Not that things'll go as easy everywhere as here. There'll be a long uphill struggle."

He walked in silence for a few mintues. "I'll be dead," he said to Ralph, more gently than usual, "before much is done. If I were sure you'd do your best to help it along when you come out of Maynooth I'd be less agin your being a priest."

"I thought you had no ideals," said Ralph, smiling.

"Nor have I. Sorra one. But this is a plain everyday thing – to keep a decent roof-tree over poor people's heads. That talk about the blessings of poverty can be overdone. The people that talk that way have pretty full bellies. It's not easy for a man to have religion itself when he's worried to death over providing a bite or a sup for a hungry family."

Hilda, who had found the conversation rather trying, intervened. "But fasting is one of the holiest exercises of religion!"

Father Duff laughed. "This is getting too deep for me," he said. "I've no doubt fasting is very good for those who eat too much; and there's always the thought of a full meal at the end of it! I was thinking of something else. Ralph must do his best to see that if people like fasting they must take to it of their own accord, not because there isn't a scrap of food in the house."

Chapter 11

AUGUST WAS DRAWING to a close, and it was within a week of Ralph's departure for Maynooth when Boyle was due to arrive at Inniscar. Railway fares, he wrote to Ralph, being a consideration, he fixed his visit so as to be able to go direct to the Seminary when it opened. Ralph drove to meet him at Bunnahone, calling on Father Doyle on the way for some necessary papers for Maynooth.

When he entered the hall the sound of music came from Father Phil's room, a soprano and a baritone singing a duet to a piano accompaniment. When he asked to see Father Phil the maid hesitated and said if he waited there she would tell his reverence. The music stopped suddenly when the maid entered. Ralph heard a woman's voice emerge from a subdued conversation.

"Oh, do bring him in, Father Phil. There's a dear - I'm dying to see him." Father Phil appeared in the wake of the maid, shook hands with Ralph with one hand and patted him on the shoulder with the other.

"Come in, come in," he said; "there's nobody but the Miss Hinnisseys and Father Tom. You're out of my hands now and there's no reason in the world why you should be kept at an arm's length."

Ralph felt embarrassed as he followed Father Doyle into the room. He said that he had come for the Maynooth papers. Father Doyle waved his hand airily, saying, "Oh! they're all ready. Don't bother your head about them until you have some tea. May I introduce Mr O'Brien?" he said to the young ladies standing by the piano. "The Miss Hinnisseys, Miss Katie and Miss Julia."

The Miss Hinnisseys were dressed alike in white muslin. Miss Katie, the elder, was plump and fair; Miss Julia was thin and fair. Both had large eyes. They were prettily flushed by their exertions at the piano, on the top of which lay their hats, white straw with immense blue bows.

"I'm very happy to make your acquaintance," both said in a duet.

Father Tom Molloy sat at the end of a table, a steaming glass of punch in front of him, his rubicund face glossy with perspiration. He held out his hand to Ralph and beamed on him.

"Hullo, young man," he said with a laugh. "You're being initiated early."

"We were just going to have tea," said Father Doyle, "so you're just in time – though I'm afraid it's cold by this, we were so busy at the singing. Won't you pour it out, Katie?" pointing to the tea things at the end of the table opposite Father Molloy.

Miss Julia Hinnissey frowned poutingly. "Oh, it's Julia's turn today. She'd tear my eyes out if I poured two days running," said Miss Katie, tossing her head.

"I was so distracted by the singing that I forgot," said Father Doyle, with a mock bow.

"Isn't he a happy man," said Father Molloy, drawing a deep sigh, to Ralph, "to have two such fine young ladies fighting over him?"

"Do you hear him now? As well as if he hadn't the Miss Darcys himself," said Miss Katie, coquettishly.

"None of you deserve any tea. I think I'll just pour out a cup for Mr O'Brien and myself," said Miss Julia, looking archly at Ralph.

"Mind that your eye isn't put out," said Father Molloy, winking at Father Doyle.

"Hum, hum," said Father Doyle, pursing his lips.

Ralph drank a cup of tea hastily. Miss Julia plied him with questions, when he answered curtly and awkwardly. She was very much interested in Inniscar.

"I'd give my eyes out to live in a house like that. It's not at all genteel to live over the shop in the main street, but pa won't leave it. Ma and Katie and myself are always trying to get him to buy a house out in the country, but he says the shop is good enough for him. We have a lot of friends that we knew at the convent who live in big houses in the country, but we can't ask them here, for the nuns told us never to let on about the shop. It would lower the tone of the convent, they said. Of course, there's no hiding it within twenty miles of Bunnahone – everyone knows we're Hinnissey's Emporium."

"It's a fine shop," Ralph said lamely.

"What are you two colloguing about over there?" said Father Molloy. "Keep an eye on him, Father Phil, or he'll never go to Maynooth. Not that I'd blame him much," he said, shaking his finger at Miss Julia. "Sure if I was young again myself, Julia, there's no knowing what mightn't happen."

He laughed heartily.

Ralph excused himself. He had only just time to catch the train. Would Father Doyle give him the letters?

"Don't let me frighten you off," said Father Molloy, winking at Katie.

"I'm sure I'm not keeping him," said Miss Julia, opening her large eyes widely. "No doubt he's in a hurry to meet some grand ladies at the station."

"I'm jealous, you didn't speak to me at all," said Katie, holding his hand when he was saying goodbye. "You must come and see us some afternoon. Unless we're here with Father Phil, we always have four o'clock tea at home. There's a side entrance, so you needn't come through the shop."

Boyle was moody, depressed and irritable. During the drive home Ralph tried to interest him in the creamery, but he was unresponsive. After a long silence, Ralph said that he had met the Miss Hinnisseys at Father Phil's.

Boyle blushed, shrugged his shoulders and said, "I suppose Julia made eyes at you?"

"You know them then!"

"Know them! I should think I did! They're not a bad sort," he said excitedly, "but their bringing up has ruined them. They divide their time between doing up the altars in the Cathedral, praying at the altar of St Joseph for husbands and philandering with Father Phil Doyle. Their idea of marriage, picked up from silly nuns in the fashionable convent they were at, is half a fairy tale and half a miracle. If they only burn enough candles at the statue of St Joseph, Prince Charming is to come along and rescue them from the shop which they despise. Human nature has been so crushed out of them that they would not recognise love if it came their way. The prince doesn't come," he added bitterly, "so they'll do as other girls of their class always do, enter a convent and bring up other girls in the same make-believe."

He was silent for a few minutes, then laughed harshly. "It must have been the smoke in that beastly train. After all, it's not a crime in the Miss Hinnisseys to have big eyes and to use them."

At dinner, Boyle was in high spirits. His delicate appearance appealed to Hilda. She remembered his mother, who always knelt at the end of the front seat at Clarendon Street Church at eleven o'clock mass. She seemed such a holy, good woman, she said.

"She looks what she is," Boyle said earnestly.

He spoke much of a new literary movement in Dublin and admitted shyly that he had himself written poetry. Hilda said she had never heard anything more beautiful than a few short lyrics he read in the drawing-room after dinner. They were written in a conventionalised peasant dialect, full of quaint imagery.

"I feel so happy," she said to Ralph, as she bade him goodnight, "that you are a friend of Mr Boyle's. He has such a beautiful mind. No one but a saint could write of the Blessed Virgin as he does. How pleased his mother must be with him! Her prayers have certainly had effect."

"My mother has already canonised you," Ralph said next day, as he and Boyle were looking at the ruins of a Romanesque church a few miles from Inniscar.

"I felt a fraud in reading those poems to her," Boyle said gravely, "just as I felt when I read them to my mother. She fell on my neck, and called me her good, holy son."

"But they are extraordinarily religious in feeling."

"I think so. They are meant to be; and all poets have the weakness to swallow praise of their verse."

"Have you ever had a doubt about religion, O'Brien?" he asked abruptly, after a short pause.

"Don't look so tragic," said Ralph, laughing. "A serious doubt? Of course not."

"Of course not!" Boyle repeated angrily. "Forgive me," he added gently. "I have doubts; and they are the devil when one has been brought up as I have, with a mother like mine. If I look tragic, it is because I feel tragic."

Ralph had a feeling of repulsion, but it gave place to one of pity as he saw the look of misery on Boyle's face.

"Doubts are no harm, so long as you pray against them and put them away," he said, repeating glibly what he had heard in some sermon. He hesitated over the last phrase, vaguely conscious that it was inadequate, and was prepared for Boyle's jibe.

"I can't pitch out permanent tenants without ceremony. It's as bad as that," he added with a grimace, "and, if it doesn't shock you to hear it, I don't know that I want to get rid of them."

Ralph was shocked, but he was also interested. "You couldn't write such poems if you had religious doubts," he said.

Boyle smiled. "My feelings and emotions are Catholic. In fact, I have been more struck by the beauty of much of the Catholic tradition since my mind began to rebel against dogma than before."

"I'm sure your doubts could all be solved," Ralph said gravely. "It's a pity that I have not yet read theology. I should be able to help you if I had. Why don't you consult some priest?"

"Father Molloy, for instance?" said Boyle, with an amused smile.

"You don't feel very tragic after all," said Ralph, stiffly.

"Only when I think of my mother finding out what I really believe. The strugle within myself is over; I see my way clear enough now. Of course, there is my bread and butter. That would stand in some danger if Father Doyle knew my opinions. The loss of my job under the ban of the Church would be tragic enough. I've been a beast," he added with a wry face, "to burthen you with this. I've only pained you." He looked at Ralph appealingly.

Ralph was troubled. There was, of course, some way of solving Boyle's doubts. The Church being infallible, there was nothing she could not answer. He felt easier when he thought of Father Sheldon. He was the very man to do it. He suggested this to Boyle.

"Sheldon is all right. I don't know what good it is likely to do, but I shall have a talk with him some time. I know him slightly. He'll be sure to understand," Boyle replied.

That afternoon, during tea, the bishop called. He entered the drawing-room with an effusive greeting to Hilda. When he saw Boyle, he suddenly stiffened.

"What in the world are you doing?... How do you do, Mr Boyle?" he said, nodding curtly.

He shook hands with John and Ralph, but seemed to take no further notice of Boyle, who retired to a window-seat with John O'Brien.

"What is Mr Boyle doing here?" the bishop asked Ralph, sharply, as Hilda was preparing the tea.

"He's staying with us for a few days."

"He is such a charming man," said Hilda. "Have you read any of his poetry, my lord?"

"If it can be dignified by that name, yes," the bishop said, frowning. "A few of his pieces in an obscure Dublin periodical were brought to my notice. I have no wish to be harsh with the young man, but I had better tell you, Mrs O'Brien, that he is on trial. It is a matter of very great pain to me, as I am, in a sense, responsible for him while he is a teacher in our Seminary." He stirred his tea moodily, and Hilda flushed nervously. "I discussed the matter with Father Doyle, and we both agreed that it would be the more Christian course to give him a chance of amending his ways. It would be difficult, too, at the moment, to get another teacher. Yes, I read the poems. Taken in themselves they seem harmless enough to those who are untrained in the philosophy of the Church. Had anyone of sound religious views written them, one might put a favourable construction on them and explain them away. But I am sorry to say that Mr Boyle is not above suspicion in that respect. Father Doyle has long had occasion to regret his reading and his choice of companions. There is no smoke without fire. The poems, read in this light, are pantheistic – I need not tell you, Mrs O'Brien, how that heresy is reprobated by the Church. Of course it can be exploded in a single syllogism if put forward in a form that can be handled. But in these slight verses it is not easy to lay hold of a definitely heretical view. They are all the more dangerous for that, especially to holy minds not on the watch for heresy in poems professedly religious. They are very specious, very specious indeed."

Hilda was visibly distressed. She laid her arm protectively on Ralph's shoulder.

"It is so kind of you to warn us," she said gratefully.

The bishop smiled and waved his hand with a deprecating motion.

"Not for you, Mrs O'Brien. You are all too well grounded in the faith to need that. A faithful shepherd must, however, be disagreeable sometimes. The warning is for Mr Boyle. It is to be hoped he will heed it! Don't encourage him – though I need not say that to such a devoted daughter of the Church. You see the need for exercising caution," he added to Ralph, "in the choice of friends. No harm has resulted yet, I hope, from this indiscretion, but it is well to be on one's guard."

Ralph felt a growing dislike for the bishop. Boyle was wrong, of course; was even perhaps much worse than the bishop suspected. But it was not fair to prejudice his mother's mind against her guest. Ralph watched her face anxiously and saw her lips harden as she glanced at Boyle.

"I intended to speak on a much more pleasant topic," the bishop said, smiling. "I've just had a telegram saying that our Seminary has done excellently in the Intermediate Examinations. The lists will be in the papers tomorrow. We have ten distinctions in all. The only detail I have is that Magan has got a Senior Exhibition.

Ralph had "impossible" on the tip of his tongue, but he bit his lips and said nothing. Magan had a phenomenal memory, which might account for his exhibition.

"Your lordship deserves many congratulations. You have told me what uphill work the Seminary was," Hilda said earnestly.

"It is well out of the wood now. This is a pleasant reward for much anxiety," he said with a satisfied purr. "I must be fair, however. While I bore some of the worry, Father Doyle had both worry and hard work. You must know him better, Mrs O'Brien - my right arm, I often call him, though his humility will not allow him to acknowledge it. I regret to say there have been jealous people who sneered at the Seminary and at his scholarship, but tommorow's list will be a conclusive answer to them."

He chatted genially for some minutes of the future of the Seminary; he would get rid of all lay teachers and have priests only. They were much more amenable to control, and would have a more spiritual influence on the pupils. "I look forward to the help of two such distinguished students as you and Mr Magan, when you are ordained," he said, smiling at Ralph. "Meanwhile, you must both be a credit to the diocese in Maynooth. My predecessor, good holy man, was a little careless in these matters, but we mustn't let the other bishops have it all their own way in future. Bunnahone must have a share in Maynooth prizes commensurate with its reputation as an educational centre."

After he had said goodbye to Hilda he stopped on his way out to speak to John O'Brien, altogether ignoring Boyle.

"So you are going on with the creamery?"

"Yes. The builders will begin next week."

The bishop held a finger to his lips thoughtfuly.

"Is it worth while antagonising powerful interests?"

John O'Brien shrugged his shoulders. "Do you mean the Bunnahone gombeen men?" he asked laughingly.

The bishop frowned slightly. "Now, now, Mr O'Brien. I don't think that is quite just. The Bunnahone shopkeepers, as far as I know them, and I think I know them well, are a highly honourable body, most charitable to the poor and good to the Church. Excellent Catholics, almost to a man. You have only to look at our Cathedral to see that."

"We are going on in any case," John said stiffly.

"Don't think that you haven't my sympathy," the bishop said suavely. "Our farmers are the backbone of the country. Let them know, if you have an opportunity, that their interests are mine. But my heart is torn between the different sections of my flock. If you haven't my more open support now, later on, if difficulties arise, I shall be more readily listened to by the other side and may be able to help as a peacemaker."

"He's an adept at sitting on a fence," said Boyle, when the bishop had gone.

"I wonder what he said to Donaghue," John O'Brien said, chuckling. "What a pity Father Duff wasn't here! He'd have enjoyed that speech."

Hilda's manner to Boyle changed. She was still kind to him, but she took every opportunity of preventing him being alone with Ralph. She told John what the bishop had said. She was not a little offended when he laughed heartily.

"You are much too simple, Hilda," he said. "Why, if I went round with a microscope examining the theology and philosophy of every poem I read my whole pleasure would be gone. Don't mind the old spider. He's always spinning webs to catch imaginary flies."

The few days of Boyle's visit were awkward for Ralph, who felt renewed sympathy with him as a result of the bishop's antagonism. Ralph felt grateful to his father for making things easier for Boyle, who became so interested in John O'Brien's various farming schemes that he did not notice Hilda's growing distaste. She did not speak again of Boyle's poetry and seemed relieved when he said goodbye. She presented him with her own copy of "à Kempis", which she asked him to read, and looked rather puzzled when he said that he knew it well, as it was one of his favourite books.

The world seemed a dark wood to Ralph as he walked slowly home after saying goodbye to Boyle at the gate. Somewhere beyond, he felt, was the light, but he could not see it for the trees and the thick undergrowth. He had looked forward to his preparation for the priesthood as a time of joy and peace. This must be one of those moments of trial which the saints had experienced. He must be patient, and light would one day shine in the dark places and make clear much that was now unintelligible. It must, of course, for the Church held the deposit of truth. Some day, perhaps in Maynooth, it would enlighten him. No doubt he had failed to see the best side of the bishop and Father Doyle and Father Molloy. He thought for a long time of Boyle and prayed fervently for him. To bring all men nearer to God should be his mission as a priest. When he had learned the divine knowledge of the Church at Maynooth he would be able to help Boyle.

The few last days at home were mainly spent in visiting with his mother or in vain drives to Bunnahone for articles of clothing which Hilda made up her mind Ralph would need at Maynooth, but which the Emporium had never heard of, or were just out of, or would be stocking in a few days. There was a lunch at the de Laceys, at which Sir Charles said priests were the pest of the country; that he had no doubt Ralph would return from Maynooth with the manners of a savage, and would probably lead a party of moonlighters to burn his father's house over his head. The country was going to the dogs and the priests were responsible for it. There was only one priest in Ireland, an old Jesuit in Dublin, who had the true faith. If Father Kirtle died there would be no one left to whom he could confess. Father Kirtle was a great man, who would hang all agitators and had only a poor opinion of the Pope, whom he strongly suspected of being a Socialist. "By gad, young sir," he wound up, "it's my firm belief that Father Kirtle and myself are the only true Catholics left in the world."

After a tea at Dillonsmount, when Mrs Dillon's sarcastic tongue played freely on all his ideals, Ralph kicked against any other visit except a long-promised one to Father Sheldon, with whom he was to spend the night.

He found Father Sheldon digging in the small flower garden which separated his house from the road. The odour of white jessamine and honeysuckle, which covered the front of the old thatched cottage, filled the air. Low hedges of lavender lined the walk from the gate to the open door; well-kept beds were aglow with old-fashioned flowers: larkspur, blue cornflowers, sweet-william and marigolds.

They had tea in the priest's study, a low room, large and square, the walls, except over the mantelpiece, lined with books in open shelves from floor to ceiling. In the vacant space was a landscape, a sunset view of the mountains across the bay, night brooding over a brilliant day. A soft-toned faded Persian rug partly covered the waxed floor.

Ralph's eyes were attracted by the colour of the rug.

"I suppose I ought not to keep it," said the priest, with a sign. "It was given to me ... That is only an excuse, I'm afraid," he added with a smile. "I may as well confess my weakness for the colour of it."

Ralph thought he had never seen a calmer face. Every line expressed a rare combination of strength and gentleness.

He spoke of flowers. They gave so much pleasure for very little labour, if what was itself a pleasure could be called labour. They were full of humours but could be coaxed. A little kindness made the summer blooms live on to the autumn. "I let them have their way as much as possible. That eglantine thinks it's in a hedgerow," he said, pointing to a branch that swayed well within the open window.

An old servant announced that James Brady was in the hall and wished to see his reverence. The priest told her to show him in.

"It's sorry I am to trouble your reverence," a middle-aged farmer, dressed in his Sunday clothes, said, standing at the door.

"Come in and sit down," the priest said genially.

"Sure I won't be sitting, your reverence. It's my father that's that bad that we're afeared he won't pass the night. I thought it better to come for you betimes, than to be bringing you out in the dark."

"Poor John," said the priest, gravely. "I am very sorry to hear that he's ill. Perhaps, though," he added more brightly, "it's only one of his old attacks."

"I fear not, your reverence. My mother thinks it's the death is on him now, and no mistake. It's a fine long life he had, thanks be to God, and sure he's well ready to go."

The priest nodded his head. "I shall come at once," he said. Brady bowed, saying as he went out, "It's your reverence is always ready at everyone's call."

"Will you read here or come with me?" the priest said to Ralph.

"I may come?"

"Certainly."

The priest walked in silence to the church, beside which the house stood, and kneeling for a minute in prayer before the high altar, he took from the tabernacle a pyx containing the Blessed Sacrament, which he placed reverently with a genuflexion in an inside pocket of his cassock.

On the way to Brady's house he spoke to Ralph of the dying man. "Single-minded and God-fearing, with the simplicity of a child and a love that passes my power of expression for every living thing. There are many such," he added, in the grave recollected tone in which he spoke throughout, "in Ireland, especially among the older peasantry."

At the gate of a whitewashed, one-storied thatched cottage, an old woman stood looking eagerly down the road by which they approched. One hand shaded her eyes, under a white goffered cap. She moved her hand to her ear, as she heard the sound of their footsteps. Father Sheldon took her hand. She raised his to her lips and kissed it. There were marks of recent tears on her face, but she was now dry-eyed.

"You're welcome, Father Pat, and you too, sir," she said, dropping a courtesy to Ralph. "There's no great hurry, I'm thinking, but we'll all be easier now you're here, himself not the least."

Though it was a warm August afternoon, a bright fire was burning on the open hearth, round which were seated half a dozen men and women, "neighbours that come when they heard John was low," Mrs Brady explained to Ralph, to whom she offered a chair by the fire when Father Sheldon had gone to the sick man's bedroom.

"He was a great man at the game of hurley in his day," said an old man seated on the hob, slowly puffing a short clay pipe.

"He was that, surely," said Mrs Brady.

"Me and him were the two best bowlers with an iron bowl in ten parishes, but he could beat me easily," the old man continued, in a droning voice.

"And you weren't easily beat, Ned Griffin," said the old woman, proudly.

"You might be getting some water ready for the priest, Nellie," she said, after a pause, to a woman who was doing some housework. "It wouldn't take John long to tell all the wrong he ever did in his life."

"That's the truth," said Griffin, emphatically.

Father Sheldon opened the door of the bedroom.

Mrs Brady, her son and daughter entered the bedroom and knelt by the foot of the bed on which John Brady lay, propped up by pillows. The others knelt around the open bedroom door. Father Sheldon, wearing a stole over his cassock, took the pyx from his pocket and laid it on a small table covered with a white cloth, on which candles were lighted. He then opened a small case containing oil for the anointing of the sick and proceeded to administer the sacrament of extreme unction. The sick man's eyes were fixed on the priest, as he read the prayers from a small ritual. The anointing done, the priest opened the pyx and gave the viaticum. As the priest repeated three times, holding the particle aloft, "Behold the Lamb of God, Who taketh away the sins of the world," John Brady's eyes were fixed on the bread with a look of tender longing. When the priest laid the particle on his lips, he gave a sigh of contentment that was echoed by all those kneeling around. The priest finished the prayers, put away the pyx and oil case and knelt in prayer beside the table. The afternoon sun falling slantwise through the window illuminated the sick man's livid face. The distant lowing of a cow and the flickering of one of the dim candles relieved the tension of a silence the more profound for Brady's slow, deep, difficult breathing. At length the priest stood up and all the people with him. Brady opened his eyes and smiled faintly. He stretched out a feeble hand, which the priest took.

"I'm ready for the road now, thanks be to God and you,

Father Pat," he murmured.

"You may be up and about in a day or two," said the priest, gently.

The old man shook his head. "All my hope is the other side now," he said; "I feel it in my heart. 'Tis many a journey I gave you, but now I'll not trouble you any more. Please God, I'll put in a good word for you, beyond."

Ralph waited in the kitchen while the priest and Brady talked for a few minutes. Mrs Brady sat in a corner, her apron over her head, crying quietly. The neighbours stood around in silence.

"I'm afeard he won't be long in it," said Brady's son to Father Sheldon, as he was passing through the kitchen.

"Come for me if he gets worse," said the priest.

"Sure he gave orders that you weren't to be brought out of your bed."

"Be sure to come. God bless you all," he added, turning to the people standing by the fire.

"And you, too, Father Pat," they said.

Mrs Brady accompanied the priest and Ralph to the gate.

"I doubt if he'll see the sun again," she said, her tear-dimmed eyes fixed on the red ball level with the horizon.

"God's will be done," said the priest, reverently.

"Amen," she said, drying her eyes with her apron. "God is very good to him, and to me, too, though I hoped I wouldn't be the one to be left. Fifty-four years come Michaelmas, we were married in the chapel beyond by Father Joyce, God rest his soul.... I hope it's not long I'll keep him waiting," she added after a pause.

Ralph walked on. He could hear the murmur of the priest's voice, and the woman's voice raised as she said goodbye: "The blessing of God Almighty on you, Father, sure 'tis you're the comfort to us all in trouble."

As he walked home in silence beside the priest, in the gathering dusk, Ralph was deeply moved. He felt, as he had never felt before, a call to the priesthood, to be a minister of sympathy and love as Father Sheldon was.

The priest lingered at the garden gate on their way to the house. The west was gorgeous in broad bands of red and gold.

"Death had no terror for him," Ralph said.

"He sees God with his heart," the priest replied, his eyes on the afterglow.

They sat up, talking, far into the night, Father Sheldon smoking a well-worn pipe. He had read Boyle's poems, and liked them.

Ralph said he had heard them criticised as pantheistic.

The priest laughed and then looked grave.

"Poor Boyle," he said; "it may be made serious for him. I shouldn't laugh. Heresy hunting can't be treated lightly even in these days, though we are getting to see things a little more clearly. If we would only let people see God in their own way we should know more. Old John Brady is as near to God as anyone I've ever known, yet he has many beliefs that would not pass muster with the theologians. If you are writing to Boyle tell him to come and see me."

He spoke enthusiastically of a priest in Paris who would yet do great things for the Church. "I'm an optimist," he said, striking his pipe against the grate, "but this time I think I don't outstep the reality. You'll begin your priesthood in a most interesting time. Don't be depressed by your experience at the Seminary, or even with any disappointment you may have at Maynooth. God has always been in the world and is more manifest today than ever before. Any day the real awakening of the world may come. Bunnahone is only an accident, a little stagnant backwater of a great onrushing stream. I am too old, perhaps, to see a great change, but it may be given to you to help ... seek God in yourself first and you will then be able to find Him in the most unlikely places," he added thoughtfully.

Ralph was awakened next morning by the sun shining on his face. Father Sheldon was in the chapel, the servant told him when she brought hot water.

The canon of the mass had already begun when Ralph knelt in one of the side benches by the altar. The priest's eyes were fixed on the host in rapt absorption. Ralph could hear his slow clear enunciation of the words, "*Hoc est corpus meum*", in a mingled tone of awe and love. His face seemed transfigured as he raised the host aloft in trembling fingers. Ralph bent his head over the rails and prayed that he, too, might be made worthy to offer so stupendous a sacrifice.

"He died at six," the priest said in reply to Ralph's question at breakfast. "It was wonderful, wonderful," he added pensively. "He asked what was the morning like. 'The promise of a hot day,' his son said. 'Thank God,' he said, smiling feebly, 'the good weather is lasting for the harvest,' and that was the end."

"You were with him?"

"Yes, we priests have many consolations. John Brady was a greater help to me than he knew," he added.

"Do advise me," said Ralph, shyly, as he bade the priest goodbye. They had been talking of Maynooth. Father Sheldon laid a hand on his shoulder and looked at him gently.

"Who am I to advise anyone?" he said, "who only grope in the dark myself.... But this is entirely too didactic," he added, laughing. "Don't be a prig. Don't lock doors on yourself or others; help as many lame dogs as come in your way over stiles. Goodbye, and God bless you."

Chapter 12

RALPH SET OUT from Bunnahone station for Maynooth in a spirit of hope. His mother lingered until the last moment, repeating instructions for the avoiding of chills from possible damp sheets. A few minutes after the scheduled time for the starting of the train, the stationmaster coughed discreetly, saying, "If you are ready, Mrs O'Brien, we are."

A last embrace from his mother, a hearty handshake from his father, and it was over.

Now his preparation was really to begin! He felt in a generous mood and wished to give himself wholly to a great service. He would never be worthy of the gifts God had in store for him. He was determined, however, to do his best. Of himself he could never so free himself from sin, be so pure in heart and mind, as to be worthy to offer the inscrutable mystery of the mass. Yet if he offered himself with a humble heart God might deign to accept his unworthiness. Then, there was the advising of people in matters affecting their eternal salvation, which surely would demand extraordinary knowledge and still greater wisdom. He would work hard to fit himself for his work, and the tender mercy of God, supplying his deficiency, would be his strength and his support. Theology and philosophy would teach him much of the ways of God with men....

The train slowed down at a small wayside station, and he saw Magan rushing along the platform peering into the carriages.

"I guessed you'd be in this train," he said, stumbling into the carriage and almost falling over the carpet bag he held awkwardly in both hands. He was dressed in black, in a long Chesterfield coat and a broad-brimmed clerical hat. "You're looking at my clothes," he said; "I had to get a new suit and I thought I might as well get these. They're sure to pass me in Maynooth with a senior grade exhibition and all. Them grey clothes of yours aren't clerical enough," he added, looking Ralph over critically.

Ralph blushed at the reference to the exhibition, and Magan rambled on complacently.

"No doubt you were surprised how I did the trick," he said, grinning. "Not but it was the least anyone could expect after all my hard work. That clown Lanigan with all his airs can never pretend again he's as good a man as I am. You should see the letter Father Phil wrote me – 'a credit to the diocese,' he called me, no less; and he said his lordship himself was mighty pleased."

Lanigan and Devine joined them at the next station.

"You should have put on the Roman collar at once, Ginger," Lanigan said, eyeing Magan contemptuously, "or maybe a purple stock, now that you've got your name in the papers as a great gun."

"I've some of the money left out of the exhibition," Magan said ingratiatingly, "and I'll stand ye all a treat in Dublin as we pass through."

"Anything bought with that money'd choke me," said Lanigan, making a wry face. "It'd be the greatest joke in the world if you were spun at the entrance exam," he added jeeringly. "It'd be a great sight entirely to see you going out the gate, long coat and flat hat and all, with your tail between your legs. I'd laugh my sides out to see it. Senior grade exhibition! Faugh!"

"Charity, Mr Lanigan, charity!" said Devine, putting his finger to his lips.

"It's jealous ye all are of me," Magan said, sulking in a corner.

Ignoring Magan, Lanigan talked of their prospects at Maynooth.

"I spent a lot of time with a student during the summer, a second philosopher, and he put me up to a lot of tips for passing the exam."

Magan leant forward eagerly.

"Mum is the word," said Lanigan, "until Ginger is out of earshot."

Ralph felt uncomfortable and spoke of Father Sheldon.

"He's rather a mug, I believe," Lanigan said; "he has let the dues of his parish go down to nothing."

At a large station a number of students awaited the train. Three, dressed like Magan, but wearing clerical collars, entered Ralph's compartment. "There's a big Seminary there," whispered Lanigan, "where they priest men. These are theologians, I doubt, that have got free places in Maynooth."

The new-comers were very boisterous and made incessant jokes in bog Latin. One pulled out of an inside pocket a flat flask of whiskey and drank. He smacked his lips, wiped the neck of the bottle with his fingers and handed it to one of his companions. It was offered in turn to the Bunnahone students. Devine declined it curtly. Ralph said he didn't drink. Lanigan, after some hesitation, took a mouthful, which made him cough.

"It's the first time I ever drank any," he said apologetically.

"Oh, you'll get used to it after a time," said the owner of the bottle. "It's great stuff on a droughty day like this."

Magan took a long drink appreciatively.

"I'm sorry I near finished the bottle," he said effusively. "But I'll fill it again at the next station where there's any to be got."

"What about a game?" said the owner of the bottle. "You've got a deck, Bristowe."

Bristowe, a tall, fat man, about twenty-two years old, pulled a greasy pack of cards out of his pocket and began to shuffle them.

"They're regular radicals," whispered Lanigan to Devine, who was reading "The Little Office of the Blessed Virgin."

"Only four can play comfortably," said Bristowe. "Will one of you join in?"

Magan offered himself eagerly.

"Nap?" said Bristowe.

Magan's face fell. "I though it would be twenty-five. But I don't care; I've plenty of tin."

They closed up, two on either side. Bristowe produced a pink sporting paper, which he laid on their knees.

At a break in the game Bristowe lit a pipe with some ostentation.

Magan looked crestfallen.

"I was afraid to bring mine," he said. "I heard they were very strict agin smoking in Maynooth. I'd give anything if I had it now."

Bristowe laughed and winked at his companions.

"What a greeny! We don't intend to throw ours away. Do we, boys? I'd advise you to buy another in Dublin. Wait till I'm done and I'll give you a draw of this."

At Kingsbridge station Magan went off with his new friends.

Ralph, Devine and Lanigan drove across the city with their trunks and left them in the cloakroom at the Broadstone terminus. They had a few hours to wait for their train and had a meal at a hotel near the station.

"I never believed there was such a big town in the whole world," said Lanigan, as they walked through O'Connell Street. "I wonder how you could live in the country after it," he added to Ralph. "They must be lucky priests that have the run of a big place like this."

When they arrived again at Broadstone, the platform from which the Maynooth train was to start was crowded with students, who were hustled about unceremoniously by porters.

Magan came up to Devine, his face flushed, and said, with a sneer, "I hope ye found a chapel to say the rosary in. I wouldn't be seen travelling with a lot of greenhorns like ye;" and he shuffled off.

As the train was about to start, a neatly dressed student, with sharp pallid features, entered Ralph's compartment. His trousers were carefully pressed and his black hair abundantly oiled.

He looked at Lanigan superciliously.

"Maynooth?" he said to Ralph doubtfully.

Ralph nodded.

"What a rough lot of fellows," he said, waving his hand vaguely. "I"m Duncan, Dublin Diocese, three years in Clonliffe," carefully pulling up the legs of his trousers. "Clonliffe is top hole - not like Maynooth. We had the son of a baronet there once. What diocese?"

"Bunnahone."

Duncan pursed his lips and was silent for a few minutes, during which he eyed Ralph closely.

"You look more like a Clonliffe man," he said condescendingly.

The Maynooth platform was packed with groups of excited young men, tin trunks tied with ropes, carpet bags, black glazed-cloth bags and a few new Gladstone bags. Ralph and his companions followed the crowd across the wooden bridge, through a rather forlorn street. The entrance to the College, with its yellow paint and white lions, flanked by the ivy-covered ruin of a Geraldine castle on the right and the Protestant parish church on the left, was not unattractive. A group of students stood round the porter's lodge, where each entered his name under the supervision of a plethoric gate porter, who, Ralph heard in an awestricken whisper, was called Cerberus.

Maynooth had a charm for Ralph on that first evening that he never quite forgot: in front, an old-fashioned country house of the eighteenth century, of no particular style; the Junior House, the grounds of which he entered through a gateway on the left, with its barrack-like buildings dedicated to St Brigid and St Columba, in the latter of which he was lodged; quaint creeper-covered Tara; the long shadows cast by majestic trees in the afternoon sun; the severe simplicity of the quadrangle of St Joseph's, with its well-kept flower-beds and its cedars that were old when Silken Thomas rebelled against his over-lord; the rather fine modern gothic of the immense pile of St Mary's, designed by Pugin in his best period, with its cool flagged cloisters; and, beyond, the extensive grounds with their noble avenues of limes and horse chestnut. A curious progression of ideas marked the buildings. First came the country house; then the quasi-military barracks; lastly, the severely religious convent. A gothic church, less severe than Pugin, formed the fourth side of the quadrangle of St Mary's. Its internal beauty of line was marred by lifeless carving, a finicky altar, gaudy mock frescoes covering hundreds of yards of wall space and stained glass whose muddy colours obscured the light.

When his luggage arrived Ralph sought his room, one of many all alike, in a long corridor. It was a narrow cell, well lighted by a large window, with a fanlight over the door for ventilation. An iron bedstead, a mattress, a small deal table, a desk, a metal washstand and a small press intended to serve also as a dressing-table made up the furniture.

At supper, in the Junior House dining-room, which reminded him of Bunnahone on a larger scale, he sat next Duncan, who was cross and grumbled loudly.

"At Clonliffe we were treated as gentlemen – the waiters knew how to serve. They weren't like these fellows – mere country boys picked up on the roadside. We had tablecloths, chairs to sit on and cups to drink from. Bad as I thought Maynooth would be, I never dreamt it would be anything like this. Look at the dirt on that table, and these filthy bowls. You can see the marks of the dirt of the trays on the bread. This isn't a bad-looking place on the outside, I admit. But inside! The boards of my room weren't washed since the place was built, and I don't believe, 'pon my word I don't, that that servant lounging against the wall over there washed since he came into the house. Do you see his hands?"

Ralph was amused. His experience at Bunnahone had inured him to dirt and coarse food; and he had long since decided that it was part of his religious duty to put up with disagreeable things.

He said: "The grounds and buildings are rather charming. The senior library is most attractive."

"Humph!" said Duncan, "not bad as a building. But the books! Would you believe me? Not a single copy of Tennyson. Fusty job lots of theology and philosophy! The only decent books in the place were left by a priest who died many years ago. No books seem to have been bought since. In Clonliffe, now, we have all the best modern books. I like dipping into the modern. Have you read *The Egoist*? No? It is wonderful! As fine as Marie Corelli's best. Personally, I like Newman best of all. I make cuttings of all the articles on him that I come across. I have Lubbock's hundred best books with me; a little dry, some of them, but I believe in having the classics by me. Of course I supplement them with dear old Matthew Arnold, Hall Caine, Birrell and Mrs Humphry Ward. I should not, however, advise you to read her, until you have mastered Barbara, celarent – you didn't know I had read logic? I apply it, too. It gives me huge pleasure to catch old Mat and Mrs Ward tripping. I like sounding the depths. She has depths of mind as Ouida has depth of passion. With a well-balanced mind like mine, fortressed by logic and anchored in the truth – that is a good phrase, don't you think? – I can read these authors, but I need not tell you they are not for the general – Shakespeare you may remember."

Ralph escaped after supper on the pretence of seeing Devine, followed by Duncan's voice: "We must have another literary talk. It has been most interesting; fascinating, I should say, indeed."

The examinations dragged on slowly. The papers were easy. Magan, who swaggered a good deal the first days and boasted that he had heard groups of students say as he passed, "That's Magan, a great gun, senior grade ex," grew visibly uneasy. He pestered Ralph with questions on the subjects for examination, made notes on separate slips of paper, which he deposited in assorted bundles in his various pockets. He complained that Father Phil's list of answers was not of much use and confessed that he rather dreaded the oral examination. Ralph, who had just been through it, had found it somewhat of a farce. It was merely the translation of two short pieces, Latin and Greek, from the appointed texts, before a board of three examiners. Ten minutes' preparation was allowed in an empty room, popularly called "The Sweating Hall", and the actual examination lasted less than ten minutes.

Magan came out of the ordeal radiant.

"That Sweating Hall is a great invention," he said excitedly; "that is," he went on lamely, "I had time to pull my wits together."

"Ginger and wits!" said Lanigan, derisively. "Gave you time to read up the translation you have in your pocket there, you mean."

Lanigan, Devine and Ralph got their class, logic, but Magan was allotted to the rhetoric class, a class lower than his companions and the lowest in the College.

"The examiners weren't quite the fools I took 'em to be," Lanigan said.

"I had a faint during the principal papers and I couldn't write a word with the megrim in my head after," said Magan, brazenly. "I'll go to the President and explain, and you'll see I'll get my class."

That evening a notice was posted up, announcing that Mr Magan was allotted to the logic class.

"I'll let all the lads here know the truth," Lanigan said.

"You shut your lip, Mr Lanigan," said Magan, "or I'll write to Father Phil and tell him you're taking away my character, and the character of Bunnahone Seminary. When I told the President that I was a senior grade ex, he apologised to me, no less, and said it must have been some mistake. He hoped the bishop wouldn't hear of it. I told him it was my headache was to blame, and he shook my hand at parting. Great man that he is, I seen that he was in mortal terror of the bishop," Magan added, grinning, "so I told him early in the talk the compliments the bishop passed on me."

There was much excitement in settling in, and many visits to "the mart", a sort of market in which traders from the town had stalls, open once a week for the convenience of the students, but now open every day, as freshmen needed so many things for the equipping of their rooms and persons. Ralph bought a soutane, biretta, stock and a supply of clerical collars, the regulation indoor dress for students, and a few books, in pity, from the benighted old man who sold books, tattered and dogs-eared, the remnants of third-hand bookshops.

During the few free days before the arrival of the general body of students Ralph, accompanied by Devine, explored the College: the poky, ill-supplied divisional libraries, without catalogue, order or classification, or any book that one wanted to read; the rather fine College library, not quite as despicable as the admirer of Marie Corelli found it, but still pitifully unrepresentative of any general culture. The Pugin cloisters of St Mary's was their favourite walk: lined on one side by photographs of the ordination classes, for many years back; on the other by immense, glaring oil paintings of bishops, archbishops and cardinals, who had been students of the College, fashion-plate reproductions of magnificent full-dress ecclesiastical garments.

In the afternoons most of the freshmen played handball, seemingly the only College game, in the courts with which each division was plentifully supplied. Ralph and Devine contented themselves with walking through the grounds, the greater part of which would be shut to them when regular work began, as the three divisions were kept rigidly apart, the junior house for all purposes, the senior and middle divisions meeting only for meals, eaten in silence. They paid many visits to the little cemetery, with its simple memorials of dead professors and students; or sat reading under the immense horse chestnut in the Junior House grounds, making plans and resolutions for their future.

Ralph felt isolated on the evening of the return of the old students. As a rule, the freshmen knew all the students of their diocese, having been at the Seminary with them. But as Ralph had been only six months at Bunnahone, he knew none. Devine introduced him to several men as "the diocese". A few were friendly, but the majority looked him over superciliously without speaking. A tall pasty-faced youth, lank and awkward, slapped him on the back, saying, with a guffaw, "I'm the only old rhetorician from the diocese, you know, so I'm your senior. See if I don't keep ye all in order."

"Mr Daly," said Devine.

"Oh! he has likely read me up in the prize list. I led the class in Christian doctrine," Daly said importantly. "If you want any tips," he said to Ralph, confidentially, "come to me, and I'll put you up to things. I know the ropes well."

"Sure that's only a catechism class he boasts of getting a prize in, and none of the guns'd bother to go in for the like of that," said Lanigan, as Daly rushed off to greet some friends. "He's not a bad fellow all the same, only he has a slate or two off – 'swell Daly' we used to call him at Bunnahone. He used to spend half the day putting shines on his boots. Did you notice they hadn't a speck on 'em? You'll find he done them the minute he got in."

Ralph succeeded in keeping permanently the room which had been given him for the examination week. He now learned that it was avoided by most of the students through fear of the ghost room next door. This room, the door of which had been removed and the doorway enlarged, had been converted into an oratory, in which stood a small altar. In large letters round the doorway was the inscription, "*A subitanea et improvida morte, libera nos Domine.*" A student had died there. The next student who occupied the room was found dead on the pavement beneath the window, having evidently thrown himself out in the night. The legend was that the second student had seen the ghost of the first. Ralph laughed at the tale when he heard it, but it was some hours before he lost a horrible nervous feeling of expectancy as he lay awake that night. He experienced a recurrence of his old fears as a child of death and hell, which persisted despite all his efforts to put them away. At last he fell into a broken sleep from which he was awakened by a crash followed by a smothered laugh. He sat up in bed terrified, but could not resist the desire to investigate. He lit his candle, opened his door and saw a student gazing at him open-mouthed. In one hand he held half a huge cake and firmly gripped in the other hand was a ham, from which most of the meat had been cut away.

"Good God! I thought at first you were the ghost," said the man in the passage, in a relieved tone.

"I thought I heard it," said Ralph, still a little limp.

"It must be the water-jug! We were having a little spree in the room opposite. By the way, of no harm, you know. I'm a rule-keeper myself in general. But on the first night!" he laughed feebly. "One of the lads let the jug fall. I hope the Dean didn't hear it. Put out that light. That's against all rules. If you were caught with it lighting at this hour, first night and all, you'd hardly escape a cat," and he shuffled off in the dark.

Next day was free and the mart was open all the morning. There was a general fitting up of rooms and hammering of nails. Students laden with heterogeneous loads – a sweeping brush, bedroom ware, a mat, candlesticks – were to be met at every corner. Ralph made an effort to buy a sponge bath, but no such thing was to be found in the mart. As at Bunnahone, there was no baths except one in the infirmary, which students were allowed to use occasionally. "You'll find there won't be much of a rush on it," a servant assured him, when he expressed a doubt of his being able to use it.

After dinner all the students assembled by dioceses and walked in large bands around the grounds. At six a separation bell would ring, and a four-day retreat would begin soon afterwards.

The Bunnahone group consisted of about twenty students ranging from Melod, an elderly student of about thirty, whose black hair had begun to whiten, to Ralph, who was the youngest. Melod, a grave man with thoughtful blue eyes, spoke to Ralph of Father Sheldon and Father Duff. He expected to be ordained the following summer.

"I shall be sorry to leave Maynooth," he said, "but if I could only hope to be Father Sheldon's curate, I should be glad."

"You'd never have any fun with a voteen like him," Lanigan said.

"Oh! that's why Melod likes him," said a dark, forbidding-looking man named Brown, with a sneer; "as far as I can gather they're as like as two peas."

Melod blushed and was silent. Brown took possession of the conversation and spoke of the relative values of parishes in the diocese. He hoped Bunnahone would be vacant when he was ordained. The mass offerings there were always large. "Instead of half a crown you often got a pound from some of the rich shopkeepers," he said impressively.

"This is a great place entirely," said Magan; "some of the fellows don't give a hang for the Dean or the professors."

"They'd sneak through a gimlet hole if the Dean came round the corner," said Lanigan.

"A man is none the worse for being able to navigate well," said Brown, scowling. "I've never got a cat or even been councilled, and I've been here five years. It's only a fool ever gets caught."

"Escaping a caveat is hardly the whole duty of an ecclesiastical student," said Melod dryly.

"The batch can't stand old Sobersides since he was made a Junior

House monitor. He'll lead you the life of a dog, Ginger, if you don't mind. Thank the Lord, we'll see less of him in Mary's; we're about tired of his preaching," said Brown, insolently, addressing Magan.

Melod ignored him.

Brown carried on a whispered conversation with Magan. Melod spoke to the newcomers of their studies and of the long walks he would take with them as monitor on half-holidays.

When the bell rang for the divisions to separate there was a general handshaking.

"Enjoy yourselves and keep a weather eye open for the Dean. That's better advice than you'll ever get from Sobersides," said Brown, grimacing.

Four lectures a day were given during the retreat in St Joseph's chapel by an eloquent Jesuit. In the intervals the students were supposed to meditate on the subjects of the lectures, a modified treatment of the spiritual exercises of St Ignatius. All were expected to keep rigid silence.

The preacher was vivid and theatrical. In this household of the faith, he said, he assumed all the great truths as proved, so he would deal only with their application to souls specially favoured by God. Faith was the great staff of the priest, and acceptance of authority his safeguard against the snares of the enemy. His mind was secure through the teaching of Holy Church, but the will had to be trained to obedience and observance. He sketched a high ideal of conduct for ecclesiastical students. He painted in lurid colours the terrors of death, judgment and hell for the proud of mind and the wicked of will. He laid stress on the student's special call to the service of God; this was perhaps the irrevocable moment when the choice had to be made. For those who were called and turned a deaf ear, the grand refusal might lead to service through life under the standard of the devil instead of the standard of Christ.

Ralph was deeply moved. He walked for hours under the trees after each lecture, his eyes fixed on the ground, unseeing, meditating on its application to himself. He had been called to the standard of Christ. He assumed the truth of this as axiomatic. He would cling to this standard firmly and do his best to hold it aloft to hearten others in the strife with the evil one. He would guard himself against evil desires and the promptings of his wicked will. He would freely accept the voice of authority as the voice of God, and render it absolute obedience.

For two days he was borne on the wings of his spirit and found it easy to summon fervour at will. He saw vague forms moving about the grounds, ate food mechanically and seemed to be conscious only of an exalted self and of an inspired voice in the pulpit speaking on behalf of the mysterious just God dwelling in lonely majesty in the tabernacle, to which Ralph's eyes turned in silent supplication when the speaker made some telling point.

On the third day he awoke with a headache and felt irritable and dissatisfied. He shivered with cold as he sat at the first meditation, and the stuffiness of the small chapel, crowded with students, depressed him. The man next him was bobbing backwards and forwards in his seat, giving short stertorous grunts, sleeping unpeacefully. Several men were yawning; others taking snuff. A lean man in a professor's toga was smiling cynically. Ralph noticed the toga minutely, a faint blue shade in the cashmere, the velvet a dull black. The Professor held the front tightly gripped over his hands like a muff, as Ralph had once seen Cassius hold his toga in Julius Cæsar at the Theatre Royal. He listened to the preacher and smiled at a series of mixed metaphors in which he was describing, by analogy, the tortures of the damned. Ralph became critical. God surely wasn't a petty revengeful tyrant, gloating over the tortures of the damned. He felt himself nodding in unison with his neighbour. He braced himself to listen and smiled as he saw Devine in a side bench, his rapt face fixed in admiration on the preacher. The almost general coughing was annoying and he longed to get out in the open air. "He's damned long-winded," some one muttered in a loud whisper. In the back bench by the door an intermittent conversation was kept up.

After breakfast, as he sat reading under the spreading chestnut in front of the Junior House, Magan shuffled up.

"Aren't you tired of it, yet?" he said, putting his finger to his lips and making a face.

Ralph shook his head and went on reading, but he blushed as he felt that he longed to talk to someone, even to Magan.

"If you're going to be such a mug, it's easy to find people with some sense," Magan said, looking at Ralph angrily. He joined a group on a seat near by and was soon engaged in conversation.

For the remainder of the retreat, Ralph's mind was distracted. He made many efforts to keep it fixed on the meditations, but either he couldn't keep awake or he was constantly noticing little tricks of manner in the preacher. About half the students kept the rule of silence, but small groups gathered for conversation in out of the way corners or in the students' rooms. Once Ralph found himself talking to Duncan for five minutes before he remembered that he was breaking a rule. As he walked away Magan ran after him.

"You're a navigator, you are!" he jibed. "I caught you at it. If I'd only the time I could catch all the fellows that go round with long faces pretending they're better than their neighbours."

Ralph turned away disgusted. He went to the chapel and renewed all his good resolutions. But it was of no use. He could not regain his lost fervour. He found himself standing at the top of the high field, beyond St Brigid's, admiring the sunset, brilliant red fading into pink and, in between, a band of translucent grey cloud. The scent of tobacco from the walk on his left brought back his thoughts from the sunset to his soul. He was keeping the rules; that, he supposed, was something. He doubted if it was from any spiritual motive. If it was merely from a sense of honour, as that was only a natural virtue, he should gain no spiritual profit. He went to confession to an old priest, Father Bradley, and spoke of his aridity of soul. The priest, who seemed tired, gave a long and incoherent disquisition on aridity. As far as Ralph could gather it was rather a sign of sanctity, was certainly no hindrance to sanctity; a feeling of fervour was a delusion.

Still tepid and arid, he went to communion listlessly at the close of the retreat and felt a sense of relief when breakfast was over and talking was allowed. Devine was full of admiration for the Jesuit who gave the retreat. No heart, no matter how hard, could resist such persuasive eloquence, prompted, he was sure, by the Holy Ghost Himself.

Daly said a retreat was a fine time for fixing up one's room and doing odd jobs to pass away the time. One could have a sleep too in the mornings, without much fear of the Dean finding out. The lectures were a great bore and always put him to sleep – he preferred to sleep in his bed: it was more comfortable than a hard seat in St

Joseph's chapel. Besides, the lecturer was showing off too much.

Ralph did not try to reconcile the conflicting views. Lanigan had gone to the ball courts and Magan to the "John's" for his after-breakfast surreptitious smoke. Ralph walked in silence, not even listening to the argument that arose between Daly and Devine. He did not wish to hear of the retreat, much less to talk of it. He was disappointed with himself and his surroundings. He had looked forward in Maynooth to a progressive spiritual development. The phrase interested him. He dwelt on it and tried to analyse it. It meant, he supposed, some sort of progressive intensity of religious feeling. His failure was, perhaps, due to himself more than to his environment. During the retreat he failed miserably. He had an opportunity and missed it. For the rest, Maynooth was rather like Bunnahone. Devine was still Devine, Magan Magan, and O'Brien, he felt bitterly, was a worse O'Brien. Devine, of course, was a good fellow, but he had blinkers on both eyes and built stone walls at the end of his nose. Daly was Daly. Yet with these three he should have to spend most of his free time for a year. The Maynooth system of diocesan batches, which practically compelled the students of each diocese to take all their recreations together, except at handball, made him angry and rebellious. He was tired already of the dull round of the batch conversation. He envied Lanigan at the ball courts, who had, at least, the opportunity to vary his conversation, trivial though it might be. For a moment or two he gave a longing thought to Magan's smoking companions. But there he pulled himself up. That was dishonourable, against all rules and, therefore, morally wrong. He dwelt on the possibilities of the after-supper batches. During the after-supper recreation, one could arrange with any two companions to walk around together - a different set for each night of the week, the arrangement lasting for a year. As he did not know any of the men, the possibility of congenial companions was small, but there was a chance ...

At midday, there was a long walk across country, beyond Kilcock. Melod, as senior monitor, led the junior division, accompanied by his diocesans. The country was flat and uninteresting, the pace rapid and the jumping good. The route was through part of the Meath hunting country and many of the fences were pretty stiff. Conversation was sporadic. Melod knew nothing of history and shed no light on monuments rich with Geraldine traditions. He was keenly interested in farming and pointed out the best fattening lands. For the most part the talk was small diocesan gossip which bored Ralph, but seemed of intense interest to the others. As they drew near the College on their return, Melod spoke seriously on the observance of rules. As monitor, he said, he had not much authority, but what he had would be exercised impartially. If any rule-breaking came under his notice he should be as severe with his own diocesans as with others.

Magan laughed uncomfortably, and gave a derisive "Hear, hear."

On their return, fruit stalls filled the whole semi-circular space in front of the College railings. It was against the rules to have food in students' rooms, but, as Ralph was told gravely by Melod, some rules were abrogated in whole or in part by custom. The buying of fruit on walk-days, while not recognised by rule, was winked at by custom. The more or less orderly division became a disorganised mob; apples, plums and oranges were stuffed into pockets or carried in handkerchiefs or birettas.

The following day work began. The big bell of St Mary's gave the signal for rising at six and was echoed or enforced in jangling tones by the several divisional bells. Rule-keepers rose at once, washed and dressed, or dressed and washed, hastily; made beds, cleaned boots, swept rooms, and were in the oratory for morning prayers when the warning bell rang at twenty-five minutes past six. Those who gave a legal interpretation to rules, or ignored them, got up at varying intervals. One man boasted that he always got up at twenty-past, when the angelus bell rang, did everything necessary and was in the oratory fully dressed at half-past. Stragglers in various stages of deshabille continued to arrive long after morning prayer had begun. Ralph caught a glimpse of pyjamas stuck into the unlaced boots of the man who knelt beside him. Morning prayer was followed by twenty minutes' meditation, in the strictly Ignatian method, for many; others yawned and fidgeted, while a few frankly slept. When the Dean had finished marking his list of absentees and had settled down to his own meditation, a few slipped quietly away to complete somewhat sketchy toilettes or interrupted slumbers. At seven low mass was celebrated by one of the professors, who was some minutes late.

"It must be Devlin," said the man next Ralph; "he doesn't get up even at the warning bell."

From half-past seven there was supposed to be an hour's study in rooms until the weather got cold, when, as the rooms in the Junior House were not heated, the study halls were used. As no business, however, had been appointed, the majority of the students busied themselves in fitting up their rooms, whispering at each other's doors or parading the corridors, effectively preventing any reading by strict rule-keepers or the more serious-minded.

There was much speculation during the walk after breakfast as to the professors. Daly contributed some of the gossip of his year's experience.

"Dave is a terror," he said; "we'll have most to do with him. He's mathematics and physics, and Jimmy logic. There's no getting over Dave. He looks through you if you make an excuse, as much as to say, I don't believe a word you're saying. It's easier getting over Jimmy. He likes the sound of his own voice. But what matter? Sure there are so many in the class that one doesn't get called more than once in a half-year. And the exams are dead easy. If they think you're any good they rake you fore and aft a bit, like as not to show off before the other pros what a power of things they've been teaching. But if you're not up to much, there's always a few leading questions that are sure to be given, so unless you're a fool entirely you can save your bacon. They're the two principal classes. Then there's English. You needn't trouble your head about that if you don't like. It's not of much importance, and no matter how badly you get on you wouldn't be kept back a year for such a footy thing as English. French is of little account, and no one bothers a pin about the Irish. That's about all."

The logic class opened with an hour's lecture at ten to about eighty students. The Professor, the Rev. James Hay, sat in a raised pulpit facing the students. He was slim, round-shouldered and florid, with a long, rather flat, nose, down which his somnolent brown eyes seemed to glance. He allotted the business for the next class and explained that he would, as a rule, call four students at each class, the language of which would be Latin. He then gave, without stopping to take breath, at a speed of over two hundred words a minute, a general lecture on logic, mainly a defence of scholastic logic. He was clear and dull and did not long hold the attention of the class. After about ten minutes there was a buzz of conversation throughout the hall, but his fluent, sing-song voice, thickened by adenoids, rolled on unheeding until the eleven o'clock bell interrupted him in the middle of a sentence. He stopped abruptly, said a short prayer and rushed out of the room.

"Glory be! what a lepper! He took every fence at a gallop," said Lanigan, as he passed Ralph.

There was an hour's study before the Rev. David Bannon's lecture. The students were seated, lounging listlessly, prepared for another idle hour, when he strode briskly into the hall, his right hand describing figures in the air, his head well thrown back, a frown, accentuated by black bushy eyebrows and a strong square jaw, on his stern face. Having said a preliminary prayer, instead of going into the pulpit, he stood beside a blackboard, a piece of chalk in his hand, and wrote out a problem in trigonometry. Consulting a list which he had in his hand, he called a student, an ungainly black-haired youth with a squint.

"Solve that," Bannon said, handing him the chalk and walking up and down beside the board, his hands clutching his toga.

The student gaped at the board, holding the chalk in a trembling hand.

"Can't do it! Go to your place, sir. A boy of six, if he used his brains, could do that."

Half a dozen were called in as many minutes and dismissed with scathing remarks on the inefficiency of Maynooth entrance examinations, the decadence of education under the Intermediate system, and the deterioration of Irish brain power.

Ralph, when called, began to write.

"That will do. I see you know it," said Bannon, flicking chalk dust off his fingers. "I merely wished to know where we are. One out of eight with a glimmering of intelligence! There are a few, therefore, who will understand a simple talk on what we mean to do for the half year. Long experience makes me satisfied with small mercies. What I have to say now is intended for this *nth* part of the class. As for the rest ..." He shook his head and pursed his lips.

His short sentences, crisp and pointed, accompanied by constant graphic illustration on the blackboard, were a contrast to Hay's weedy vapidity. His eyes lighted with pleasure as he worked and the worn features became almost youthful in expression.

Ralph smiled over his luncheon of bread and thick, greasy soup as he recalled the alternate looks of enthusiasm and contempt that passed over Bannon's face.

"Dave was in great form," said Daly, at recreation afterwards.

"Sorra head or tail I could make of anything the two pros said," said Magan, moodily.

"Listen to the senior ex," said Lanigan, jeeringly. "Dave seems to think we're all dirt under his feet," he added.

"He's an excellent teacher," said Ralph.

"You want to draw attention to your being able to do the problem," said Magan, angrily.

"Imagine making a fuss about poor Dave," said Daly, airily. "The lash of his tongue, when he keeps you standing like a fool before the blackboard, is a trifle unpleasant, but it wears off, and he never spins a man. You need never look at a book for him until the night before the exam. The trick is to answer nothing when you're called in class; then you're let off easy at the exam. I've a list of the questions he gives to them he calls 'the brainless many'. Ginger with his memory'll learn them off in ten minutes."

"Ginger, brainless!" said Lanigan, holding up his hands in horror. "Did anyone ever hear the like, and he going to head the prize list!"

Magan, with a scowl, strode off in the direction of his room.

The class work of the day wound up with an English lecture at half-past two. It was a close stuffy afternoon, and many of the students were inclined to sleep, their heads on their outstretched arms. A few of the senior students, the rhetoric class of the previous year, clapped the Professor as he entered. He walked with mincing steps, bowing repeatedly, a bundle of books under his left arm, waving his biretta with his right hand at each bow. He was a tall man with black hair, chubby cheeks, girlish in their pink simplicity, an undecided chin and mouth and faded blue eyes. In the College calendar he was described as the Rev. Thomas Delahunt, D.D., but was known to the students as Miss Muffet.

He simpered his thanks for the hearty reception, which, he said, had been given him, unmerited, he was sure, for his humble efforts to make known the beauties of a great literature. He hoped that their vigorous appreciation wasan indication of hard work for the coming year.

This was received with cheers and renewed clapping of hands.

"He's a prosy devil," Lanigan said, yawning.

"We shall do a play by the noble Swan of Avon," the Professor went on, "as well as one of those incomparable essays in the glorious scintillating prose of Macaulay."

"Rats," said Lanigan, settling himself for sleep.

"Perhaps the best preparation for our work would be a recitation of some of the more beautiful passages. Notice especially the way in which I manage my lips and my gestures."

He stood in the pulpit, pulled back the loose sleeves of his toga, drew down his white cuffs and began Marc Antony's speech over the dead body of Cæsar.

"It's just like Pizarro I once saw a play-acting lad do in a barn," said Lanigan, who had again become attentive, admiringly.

The strong voice, pitched in a high key, rose and fell monotonously. Now one arm sawed the air, now two, his eyes fixed in a stony stare at a window at the back of the hall.

Ralph pitied the orator as he heard some one behind him snigger. He disliked seeing a priest in a ridiculous position. He even felt some resentment against the priest, who sat down, a glow of satisfaction on his face, when he had finished with a resonant bellow.

"These great efforts are rather trying," the priest said, patting his forehead gently with a coloured silk handkerchief. "But if they do good I am amply repaid. I hope you noticed the voice inflection and the production of the vowel sounds. You hold your mouths as if you had an egg between your lips. These things may seem unimportant to you now, but afterwards, when, as priests, you have taken up the noble work of preaching, you will remember them with gratitude. I only wish I had such advantages in my day. I may mention that nothing adds more to the effect of a sermon than graceful gesture."

Ralph was glad to escape from the hall in the wake of Father Delahunt, who was cheered derisively as he went out, some one singing, "Little Miss Muffet sat on her tuffet."

Chapter 13

AUTUMN FADED INTO winter; fires were lighted in the study halls, the students using their cold rooms for sleeping only; the red-gold creepers on Tara shed their leaves; cold, damp, penetrating fogs, impregnated with the smell of gas, hovered constantly over the low-lying ground; some students who were ill, and many who were well, went "on" the infirmary for the sake of fires, freedom from class, unlimited leisure for gossip and buttered toast. Around the door of the Dean's rooms a horde gathered every night seeking permission for a morning sleep, a few because they were ill, the majority because they were lazy or disliked the gloom of a winter morning. Others who had not asked permission, when awakened by the six o'clock bell, tucked the bedclothes around them comfortably and decided to get up at twenty-past, then bethought themselves that the Dean, possibly, would not be in the oratory; what matter even if he were? the offence was not very serious! turned over and slept as soundly as noisy servants emptying slops and sweeping corridors allowed. Those who were really ill often got up for a late mass; many of the others "soaked" over breakfast, bribing a servant to bring them a bowl of sloppy tea and a plateful of buttered toast, a greasy mess, the butter collected in driblets off plates in the refectory after the students' breakfast.

Ralph settled down to work. He had been told that Father Hay's class was the most important, but he found it unsatifactory. The textbook, Zigliari, was dull, but bad as it was, was brilliant compared with Father Hay's duller notes. Father Hay spent the last half of class time in dictating notes in slipshod bog Latin, which formed the subject for questioning for the first half-hour at the following class. Melod told Ralph that Hay was extraordinarily clever, that it was unnecessary to read any book on his subject, that everything was in his notes, which alone sufficed for examinations and class pieces. Indeed, one was more certain to get prizes by reading only the notes, for Father Hay preferred replies in his own words.

Magan, who had begun to despair of being able to translate Zigliari – on Lanigan's advice, he had written in vain to an imaginary Paris publisher for a translation – plucked up hope at Melod's words. Hay's impossible Latin, which left Ralph doubtful as to his meaning, and even when his meaning was clear, doubtful as to the value of his dogmatic assertions without a shadow of proof, was a joy to Magan, who learned the whole by heart and made such a brilliant call in class that he began to dream of prizes.

One evening in the study hall, Ralph, who sat next Magan, was puzzled by a passage in Hay's notes and asked Magan what he made of it.

Magan repeated the Latin words glibly.

"I know that," Ralph said, "but what does it mean? Say it in English."

Magan looked at him blankly. "Oh, I never bother about the meaning in English," he said, "as long as I have the Latin words. Sure no one can deny the meaning is in them right enough. What more can any man want?"

Ralph watched him, fascinated, as he read over a passage several times, then shut the notebook and his eyes; his lips moved. He took another look at the notes and repeated the process. A look of pleased satisfaction glowed on his face when the words were thoroughly commited to memory.

Conversation in the batch often turned on class work. In the course of a discussion Ralph offended Devine by saying that Father Delahunt's class was mere drivel.

"I know you don't mean any harm, Mr O'Brien, but still one shouldn't speak like that of a priest. Besides, he speaks beautifully, and his recitations are the grandest things I ever heard; finer even than Father Doyle's, and I always thought him great."

Ralph smiled at the recollection of Father Delahunt's Rathmines accent, but disclaimed any intention of reflecting on Father Delahunt as a priest.

"I'm sure," he said seriously, "he's a very good priest. All the same, even in the junior grade at the Ignatian school, I got well caned for saying many of the things he teaches us. And I can't close my eyes to the fact that the worst actor I ever saw doing Shakespeare at the Theatre Royal could teach him to recite."

Devine shrugged his shoulders and looked at Ralph sadly.

"Father Doyle told me once that the Jesuits aren't the best judges of things to suit a missionary priest. I'm sure, with all their experience of the mission, a Maynooth priest knows best the sort of English to suit us. And I'd never dream of comparing an actor to a Maynooth professor. I'm not sure that it's not sinful. I hope you won't grow worldly through all these plays and things you've seen?" he added wistfully.

"Good old Devine," Ralph said, slapping him on the shoulder, "let's talk of Father Bradley's lecture on meditation." Devine grew enthusiastic and spoke at length of the sanctity of the old priest and of his kindness. Ralph agreed, but he had said and heard all this before, and his thoughts wandered again to Father Delahunt and his liking for a textbook of Julius Cæsar, with elaborate notes at the end. "Rubbish that would make Shakespeare turn in his grave," his old Jesuit teacher of English had called it years ago, when Ralph brought it to class one day, a great find from a second-hand book shop on the quays. Father Delahunt's method of lecturing was to get a student to read a passage and then to ask questions on the text. As he raised all, and only, the points referred to in the notes, Magan one day made a brilliant call by opening his copy at the notes, which he read for the first time in response to Father Delahunt's questions.

"Very good, very good indeed, Mr Magan," the Professor interjected. "But you needn't be so modest. Hold up your head so that the class may hear."

As Magan's ability to answer depended on keeping his eyes fixed on the book in front of him, he was modest to the end.

"You're not listening to a word I say," said Devine, who asked Ralph a question to which he did not reply. "Wool-gathering as usual! You won't mind my leaving you?" he added gently. "It's within a few minutes of the bell and I want to go to the chapel for a while."

As Ralph went to his room he thought how much better than himself Devine was, accepting everything, never questioning, keeping rigid guard on every thought and word. He sighed and hoped that some day he would have Devine's even spirit.

He enjoyed Father Bannon's class. He had done most of the work before and wasn't deeply interested in mathematics, but he liked the old priest's sincerity and thoroughness. It was a pleasure to see the stern, thoughtful face yield for a moment to boyish enthusiasm; and a constant wonder how the priest kept up his keen interest in the routine work of teaching. The majority of the class did not know and did not care what he talked of. The "nth number" he generally addressed were about a dozen, and perhaps twenty others followed his lectures half-heartedly.

The same lack of interest prevailed in the French class, which was treated as a joke. The professor, Father Ryan, was a cultivated man, shy in manner. Educated abroad, he was new to Maynooth's ways and suffered tortures. Ralph felt all his chivalrous instincts aroused by the ill-treatment Father Ryan had to bear at the hands of the rougher students. It felt somewhat as if his mother was jeered at by corner-boys. The priest being sensitive to unpleasant sounds, a favourite method of annoying him was by making grating noises, kept up, at intervals, from the beginning of class to the end. The greater number of students did not know French and were determined not to learn. Many were firmly convinced that anyone who attempted to read French correctly was imitating the Professor.

"Bedad, O'Brien is turning into a Radical. If he's not imitating Owney's accent to a tick!" Magan said to a neighbour, when Ralph was first called on to read.

For the only remaining class, Irish, held once a week, Ralph studied hard. Melod advised him against wasting his time on such a useless subject. Even Devine studied only the bare minimum necessary to salve his conscience, which pricked him if he neglected any of the College duties.

"Everyone knows," he said, "that only for some Irish League outside in Dublin, no Irish professor would have been appointed. Melod tells me the President laughs at the language and the pros are always joking about it. Father Doyle told me that our bishop meant to raise a row about it at the trustees' meeting. However, as there is a professor and a class, I suppose I must study a little."

"I won't spend a penny in buying a book for it then, if that's the way the land lies," said Magan.

Lanigan always jeered at Irish, but, after attending a few classes, he said to Ralph, "You help me with the grammar and I'll talk as much

Irish to you as you like. Here's, maybe, a great opportunity for me of getting a prize. There won't be much competition, I'm thinking. If the Irish isn't much use itself, as I'm nearly certain to get a bad report from Dave, it might help me along to be on the prize list. The bishop don't think much of the Irish, but he's so anxious to have the diocese kissing his ring on the prize day that he'll give little heed whether it's a prize in theology or in pitch-and-toss."

Ralph soon got on friendly terms with the Irish professor, Father Gogarty, a shy, delicate looking, gauche young man in spectacles. Melod had told Ralph that Gogarty was rather looked down on by the other professors, partly because Irish was considered such an unimportant subject, partly as he, unlike themselves, was not a prize-man in the Maynooth classes during his student days. "He wasted so much of his time over the Irish," Melod explained. It seemed that Gogarty, who knew no Irish when he came to Maynooth, suffered very much from ill-health, and being attracted to Irish – "why, nobody could ever imagine" – had studied the language during his long periods of illness and was now one of the recognised leaders of the popular movement for its revival.

Ralph found him dry and not nearly as interesting on Irish subjects as Teig Moriarty, but was attracted by his simplicity and earnestness. One day, after Gogarty had called him in class, Ralph was surprised to get a note from the professor, asking him to call at his rooms that night at seven. It was the first time that any of the superiors had taken any notice of him outside class. Indeed, he had not even spoken to any, except once, formally, to the Dean on his arrival. As far as he could see, there was no intercourse between the professors and students. The professors had a separate dining-room and never joined the students at recreation. After breakfast they walked around in batches as the students did, the professors of each ecclesiastical province walking together.

Ralph spoke of the invitation in the batch, with a view to find out whether it was necessary to get permission from the Dean to leave his division, as Gogarty lived in St Joseph's.

"Lucky man," said Magan, "I wish I was in your place. He's sure to offer you a drink. What a waste! and you a T.T. too."

"I'm sure a professor wouldn't do any such thing," said Devine, primly.

"It's little you know about the place, goody-goody," said Magan, grimacing. "What earthly good is a pro, beyond annoying fellows in class, if it isn't to give a student a drink when he wants it badly? I went to two already and I'll pay them all a round before the year is done. You just knock at the door," he went on garrulously, "after dinner is the best time, about seven o'clock. They're in the best humour then. When he says 'come in', it's well to have some excuse to start with. I asked Owney about a French text, and he went into long explanations about it that I couldn't follow, and in the middle of 'em, took out a bottle of port, and I had two glasses seated fornint his fire. Dave, I admit, was a bit stiff. He asked my name and looked at his list. I mentioned something about trigonometry, but he pretended not to hear me and handed me a small glass of wine, which he filled himself. He never asked me to sit down, and in half a minute, almost before I could finish the glass, he said mighty stiff, 'I'm afraid I must say goodnight, Mr Magan, as I'm busy,' and before I knew where I was, I was outside the door. He's the worst though - none of the others make any bones about it. It's only wine, of course, but it's better than nothing in a dry place like this," he wound up, champing his lips.

With some difficulty Ralph found Gogarty's rooms at the end of a corridor in St Joseph's. When Ralph entered, Gogarty rose from a table covered with galley slips, which he had been correcting.

"Something I should like to have had when I first started learning Irish - just a primer," he said, blushing, greeting Ralph awkwardly. "I'm glad you have begun to learn Irish. We need some enthusiasm for it here. I heard all about you from Charles Dillon - what a fine fellow he is! He should be doing this work, not I."

The words tumbled over each other nervously. He spoke on, deprecating any claims to scholarship.

"There are many who know Irish better than I, many of the professors here even, and some of the students. But - that is," he hesitated painfully, "I care - no doubt they don't yet see its importance. I was as bad myself once," he added with a smile.

Ralph's heart went out to the awkward little man, who peered at him wistfully with short-sighted eyes. He seemed such a pathetic figure in his bare, half-furnished room, with its rows of gaping rough wood shelves - a few books on Ireland, history, philology and archæology scattered here and there.

"I'm not a poet, like Dillon," he said, "only a plodding worker. He appeals to the imagination of the people. I'm only a maker of baby food to start them on the way."

In the gloomy foggy days that followed, Ralph often recalled the shy enthusiasm of Gogarty's monologue which continued until the bell rang for spiritual reading. He felt that one man at least in Maynooth had an ideal and lived up to it, despite ill health, neglect and contempt.

He often spoke of Gogarty in the night batches. He had not been very successful in getting congenial companions and on most nights had his own diocesans. On Tuesdays, he had Devine and Duncan, and on Thursdays, a saturnine elderly student named Ramsay, with a cynical view of life generally, who had unexpectedly asked him to join his batch. The third member didn't turn up, so it was a batch of two. Duncan had the greatest contempt for Gogarty and all that he stood for, so much so that Devine was roused to defend him, chiefly because he was a priest. Ramsay said the Gogarty was the only man in Maynooth with any red blood in him. He did not believe in Irish himself, he said, but he liked a man who believed in something.

One night, as they walked briskly, a keen wind cutting their faces, cloud rack scudding now and again over a brilliant moon, Ramsay broke the silence that had lasted for about ten minutes.

"Are you sick of this place yet, O'Brien?"

"One has to put up with things."

"I ran away to sea from school and went round the world as a cabin boy to escape what was better than this. I wish to God I was back at sea again. Stoking, even, would be pleasanter work than listening to Hay and Delahunt."

"But your vocation?"

"Vocation be damned.... Remember I was a cabin boy," he said very gently. "I haven't a vocation. I have an old grand-uncle, a parish priest, with pots of money. He said he'd leave it to me if I became a priest. I hadn't the least notion of being one. Despise me for it, or not, as you like, but I came here on the off chance of his dying while I was a student. The meanness and hypocrisy of so many fellows here, conscious and unconscious, have made me ashamed of myself.

I'm only a mean skunk myself, but there are depths to which I'm glad I can't descend. I'm off to sea again in a few days."

For a brief moment Ralph experienced an intense longing to be out of Maynooth, too, but he remembered his mother and the strict line of duty he had laid down for himself at the retreat. He did not feel shocked at what Ramsay said, yet he felt he ought to say something. Surely Ramsay must be wrong.

"You ought to see Father Bradley," he said.

"Poor old Bradley! he intends well, but I'm beyond his help. I believe in God still, but very soon I shouldn't, if I stayed here. I told Bradley that, and he said perhaps I was right. He's a wise old man in many ways."

"But Father Bradley and the many holy people here might even now give you a vocation."

"There are Bradleys, too, in the foc'sle of a ship. There are other sorts also, and I prefer them for not pretending to be what they're not. It'll take many a drenching of heavy seas to wash my own meanness of the last few years out of me."

"I wish I could share my vocation with you."

Ramsay looked at him curiously.

"You may one day help to rake up the muck heap. Heigh-ho! We must find our own track ... or make it," he added, musing. "I hope to God you're on yours."

There was a sensation a few days later when Ramsay left.

Magan joined his batch in much excitement.

"Did ye hear the news?" he asked breathlessly. "That black chap, Ramsay, has cut. I doubt but he was caught at something bad that would mean expulsion and was cute enough to be off before he was councilled."

"Not at all," said Ralph, stiffly. "He's a very decent fellow and left because he thought he had no vocation."

"Tell that to the marines," said Magan, seriously. "Run away to sea, I believe he has. Imagine any man giving up the chance of a comfortable life for the like of that without being forced to it."

"Conscience is a force."

"Keep that for Bradley," Magan replied, tipping his nose with his forefinger. "He looked at you in such a damn superior way that I'm glad he's out of the place," he added to Lanigan.

Ralph looked forward to a short vacation after Christmas. Most bishops allowed their students home during the fortnight's recess that followed the Christmas examinations; but a special application had to be made each year by the senior student of the diocese.

Ralph found the examinations a mere form. A public oral examination was held in each subject by a board of three professors, the teacher of the class and two others. The professor of the class alone took any interest and carefully gauged his questions to the capacity of the student. "Tact and glibness of speech," Duncan said, "would get any man through. Those who fail to pass deserve to be expelled as fools." This he found was a mistake in regard to Bannon, who put some searching questions, much to Duncan's confusion. Magan, who would have fallen to Bannon, left the hall when his turn came and managed to have himself examined by one of the Deans, who evidently knew nothing of the subject. In a portentous manner, he put some simple questions which Magan was able to answer. Bannon frowned and fidgeted, but said nothing; and Magan came down smiling triumphantly.

Much to the disappointment of the batch, Mclod had a reply from the bishop refusing permission to leave the College during the holidays. "I find," he wrote, "that a break in the year tends to worldliness and is apt to retard the spiritual growth so necessary in ecclesiastical students. Of course, if a vacation is absolutely necessary for the physical health of any student, the President has my permission to give him a holiday, on the recommendation of the doctor. The hard work of the mission demands the *corpus sanum* as well as the *anima sancta*. But I needn't remind any student availing himself of this permission that the *anima sancta* is infinitely the more important; or impress on him, during his brief stay in the world, to practice assiduously all the spiritual exercises with which our beneficent mother Maynooth nourishes her spiritual children."

"Bunkum," said Lanigan. "I can't afford to go home, anyway, so I don't care. Are you going, Mr O'Brien?"

"I'm not ill," said Ralph.

"I'm off to the doctor at once," said Magan; "my mother always told me that with my red face, if I wasn't careful, I might die of a stroke."

The long winter depressed Ralph. He did a lot of desultory reading and spent more and more time in the chapel praying before the Blessed Sacrament. Yet his prayers seemed to avail nothing against a growing distaste of his surroundings. Spring only increased his lassitude and filled him with vague longings that caused him much anxiety. "Prayer and abstinence," Father Bradley told him at confession, "are the best remedies, and absolute obedience to rule."

In June he suddenly felt brighter and for the first time for many months took pleasure in external things. The chestnut trees were in full bloom. Class was over for the year, and the summer examinations had begun. He agreed with Devine that Maynooth was a beautiful place in summer and laughed over a phrase in a letter he had from Ramsay, posted at Rio, calling Maynooth "a miasmic pest-hole enveloped by intellectual and moral fog". The lilac was late in blossoming, and now its pervasive scent was everywhere. Tara was again covered with creepers. There was something joyous in the jeering faces stretched out of the windows of Mount Rascal, a haunt of Radical Josephites, overlooking the Junior House grounds. Ramsay was no doubt right when he said that he could see God best under a night of stars from the deck of his ship, surrounded by the mystery of the sea. But God was in Maynooth, too, in one of those wonderful six-part motets of Palestrina, sung by the choir, trained with German thoroughness; in the brilliance of an occasional day of perfect heat, when all nature seemed keyed up to the same pitch of gladness. The noise of the students at play, the song of birds, the humming of insects and the beating of one's own heart seemed harmonic parts of one universal pæan of joy. It felt good to be alive on a long walk across country, the hedgerows glowing with June flowers; past the meadows of sweet-scented clover by Mary chapel; cows standing knee-deep in water in the Liffey at Cellbridge, flicking busy flies with lazy tails; down the river bank, with the cottage sacred to the memory of Stella, nestling in trees at its edge; to the Salmon Leap at Lucan; through the De Vesci demesne, still following the beautiful winding Liffey, with weeping willow and ash reflected in its glassy depths, and cool woods stretching far back and up on the other bank; and home by the valley of the Black Pig, ablaze with yellow iris.

Hay's notes on psychology seemed even more foolish, as Ralph read them now in preparation for the examination – they were so far away from the realities of his own feelings and of the life around him; yet he had none of the resentment that filled him when he wrote them down in the gloom and fog of winter. A slight breeze through his wide-open window tempered the heat of the sunlight that danced on the bright surface of his scant furniture. After all, what did Hay's empty formulas and weak solutions of obvious difficulties matter? In a few weeks he would be at home and could climb the mountain across the bay with Teig Moriarty....

Almost all the students took the summer examinations seriously. On success or failure, supplemented by the Dean's report as to conduct, depended the call to Orders. Students in the logic class, if all went well, were "called" to tonsure. Moreover, according to their success at the oral examination, a selected few were called to a written examination for prizes, the primary goal of the "good" as well as the ambitious student.

Ralph was called to all the class pieces, as the written examinations were called, Magan to all except Bannon's and Gogarty's, Devine and Lanigan to Gogarty's and Hay's, and Daly to none.

"Ye're only a lot of fools," Daly said, "to be going in for prizes in the fine, warm weather there is, and pounding hard in your rooms, and I lying on my back in the sun, reading a novel."

"If Ginger has sense he'll come out without writing any, like I'll do, except in the Irish," said Lanigan. "Then he can pretend he could write them if he had a mind to."

"Wait, and you'll see," said Magan. "I'll prove to ye all yet that I've more in me than ye think. There was no getting over Dave," he added regretfully, "but I've got the hang of the other lads all right."

Ralph was troubled when he read Hay's examination paper. Dissatisfied with Hay's lectures, he had read a number of books in English and French on logic and psychology, recommended him by a brilliant young Jesuit professor. Should he answer the questions, which Hay had dealt with elaborately in his notes, according to Hay or independently, in accordance with the views he had himself formed? Though he was not long in doubt as to what he would do, he dallied with the problem. He had tried to excuse Hay's method of teaching on the plea that he was making an effort to put a connected view of his subject in such simple form as the least intelligent in the class would be able to grasp. In the effort to make it simple he made it inconsistent. Anyway, this paper was a test. Ralph wrote a careful paper and felt, when the time was up, that he had done well.

The retreat which preceded the giving of Orders was somewhat similar to that of the opening term, but dwelt more particularly on the responsibilities of the priesthood.

Ralph brooded for several hours on his lack of fervour. As far as he could see, he had made no progress spiritually during the year. No doubt the fault was largely in himself, but he had expected help in Maynooth which he had not got. It was wrong to be critical, yet his mind would dwell on the differences between profession and practice, not only among the students but among the superiors. Father Bradley was a saint, but many of the difficulties that troubled Ralph Father Bradley brushed aside as unworthy of consideration. He said one must always shut the door on the devil and not let him get a word in edgeways. Ralph questioned the wisdom of this. He could not ignore difficulties like Father Bradley; he had to face them. Philosophy, he was told, was the handmaid to theology; but as Hay taught it, it was sheer nonsense. Zigliari, with his eternal appeal to the mind of St Thomas and the mind of St Augustine, in order to refute Kant and Hegal, was grotesque, but Hay was worse; he was foolish. Perhaps philosophy was not important. All his doubts would probably be solved and his mind set at rest when he read theology....

The ceremonies of ordination were long and dull, except for those who were being ordained. There was a general feeling of relief, expressed in much horse-play, when the prize day came, on the morrow of which the summer holidays would begin.

For several days bishops had been arriving, their gorgeous purple robes making bright patches in the grounds.

"It's great to see the pros kow-towing to the bishops," Lanigan said gleefully. "From the way they lorded it over us during the year, you'd never believe how well they're able to lick the ground."

The prize distribution took place in the McMahon Hall, a gaunt new building remarkable for its size and stuccoed ugliness. The students occupied the body of the hall. On a raised platform at the end sat a row of over twenty bishops in their robes. Seated modestly behind were the superiors of the College.

The College President, facing the presiding bishop, read a report:

"The College during the past year has maintained its high reputation for learning and holiness. With some exceptions, so few as to be negligible, discipline has been excellently kept. This was due in large measure to the watchful care exercised by your lordships in selecting the students you send us and to the fatherly guidance you give my colleagues and myself in the management of the College."

This was greeted with salvos of applause from bishops, professors and students.

The presiding bishop arose and waved his hand for silence.

"My dear young friends," he said, "your excellent President has not dwelt enough on his own share in the good work of the past year. By his own learning and sanctity he keeps up the best traditions of the Irish Church" (loud applause). "From the report of your good President, I have no fears for the Irish Church in the future. I shall be seeing our Holy Father the Pope within the next few months, and I shall tell him how pleased the other holy bishops and myself are with our great College, the greatest seat of learning, I have no hesitation in saying, in the whole world. Its piety I needn't dwell on, for it is known to everyone."

All again united in cheers that lasted several minutes. When they had died away, the President read the prize list.

The prizes were handed to the bishops, who presented them, each to his own students, together with a kiss of the episcopal ring and a blessing. Those bishops who had many prizes to give looked pleased. When the Junior House prize list was reached, Magan was read out as first prizeman in Hay's class and third in Delahunt's. Ralph's name did not appear in either list, not even among the *proxime accesserunt*, which included practically everyone who had written the class piece. He, however, got a prize from Bannon and one from Gogarty, whose class was led by Lanigan.

"The bishop said he was proud of me," said Magan, excitedly, as the batch walked around for the last time after dinner.

"I don't doubt but you've notions of sitting up there one day yourself," said Lanigan, derisively.

"Will you all be going home by the nine-thirty in the morning?" asked Devine.

"I shall," Ralph said.

"Not me," said Magan. "I'll have a good sleep. A few of the lads and myself are going to spend the night in Dublin and have a spree."

Chapter 14

FOR THE FIRST few days at home Ralph felt a sense of freedom that he had never before experienced. He walked the meadows with a springy step and drew deep breaths of air scented with the perfume of new-mown hay. Inniscar looked more gay, the sky more blue than his memory led him to expect. Maynooth was a confused memory of the reality and Silvio Pellico's prison house – he was reading *La Mia Prigione*. Ann Carty had told him that he "had grown up a fine figure of a man, and if you didn't use the razor on your lip, you'd be the dead spit of your father". His mother thought him pale, which he was, and more spiritual looking. His father seemed shy with him and told him petulantly to keep out of black clothes – the official garb of the ecclesiastical student – as much as possible while at home.

Teig Moriarty was delighted with his progress in Irish. Father Gogarty was a real Irishman, Teig said, though his little books had many of the faults of a "new beginner. But the spirit is the thing, and you feel it in every word he writes," the old man said enthusiastically.

One morning a week Father Duff said mass at Inniscar. On the other mornings Ralph walked to Father Duff's chapel for eight o'clock mass, and often breakfasted with the priest, who was full of curiosity about Maynooth.

"The professors there now couldn't hold a candle to the men in my time, but in most ways it hasn't changed a bit. I suppose there's always a crowd in 'Rascal'? There would be," he added when Ralph nodded.

"That fool of a grand-nephew of mine is a high prizeman, I hear! Well, well, wonders'll never cease. He didn't get much change out of Dave Bannon though. Dave is one of the old lot and sizes a man up right. The old professors knew their business, but most of the new men are too busy keeping their eyes on bishoprics to do much work. It's queer what attraction a bit of purple has for men!"

"Many of the professors are a good sort," Ralph said.

"Maybe they are, but I don't see much signs of it. There's Charlie Magan, who hasn't the brains of a tom-tit, leading the logic class and on the high road to a bishopric! all because he has the memory of a parrot. And the saints in heaven couldn't make a decent man of him. What he'll be when he's a priest, the Lord only knows!"

Ralph found that his mother's outlook had not broadened during his absence. She had become more self-centred and was almost entirely preoccupied with her own soul. She had practically shut herself up in Inniscar and rarely went outside the grounds except to mass or to Bunnahone to confession. She received no visitors willingly except the bishop, who was her confessor.

Ralph felt a change in her attitude towards himself. Her interest in him seemed to have narrowed itself entirely to his vocation for the priesthood. This interest had always been prominent, but hitherto it had not been so exclusive as he now felt it to be. He was no longer a son, but a sacred object dedicated to God which she regarded as a sort of fetish.

She took no interest in the lives of the tenantry and rebuked Ralph for wasting his time in such worldliness.

"Your mother is turning the house into a convent," his father said gloomily.

Ralph was invited for a week to Dillonsmount by Mrs Dillon. Charles and her daughter Eva were both at home and were anxious to see him about some Irish project, she wrote.

Hilda objected to his going. "The Dillons are so worldly," she said; "they criticise the Church."

"We can't all treat priests as little tin gods as you do," John O'Brien said fretfully. "Ralph must go. We can't shut ourselves off from all our relatives like this."

For the first time Ralph looked forward to leaving home with pleasure.

A week later, when he arrived at Dillonsmount, a rambling Queen Anne house, much added to, with the remains of a thirteenth-century castle at one corner, he found Mrs Dillon and Eva at tea.

Ralph had not met Eva Dillon before. She had been at school in Paris and had spent the previous summer's vacation with some school friends in Brittany. She was a tall girl of about eighteen, slight and graceful, but well knit. Her blue eyes had a tinge of the brown of her hair, and sparkled when she smiled. Thoughtful looking in repose, her expressive face lit up on the slightest provocation. When she laughed, the colour of her eyes deepened; two bright points, as of lurking humour, shone from the depths; the dimples on her rounded cheeks grew more pronounced and her white and somewhat irregular teeth seemed to gleam with mirth.

She laughed as she shook hands.

"I couldn't help it," she said, still smiling. "It was a laugh of relief. I expected to see you in the long soutane and bands of the French seminarists. They came sometimes to Les Cigales for ceremonies."

He felt ill at ease, blushed furiously, and asked was Charles at home.

"You must put up with us for a while," Eva said, handing him bread and butter. "Charles is in Bunnahone."

When Charles Dillon came in he greeted Ralph warmly. A year or two older than John O'Brien, he looked seventy.

"Not a priest yet," he said, his eyes lighting up with a humorous smile, like his daughter's.

"He has still time to change his mind," said Mrs Dillon, dryly.

"Tut, tut, Honoria, you can't expect to run the world. We must have priests. Why shouldn't Ralph be one?"

"We must have nuns, too. Why shouldn't Eva be one?"

"Now, now, my dear, what nonsense! I have proved in my pamphlet that nuns are of comparatively recent origin in the Church. Not but convents have their uses. Think of all the gabbling old maids we should have without convents. That's one great pull we Catholics have over the Protestants," turning to Ralph; "they have no place to which to send their old maids."

"I'm glad I shall have a refuge in my old age," said Eva, demurely.

"I'm sure Eva has a vocation," said Mrs Dillon, mischievously.

"I guarded against that, my dear," Charles Dillon said, stirring his tea, with a smile.

"A cousin of ours," he said to Ralph, "Matilda Dillon, a distant cousin of yours, too, is superior of Les Cigales. Honoria bothered me about sending Eva to some swell convent to finish her – that's usually what they do to a girl; not a bad word at all," patting his knee gleefully. "Honoria and I were in Paris at the time. One day, I slipped away quietly to Les Cigales and saw Matilda – Sister Michel or some such name they call her. 'On your honour, Matilda,' I said, 'you won't give Eva a vocation.'

"'Do you take me for a fool,' she said snappishly. 'We have to keep up the numbers at this school. If all our girls became nuns what would become of the school?'

"A remarkable woman is Matilda," he added musingly, "ninety per cent of the pupils of Les Cigales marry, and most of the others are accounted for by the difficulty of marrying abroad without a dot."

"Come and play tennis, Cousin Ralph," said Eva, rising hastily.

"I was just going to tell him about my pamphlet ..." her father said eagerly.

"He will be here for a week at least, Dad. Have him to yourself in the study some day. Come along, Cousin Ralph. You can wear Charles's tennis shoes if you haven't brought your own."

Ralph rose with alacrity and followed Eva through a French window.

"Young people, young people," said Charles, resignedly.

"And they are just suited to each other," said Mrs Dillon, with a sigh.

"An ecclesiastical student! What nonsense, my dear."

"That's the pity of it. It's all Hilda's doing. John O'Brien has more sense."

"Besides, we don't want her to marry. Why, she's only just home from school."

"You men are all the same," Mrs Dillon said, looking at her husband pityingly. "John O'Brien lets his wife make a priest of his son. You'd let your daughter grow up an old maid."

"No good comes of made marriages," said her husband, testily. "In our own case we married without external interference."

"Is that all you know of my mother?" said Mrs Dillon. Her face softened. "Come and read me some of the pamphlet," she said gently. "She's young yet; I think we needn't worry about her."

Ralph and Eva played several sets, alternately playing and wandering about the old-fashioned garden. She won most of the games. Strands of her brown hair fell over her forehead and shone golden in the sun. Ralph found himself watching her vivid face, delicately flushed, as she stood giving an overhand serve, her short loose sleeve falling back to the shoulder of a finely chiselled arm. She was very beautiful. He was glad he had come to Dillonsmount. It was so jolly here. He liked her open unreserved talk. He missed a ball once, watching the sun at his back send its rays through her hair, spun gold! He had read the description somewhere of some woman, but he had never seen it before.

"Game and set: six, love," she said; "you're wool-gathering. You shouldn't have missed that last ball."

He blushed. Why did he feel towards her as he had never felt for any woman before? He remembered Father Bradley's warning to avoid female society, especially never to be alone with any woman. He said a short prayer for grace to strengthen him against temptation. After all, she was his cousin. Life would be intolerable if he was forced to avoid meeting pleasant people....

"What are you dreaming about? Come, let's walk," she said, looking at him with half-shut eyes.

How musical her voice was, like the sound of a bell across a plain, clear and soft, with a slight touch of a brogue. She drew him out about Maynooth.

He gave a rosy description of it, but was conscious that, flattering as he tried to be, the picture was unsympathetic.

"What a beastly place," she said with a frown.

"You should see it in early summer...."

"It's the whole atmosphere I object to. No wonder it turns out such sneaks."

He looked at her in astonishment.

"I don't think it has affected you ... yet," she said, smiling quizzically. "I was thinking of Father Hardy," she added, frowning thoughtfully. "He's a pig. He was here the other day telling mean tales of Father Sheldon. I'm sure he invented them. They were just the sort of things he would do himself. He maundered to me about convents and vocations and began patting my hand. I feel his slimy touch still," she shuddered, and then laughed gaily.

"Don't look so tragic. I knew how to deal with him. Cousin Matilda had warned me against that type. He won't try to hold my hand again. What they don't know about priests and seminarists at Les Cigales isn't worth knowing," she said, a humorous twinkle in her eyes.

Ralph had felt at first that he should like to kick Father Hardy. But surely Eva was mistaken.

"It was only his priestly interest in you. After all, why shouldn't he wish you to be a nun?"

She looked at him squarely. "You are learning the jargon; but in your case it's youth and not guile. I'm feeling about thirty this minute," she said, drawing herself up, "and you are a boy of ... shall I say ten?"

Ralph squared his shoulders. He felt angry that she should make fun of him, but he managed to control himself and replied lightly, "What a woman of the world you are! Just out of a convent!"

"Don't forget Cousin Matilda," she said, flippantly, and ran excitedly after a green dragonfly.

The days passed quickly, "flew away", Ralph wrote to Devine, who had written him a kindly apologetic letter asking Ralph to stay with him for a few days. Charles Dillon was busy over the organisation of the language movement, enthusiastic and depressed in turn.

"The young people are inclined to take it up," he said gloomily, "but it is impossible to move the older people: and the priests! But I mustn't speak my mind about them, and Gogarty may be able to do something. It will be years before we make any headway. I wish someone would induce the majority of the bishops and monseigneurs and canons and parish priests and a dozen or so of Maynooth professors to go on a trip to the North Pole and swamp them on the way...."

"Charles, don't be revengeful!" Eva interrupted. "It'd be much more kind to wreck them on an uninhabited island on the South Seas. They'd have to think for the first time in their lives, and the clever ones would soon discover that the only thing they really knew was Irish. They'd become so proud of it that they'd insist on teaching all the others. In a few years they'd have forgotten the little English and Latin they knew and would speak Irish only. Then they'd be rescued, and we could use them as organisers in the Irish-speaking districts."

"Gabble, gabble, and the language dying all the time," said Charles, bitterly.

"Don't put on that mourning voice. It's not dead yet. I'm rich in suggestions, and no one listens to me," Eva said, walking up and down the room, her forehead wrinkled.

"It's not a joke," said Charles, frowning.

"You are all the same," Eva said, the dimple on her chin, which Ralph noticed for the first time, contradicting the gravity of her eyes. "Cousin John with his old co-operation and you with your Irish, as grave and as dull as ditchwater. I've a new frock upstairs for the de Laceys' garden party. I shall canvass the bishop and Father Molloy in it and bring them here in triumph at my chariot wheels – that is, if the old victoria is fit to make a journey. One of the wheels was loose the last time we had it out. I'd try Father Duff, but I fear he's beyond feminine charm."

"Chatterbox!" Charles said, looking at her affectionately. "What do you say, Ralph?" Ralph thought her more charming then ever, but very foolish. He blushed and stammered, "It is a serious subject, Eva, and ..."

"Don't preach at me, your reverence," she said, making him an elaborate mock courtesy.

"That's not fair ..." he began angrily.

She blushed a deep pink, and flounced out of the room. She hesitated at the door, turned half round, and said, "If you had a sense of humour, you wouldn't be in Maynooth," and banged the door after her.

Charles Dillon laughed. "Women are kittle cattle. You're well out of them, Ralph." Ralph felt angry with himself and angry with Eva. He heard very little of an account Charles gave him of an attempt to start an Irish class in Bunnahone, which Father Molloy managed to break up. Eva had never looked so beautiful as when she attacked him. He had not meant to offend her. She must have mistaken something he said....

He was glad when Charles suggested going to bed. He lay awake for some hours, thinking of what he would say to Eva to make friends again. He was leaving the next morning, and she must forgive him.

At breakfast Mrs Dillon told him that Eva sent him many friendly messages. She had driven over early to the de Laceys', to see her friend Mildred, who was going abroad.

Ralph felt very unhappy as Larry Gallagher drove him home. He dwelt on every word that had been said the night before. What had he done? He ...

"'Tis Miss Eva's the fine girl, now," said Larry.

Ralph started, but did not reply.

Larry flicked a fly lightly off the horse's right ear.

"It's the fine wife she'd make for the right man, and no mistake."

"I dare say," said Ralph, shortly.

"Sure it's the pity of the world it's not yourself is making her the young mistress of Inniscar," Larry said imperturably.

Ralph stared at him for a few seconds, without taking in what he meant. "Drive straight and don't be looking around," he said sharply. He felt the blood rushing to his face and kept his back well to Larry.

"No offence meant. Sure, I only meant if you had the luck of not to be going to be a priest now."

Ralph stared at the road in silence. Larry's words made his heart beat rapidly. He clung to the rail at his side. The image of Eva, flushed and angry, rose before him, and he seemed to enjoy her anger. A curious faintness overcame him, and he felt inexpressibly happy. She seemed so real, her lips seemed to lure him - he clutched the railing until his fingers ached.

A cold sweat broke out on his forehead. "God, God, save me from temptation!" he said, between his clenched teeth. He said an act of contrition and felt relief. It was a temptation of the devil to destroy his vocation! He did not care for her in that way. No, he had not fallen. It was, however, a warning. Father Bradley was right. Not even the saints are safe against love. Not that there was any fear of his falling in love. His vocation was too strong for that. Still, he was too much in her company and he thought of her too much. No wonder the devil made use of her image as a means of tempting him. He must be more careful....

He was ill at ease for a few days. He went to confession to Father Sheldon, who was very gentle and kind.

"You are sure you know what it means to be a priest?"

"Quite. It was only a momentary madness," Ralph replied decisively.

"Then keep away as much as possible from occasions of these distracting thoughts."

Ralph felt that his father eyed him curiously during these days and began to think that he suspected his lapse.

"Anything wrong, Ralph?" John said one day.

"Nothing whatever. What made you think so?" Ralph said apprehensively.

"You look worried. That's all."

Hilda spoke much of the perfections of the priesthood. Every word seemed like a cut of a sharp knife. God was using everyone, he felt, as instruments to punish him for his infidelity.

He prayed for hours in the little chapel. Reading bored him. He took no interest in the creamery or in his father's plan for extending the sphere of work of the co-operative society. He felt relieved when Devine wrote again, urging him to come to Baltubber, where he would get a warm welcome. It was only a plain farmer's house, but his mother would do her best to make him comfortable.

Hilda had some doubts as to whether he ought to go, which his father brushed aside impatiently.

"You mustn't keep him tied to your apron string, Hilda. As to the Devines being only small farmers, that's all right! The more he mixes with the people the better. As for his religious exercises, you may set your mind at rest. I know old Jack Devine – he's more religious even than you are," he added dryly.

Ralph found Devine waiting for him outside the Lisslea station with a freshly painted side-car. The horse, a stout cob covered with a heterogeneous collection of harness, pawed the ground impatiently.

"You are heartily welcome," said Devine, shyly. "I'd have gone on the platform but I couldn't leave the horse. He's not used to a side-car and might run away. We put the winkers of the cart harness on him so that he mightn't know he was under a side-car."

The car swayed with the motion of a small boat in a rough sea. The horse jogged soberly along a pretty road by the shore of Lough Brine. Rain had fallen in the morning, giving a delicious odour to the grass and hedgerows, now bathed in brilliant sunlight. The lake reflected the deep blue of the sky, with here and there a group of filmy cirrus clouds.

Devine stopped at a wooden gate, old and dilapidated notwithstanding its emerald-green paint, and led the horse through a short rutty boreen leading towards a two-storied slated house, rough cast and whitewashed, the door and window sashes painted the same colour as the gate. Freshly cut rushes were strewn over a gravelled yard in front.

A buxom woman of about forty-five in a white apron and, hot as the day was, a small coloured shawl pinned over her shoulders, stood at the open door. When the car stopped she came forward and shook Ralph's hand, her grey eyes glowing with kindly welcome.

"Sure it's glad we are to have you under our roof, Mr O'Brien, a hundred thousand welcomes," she said, taking some small things he had beside him on the seat. "Take the car round, Joe, and put up the horse, and I'll bring Mr O'Brien into the room. Your father and the children are down in the ten-acre meadow giving the hay a turn after the showers, or you wouldn't have to put up the horse."

She led the way into a small sitting-room, newly boarded and papered and hung with cheap coloured religious prints. A rag mat of many colours in front of the fireplace, decorated with green tissue paper, was the only carpet. A painted deal table in the centre of the room, an old hair cloth armchair covered with a spotless crochet antimacassar, a few new windsor chairs and some books on the window-sill were the only furniture.

"Take a seat in the armchair and rest yourself after your journey," Mrs Devine said, laying aside her burthen on one of the chairs and dusting the armchair with the corner of her apron. "I hope you'll be comfortable."

"I am sure I shall."

"We did the place up for Joe," Mrs Devine said, looking around complacently. "After all the grandeur he's used to in Maynooth, with its great halls and rooms that you could fit the half of a parish in, the husband and myself agreed that the least we could do would be to smarten the place up a bit as far as a few pots of paint and a lick of lime and some wallpaper and a few boards go.

"It's a great place entirely, Maynooth is," she added, sitting on the edge of a chair. "Joe do be telling us about it an odd time, around the fire of an evening. 'Tis proud a woman ought to be to have a son in it, thanks be to God for His goodness. Sure I hope to see it one day before I die, maybe when Joe is ordained, if I can persuade Jack Devine to make the journey. 'Leave it at that, woman,' he says to me now when I mention the matter, but sure I know by a hundred tokens he's prouder than I am that we have a son a student; and I'd be willing to stake a good deal that if he had to go to America itself, and had to scrape the money together by half starving himself for a year, he'd be in the chapel the day Joe is priested."

She was suspiciously near to tears and got up hastily as her son entered.

"It's sorry I am, Joe, to have to ask you to soil your hands to do work like that. I'll hurry off now, Mr O'Brien, to get ready a bit to eat for ye and leave ye to yourselves. The other'll be in to their dinner at one o'clock."

The meal for Ralph and Joe was served in the sitting-room, the family dining in the kitchen. Ralph enjoyed the boiled chicken, ham embedded in white cabbage and flowery potatoes bursting their jackets.

"Take a little butter – you'll find it's good, I made it with my own hands – with the new potatoes, Mr O'Brien. Have ye everything ye want now, Joe? If so, I'll leave ye and have a bit for myself. After dinner I'll get ye a nice cup of tea to wash down, not but we have other drink in the house, but Joe says you don't take any, Mr O'Brien. It's a dry kind of welcome when there isn't a drop of drink going. Give Mr O'Brien another bit of the breast, Joe."

While they were taking tea Devine's father, brother and sister came into "the room" and were introduced to Ralph – Jack Devine, a straight, clean-shaven old man of about seventy, with a face like a russet apple, Thade, of a heavier build than Joe and more awkward in manner, and Bridget, a shy girl of seventeen, brown haired and florid faced like her mother.

"Don't get up, Mr O'Brien," said the old man, putting his hand on Ralph's shoulder and pushing him back gently in his seat. "Go on with your tea. Sure we wouldn't disturb you like this, but I couldn't leave the house and go back to the hay without bidding you welcome."

Thade and Bridget shook Ralph's hand shyly, without speaking.

"We must be running away and try and get the hay into breast cocks before night. I hope you won't be thinking it unmannerly of us, Mr O'Brien," the old man said courteously. "Maybe you'd both give us a look in at the field?" he added, doubtfully, to Joe.

"Certainly, and give a hand with the hay, too," said Ralph, jumping up.

"Oh, that's too bad entirely," Devine said. "I oughtn't have mentioned it. The idea of ye working and ye going to be priests, too. But sure if you think it no harm, Mr O'Brien, I'm sure it's all right. We're loth to let Joe do any work, not that he's not willing enough, thank God, but for fear it wouldn't be respectful like."

Ralph forgot all his troubles of conscience in the pleasant, but by no means easy, work of hay-making.

"Bedad, but you have the makings of a great worker in you," old Devine said admiringly. "Joe always took more kindly to the books. Have a drink of buttermilk, now. It'll knock some of the drought out of you."

Ralph paid frequent visits to the jug of buttermilk, standing immersed in a flat pan of water covered by cool green fern fronds, by the shaded side of a haycock.

"Bridget is dead set on being housekeeper for Joe when he's a priest," said the old man to Ralph, looking towards her as she worked at a distance, "if she's not picked up in the meantime. It's many a man'll be after her, I'm thinking. But sorra one, I believe, she'll look at. She thinks the sun rises and sets for Joe and that nothing's good enough for him. Sure she goes in, off and on, to the convent at Lisslea to learn the cooking so that she'll be able to give him grand meals entirely.

"There's Thade, now, the sly fellow," he said, another time, winking elaborately; "to look at him you wouldn't think he had a word in him, but if he isn't courting Ann Deasy in that house you see the smoke rising out of beyond. He thinks none of us know anything about it but Bridget and she doesn't let on a word. But troth, it's hard to escape Bedelia's eyes, his mother you know, and we often talk of it of a night. She's a decent slip of a girl, but they're both young and they'll have to wait a bit, till Joe and Bridget are out of the way. Bedelia is too young yet to be resigning things into a daughter-in-law's hands. Not but she likes the girl. The best woman in the world, Bedelia is, but a bit masterful like with females."

He spoke at length of Joe. "I'm a bit old, seventy last Martimas, and though I haven't a pain or an ache, it's not long more I can be for this world, but I pray every day to God on my bended knees that he won't take me out of this till I see the bishop's holy hand laid on Joe. I married late in life, and it's well for me I waited, for the like of Bedelia wasn't to be had; never to this day did she throw my age in my face. She was such a great manager that we were able to put a little money by, and we agreed if we had a son we'd make a priest of him. The first boy, Thade, we were loath to part with and we said we'd keep him for ourselves, but the next, we took a solemn oath on it, we'd give to God. And Joe seemed cut out for the life from the start. It would do your eyes good to see him serving mass at the altar on a Sunday, and sorra curse he ever let out of him in his life, and he took to prayers like a fish to the water. Thanks be to God for all His blessings, sure Joe's a comfort to us all," he added, lifting his battered straw hat reverently.

As the sun went down in ruddy glory, "Not unlike rain tomorrow," Devine said, the last cock was finished. After a simple supper of oat-meal stirabout and milk, followed by tea and soda cake, the whole family gathered round the fire in the kitchen. A few neighbours dropped in and were formally introduced to Ralph. Pipes were lit by the men. Bridget sat by the lamp knitting, while Mrs Devine polished some old brass candlesticks at the fireside.

"Them politicians is the great playboys," one of the visitors said. "It's a sight of promises they make and mighty little is done for the poor farmers."

"They're not too bad, now. Sure they got us the three F's," old Devine said.

"But where's the Purchase Act they promised? I'm thinking it's until Tibb's Eve we'll be looking for it."

"Give 'em time. Give 'em time," said Devine.

"It's little you trouble about politics up in Maynooth, now," said the same visitor to Joe. "Sorra newspaper allowed inside the walls, I'm told."

"Not to the students," said Joe.

"And the power the priests know about politics when they come out! sure one would think they read the *Weekly Freeman* as regular as the clock. But I suppose once you know the seven languages you know everything, and it's little there's left to learn out of a paper except an odd murder or the like."

"It's great power entirely the priests get out of all their learning," said another visitor. "I'm told for certain, though it's only an odd one of them lets on about it, that they could change a man into a goat by reading over him, while you'd be winking the eye."

"I wouldn't be too certain of that," said another, sceptically. "I put it to you now, Joe, could they do the like?"

Joe blushed. "I haven't read theology yet. Priests have great powers, of course, but I don't think they exercise them all nowadays."

"It's best not to anger them, anyway," said the first visitor, "or you never'd know what might happen."

When the old grandfather clock in a corner of the kitchen struck ten, Mrs Devine stood up and proceeded to wind the heavy weights.

"It's that lightsome you'd never think it was ten o'clock," she said yawning.

"Sure it's time we were bidding ye goodnight, may God keep ye all," said one of the visitors as they rose to go.

"God see ye safe home," said old Devine. "Trim the lamp well, Bridget, to light them out the boreen."

The family and Ralph knelt by their seats in the kitchen and the old man said the rosary, the others giving the responses. Tired out, all went to bed the moment the prayers were finished, Ralph in a small room off the sitting-room. "It used to be our own room, but sure now that he's the makings of a priest, we fixed it up for Joe, and half good enough it's not for him," Mrs Devine said, as she bade Ralph goodnight.

Next day Ralph insisted on helping to make tramp cocks, working for the most part with old Devine.

"It's a great calling entirely you're going in for," he said, patting the side of a cock with a rake: "sure there's nothing like a priest in the whole world. It's often a wonder to me that God'd lift up a son of mine so high, and I doing nothing to deserve it. And all the good you and Joe can do, when the holy oils are laid on you, for the sick in mind and body and everyone that's in trouble and misery. No wonder ye are good and holy, living in the Seminary and in the blessed College of Maynooth, with nothing but prayers about you from morning till night. Not that ye could ever be good enough for the work ye'll have to do, taking the place of the Lord God Himself every morning in the mass and washing out the sins of sinners like myself with a couple of words. At the thought of what my son is going to be I feel like taking off my hat to him every time I meet him and asking his blessing."

During his visit the thought of his calling was urged on Ralph every hour. God was spoken of as a familiar of the household, whose help was always at hand in the most trivial action. Life was a pilgrimage of joy and sorrow, both to be accepted because they came from the hand of God, and death but a gateway to a nobler and more glorious life. The priest was reverenced as God's representative, and homage was paid even to Joe Devine and Ralph, who stood in the shadow of the priesthood. As he knelt at evening prayers, he felt that he knelt in the presence of God, with more certainty than he ever felt at Maynooth, or at home, or at Clarendon Street in his childhood. What did Father Hay's superficial philosophy matter, or the contradictions of profession and practice at the Seminary and at Maynooth, or his mother's spiritual timidity? Nothing mattered but old Devine's calm faith in God and his broad charity and his high ideal of the priest as the minister of God. He fell far short of that ideal. He shuddered as he thought of his backsliding at Dillonsmount and prayed fervently that God would purify his heart and give him the necessary strength to overcome all temptations that stood in the way of his becoming a good priest.

Chapter 15

YEAR FOLLOWED YEAR at Maynooth. The gloom of winter yielded to the fresh joy of spring, and Ralph experienced frequent alternations of hope and feelings that were almost akin to despair. Father Hay's lifeless abstractions and the crude legalism of moral theology left his heart cold and repelled his mind. He spent many hours during retreats trying to reconcile the futilities of the classes and the claims of the Church to learning. He read widely round every subject and was relieved to discover Catholic writers who felt as dissatisfied as he did with the modern teaching of the Church. He read again and again Blondel's Sorbonne thesis, maintaining the possibility of religious certainty independently of the teaching of the schools. The Church had taken a wrong turning and used the out-of-date implements of the thirteenth century in the nineteenth. As the Church could not err fundamentally, all was sure to come right in time. The Pope was believed to be in sympathy with change. Meanwhile, everywhere, except at Maynooth, Catholic teachers were advocating a new philosophy and a fresh presentation of dogma. As Ralph read the older mystics he felt that the new view had been there all the time, obscured by the formalism of the schools.

While staying with Father Sheldon one vacation he told him his difficulties. Ecclesiastical history as taught in Maynooth was unconvincing. The textbook was illiterate. Was the writer merely stupid and incompetent, or was he dishonest? No thinking mind could accept the reasoning of the philosophy and theology schools with their puerile major premises assuming things as proved that bristled with difficulties. Scripture teaching was a series of evasions. He had no difficulty in believing in God, but it was only by constant prayer and the study of other teachers that he warded off the scepticism to which Maynooth teaching tempted him.

The priest shook his head sadly. "For years I have been hoping for better things, which are slow in coming. But," his face brightened, "they are coming. France and Italy and Germany are showing the way. Some day Ireland will move too. Who knows but you may have a part in a great work? Don't mind the quibbles of the schools. Try to get to the kernel inside the husk. Live your life as closely as you can on the pattern of Christ's. You'll never convert a soul from evil nor help it to heaven by a syllogism."

In the arid months that followed, the thought of the Devine family, ignorant of all theological subtleties, full of simple faith and good works, consoled Ralph in hours of depression. In walks with Devine he often spoke of his family.

"Of course they are very ignorant of theology," Devine said apologetically. "I don't believe my father even remembers his catechism. I make notes of the lectures in theology here in a form that I can use afterwards as sermons. They will be very useful to people like my father.

"That lecture on the Trinity, for instance?"

"Yes, of course," said Devine, simply.

To Ralph the lecture with its array of wordy distinctions had been unintelligible gibberish.

"Don't you think your father realises God better than we do?"

"You are a queer fellow, O'Brien! Why, if you questioned him on the Trinity he'd be sure to fall into several heresies."

As a refuge from scholasticism Ralph read many books of mystic theology: St Catherine of Sienna, St Teresa, Eckart, St John of the Cross. He had long conferences with Father Bradley, who had never heard of Blondel or Loisy or any modern apologetic; who, if he ever knew much of scholastic subtlety, had long since forgotten it. Christ was the Way and the Life, and it was by living His life, he said, not by discoursing learnedly of the Trinity, we entered the Kingdom of God.

The same idea Ralph gathered from the lectures of the only professor in the College from whom he ever got any spiritual help, Dr Fraser, who lectured a somewhat obscure class which Ralph attended during his two last years at Maynooth. By far the most original thinker in the College, in fact the only thinker there, as far as Ralph could judge, Fraser illuminated his lectures by *obiter dicta* that spoke directly to Ralph's soul. In Fraser's hints of a philosophy of action,

Ralph felt, was the only possible escape from the dry bones of scholasticism.

After a lecture in dogmatic theology by Father Malone, who demolished all the thinkers of four centuries with an axiom culled from Aquinas, delivered in a loud self-satisfied voice and accompanied by much tub-thumping, Ralph often sat in his room, limp and confused, hopeless of his own future and of the future of the Church. Several times he was on the point of leaving the College, but at the supreme moment of crisis came some inward voice urging him to stay. It brought him a fleeting peace, followed by doubt that it was some illusion, or an echo of his mystic reading. Father Bradley had no doubt on the point: it was the voice of God. Ralph tried to explain how Father Malone worried him. The old priest did not understand and showed signs of boredom, interrupted Ralph, and spoke of the wonders of the love of God.

Ralph had heard much talk of a professor of theology, the object of hero-worship in the College, a Father Dunlea, and looked forward eagerly to attending his lectures. He was said to be the ablest professor Maynooth had ever produced. Tall, brown haired, thoughtful looking, with a rather weak mouth, which he kept tightly shut except when talking, he carried himself with a commanding air. Ralph was disappointed to find that with much ability his mind was more narrow than Malone's. He was merely lucid and superficial. Ralph once ventured an opinion contradictory of Dunlea's notes.

The Professor flushed angrily, but said suavely, "What is good enough for St Thomas and me ought to satisfy you, Mr O'Brien. I'd advise you to read my notes carefully. They contain everything necessary to be known on the subject."

That evening during study Ralph read these meagre notes, the fine flower of Maynooth teaching, a superficial application of a knowledge theory to religion that carried no conviction. If this book was the best Maynooth could do, why had he wasted the best years of his life there? It reduced God to a series of abstractions, unreal and meaningless. He pitched the book on his bed and walked up and down the room. He stopped to look at his bookshelves and read over the titles of the books on which he had spent most of his pocketmoney for the last five years. He recalled with a smile an expression of Magan's, "Why do you waste your time reading that trash?"

Dunlea would probably say the same. Malone would go further and say "heretical trash". Was the whole thinking world gone mad? the scholastic seminarists alone right? He picked out a book of Loisy's and read a few of the dispassionate vivid sentences, and laughed aloud at the memory of Malone's spluttering incompetency in dealing with the same point.

His thoughts came back to Magan, who was now leader of their class. After the partial success of his first year Magan gave up his radical companions and worked hard at his class work. He wrote down feverishly every word that fell from a professor's lips and committed his notes afterwards to memory. With the exception of Bannon's class and Fraser's, after the first year he had been a prizeman in every class he attended. He never read a book but relied entirely on his notes, many of which were meaningless to him. "The meaning doesn't matter; give them pros back the thing in their own words, that's what they like," he once said. Did Magan typify Maynooth learning? What was the object of it all? Magan's own answer seemed to fit the facts. "There was the honour and glory of being leader of a class, and after a few years' teaching in the Seminary, or maybe sooner, a professorship in Maynooth, and who knows what mightn't follow that?"

Yet the students and professors were not all Magans. Many were intellectually able and of fine character. Devine had the simple faith of his father beneath all his devotion to theological definitions which he never understood. Lanigan said that he knew what was right even if he didn't always do it. Malone, with all his ineptitude, was the kindest-hearted man in the College. Father Bradley walked about, under the limes, fingering his beads, a happy smile on his tranquil face, seeing good in everyone and everything.

The memory of Father Bradley set Ralph in another train of thought. There was something in common between Father Bradley, uneducated as he was in an intellectual sense, and Father Fraser with all his learning – something that recalled Jack Devine, who had never heard of a theological definition, something that linked all three to the mystics. For them as for Father Sheldon religion was a living experience. They spoke not in senseless jargon, but out of the depths of their own feelings.

He knelt beside his chair and prayed for strength of will to tread the rough path so many of the saints had trodden. He would labour to make known the Life, the Way and the Kingdom. But first he should live it then; perhaps, he could help others, as Father Bradley helped many.

As the spring days lengthened into summer during Ralph's last year at Maynooth, there was daily a growing excitement in the Bunnahone batch. Daly, Magan, Devine, Lanigan and Ralph were to be ordained in June. Devine was already in deacon's orders and Daly a sub-deacon. Ralph and Magan, though called to Orders regularly, had not taken them: Ralph because his mind always got worried when the time of ordination came on, with the result that he was in his sixth year without having taken tonsure; Magan said that preparing for Orders, and the saying of the office involved by sub-deaconship, would interfere too much with his studies.

"Another couple of months and we'll be out of this, thank the Lord," said Daly, one afternoon, as the batch walked by the cemetery.

"I have been very happy here," said Devine.

"You made your name for piety early," said Daly, with a sigh, "and you've no fear of the Dean. Not that I've much to fear, seeing that I've put up the sub-deaconship. They can't send me out into the world with that on me and not make a priest of me."

"Can't they though?" Lanigan said mockingly. "I heard of a jarvey, in the south, too, who used to say to the people he was driving and he going slow up a long hill, 'by your leave', and he'd pull out his breviary and read a bit of the office. He was a sub. I doubt that he made a good thing out of it from American tourists as a curiosity like. If anything happens you, sure you can take up something of the kind."

"Oh, I think I'm safe enough in the last lap. It's just habit that makes me fear a dean round every corner," said Daly, thoughtfully.

"Where do you think you'll be sent to, Devine? I hear there are going to be great changes in the diocese," said Magan, eagerly.

"I don't know," said Devine. "I shall be glad to go wherever I'm sent."

"How modest we are!" said Magan, mockingly, "and you angling all your career for a Junior House monitorship."

"You're the fellow that ought to talk, surely!" said Lanigan, with a sneer. "You wouldn't know an honest man when you see him. Why didn't you tell him, Devine, what he wanted to hear, that everyone in the diocese is saying that the great Magan ought to go to the Seminary?"

"I don't know who has a better right," Magan said complacently.

"You wouldn't! I suppose you're right," Lanigan said musingly. "No one is up to the tricks of the place, anyway, half as well."

"I dare say we shan't be consulted as to where we shall be sent," said Ralph.

"Who asked you to interfere?" Magan said angrily, his face flushed a poppy-red and his small eyes gleaming. "Everyone of you have been dead jealous of me since ever we came to Maynooth; and you especially, O'Brien! I've seen it often and often in your eye, the way you look at me – you, that never showed your nose on a prize list since your second philosophy!"

He walked away from his companions muttering, "I'll let you all know who I am yet."

"We know you better than you know yourself, Ginger," Lanigan shouted after him.

Devine looked at Lanigan sadly.

"You oughtn't to do it, you know, Mr Lanigan," he said gently.

"I'm sorry if I hurt you, Joe," Lanigan said, "but Ginger rouses every bad feeling I have in me."

"It's a good job, too, to bring him down a peg," said Daly, gleefully.

"He's a very great theologian," said Devine, simply, "and we ought to show him great respect."

A servant approached and said that a visitor was waiting in the parlour for Mr O'Brien.

Ralph was surprised to find that it was Boyle, looking shabbier than when he last saw him at Father Sheldon's, two years before, the only time he had seen him since his visit to Inniscar.

"I'm not sure that I'm not afraid of you in that ecclesiastical get-up," said Boyle, cheerfully, looking Ralph all over, "especially as I'm in bad odour with the clergy at present."

While they walked round the grounds Boyle said that he had left Bunnahone a week ago for good. He had been offered the editorship of a new weekly in Dublin and had jumped at it. The salary was small but he should have independence.

"That is, such independence as anyone can have in this benighted country with the guns of all you ecclesiastics turned against him," he said with a smile.

The paper was to be literary and would deal with religious, social and intellectual problems generally. "We'll cause a flutter in the clerical dovecote, anyway," he said aggressively.

"How?"

"We shall have a tilt at Maynooth education."

"It needs a shaking up," said Ralph, dryly.

"You've found that out! If there are others here who see it, things may be more hopeful than I thought."

Ralph shook his head doubtfully.

"There's Father Fraser," he said.

"I've heard of him. I hope to get him to write. Any others?"

"Gogarty, but I am afraid he's interested only in Irish. There may be others – I know little of the professors beyond what I learn in class; nor of the students outside my own diocese."

"And these? But I needn't ask. I know them all. It will be an uphill fight, I'm afraid."

They walked in silence a few minutes, then Boyle laughed mirthlessly: "The old castle at the gate is a symbol of the Maynooth mind. Both are thirteenth century."

"Father Sheldon sees signs of a change and is full of hope."

"I know. We have had many talks. He has saved me for the Church. Not that the official Church would thank him for it. I wish I could share his hope. But he has all the optimism of his own generous soul," Boyle said doubtfully.

"I am becoming a priest on the strength of his optimism and my own," Ralph said. "What are you afraid of?"

"I haven't been eight years teaching in a clerical Seminary for nothing. Sheldon thinks the leaven will work in the clerical camp. I hope from my heart he's right. The Sheldons always think there are many like themselves. They are only a handful, and never realise the numbers and strength of the Devoys, the Doyles and the Molloys. Father Sheldon spends his days doing good. The others are pastmasters of intrigue. In a struggle the Sheldons would go under at the first blow."

"But if the others can be brought to understand the danger to religion in the present system ..."

"These fellows don't care. They don't want to understand. The present system suits them best. They may understand beyond the grave – I don't know what happens there – but never in this life. My only hope is to get the younger men, and I am not even sure of them. However, there is a chance. In France and Italy things are different. There the clergy seem to think. The seminaries are full of new ideas, which have even found their way to the episcopal bench. But poor old Ireland has only Fraser and Sheldon, and a few students and curates perhaps. However," he added, brightening, "every day there are more educated Catholic laymen who are dissatisfied with the fetters of a medieval ecclesiasticism."

"The Church has adapted itself before to the needs of its growth," Ralph said hopefully.

"Not since Trent. It stopped growing then and has lived since by coercion and repression. It has to be proved whether it has still enough energy to change – or desire. It is all to the good that you think so. Some day, when you are far from this hole, you may be able to help."

He looked round the grounds and sniffed the fragrance of the limes now in full bloom.

"It is a beautiful place," he said, watching the glow of the afternoon sun on the green turf between the long shadows of the trees. "Lord, what a force this College could be!"

They walked along the cloisters and he stood before one of the portraits of the bishops. "Smugness and self-satisfaction in every line of it. That is the Irish Church all out ... if not the whole Church," he added drearily. "Nothing short of a spiritual earthquake would make them even question their belief in themselves. They don't know that anything is wrong and they are unteachable. They prefer to be what they are – autocrats, domineering over a sycophant clergy, holding an ignorant laity in check through fear of eternal damnation. The medieval idea of absolute government is written on that man's face. He won't yield an inch of his power willingly."

Ralph told him of Father Bradley.

"There are the Bradleys, of course. They keep the simple faith of their childhood. They live Christ and don't argue about Him. We want men, however, with Bradley's faith, but with intellectual power as well: intellects that won't smother faith in worn-out formulas, that will make religion intelligible in the light of progress. We ought, however, to be thankful for our Bradleys," he added, shrugging his shoulders: "they have kept the faith alive. They are the salt of the most ideal Church. But we must express our religion in a form that will meet all the needs of the day. The Bradleys can't do it. These men won't do it" – waving his hand towards the portraits of the bishops. "Can't do it. For even if they had the will their brains are atrophied. But they haven't the will. They take no interest in religion, nor in any ideal – power, authority, their own petty careers, the interest of the organisation with which their careers are bound up, are all that appeal to their minds and hearts – if their narrow little organs can be called by such dignified names. They don't care a pin for ideas, for theology or philosophy, except as instruments for maintaining power. They are wise in their miserable worldly wisdom for this generation at least. As long as the people are drugged, the best prop to a medieval authority is a medieval theology from which all religion and reality have been crushed out."

"Then how is the transformation to come about?"

"God only knows. My own opinion is that nothing short of a break-up of the whole system will do. Father Sheldon and others think that there is hope of a reconstruction. The path to it has not yet been blocked. I'm willing to work for it, but, always, I feel at the back of my mind that our work will lead nowhere."

"I share Father Sheldon's hopes," Ralph said eagerly. "Ireland is sure to wake up ..."

"I hope so," Boyle interrupted. "But with the waking up will come action on the part of the authorities. They are in possession ... but I shan't flood you at the start with my pessimism. Besides, my vision is perhaps distorted. Eight years' schoolmastering under the heel of priests and bishops is enough to crush hope out of a man. When Sheldon rescued me from the pit I had come to look on the Church as identical with its rulers, hard, pitiless, without religion or humanity. He showed me another vision, but the old one still obtrudes itself in argument. There is religion in Ireland still; I saw it in the lives of his parishioners, in himself, and it revived my memories of my own mother and of the many who have kept the spirit of God in the world from the beginning."

As he said goodbye his eyes lighted up. "It did me good to let off steam," he said, "in this home of obscurantism. I was half afraid to come to see you. But you have grown. I remember your unspoken disapproval of me at Inniscar. What has happened in your case may be happening with many others. Who knows but we shall yet make the old ivy-grown castle, battered, roofless and windowless, fit to live in."

Ralph made efforts in the days that followed Boyle's visit to win people to his project. He tried Gogarty, who was the only professor he knew well, but Gogarty was interested only in the possibility of utilising Boyle's paper for the propaganda of the language movement. He said he understood very little about theological questions. If he had a doubt on any point he always went to Dunlea, "a wonderful man," he said, "though he looks down on the Irish language." His diocesans were unresponsive. Magan said it was "infernal cheek of laymen to write about religion at all. What do they know about it?" Devine said he was glad a religious newspaper was to be started. Ralph lent him some books giving a popular account of the new religious movement. He returned them in a few hours, a scared look on his face.

"They are bad books," he said excitedly. "You ought to burn them. I'm sure you can't have read them yourself. I'll have to go to confession and tell that I read a few pages. The beginning was so holy, like the spiritual reading book I'm using now in the oratory, that it led me on. The way dogma was spoken of, and the whole system of theology, was shocking. You won't read it, Ralph? Do promise me; there's a good fellow."

As the day of his ordination drew near, Ralph was troubled by his state of mind. With his views, ought he to take Orders? He had no doubt that the Catholic Church was the Church of Christ. He couldn't imagine himself anything but a Catholic. Most of the Maynooth professors would say that his views were wrong. Still, these views were held by professors who were priests and had not been condemned. He had a strong feeling that his reasoning was somehow dishonest, and determined to go to the President and explain things to him. First he would consult his confessor, Father Bradley.

"These doubts are only all temptations of the devil," the old priest said decisively, taking a pinch of snuff. "He's extra busy at a time like this. Would you tell me now what did the Curé d'Ars know about theology? My head is moidered in the professors' parlour hearing them arguing theology. That same theology, it seems to me, would prove that black was white, or white was black. I'd rather you'd love God and do his bidding than that you'd be able to explain to me all about God in the most beautiful language that was ever written. Take your Orders, my boy, and God bless you. Keep from sin and say your prayers and help people all you can to keep the love of God in their hearts - preaching theology won't help you much - and you'll be a good priest."

Father Bradley's opinion did not settle Ralph's difficulties, but they almost disappeared under the influence of a Jesuit of modernist views who gave the ordination retreat. It was a series of simple lectures on the life of Christ - the type of the Christian life, lay and clerical. The ideal priest, forgetful of self, would give himself wholly to service. Work for others was work for the God in them. Men were to be gained to God by example and love rather than by precept. The truth of God was simple and intelligible to the heart. The same faith saved the simple and the learned.

Ralph prepared for a general confession of his whole life. For the first time he felt that he had been swayed by every mind with which he had come in touch: by Ann Carty, his mother, Father David, Father Best, Father Sheldon. His religion had been something external to him; yet it ought to be something more than formal exercises, fears, rewards and punishment. Real religion came from within, not from without. His mind had knocked at many doors in vain. The solution of all his difficulties was to be found at the Seminary; when that failed, at Maynooth, which was destined to be the supreme failure. Yet all the time God was within his own heart. Father Bradley was right; theology did not matter; all that mattered was the will to be united with God, and the doing of His will. To help to break down the barriers that kept men from God: this was his vocation in life.

As he received the various Orders, day after day for nearly a week, at the hands of a bishop in the College chapel - tonsure, porter, lector, exorcist, acolyte, sub-deaconship and deaconship - he thought of them as steps of service – keys placed in his hands to open doors to life.

He was awakened on the morning of his ordination to priesthood by the tramp of feet in the corridor. He had not heard the bell, and was only just in time to join the procession of deacons, in albs, stoles and shortened chasubles, as it entered the church. At the door he caught a glimpse of his mother standing in the background, smiling at him through tears.

He went through the ceremony mechanically, obeying the harsh, sharp voice of the master of ceremonies. He felt none of the ardour of the retreat and noticed all sorts of small details: Magan's face was pale and his hands trembled; small drops of sweat stood out on the bishop's upper lip; the chalice and paten were from the Junior House – he remembered seeing that dent in the boss of the chalice when he served mass there years ago.

"Thou art a priest for ever, according to the order of Melchizedek." The words repeated themselves in his ears like a refrain. The mass, which he had always loved for its silence and mystery, jarred on him when all the prayers were said aloud by the bishop and repeated by his companions. The bishop was so like the old schoolmaster in the National School near Inniscar!

He was a priest. He took off his vestments slowly. For years he had looked forward to this day as the crowning day of his life, when his whole being was to be transformed. Yet he felt the same. He leant his arms on the vestment press, his alb still on, his eyes fixed on the crucifix. The outstretched arms on the Cross! Yes, that was his work. To help to bring the whole world of suffering humanity within these arms. He was weak, but God would give him strength. He had set the seal of His service upon him. These arms were extended to all, the lowly and the learned, the ignorant and those high in place and power. The Truth, the Way and the Life were for all. It was for him, as a priest, to use his mind and will to bring man into harmony with the Divine will.

Outside the sacristy door stood his father and mother. As he hastened forward they knelt on the wood pavement of the cloister. He blushed and looked confused.

"Won't you give me your blessing, Ralph?" Hilda said, bending her head. He hesitated, trying to remember the words, held his hands over her and murmured, "*Benedictio Dei omnipotentis, patris et filii et spiritus sancti decendat super te et maneat semper tecum.*"

She caught his hand in both of hers, and kissed it passionately – he felt her warm tears drop on it. She was the mother of his childhood again, he thought.

"Well, Ralph, old man, you've gone and done it," his father said, shaking his hand, his voice somewhat broken.

All around were groups of relations of the newly ordained priests, waiting for a son or a brother.

Ralph felt a tug on his sleeve, and turning saw Mrs Devine, her round face red and full of smiles.

"I hope you've a blessing left for me, Father O'Brien," she said, flopping on her knees. "This is the tenth I'll have got, and we'll make the round of all the young priests before we've done."

"And there's Father Magan!" she said. "Sure, Father, I saw you once with your mother in the street in Bunnahone. Many a time since of a market day she tells me about you and how you swept the halls of Maynooth from start to finish."

Old Jack Devine approached Ralph.

"You won't mind my not kneeling, Father? Sure the knees are gone on me, and if I once got down, sorra one of me could rise again till I was lifted."

He bent his head, aged since Ralph last saw him, for a blessing.

"The blessing of God and His Blessed Mother and all the saints on you, too," he said fervently.

"Let ye hurry off now, Father Joe!" said Mrs Devine to her son and Ralph, "and get your breakfasts. My heart went out to them," she added, curtsying to Mrs O'Brien, "pale and peaky, kneeling there before the altar fasting all these hours without a cup of tea itself. And me having my breakfast as comfortable as you like before I left the lodging-house in town. It was little appetite Jack had, he was that excited, but I made him eat a bit all the same."

Ralph never found Maynooth so genial as on his ordination day. Rain had fallen during the ceremony, but now the sun shone from a cloudless sky. All the students seemed friendly. At breakfast the young priests, more grave than usual, beamed on him. Lanigan wore a set look, as if he were afraid to smile. Daly alone seemed unaffected.

"What I'm longing for now," he said to Ralph, as they left the refectory, "is to meet a dean round the corner. I'd soon let him see I was independent of him."

Ralph met his father and mother on their return from breakfast and walked round the grounds with them. Every hundred yards they came on a line of kneeling students or lay visitors being blessed by some young priest. Father Dunlea detached himself from a group of professors and knelt on the gravel as Ralph passed.

"This is a day to forget all disputes," he said, as he got up from his knees. "Neither schoolmen nor innovators object to a blessing."

"I'm sorry I haven't given you satisfaction," Ralph said.

"Young men and novelties!" said Dunlea, laughing. "You'll come back to the *Summa* yet - but I mustn't keep you from your people. Your mother? I thought so. I knew it by her happy face. Don't ever make her sad. God bless you."

John and Hilda remained in Maynooth for Ralph's first mass on the following day. Father Gogarty attended him at the altar to see that he omitted nothing essential. He had practised the mass from his childhood, and as he walked to the altar he recalled his desire at mass in Clarendon Street, "to be the man walking towards the altar with the veiled chalice in his hand". His dominant feeling throughout was one of unworthiness. As he said the words of consecration of the bread, his fingers holding the host trembled and his heart seemed to stop beating. He felt himself standing before a mystery from which the veil was suddenly to be withdrawn. He paused perceptibly, half expecting something wonderful to happen. Nothing happened but the penetrating sound of his own voice, "*Hoc est corpus meum*," sounding from afar of in a tone that was strange to him. He could hear his mother sigh, a glad sigh and not a sad one, he thought with relief as he took the chalice in his hand for the consecration of the wine. He felt, as he laid the bread on his mother's tongue at the communion, that it was the symbol of his work though life - the breaking of the bread of divine love to all who would eat of it.

Chapter 16

RALPH SPENT THREE weeks quietly at Inniscar, saying mass every morning in the little chapel, much to Hilda's comfort. Her maternal feelings were again awakened, and she looked forward to having him with her for a few months. She was much disappointed when he read a letter from the bishop, one morning at breakfast, appointing him as additional curate to Bunnahone.

The letter was long and explanatory, suave with a distinct tone of command. The bishop had long wished to send another curate to Bunnahone and was prevented only by lack of priests. He wished to have all the parish work in the hands of the parish clergy so as not to be dependent for help, as was hitherto the case, on the good Dominicans. There was no room in the parochial house for a fourth priest. Father O'Brien would, therefore, provide lodgings for himself. The revenues of the parish, which he was to share equally with the other curates, would enable him to do this with comfort. He would take instructions as to work, etc., from Father Molloy, the administrator.

Father Ralph, as he was now almost invariably called, was fortunate in finding a suitable small house close to the Convent of Mercy. He furnished it simply, with odd pieces from Inniscar, annexed freely by Ann Carty, who was installed as his housekeeper.

There had, it seemed, been a regular shake-up among the younger clergy, consequent on the promotion of Father Phil Doyle from the Seminary to the parish of Lisslea and the vacant vicar-generalship. Magan was appointed to the Seminary, with Lanigan as assistant. Father Dempsey and Father Hardy were Ralph's fellow curates.

Ralph found both curates with Father Molloy when he called to report himself. Father Molloy was stretched on a sofa in his sitting-room, the others in comfortable armchairs in front of an empty grate. All three were smoking, Father Molloy with his soutane and waistcoat unbuttoned and his collar loose.

"The convent mass of a morning knocks it out of a man," he said apologetically, as he greeted Ralph: "I get that tired that I must have a lie down after it. Twenty-past seven even in summer is too much for any man. Sit down, won't you, and stoke up. I'm glad you're all here together so that we can have a talk about things. So you're taking that little house by the convent. A sunny little place enough, but you'll be lonely there. I'm sorry we couldn't fit you in here. Four is a better number than three in a house – it's convenient to have even numbers for a game of cards; but you won't be far off if we want you. I like to have the lads about me myself. It passes the time better when there's nothing else doing. You must take to a pipe," he added after a pause. "I don't know what the young fellows nowadays are coming to. Give up them cigarettes you're smoking. These fellows are nearly as bad; they smoke some kind of rotten mixture – there's nothing like a whiff of good strong twist."

"I called about the arrangement of work," Ralph said.

"Oh! the day is long! You needn't be in any hurry. You'll stay and have a bit of dinner with us. The Seminary lads will likely drop in and we can have a game of nap afterwards."

"I am afraid I must see about the removal of some furniture."

"Don't begin by being a spoil sport. But I suppose if you can't stay you can't. You might have known I'd want you to stay to dinner."

"What about the masses?" asked Hardy, sharply.

"You mightn't be so ready when you're wanted to say them," said Father Molloy, sighing deeply. "There are four masses every day," he went on wearily, "and the four of us take them turn about – the Cathedral, the convent, the asylum and the workhouse."

"I don't know what the lunatics want a daily mass for," Hardy said.

"I don't either, but we're well paid for it; that'll be some consolation to you," he said, pointedly, to Hardy.

"The second priest at the Seminary will be a kind of relief man for mass an odd time," he continued. "Generally, ye young fellows'll have to duplicate on Sundays. I'm getting on in years, and ye must let me down easy in case the bishop or Magan or Lanigan says any of the fixed masses."

"We must all get our turn of the relief, too," said Hardy.

"Isn't he a great lawyer, now?" Father Molloy said, winking at

Dempsey and Ralph. "I'm the easiest man in the world to get on with as long as there's give and take. But there's two things against which I'd kick like the devil, poaching on my preserves and interfering with the running of the parish." He laughed heartily and took a pinch of snuff.

"The man who says the church mass takes the sick calls; and the preaching is easy, not more than a sermon a month apiece. The bishop likes to hear himself talk and he takes a good many sermons off our hands.

"I don't think there's anything else but the confessions on Saturdays and the eves of holidays. That's light work enough, more's the pity! The Dominicans have too great a pull in the town and get all the confessions and most of the mass offerings, too, worse luck." He frowned thoughtfully.

"It was to put a brake to their wheel you were sent here," he said to Ralph. "The bishop had it in his eye for a long time. We can be stiffer with them now since we don't depend on them for any of the regular work."

"But there is other parish work?" Ralph asked hesitatingly.

Father Molloy looked puzzled, and then smiled.

"If you hunt the children to school the nuns'll make a pet of you," he said. "There are a lot of other things that young fellows often begin, but they soon give 'em up. I believe myself in not interfering too much with the people. They don't like it, and it makes life easier for us."

"It's a bit hard to be bound to a daily mass," said Hardy, yawning.

"It is then," said Father Molloy, sighing. "I often thought of getting the bishop to give me an easy country parish where I could throw most of the work over on a curate, but I couldn't tear myself away from the town. I like company, and I'd die from loneliness in the country in a week. Except for the mass, however, you'll find things easy enough."

Dempsey got up impatiently.

"I'll go part of the way with you, Father O'Brien; I'll be back for dinner," he added to Father Molloy.

"Three o'clock sharp, the joint is always on the table," the latter said, waving his hand. "If Hardy'll only sit quiet or go out visiting some of his friends in town, I think I'll have a little snooze."

"Don't you fear," said Dempsey, as he and Ralph walked away, "but there's plenty of work to do. You must go cautiously, however. Molloy doesn't like things stirred up; he has the ear of the bishop, too, and could get one moved quick enough."

Ralph was disappointed by his visit to Father Molloy, and felt depressed. He did not, however, wish to discuss him.

"I dare say I shall fit in all right," he said.

In a few days Ralph was settled in his house. For the first week he said mass every day at the asylum, and one day, in the absence of the other priests, he had a sick call. The woman whom he was called to attend was dead when he arrived. She lay, fully dressed, on a straw pallet on the earthen floor of a miserable thatched hovel. The sun, shining through the open door, fell on her worn, starved face. A baby shrieked loudly in a packing-case beside the smouldering embers of a turf fire. Two unkempt children of about three and five wept loudly in a corner. A broken deal table on which stood a few dirty chipped cups and a board supported by stones, evidently serving as a seat, were the only furniture. A few women stood by the door.

"She's dead, poor woman," one said to Ralph.

He looked round the room.

"What's to be done?" he asked helplessly.

"Sure 'tis you that knows best, your reverence."

He tried to comfort the children.

"It's hungry they are, I doubt," one of the women said.

He gave her some money to buy food.

"Her husband, Mike Reardon, left her a month ago, and she lived on the bits of furniture ever since. Starved to death likely enough she was."

"Was there no one to help her?" he asked.

"She was that proud and close, there was no helping her. She wouldn't go into the poorhouse. There was many would give her a bite or a sup, but she wouldn't be beholden to anyone."

A policeman came to the door and heard a voluble account of the death from a bystander.

"Nothing must be touched. There'll have to be an inquest," he said, authoritatively.

The relieving officer, a solemn, stupid man, soon arrived. He scratched his head, and said, doubtfully, "I think I have the power to take the children into the poor-house."

Someone suggested that the nuns might do something.

Ralph gave a sigh of relief. Of course, that was the solution. He asked the woman who had fetched food for the children to take charge of them in his absence and he walked quickly to the convent. He hadn't yet visited and knew very little of nuns. He had read a copy of the rules of the Sisters of Mercy and remembered that they were vowed to the service of the poor, sick and ignorant.

He was awed by the magnificence of the gate-house. The long carriage drive wound alongside a stream, through well-kept grounds shaded by trees, crossing a rustic bridge in front of the magnificent cut-stone convent, a fairly good example of modern gothic. He pulled the bell at the gate-like doorway with some trepidation. The contrast between the house he had just left and all this splendour chilled him. The door was opened at once by a small girl, from the orphanage attached to the convent, he knew by her dress. He asked for the superior and was shown into a reception-room, the oak floor and woodwork shining with wax and furniture polish.

A tall elderly woman in nun's garb entered after a few minutes. Her strong features were saved from sternness by kind brown eyes which peered at him eagerly above spectacles hung rather low on a long nose.

He told his tale nervously. She kept her eyes fixed on the floor and fingered the rosary beads hanging by her side.

She sighed when he finished.

"I can have the children looked after," she said decisively. "The baby will be put out to nurse; the others can come to the orphanage."

He muttered his thanks.

She looked at him keenly.

"I'm glad you take such an interest in things. Don't hesitate to come to me if I can help," she said, ringing a bell.

She told the young nun who answered to go with another nun to Mrs Reardon's and look after the children. Ralph was struck by the fulness of direction she conveyed in a few short sentences.

When the young nun had gone Reverend Mother said anxiously, "The woman might have lived if she had food. One of the stones in this convent might have kept her alive."

She shook her head sadly.

"When I was as young as you I thought it so easy to do things. It was only a dream. The little I can do now – I'm not even sure that it's for the best."

"You have been very good about this," said Ralph, gratefully.

"The mother died of starvation," she said. "This is a village of about four thousand – about nine or ten hundred families in all. There is a workhouse with a large staff of officials, a dozen policemen, town commissioners, one convent here with over forty nuns, the Dominican convent with about twenty, a bishop and five – or is it six now? – secular priests, half a dozen Dominican priests and lay brothers – all these bodies make some profession of looking after the poor. We nuns made a solemn vow to do it. Yet a woman can live in a house that's not fit for a dog-kennel and die of starvation. We all make some show of doing things when the evil that could be prevented has happened. There must be a way out. I can't rest at night in this palace with the thought of these things happening at our door."

She fidgeted with her beads.

"But I shouldn't criticise like this. It is not right. The bishop of course knows best ... my tongue runs away with me."

Ralph pitied her evident distress. Thanking her again, he rose to go. She led him through a back way which she said was the shortest way to his house, through a low ivy-covered house abutting on the street.

"This was the original convent," she said. "The happiest days of my life were spent here before we lost our heads in stone and mortar. I may be able to help you in some ways if you let me know," she added, as she said goodbye. "We only visit at the request of the priests, and I know comparatively little of the town, although I have lived here for forty years."

Ralph called at the parochial house and found that Father Molloy had just come in. He shouted to Ralph to come to his bedroom, where he was busy packing.

"I'm just off to Lisdoonvarna for three weeks," he said, as he folded a shirt. "I was going to write you a note. Hardy is going with me. Dempsey and yourself will have to mind the parish. Keep up the church and the convent masses. If you can get Magan and Lanigan to say mass at the asylum and the workhouse, well and good. If not, you can let them slide. The officers are well trained and you won't hear of any complaints."

Ralph told him about Mrs Reardon.

"I'm too busy now," he interrupted in the middle. "I've only a few minutes to catch the train. I remember now, that woman did come to me about a month ago and told me some cock-and-bull story. I intended to speak to the nuns about her, but I forgot. It's all right now, anyhow. The relieving officer'll bury her and the nuns'll take the children. What more do you want? I'm sorry you're not coming to Lisdoonvarna," he added, brushing his scant locks carefully in front of the looking-glass. "There's no place like it in the world for a bit of fun. It bucks a man up greatly for all the work I have to do in this place."

Ralph walked home weary and depressed. The sunlight somewhat relieved the squalor of the town, but he could not help shuddering as he passed dingy public houses, flanked by dingier private houses. He couldn't get the thought of Mrs Reardon out of his mind and felt that behind every battered door was some tragedy of poverty or misery.

The expensive ecclesiastical buildings stood out in strange contrast against the surrounding poverty. A bank, the post office, Darcy's imposing frontage, the Emporium, a few other big shops, a dozen houses belonging to doctors, solicitors and retired shopkeepers alone gave any evidence of secular wealth. The whole town, he thought, exclusive of the Church property, could be built at a third of the cost of the ecclesiastical buildings! Men lounged idly at street corners, stood chatting at shop doors or leant against shop windows. They saluted Ralph as he passed and looked after him curiously. "The new priest," he heard someone say in answer to an inquiry. He was conscious of drawn-back lace curtains in the living-rooms over shops and faces flattened against the glass in an effort to get a good view.

There was little or no industry. The smith, usually employed shoeing horses or mending farm implements, disappeared into an adjoining public house and the smithy was silent. A carpenter was listlessly making a plain deal coffin, probably for Mrs Reardon. A policeman came out of a public house wiping his long moustache, straightened himself when he saw Ralph and, putting on an air of business, gave a military salute. A beggar whined an appeal. A few ragged children played noisily on the pavement, the only sign of real activity in the desert village.

"Hallo!" Lanigan said, slapping Ralph on the back as he stood gazing down a side lane, watching the sunlight on a dilapidated house washed with red ochre and now glowing in the bright light. "I was going to look you up. I'm on guard at the empty Seminary. Magan is off in Dublin or Lisdoonvarna."

"How do the people here make a living?" Ralph asked, still gazing moodily at the somnolent street. "There seems to be no business."

"Market days and fair days are their harvest. The place is busy enough then. They live on the farmers, of course," Lanigan said indifferently. "Will you come to the Seminary with me or will I go home with you? I'm tired of taking the air of the town. The Miss Hinnisseys are out and there isn't a soul to talk to."

They sat in the small garden, on which a French window gave from the study at the back of Ralph's house. In the distance was the sea breaking white on a shelving rock beach, with, further off, mountains, their mysterious ravines lit up by the afternoon sun.

Ann insisted on their having tea, though Lanigan protested that he never took any.

"There'll always be meals at the proper time in this house while I have anything to do with you," she had said to Ralph the first day they settled in. "You can ate them or not, as you like, but I'll have done my duty. You won't descend in my hands to three o'clock dinners and eight o'clock teas, and the like. I'll see that you ate like a Christian."

"It's a great joke me and Ginger being at the Seminary," Lanigan said, stirring his tea vigorously, "and Boyle gone, too!"

Ralph murmured something, and Lanigan went on, "Ginger is cute enough, and though he won't admit it, he knows we're in a hole and that we'll be in a worse one at the end of the year if he can't pick up as good a man as Boyle cheap. That's what he's going to Lisdoonvarna for, to try and hear of some man from the priests that are gathered there. Heigh-ho! it's a queer world. Here I am, Professor of Greek, no less, and spending every night already over the texts for the year, with a couple of translations and a dictionary and a grammer, trying to spell out a few lines to keep ahead of the class. I hope there won't be any clever fellows in it or they'll soon find me out and play the dickens with me. And with all his pretences Ginger'll be worse."

Ann came out frowning and called Ralph aside.

"Hinnissey the shopkeeper's daughters are within in the dining-room, and I can't get them out of the house."

"Show them out here."

"Is it the likes of them riff-raff? I asked 'em if it was a sick call, and they said it was not then. So I said you were engaged. 'It's only Father Lanigan,' they said; 'we saw them go in.' The impudent hussies! Sorra foot they'd leave the place, though I showed them plain I'd rather their room than their company."

"You must be more polite to people, Ann. Please show them here and bring two more cups," Ralph said, frowning.

"Politeness and them are well met! I expected more of you, Father Ralph! Don't be vexed, *a gradh*," she added hastily, as he continued to look annoyed.

He smiled at her affectionately.

"Well, I suppose I must do it," she said resignedly. "But I have my feelings, too. All my life living with the gentry and now having to get tea for old Hinnissey's daughters that I'm every bit as good as myself, if not better, for I don't spend my time traipsing the streets of Bunnahone and running after my betters!"

Ralph made a movement to enter the house.

"Oh, I'll go and be civil enough if you want me to," Ann said, with a look of offended dignity. "If I feel I'm demeaning myself, I can pocket my pride. I know my duty as a servant."

The Miss Hinnisseys looked somewhat subdued when they appeared under Ann's escort. Miss Katie was fatter, Miss Julia thinner than Ralph remembered them six years before, but they were more youthfully dressed – Miss Katie in white, and pink ribbons; Miss Julia in white, and blue ribbons.

When Ann disappeared after bringing the tea-cups, they recovered their spirits.

"Imagine now," said Miss Katie, simpering, "gentlemen having tea by themselves, all alone, and no ladies present! The height of fashion, I call it. And out in the garden, too! We must have tea in our garden, Julia." Her face fell. "I forgot we'd have to cross the yard, and pa will not have it kept clean," she said. This thought distressed her so much that she was silent for some time.

"It was very bold of you," said Miss Julia, shaking her finger archly, "never to come to see us, Father Ralph, all these years. I often saw you passing and you'd never even look up at the window, and I looking out for you."

Ralph muttered some excuse.

"But we'll make up for lost time now. No, I won't take a chair, thanks; I prefer to sit on the grass."

"You skittish young thing, you'll never grow up," Miss Katie simpered.

"With two priests in the Seminary and an additional curate in the town, there'll be great times in Bunnahone," said Miss Julia, opening her eyes wide. "Don't look so sad, Katie. You haven't lost Father Phil for good. He's sure to come to see us often. What is Father Magan like? We've never met him yet," she said eagerly. "He was away in Lisdoonvarna when we called. Indeed, I think he mightn't have run away from Bunnahone so soon. We have a lot of nice young ladies here – more ladylike than many I've seen priests go about with at Lisdoonvarna."

"He's a regular ladies' man," said Lanigan, solemnly.

"But not as nice as you, Father!" said Miss Katie, "or he'd be at home, like you, when we called."

"Sure, I didn't stir out of my room for days for fear I'd miss the pleasure," said Lanigan, gallantly.

"Do you hear him now, Julia? I'm sure he's after saying the same thing to the Miss Darcys," said Miss Katie.

"I never set eyes on 'em yet, but I'm sure they couldn't hold a candle to the present company."

"They're very sly, the Darcys," said Miss Julia, frowning. "I wonder what they're up to in not calling yet. Perhaps they're making up to Father Hardy and Father Dempsey. But it's little good, for Father Hardy is an old friend of ours and he promised that Father Dempsey should come to us."

Ralph felt tongue-tied and regretted that he had not allowed Ann to have her way.

"Who's to be the new director of the Children of Mary, Father Ralph?" said Miss Julia, after a pause.

"Is there a sodality? I hadn't heard of it."

"Indeed, there is, and a fairly select one, too. Sister Margarita, who's in charge of it, tried to keep it for young ladies who've been at least a year boarders at a convent. Reverend Mother, who has odd ways, insists on some quite low girls being allowed in. Sister Margarita manages to circumvent her mostly, but she has to give in if Reverend Mother rides the high horse. I'm surprised at Reverend Mother, and she of a good family, too. But, on the whole, Sister Margarita has her own way. You'll find it's quite the thing. Miss Eva Dillon even is a member of it. She doesn't come to many of the meetings, but we have her name and that's something. I do hope you'll be made the director," she added, in a low voice, so that Father Lanigan couldn't hear. "I know Sister Margarita would give her eyes out to have you, and we're all the same. It depends on Reverend Mother, however, and there's no knowing what she'll do."

"I'm sorry," Ralph said, "but I'm afraid I have to leave you now."

"Just when our conversation was getting interesting, too," said Miss Julia, reproachfully.

"It is very rude of me, but I must see that everything is fixed up in regard to a poor woman, Reardon, who died suddenly today."

"People ought to die at night and not be interrupting us like this."

"You mustn't absorb *all* Father Ralph's time, Julia dear," said Katie. "I noticed when we passed through how bare your rooms looked, Father. Couldn't we make you some embroideries for the backs of the chairs? Julia does crewel work beautifully, and I know she's longing to do something for you," she said, looking at Ralph languishingly.

He saw them out. "Don't think I'm interfering," Katie said, on the doorstep, "but priests are so unprotected, having no one to look after them. I said to Julia I ought to tell you and she said it would be a charity. Your servant is very rude. I'm sure you can't have noticed it. She's evidently not at all used to ladies."

"Thank you," Ralph said dryly.

"Has one to do much of this?" he asked Lanigan, ruefully.

"What's wrong about it? They're a fine pair of girls and great fun. You needn't be making faces as if you didn't like it. It's a plain as a pike-staff that Julia is soft on you."

"Don't be an ass," said Ralph, angrily.

Lanigan laughed. "You'll never do on the mission, O'Brien. If you don't make up to Katie and Julia, old mamma Hinnissey won't open her purse with mass offerings. However, if you cry off I might have a chance myself."

"Don't, Lanigan – it hurts! Surely we ought to be beyond all this," Ralph said appealingly.

Lanigan looked at him for a few moments, and smiled.

"Poor old O'Brien!" he said, patting Ralph on the shoulder. "Try and work up a sense of humour. We must take things as we find 'em. When I'm in the dumps I think of Ginger and that always sets me right. If you don't like things, lump them, and knock what fun you can out of them. Why, man alive, if I began to think I was responsible for things, what would happen to me? and I having to teach Greek, which I never knew right, and the alphabet of which I hardly remember. I'd shoot myself as likely as not. I had a bad half-hour the night before I was ordained sub-deacon and I was within an ace of leaving the whole bag of tricks. I took the jump and I'm going to let sleeping dogs lie now. I'm not going to give a mission to cure Molloy of drink, or to put some decency into that little sneak Hardy, or make Magan believe in God ..."

"You shouldn't say these things," Ralph interrupted. "I don't believe ..."

Lanigan whistled. "Don't go round in blinkers," he said sharply. "If these things surprise you, Lord! where were your eyes when you were in Maynooth and during your vacations? You throw up your eyes at the Miss Hinnisseys. If that's all there'll be to shock you ... but you'll have to find out things for yourself."

Ralph was so disturbed when Lanigan left that he sat on in the garden instead of going at once to Reardon's. His mind was full of confused impressions. He made an effort to disentangle them, but they seemed to grow more blurred. He watched the sun, now low in the west, throw a bar of molten gold in the track of a small paddle steamer, while the mountains enfolded themselves in purple gloom. There was light somewhere, if he could only find it, to make clear the dark places of his soul....

Ann stood at the window, and said, sternly, "Do come in out of that, Father. You'll get your death of cold sitting with your feet in the dew. I can see the grass all wet from here, and the dinner is on the table, too."

In the middle of dinner he got up suddenly and went out. As he walked through the dimly lighted street, paraffin lamps at long distances apart seeming to add to the gathering darkness of the sky, he pulled himself together. He was only a prig after all. The world was what it was, and if he was to do anything it was not by moaning, but by working. He was only a mixture of good and bad himself, like everything in the world. The Church was the same....

The lights gave out in the street leading to Reardon's house. He stumbled into something. A man cursed. A woman peered into his face, hastily drew her shawl over her head and shouted hoarsely to her companion as she ran off, "Run, run, it's the priest!"

Light streamed through the Reardons' open door. In the far corner by the fireplace lay the corpse on the straw pallet, which now rested on some chairs. Three candles were lighted at the head and foot and cast an unsteady glow on the emaciated face, calm and beautiful, of the dead woman. Her hands were crossed on her breast, the long, slender fingers holding a rosary beads. The lips were set in a faint smile. The room was clouded with tobacco smoke. A dozen men and women knelt facing the corpse, their backs to the door, saying the rosary aloud. Ralph knelt by the door and joined in the prayers.

"May the Lord have mercy on her soul and on the souls of all the faithful departed," said the man who led the prayers, sprinkling the corpse with holy water.

He came forward when he saw Ralph and said, "Sure I wouldn't have taken the liberty, your reverence, if I knew you were there. It's a beautiful corpse, entirely, she makes. She's well out of her troubles, poor woman."

Ralph asked about the children.

"Reverend Mother, may the blessing of God be on her, took two of them to the orphanage and put the baby to nurse with a decent woman."

"Can I do anything?"

"Well, if you wouldn't mind giving a trifle to help to bury her? She never went on the rates while she was alive, and we thought it was a shame she'd have to do it and she dead, and she not able to have a say agin it. So we're making up a collection to cover the expenses of burying her.... That's too much entirely. The half of it'll be more than enough."

"If you can have the coffin brought to the Cathedral tomorrow by eight o'clock I shall offer mass for her."

"Is it the likes of her, Father? Sure we'd never be able to raise the money for that. Father Tom puts on a high charge and we'd never be able to meet it."

"Bring her in any case."

"May God Almighty bless you! Sure it never rains but it pours. 'Tis proud Kitty Reardon'd be to see herself in front of the high altar and the big yellow candles lit around her coffin. Sure it's not often the poor has such a chance. May heaven be your bed for that."

A hard-featured man with a grizzled moustache joined Ralph on his way out.

"I'm going your way, Father, and I may be better company than none in the dark of the night."

They passed several couples on the way.

"I'm glad you don't rise your stick to them," said the man with a dry laugh.

"I don't understand?"

"When you will understand, I hope you won't do it either," with the same dry laugh.

They had again entered the dimly lighted street. The dingy public houses looked more dingy at night, their dirty windows, filled with bottles, obscuring the light of the hanging paraffin lamps in the shops behind.

"The saloon keeper is a great person in Bunnahone. He hadn't much of a show in Lee, Massachusetts, where I spent the best part of my life. I'm a shoemaker, John Byrne by name; my health broke down in the States and I had to come back to this God-forsaken hole."

"It is dreary," Ralph said. "Bad as the public houses are – I suppose there are too many – they seem the brightest spots in the place. What can be done?"

Byrne eyed him closely.

"There's many things that need doing," he said cautiously, "but it's not for me to be giving advice to a priest."

"Come in, and let us talk things over," Ralph said, when they reached his gate; "if you have no engagement," he added, seeing that Byrne hesitated.

"It's not that," Byrne said, shuffling from one foot to the other. "I'll tell you when I get in."

In the study he looked at Ralph aggressively.

"Before I sit down," he said, "I want to tell you that I haven't been to the sacraments these twenty years. I don't want to be here under false pretences."

"Take a pipe," said Ralph, smiling, pointing to a rack full of new pipes. "There's tobacco, or would you prefer a cigarette?" He felt a sense of relief that he was able to take Byrne's announcement without resentment.

"You mean it?" Byrne said anxiously. "It's the first time I was ever beyond the door in a priest's house, or even asked in either," he added, as he filled his pipe carefully. "I'd be almost tempted to speak to you as a man," he said, puffing his pipe with relish.

"Am I not one?"

"That remains to be seen. You see you're a priest and, somehow or another, the priest sinks the man out of sight. I don't like the class, that's the truth. You're young yet and maybe one can speak to you as between man and man. You haven't the domineering ways of a priest, for one thing."

"Now, what's wrong with the town?" Ralph said, lighting a cigarette.

"It's run by priests and gombeen men, saving your reverence's presence," said Byrne, bowing mockingly.

"What are the rest of the people doing?"

"Kicking agin it under their breath."

"Why don't they kick and shout?"

"They're bound hand and foot."

Ralph, unable to disentangle the metaphors, looked puzzled.

"The way of it is this," said Byrne, laying his pipe on his knee. "The whole town depends on the shopkeepers. Not only do they own the shops, but they own the other houses as well and all the land round about and they have most of the farmers, except in a parish here and there, in their books. There's Hinnissey and

Donaghue. Between them and Darcy they have half a score of farms seized for shop debts. If a man opens his lips agin them he might as well leave the country. There's near three-quarters of the town working for the other quarter at nine or ten shillings a week, and living in houses that aren't fit for pigsties."

"The sanitary authority should see to that."

"The sanitary authority! Why they're the same shopkeepers that own the houses. If the plague was in them never one of them'd ever be condemned."

"Can the priests do nothing?"

"Whatever they could do, they don't do it. The gombeen men pay most of the dues and the priests stand by their friends through thick and thin. There's nobody in the town for the priests but Hinnissey and Darcy and the like. If a man won't go to mass Father Tom abuses him and threatens to get Mr Darcy or Mr Donaghue to give him the sack. And if a man objects to the wages he gets from Hinnissey, Hinnissey threatens him with hell and damnation and Father Tom. Before God, that's a good deal the reason I don't go to the sacraments. Every time I go into the Cathedral and see gombeen publicans' names tacked on to every stained glass window and every seat – advertisements for porter and whiskey every one of them – I see the whole place red with the sweated blood of the poor. I don't believe God'd set foot in a place of the kind.... My temper rises when I think of it all," he added apologetically. "I was thinking when I saw you at Reardon's that you might be a different kind of priest – there are a few that are real priests, I believe, though I haven't come across 'em much – and I made bold to speak to you."

It was long before Ralph slept that night. Making all allowances for Byrne's prejudice and exaggerations, things seemed to be in a bad way in Bunnahone. Half asleep he saw himself tilting against an immense windmill, shaped like a church, covered with porter and wishkey advertisements. He poised his lance ...

Chapter 17

FATHER O'BRIEN SOON became a well-known figure in the streets of Bunnahone. In the three weeks of Father Molloy's absence he had visited most of the houses. The Miss Hinnisseys confided to their rivals the Miss Darcys that they had found him "either shy or stuck up" when he returned their call. The Miss Darcys were not quite sure about him, but thought "he had no conversation", Kate Riley, the hard-working slatternly wife of one of Hinnissey's labourers, said he was "a laughey young priest without any harm in him, who took notice of the children, no bad sign". The Miss Cullens, still young in the fifties, daughters of a defunct land agent, who visited no one in the town except the bishop and selections of the clergy, drove to meets and were occasionally asked to luncheon in country houses, said that he reminded them of their friends the Dublin Jesuits, his accent and manners being everything that could be desired. The Dominican nuns were reserved at first and complained of being neglected by the parish clergy.

"Of course as we are enclosed we know little of parish affairs," the prioress said. After a while she thawed and told him with some gusto all the parish gossip and showed an intimate knowledge of his own movements. At the Dominican priory old Father Lyons gave him a hearty welcome, "though a little bird tells me you're the first step towards driving us out of the place. Well, well, the Church is a wonderful institution. I bear no malice. I'll get a cell somewhere to die in - though I can't carry away that view of the sunset with me," he added, wistfully, his eyes on the sea. His shrewd but kind, grey eyes twinkled mischievously when he spoke of the parish clergy. "I'm not a man of affairs, like the bishop and Father Molloy. I'm even too old for some of our own young men here and am good for nothing but reading musty old books." Ralph saw on his table side by side with the *Summa* of St Thomas, books by Laberthonniere, Le Roy and Loisy.

"As musty as these!" Ralph said, smiling and pointing to the books.

The old priest's ascetic face flowed with enthusiasm. "You know them? Come in and have a talk sometimes. It will be a kindness to an old man."

His fingers lingered lovingly on the books.

"These men have caught the spirit of St Thomas. They say what I always felt St Thomas would say, if he were alive today. They make the dry bones live again."

At the National School he was received with much deference by the head teacher, Mr Grogan, a brown-bearded giant with timid scared eyes, who added "Father" or "your reverence" to every sentence. Ralph had expected to find the school, which was Church property under Father Molloy's management, in keeping with the other ecclesiastical buildings, and was at once struck by a contrast. It was a ramshackle, low, one-storied building, once whitewashed, the walls within and without discoloured by the drip from broken eave-shoots. From the gate of the school-yard, which hung off its hinges, to the dilapidated teacher's rostrum, everything – doors, windows, desks, floor – was out of repair. A few torn maps hung on the walls. The room had not been dusted or the floor washed for years.

Grogan saw Ralph's disapproving eye.

"I intend to do something with it this vacation. I'm a poor man with a long family and can't afford much," he said in a shrinking voice.

"Is it your duty to keep the schoolhouse in order?"

"In a way it is and in a way it isn't, your reverence. I promised Father Tom, when I was appointed, I would," he said evasively. "Father Tom is a grand man, your reverence, but he's that busy he doesn't have time to come here once in an age. But he's easy to get on with, the easiest gentleman in the world. It's the inspectors there's most to fear from. Father Tom snaps his fingers at them, but still they will keep on sending down bad reports."

The helpless-looking teacher, the room itself, the unkempt pupils and the dreary incompetent teaching – Ralph waited to hear a lesson – were depressing. Some boys in the back benches, awed into silence by his entrance, soon became disorderly notwithstanding the violent efforts of the teacher to restrain them. It was the one sign of life Ralph saw during his visit.

It was a relief to go afterwards to the girls' school attached to the convent, under the management of the nuns. The rooms were bright and clean, the walls hung with pictures, poor German subject reprints, but pleasing to the eyes of children. The pupils were clean and looked happy. The teaching was haphazard as the nuns were untrained and, for the most part, young and inexperienced.

"They are great fun," Sister Veronica, the young nun in change of the infant school, said to Ralph, waving her hand at her romping pupils.

"The infant school at the convent is the one bright spot in Bunnahone," Ralph said to Father Dempsey, as they sat together in Ralph's study.

Dempsey laughed. "You'd better be careful," he said. "That's Father Tom's preserve. He's a bit soft on little Veronica and she's quite gone on him. He'll think you're poaching. Besides," he added seriously, "I'd leave the nuns to God. When you're on the mission as long as I am, you'll find they're dangerous to have anything to do with."

He blushed and changed the subject. "Old Byrne, the shoemaker, was blowing your trumpet to me today," he said awkwardly.

"Why are the nuns dangerous?" Ralph asked.

"Oh! you'll learn that soon enough."

"Why not now?" Ralph persisted. "It seems to me that all through my life the explanation of things has been put off to some indefinite future that never seems to arrive."

Dempsey's face became redder than his hair. After a long silence he said, "Well, they have hearts and feelings, and so have we."

"Well, what of that?"

"One of them might fall in love with you, or you with one of them, or both of you together, and then there'd be the devil to pay."

Ralph laughed boyishly. "What of our vows?" he said.

"The best way to keep vows is to keep out of the way of breaking them," Dempsey said sententiously.

All the prurient things which Ralph had blushed over when reading moral theology flooded his memory, and he became more red than Dempsey.

"It's that horrid moral theology that puts these thoughts into your mind. I always thought it was wicked," he said angrily.

Dempsey stared at him open-mouthed.

"Do you know you're accusing St Liguori of wickedness? He's the great authority on moral theology."

"I don't care," Ralph said obstinately. "His books are disgraceful."

"Look here, O'Brien. You're excited and I don't believe you mean what you're saying. If Hardy or Molloy heard you saying anything like that they might make mischief. I always liked you, though I did hear you had odd views," he added thoughtfully.

"You seemed to cast a reflection on nuns," said Ralph, lamely.

"By saying they were human beings like you and me? But maybe you think you're a plaster saint yourself?" Dempsey said dryly.

"You know I don't," said Ralph, more soberly. "I wasn't thinking of myself, but nuns surely ..."

"Are like any other lot of women you meet, or men either, priests included," Dempsey interrupted. "Some are strong, some weak; some good, some bad - with the great majority somewhere in between. Some are as cold as icicles, some have hearts and control them, others have hearts and don't. Leave them alone ... I tell you, I know what I'm talking about."

Dempsey was again growing excited, and it dawned slowly on Ralph that in some way the discussion touched him personally.

"I dare say you're right," Ralph said, lighting a cigarette. "Of course, I have no experience. Does what you say mean that I am not to go to the convent at all?"

"I've no doubt that would be best," Dempsey said gravely. "You must go there on business, but let it be on business always, and have as little to do with the young nuns as you can."

Ralph tried to draw Dempsey into a discussion of theology, but he was not interested.

"I have a small compendium of Gury's *Moral Theology*," he said, "and it has more than I'll ever want to know in it." He never read any dogmatic theology or philosophy and had entirely forgotten the little he had learned at Maynooth. "The penny catechism," he said, "would see a priest through on the mission, if it weren't for clerical conferences, and a look over a few pages of Gury the night before is enough for them."

"But there are some people who are dissatisfied with Gury and the penny catechism," Ralph said. "Ought we not to make an effort to adapt our teaching of Catholic truth to them?"

"It's their loss if they don't take the truth that's given them," Dempsey said complacently. "There's no going behind what we were taught in Maynooth. If they prefer to walk straight into hell, let them. You'll find, if you only look deep enough, that it's not questions of faith that trouble these people, but they want to follow their own wicked passions."

Ralph smiled as he recognised a phrase of Malone's, who always disposed of heretics, unbelievers and even Catholics who questioned the received theology in these words.

"Are you quite satisfied, then, with the present teaching of the Church?"

"Well, you're a queer fellow! Why shouldn't I?" He paused and frowned. "Except in regard to the Irish language," he added.

"What in the world has Irish to do with either faith or theology?" Ralph asked laughingly.

"It's no joking matter. The people aren't nearly so strong in the faith since they gave up speaking the Irish. It was a bad day for the Church when it took a hand in killing the language...."

Ralph listened in amazement to a long dissertation in which Dempsey proved to his own satisfaction the dependence of Catholicism in Ireland on the language, and the blindness of priests and bishops in not seeing the connection.

"The best work I can do for religion is to start an Irish class in Bunnahone, and I'm going to do it, no matter what the bishop and Molloy think. Charles Dillon made several efforts to start one, but no priest had the courage to support it and Molloy was always able to kill it. All they can do to me is to move me to another parish."

"I will help you," Ralph said, smiling. "I haven't much belief in your reasons, but I believe in the language, and have always wanted to work for it."

"Oh! you'll come round to the right reasons in time. The important thing now it to get the class started," Dempsey said with enthusiasm. He kept Ralph out of bed for hours discussing all the details of his project.

The bishop, who had gone for a vacation on the continent the day before Ralph arrived in Bunnahone, returned about a week after

Father Molloy came back from Lisdoonvarna. Ralph called but failed to see him.

"His lordship told me to tell you in case you called to come to dinner at three o'clock on Thursday. I'm to tell all the priests, or send them round word," the servant, who opened the door, said.

"It's an odd way of inviting one to dinner," Ralph said afterwards to Dempsey.

"What the man told me was that the bishop ordered me to come. You'll get used to these little ways in time. There's always a good dinner, anyway. 'Mum' about the Irish class until we get it started. The lord might stick in his oar too soon."

The bishop received his guests in his study, all kneeling to kiss his ring. When the clock on the mantelpiece struck three, he became uneasy.

"Ring that bell, Father Hardy," he said with a frown.

"Why isn't the dinner up?" he said, sharply, to the servant.

"The cook says it'll take a few minutes yet, my lord," the man said nervously.

"Put the soup on the table at once."

"Yes, your lordship."

The bishop stalked into the dining-room, followed by the silent priests.

"You take the vice-chair, Father Molloy. Sit here next me, Father O'Brien – Father Magan." He said grace and fidgeted with his spoon until the soup arrived. When he had taken a few spoonfuls, he gradually resumed the suave manner to which Ralph was accustomed.

"Have you broken in the young men yet, Father Molloy?"

"I'm hard at it, your lordship. They're a bit restive in harness," Father Molloy replied, with a broad smile, his florid face glistening above the napkin tucked under his chin.

"They could have no better trainer," the bishop said, tightening his lips.

"Had your lordship and the other bishops a pleasant holiday?" asked Father Hardy.

"One would hardly designate a pilgrimage to Lourdes a holiday, Father Hardy."

The priest looked crushed, but brightened when the bishop

added, with a smile: "Though we did do a little sightseeing on the way."

"Lourdes must be a great sight entirely, my lord," said Father Molloy.

"A wonderful demonstration of faith, a standing proof that God is guiding the Church."

"Did you see a miracle, my lord?" Father Hardy asked.

"No; that blessed privilege was denied me. One of the good bishops who accompanied me, however, told me that he has been quite free from rheumatism since he took the waters. By the way, an amusing contretemps prevented me bringing you home some of the blessed waters, as I intended. One of my companions used it to mix with a little whiskey he took to refresh himself on the long train journey."

"Was it the bishop that got cured of the rheumatism, my lord?" asked Father Molloy, gravely, after winking at Father Hardy.

"Yes, I believe it was. We are well rid of that man Boyle who used to teach in the Seminary," he added, turning to Magan. "I picked up a newspaper rag in Dublin, which I found is edited by him. I intend to bring it under the notice of the bishops at their next meeting. Every sentence of it was temerarious and offensive to pious ears, if not absolutely heretical."

"I never cared for that lad," said Father Molloy, unctuously.

The entrance of a huge boiled leg of mutton, which was placed in front of the bishop, attracted Father Molloy's admiring gaze.

"I hope it has been kept long enough," he said anxiously. "There's fifteen pounds in it if there's an ounce. A piece of the lap, too, for me, my lord. You don't get the flavour right if you don't mix the different parts. How did you ever live on them little kick-shaws you get in foreign parts, my lord?"

The bishop and Father Molloy discussed the relative merits of foreign and home cooking until the next course of chicken and ham arrived. "Chicken and ham is nice and light after the mutton," Father Molloy said, appreciatively, as he gave himself a large helping.

Ralph made an effort to lead the conversation back to Boyle.

"I don't think we need discuss him further," the bishop said. "I have already disposed of him. Nothing now remains but to have his paper condemned."

"Right well he deserves it. He was always the stiff fellow," said Father Molloy.

"How are the friars?" asked the bishop, smiling.

"The people go far too much to the monastery still," Father Molloy said with a frown. "We'll have no peace till they are out of the parish entirely. I'll have to start in the curing line myself," he added, shrugging his shoulders. He continued to look despondent while the table was being cleared, but cheered up when the servant brought in whiskey and hot water, saying, "The bare mention of a friar makes my heart that low, that nothing short of a stiff glass of punch puts any life in me again. Will I make yours, my lord? I think I know your taste by now."

The bishop nodded. After taking a few sips of punch, he said, "I have an important announcement to make to you, gentlemen. It will put another burthen on Father Molloy's shoulders, but I have always found him a willing helper and I am confident he will not fail me now. I hope I shall be able to promise him your active co-operation."

"Hear, hear," said Father Hardy; "certainly, my lord, why not?"

"I have brought back with me the plans for a new Seminary."

"Good Lord!" muttered Father Dempsey.

"What did you say, Father Dempsey?"

"Nothing, my lord."

"I have long felt that our present Seminary, in its buildings only, I needn't assure you, was not sufficiently creditable to our ancient diocese. It is not in keeping with our beautiful Cathedral and other ecclesiastical buildings. I feel ashamed when other bishops visit me and I recall what fine seminaries they have in their dioceses. The cost is a mere bagatelle compared with what we have spent on our Cathedral – the debt on which is now entirely paid off, I am happy to say – ten, or at most twelve thousand pounds."

"It's a lot of money," said Father Molloy, balancing a spoon on the rim of his glass.

"It's a scheme that is worthy of your lordship," said Father Hardy, enthusiastically, "and shows how much you have at heart the best interests of your flock."

"The parish is so poor," said Ralph.

The bishop frowned. "You forget, Father O'Brien, that the people will be giving to God, Who can reward a hundredfold."

"Many haven't enough food for their children."

"You are young yet, Father O'Brien, and know little of the generosity of our people. They would give their last crust to the Church."

"Under the screw," said Father Dempsey, in a low voice.

"They're murmuring a good deal against the heavy charges. But if your lordship wants it, I dare say we can do it," said Father Molloy.

"It's a noble work – though it's not for me to speak," said Magan.

"No one has a better right," said the bishop, suavely. "Nothing could be more fitting than that we should build a Seminary to inaugurate the work of the most distinguished student the diocese has produced for many years."

Lanigan grimaced at Ralph.

"We must put our heads together in the name of God to see how we can get in the cash," Father Molloy said, sipping his punch, thoughtfully.

"The young priests, who owe the blessings of their sound education to the old Seminary, ought to be generous," said the bishop.

"At the most the priests will be good for no more than a few hundred pounds," said Father Molloy.

"We might utilise this new craze for the Irish language. We might hold out a hope of teaching Irish.... Father Lanigan knows the language," the bishop said doubtfully.

Dempsey became interested. "If you'd only make it a real Irish college, my lord, you'd get plenty of money."

"There's no money in that movement. Not a man with any money in Bunnahone gives a snap of his fingers for it," said Molloy, finishing his punch in a gulp.

"Don't be narrow, Father Molloy," the bishop said with a smile. "We must draw our net very wide; we should not commit ourselves definitely, of course – a hint or two would be enough, so as to secure the support of Charles Dillon and those who sympathise with his views."

"We'll have to depend for the bulk of the money on Darcy and Hinnissey and the like," said Father Molloy. "That reminds me, my lord, that we'll have to give them a hand against this co-operative movement. Hinnissey told me he lost hundreds of pounds last year through it. If we don't take their side, some day they'll leave us in the lurch. Donaghue came to see me last night and as much as said we owe them something for the help they've always given the Church, and I couldn't deny it. I think your lordship might come out against co-operation."

"Hum, hum," said the bishop, pursing his lips thoughtfully.

"Father Molloy can't be serious," said Ralph, looking at the bishop enquiringly. "Co-operation has given new life to the parish of Inniscar in a few years, and the improvement in the condition of the people is even more marked elsewhere, I'm told."

Father Molloy's eyes gleamed angrily. "I'd remind you, my lord, that your dues are drawn from town parishes, and if the shopkeepers in the towns are ruined, where will you be? and we too?" he said, looking around the table.

"Hear, hear," said Father Hardy.

The bishop waved his hands deprecatingly.

"It is a difficult situation," he said, "but there is no occasion for heat. A bishop must walk cautiously. Naturally my sympathies are with our good parishioners here, as you must know, Father Molloy. I want Father O'Brien to know too that I never lose sight of the fact that as bishop I am Father to all the people of the diocese. I shall consider the matter carefully, and I feel sure, with God's help, that I shall find a way to conciliate our shopkeeper friends without antagonising the co-operators. I shall discuss the matter with you, Father Molloy, when I have come to a decision.... To revert to the Seminary, I shall set the ball rolling in a sermon in the Cathedral on Sunday. There are some chapters of the prophet Aggæus on the building of the temple which will, I am sure, move the people to generosity. What is a Seminary if not a temple to God – the sacred abode where the mind of youth is first prepared in wisdom and knowledge for the service of the Most High?"

Ralph felt glad when he got into the street and breathed some fresh air, after the heavy fumes of the stuffy room. The priests walked along in a group.

"I don't know yet, long as I've known him," said Father Molloy, jerking his finger back at the bishop's house, "whether he's pretending or in earnest with all his religious talk. I doubt but this blessed Seminary will be the last straw. The people are kicking like the devil already. If we grab any more from them our own dues and mass offerings will be in danger."

"It's a shame to put such a job on us, and we only beginning in the parish," said Hardy, fretfully. "Why didn't you speak up against it, Molloy?"

"I thought you were in favour of it?" Molloy said slily.

Hardy laughed and said, "Catch me letting on to the lord what I thought about it."

"You'll get up early the day you make a catspaw of me," said Molloy, dryly.

"I dare say the Cathedral has pretty well drained the parish," said Hardy, tentatively.

"You may bet your life on it. It was all right for the big shopkeepers, but it broke a few of the small ones. They had to pretend to be as good as their neighbours – not paying would be admitting they were short of cash. So the Church got what the creditors should have got, and in the end there were some cases of bankruptcy."

"The Church might as well have it as the creditors any day," said Hardy.

"I don't know," Molloy said, musing. "It caused a lot of talk. People aren't nearly as biddable as they used to be."

Father Molloy pressed Ralph to go to the parochial house for a game of cards.

"It's the only proper way to finish off a dinner," he said heartily. Ralph excused himself on the plea of work.

"I'd advise you to take things easy," Molloy said seriously. "It's a bad thing to spoil the people by doing too much for them. If you go on as you're going, they'll be running to us at every turn, and we won't have a minute's peace. And – take a friend's advice – don't be airing these views of yours about co-operation in Bunnahone or you'll land yourself in a mess."

Instead of going home Ralph wandered through the streets. Faded women, worn out by childbearing and underfeeding, stood listlessly at the doors of miserable one-roomed hovels. In a street that led to the seaside the thatch had been blown off several houses. A few had been mended with old sacks, kept in place by huge stones, dangerous alike to the dwellers and passers-by. For the most part no attempt had been made at repairs. At the door of the only well-kept house in the street stood John Byrne, leaning against the door-post, smoking a long clay pipe.

"The storm last April!" he said, as he saw Ralph looking at the broken roofs. "The houses belong to Hinnissey and he's supposed to repair them. The creatures that live in them haven't the heart, even if they had the means, to do anything themselves. Coming on the winter, maybe, they'll put up an old bag; they don't give much heed to a drop of rain through the roof in the summer. The holes let in the air, too, and some of them pigstyes need it."

"Come along and get a breath of the sea," Ralph said.

"Father Tom wouldn't be too pleased to see you walking with me. I'm a marked man, I am."

"I should think I am free to walk with whom I please."

"You might then, and then you mightn't," Byrne said cautiously.

They walked along the top of a cliff, a high tide breaking on the rocks beneath. From the summit the little town seemed to nestle at their feet; lazy spirals of smoke ascended through a soft, thin windless haze. The sun lit the upper windows of the Convent of Mercy and was reflected off the roof of the Cathedral.

"How beautiful it looks," Ralph said.

"So does death," said Byrne, bitterly. "Would you tell me now what buildings you can make out from here?"

"The Cathedral, the two convents, the monastery, the asylum, the workhouse, the bishop's palace, the parochial house and, I think, the Emporium...."

"That's the history of the town in a nutshell. All that's left of the people after the Church has got her divide is the workhouse or the asylum. There's the Emporium, of course, and the other big shops. They wouldn't be long in it if they didn't pay up too. Instead of doing all the bleeding direct, the Church lets Hinnissey and his like bleed the people and then the priests bleed Hinnissey. My neighbours go without a roof to the houses that they're paying Hinnissey for. Hinnissey gave a thousand pounds to the new Cathedral. It's many a man Hinnissey and his like sent to the workhouse and the asylum; and in the end, in one way or another, their money finds its way to the Church. Hinnissey has only them two daughters of his. They were sent to some grand convent and they cock up their noses at their equals now and wouldn't think of marrying a decent man in their own station. When they're tired of tramping round after priests they'll enter a convent. That's always how the money of men like Hinnissey goes – to this church collection and to that, to fortune their daughters when they enter a convent; and, when the old people die, what's left – the priests take good care of that – is given for masses and churches and convents."

"You know you're exaggerating," said Ralph. "Why, I know dozens of priests who would do nothing of the kind – Father Sheldon, Father Duff, Father Dempsey here...."

"I'm not so far out at you think," Byrne said aggressively. "Look at the town fornint you, though the light of the sun is hiding the sores of it now; there isn't a trade in it nor an industry, and most of the money that was made by gombeening for the last hundred years is sunk in the clerical buildings you see before your eyes, or held in stocks and shares by priests and nuns and their relations. I'm not a fool and I don't say that every priest and nun is responsible. There isn't a finer woman in Ireland than the Reverend Mother at the Mercy Convent beyond. But what can she do, or the few decent priests you named, or even hundreds like them? The whole country is in the grip of the system and 'twould take a miracle to change it. Not but that I see a change coming," he added, his eyes gleaming.

"Have you come across a little paper of Mr Boyle's who used to be teaching at the Seminary here?" he asked.

Ralph nodded.

"I gather that the priests themselves in foreign parts are beginning to see the harm the Church is doing itself, and he hints that some priests in Ireland are thinking the same. Then there's that movement to revive the language. It won't do everything they claim for it, but it'll make the people think. And there's the co-operative movement. If that only goes on it'll be the end of the gombeen men and give the people some backbone. Then, if we get Home Rule to crown it all, the country might be able to make a fresh start."

"But there are priests helping in all these movements."

"They often joined in with the people in order to get control and direct things to their own ends," said Byrne, shaking his head sceptically. "It may be different now, but the proof of the pudding'll be in the eating. There may be something in what Mr Boyle says."

Ralph told him what Father Duff had done for co-operation, but could not move the old man from his fixed idea.

"One swallow don't make a summer. We'll see what we'll see," he said, again becoming despondent as he said "goodnight".

Chapter 18

RALPH SAT IN a back bench at the Cathedral at twelve o'clock mass on the following Sunday and heard the bishop announce the building of the new Seminary. It would be the pride of the town. The choicest blessings of God would descend on those who contributed to such a monument of piety, zeal and love of sacred learning.

"That's the last straw! more blood money," old Byrne said as he passed Ralph on his way out of the church. "I'll never darken the doors of that place again."

"What a beautiful sermon! thanks be to God," said Mrs Hinnissey. "Sure Thomas'll have to come down strong for such a noble work as that. What do you think now we ought to be giving, Father Ralph?"

Ralph strode forward several paces before her words penetrated his brain. He turned round to speak to her and caught a glimpse of her, for a moment, staring at him open-mouthed. The crowd emerging from the church door shut her off. He walked away quickly, his head down, and felt the blood rushing to his cheeks. His one thought was to get away from the tawdry church, from the bishop and the priests, from Bunnahone. Once during the sermon the strong sunlight penetrated the muddy red of a stained glass window and Byrne's words had occurred to him, "the blood of the poor". The garish brasses surrounding the altar, the vulgar lamps, the gorgeous vestments of the priest saying mass, the purple robes of the bishop standing smug and complacent in the pulpit, stone piled on stone in the lofty Cathedral – all were drawn by cajolery and threats from the blood and sinews of the unkempt wretches who crowded the aisles. Was his God the God of all this tinsel magnificence, who bedecked himself at the expense of hungry children and toiling underfed men and women?

He fell into a sort of stupor, and saw his life in a confused panorama: his school days, the Seminary, Maynooth, his ordination. As he gained the top of a hill overlooking the sea, a cool breeze fanned his cheeks and awakened him to a sense of his surroundings. He looked back and saw the Cathedral dominating the squalid houses of the town. Where was the Christ of the gospels?

Ralph walked on, unthinking of where the road led. Suddenly he felt more calm. He expanded his lungs and drew in deep breaths of exhilarating sea air. He settled down to a steady pace; the road became resilient. With springing steps he mounted the next short hill. Shackles had fallen from his limbs, he thought, and he stretched them with a confidence he had not felt for years. He thought again of his past, clearly and rapidly. Scales fell away from the eyes of his mind. The God he had been groping for was within him all the time. He had been in the hearts of those who sought Him from the beginning. Christ came to point out the way anew. He was the Way, the Truth and the Life, disclosing new treasures as the minds of men grew and their hearts expanded.

He thought of the Seminary and laughed aloud. Yet it was no laughing matter. *E pur si muove*. The spirit of God moved and grew on earth, notwithstanding the vain attempts of men to check it. An out-of-date man-made theology could as little narrow the idea of God as it could, by a foolish decree, stop the earth and the sun in their courses.

He smiled as the image of the bishop in the pulpit came back to him, with uplifted hand, denouncing modern learning. Poor cramped narrow mind and feeble hand. He pictured him standing on the rocks at his feet, with raised hand, ordering back the incoming tide. It was incredibly foolish, but it was sad, too. A church that was a true Church, garnering and distributing all the spiritual riches of her children, could do so much for the real life of the world. But instead of being a light, this Church that claimed his allegiance cast a pall over the mind, set up barriers instead of breaking them down, drove men out instead opening her gates wide: men cried aloud for bread and were offered stones.

The fault lay not only with her theology and philosophy, but with her whole spirit. Not only were the minds of her children fettered, but their hearts were crushed. Love and pity had flown away with knowledge. A monstrous organisation, self-seeking, material, thinking only of itself, had taken the place of the men of God whose lives manifested the God they experienced.

"What am I doing in this Church?" he said aloud. He pondered his life again. It was clearly his way to the truth. The leaven of holiness still worked in the Church, in odd out-of-the-way places, and he had picked up a crumb of food here and there. Decrees and dogmas and laws and regulations had not killed all life. The immense complex machine of Pope, cardinals, curia, ecclesiastical officials, bishops, priests and nuns, dead and mechanical for the most part, had here and there a wheel, instinct with the life of the spirit, that kept in touch with the growing needs of humanity.

His duty was to stay where he was, to work for the growth of the spirit, to do his best to bring back the Church to a sense of its mission. He had hitherto been merely receptive, influenced by the opinion of others. He felt that he had now discovered his mind; that he must use it, not merely as a help towards his own spiritual growth, but for the benefit of others who were seeking their way blindly. He was ignorant and ill-informed and could not hope to do much, but he would work with all the powers of his mind and will, of his whole being, to know God and make Him known.

He had been conscious for some time of the beautiful early autumn colouring of the trees and hedgerows, but, until he found himself on a low hill overlooking Father Sheldon's house, he had taken no notice of locality. He had not eaten since early morning, and suddenly felt hungry. He hesitated for a moment and felt a shrinking from speech with anyone. Father Sheldon was different from most people. He would be sympathetic.

Father Sheldon's midday meal had been cleared away, but he insisted on getting Ralph some food, to be followed by tea, to which some visitors at the de Lacey's, a Mr Harley, a well-known author, and a Mr Ross, a prominent government official from Dublin, were expected.

Father Sheldon spoke little while Ralph ate some sandwiches.

"Quite settled down to work now?" he said, when Ralph had finished.

Ralph looked worried.

"I suppose I do some work," he said, "but I can hardly say I'm settled."

"What's wrong?"

"I hardly know. For the first time in my life I have done some thinking on my own account, and it's the reverse of settling."

"A dangerous occupation for a priest," said Father Sheldon, smiling.

"During this morning's walk I have shed so many official views that I think the bishop would say I deserved excommunication."

"I thought it would come to that," said Father Sheldon, gently.

"The curious thing is," said Ralph, "that the more I seem to lay myself open to external censure, the nearer I seem to have come to a vital religion that satisfies me."

"Thank God," said Father Sheldon, fervently. "There is always the danger of confounding the kernel and the husk, and rejecting both together; I am glad you escaped it."

"You have been through all this?" Ralph asked eagerly.

"Long ago."

"And felt that you could continue to work as a priest?"

Father Sheldon nodded gravely. "I had doubts as to whether I could stay on. Was I right or was the official Church right? I had to decide according to my conscience. Fortunately at the time the officials had put themselves hopelessly in the wrong by their decree of Papal infallibility. If they were right religion meant nothing to me. But it was my very life," he added gently. "It was more easy to believe that a number of interested officials could go wrong than that Christ had lived in vain...."

He was interrupted by the arrival of Harley and Ross.

Ross, a slightly built man with furtive grey eyes and a brown beard, greeted the priest effusively. Harley looked at Ralph curiously when he heard his name, a cynical smile on his lips.

"Your mother has been trying to convert me," he said as he shook hands. "I wish she could," with a thin smile. "All my life I have longed for the sensation of religion, but I haven't the temperament."

"This is all a pose of Harley's," said Ross, jauntily. "Take no notice of him, Father Sheldon. He's really a Catholic."

"Never have been," said Harley, holding up a plump well-manicured hand, a look of horror in his faded blue-grey eyes. "I was labelled a Catholic as a child, but I have never believed in anything. Unless," he added, looking maliciously at Ross, "you mean by a

Catholic one who believes in nothing."

"You shouldn't jest on such subjects," Ross said angrily, his pointed beard shooting out, "especially before priests. They might misunderstand. I'm glad to say that I'm a good Catholic and I'm proud to proclaim it in these days of infidelity."

"He lunched with the bishop yesterday," said Harley. "Ross always grovels before bishops. They make the work of his Board easy. He's an extra good Catholic when he's under the eye of a bishop."

"Your mother interested me," he added, addressing Ralph. "All Catholics interest me. There are so many varieties. The de Lacey's, your father, Father Sheldon here, Ross a little, but your mother very much. She believes in real material fire in hell. She was very nice to me, but I could see that she believed I should burn there one day."

"Don't be flippant," said Ross.

"Ross hates a religious discussion," Harley continued coolly. "He never read a book on religion in his life."

"I believe everything the Church teaches."

"What does it teach?" Harley asked.

Ross shrugged his shoulders. "Harley is incorrigible," he said to Father Sheldon. "By the way, Father, your good bishop told me that he is building a new Seminary. I was glad to be able to promise him some help from my Board by way of equipment."

"Towards determining how many angels infinitely compressible can stand on the point of a needle infinitely small," said Harley.

"Dr Devoy is a very shrewd politician," said Ross, ignoring Harley.

"Ah, there you were on common ground, more familiar to both of you than either religion or education," said Harley.

A desultory conversation was kept up during tea, Harley making a butt of Ross.

When they had gone, Father Sheldon gave a sigh of relief. "Harley by himself is interesting," he said; "Ross makes him stupid. Not that Ross would not make anyone stupid. He is, however, a type – a so-called educated Catholic. Successive English governments, both Tory and Liberal, take their views of Catholic Ireland from a few official Catholics in Dublin, of whom Ross is chief. He owes his place to the influence of the bishops and keeps it by fawning on them. He hasn't a conviction on any subject. Mainly through his influence, the power of the bishops in civil administration in Ireland is enormous. He persuades the government that the bishops hold the people in their hands; that if the bishops are placated by an appointment here and a grant there, the people will be quiet. It is a theory that has had many shocks lately. But Ross, from saying it so often, has come to believe it himself. Some day his house of cards will tumble about his ears."

"But our bishop is a Home Ruler," said Ralph.

Father Sheldon smiled. "The bishop is a thorough upholder of the present Roman system of Church government – absolutist, as in the days of the emperors. Ross said that Dr Devoy is a shrewd politician. He is, in a modern sense, which confounds the word with a degraded sort of tactics. Roman absolutism and democracy are incompatible. When he gives a colourless patronage to Home Rule, he is the shrewd politician Ross so much admires, appearing to bless what he hates, for the sake of some temporary advantage. That a Roman Catholic bishop believing in the present deplorable regime of the Church, as Devoy undoubtedly does, could be a Home Ruler, is a hopeless contradiction."

Ralph moved his head up and down helplessly.

"We have got to face facts," said Father Sheldon, gravely. "I am in sympathy with the new movement in philosophy and theology, but for their full expression they need an entirely new conception of the Church – a Church that feels and voices the aspirations and ideals of every man of good-will in the world. At times I am full of hope. Again I am in depths of despair. When I think of the present iron-bound autocracy, drunk with power, wedded to a theology and a philosophy divorced from religion as well as from life, founded on authority and devised to maintain it – an autocracy, for every member of which, from the humblest curate to the Pope, success in life, power, honour, even bread and butter, depends on presenting a solid front to a derisive world and on crushing ruthlessly internal dissensions, hope dies in me. I thank God that I have a quiet corner to work in here, obscure enough to save me from interference as long as I keep my opinions to myself....

"This is a long-winded speech," he added, laughing. "You are young, and there is no reason why you should be depressed. The people have faith and are not bothered by medieval intellectual abstractions."

"There are some who have begun to think and to question," Ralph said.

"Be honest with them. Tell them that you yourself are groping in the dark, trying to find expression for what can never adequately be expressed. Be gentle with the bruised reed and the smoking flax."

"I intend to write in Boyle's paper," said Ralph, abruptly.

Father Sheldon looked out of the window, thoughtfully.

"When a crisis comes, we all find ourselves alone," he said, after a few minutes' silence. "We are tossed backwards and forwards like shuttlecocks; a hundred obscure influences act and re-act on us. No one knows the impulses of another's heart. Our most momentous decision must be taken by ourselves. May God be with you in yours...."

The sun had set when Ralph got up to go. Father Sheldon was preoccupied as he accompanied him to the gate.

"Have you been home lately?" he asked, hesitatingly, as Ralph said goodbye.

"No," said Ralph. Noticing the priest's manner, he asked, "Why?"

"I'm told your father is not well. You ought to see him, I think."

Two months before, Ralph, who had never known illness in his family, would have taken the announcement calmly, but his recent experiences of death made him nervous and uneasy.

"I ought to go now?"

"No. It is late. Better call tomorrow, casually. There is no immediate danger, as far as I know...."

Next day, Ralph went to Inniscar for luncheon. A drizzling rain swept in from the sea and gave a gloomy look to the grounds. The avenue was strewn with fallen leaves and the house looked grey and forbidding.

Hilda was pale and restless.

"I am glad you have come," she said. "Your father hasn't been well. Something is on his mind. He is very odd in manner. I shall let him know you are here."

Ralph paced up and down the drawing-room, full of forebodings. The stillness of the house made him nervous.

Hilda came back with signs of tears on her face.

"He won't see you," she said in a strained tone. "He has been moody for months; just lately, since you went to Bunnahone, he has become worse. It is only something temporary. Say mass for him. I pray constantly and I'm sure everything will come right soon."

Ralph tried to get some particulars, but she was vague and inconsequent, always winding up, "Let us both pray for him. Prayer will work wonders. God will make him all right in a short time."

Luncheon seemed interminable. Ralph could hear the faint sounds of feet pacing quickly in the bedroom overhead – his father's room. "I must go to him," Hilda said, after luncheon. "He relies on me more than ever, and likes to have me with him."

Ralph drove to see Father Duff and found him at dinner. He looked worried when Ralph entered.

"My father?" Ralph said.

"Oh, it's only some passing strangeness." He fidgeted with the back of his chair. "You'll have some dinner."

"I've just had luncheon. Do sit down; don't let me interrupt you."

Father Duff ate in silence for a minute.

"It's better to be straight about it," he said, laying down his knife and fork. "Your mother told you nothing?"

"Very little."

The old priest touched his head with his hand. "Some weakness here. I saw it coming on," he said sadly, "and he only a young man too, sixty or so. If it was a useless old man like me, there'd be some understanding it."

"Why wouldn't he see me?"

"That's the pity of it. It's all you. It broke his heart, you to become a priest. I often saw signs of it for the last few years, but it didn't come home to him entirely till you went to Bunnahone. The creamery kept his mind off it for a while, but not for long. He used to wander about the fields. 'What's the use of me doing anything?' he'd say, if I met him, 'when Ralph'll turn the place into a monastery? But I'll prevent that,' he'd say ... I wouldn't be surprised," Father Duff added, after a pause, "if he has willed the place away from you. I don't know for certain, but I do know he has been seeing his solicitor."

"It is his not seeing me that troubles me," Ralph said anxiously, "not the place."

"I'm sorry I ever lived to see this day," the old priest said, shaking his head. "There's no use in me trying to conceal it. He has taken a dislike to you. Until this fit passes he won't hear of seeing you. He has got it firmly into his head that you are intriguing to get Inniscar for the Church."

"My God!" said Ralph, "if he only knew." He leant his arms on the mantlepiece, his head between his hands.

"Don't take it to heart," said the old man, gently, laying his hand on Ralph's shoulder. "I was always agin the idea of you being a priest, always agin it ... I knew no luck'd come of it," he murmured to himself.

For weeks the shadow of his father's estrangement was between Ralph and his work. It had come as a complete shock to him. He had always taken it for granted that his father wished him to be a priest. Yet, had he known the truth, could things have been otherwise? Had he been carried down the current of life, like the little piece of wood he watched from the bridge in the convent grounds, bobbing about in the rapid stream, stopped by a branch here and there, but making inevitably for the open sea? Or could he have swum aside, or against the stream? It was almost impossible to disentangle the past. Every crisis in life, when he dwelt on it now, was coloured by his present thought. It was all an insoluble puzzle.

He called again at Inniscar, but did not see his father. Hilda said, hesitatingly, as he was leaving, "Pray for strength ... but ... I think it would be better if you didn't come again until I send for you. It disturbs him so much to hear that you come."

Ralph bit his lip, but said cheerfully, "All right, Mother, I won't come."

"It can't be long now, with all our prayers," she said.

He worked very early and late, visiting the sick, straining every nerve to help all who asked his assistance in any way, seeking out those who were in trouble. He never left the parish, and as he was to be found easily - he always told Ann where to send for him, in the expectation of a summons to Inniscar - most of the parish work fell to his lot. The inexplicable gulf that divided him from his father made him take infinite pains in adjusting even the most trivial misunderstandings. The dumb patience and resignation of many of the poor he visited made him long for a nature like theirs, that accepted the rough and the smooth of life as an unquestioned destiny.

Boyle wrote several times, pressing for copy. But he couldn't write.

All controversy seemed so futile. Nothing mattered but work. He frequented the school, taught a class, helped to mend the maps and managed to inspire Grogan with zeal for painting the doors and windows. He called to know why children were kept at home from school and often led them there. Every day he went to the workhouse and sat for hours listening to wandering tales that led nowhere, save to the present happiness of the teller in having a patient listener. He helped Father Lanigan with his Greek....

He told no one of his father's illness. Ann accused him of being an unnatural son for not going home oftener. "You're making yourself too cheap," she said angrily, "fetching and carrying for everyone." He smiled grimly. The round of petty duties, if it did not bring happiness, at least distracted his mind and, to some extent, kept him from brooding.

Chapter 19

FATHER MOLLOY CALLED on Ralph one morning in November and sat in front of the study fire, smiling and rubbing his hands gleefully.

"What a power of books you have. I never have time to read much myself. I make a point of reading the *Freeman's Journal* every day, and that's enough for any man. By the way, you're not a politician? You ought to join the League."

"I know very little about politics."

Father Molloy laughed boisterously. "Who wants to know?" he said. "Pay your shilling as a member, and there you are. Why, every man is a born politician. I'm in great fettle today," he added, giving a sigh of satisfaction; "the bishop has played trumps. You remember me telling him a long time ago that Donaghue and Hinnissey were kicking agin us for not denouncing the co-operative movement? Well, the bishop sent for me today and gave me ten pounds' subscription towards the League, not as a member – he was quite clear about that – but as a sign of his moral support."

"Well?"

"You must be very dense. Can't you see the point of it? Why, man alive, the League in Bunnahone is Donaghue and Hinnissey and their friends."

"I am afraid I am dense, for I don't see the point of the bishop's subscription."

"Can't you see that he doesn't want to attack co-operation directly, but it's like a wink to a blind man that the lord won't mind if the League gives it a dig."

"But the League is a farmers' movement to secure a better system of land tenure."

"What a simpleton you are! It may be that elsewhere, but in Bunnahone it's different. The first duty of every man is to protect himself, and why shouldn't the Bunnahone shopkeepers do it?"

"But it's using the farmers' movement to attack themselves. I am quite sure the bishop wouldn't countenance anything of the kind."

"That's where he's so clever," said Molloy, admiringly. "He subscribes to the League – that pleases the farmers; but he subscribes to the Bunnahone branch, and that satisfies the Bunnahone shopkeepers – he knocks down two birds with one stone."

"It seems dishonest."

"It's damn cute, I admit. But sure a man couldn't live if he hadn't his wits about him these days. You had better join the League, too. All the priests in the town are in it except Dempsey. He has a bee in his bonnet over that nonsensical Irish and takes no interest in anything else."

"I'm in favour of co-operation. I couldn't possibly join the League if things are as you say."

"You can easily get out of that difficulty. You needn't pretend to know – you can go on the bishop's tack."

"But I do know. You have told me. I subscribe to the funds of the co-operative movement, and I shall certainly not join a League that is bent on wrecking it."

"For God's sake keep these views dark here," said Father Molloy, earnestly. "For your own sake as well as ours. If it got out that you were a co-operator sorra much mass offerings you'd get; and it's likely enough we'd all be made suffer too, for the shopkeepers might take it into their heads to boycott the dues on account of you."

He looked around the room disapprovingly.

"I never knew much good to come out of books," he said sadly. "Your head is moidered with them, and they put all sorts of queer notions into you. When you're on the mission a while you'll get more sense. Them views of yours would suit in a country parish very well, but they're nothing but foolishness in a town like this.... Have you a bottle of beer handy? My throat is dry with all my talking to you."

Ralph got him some beer. He smacked his lips after a long draught.

"I rather like you," he said, looking at Ralph through half shut thick eyelids. "I feel I can speak my mind openly to you without any fear of your running round with tales behind my back like that little Hardy, who's always buttering me to my face and sticking a knife in me when he gets the chance. He hopes to get my job here, but I can tell you I wasn't born yesterday."

He frowned and finished the beer.

"That was good. What was I saying? Oh, that I had an interest in you. Well, so I have. You can't expect me to stick to you if you make difficulties in the parish, but as long as you go along quietly I'm your friend. That's the trick for a young man – to lie low. Always keep an eye on the bishop and say ditto to all his views. Don't offend any parishioners that keep the purse fairly open. You'd be all the better for taking a drink now and then, it makes a man more mellow. Let sleeping dogs lie. Live and let live is my motto as long as a man doesn't interfere with me. Come to me when you're in doubt about anything and I'll advise you. I've weathered many a storm in my day and no man knows better how to steer an even keel. Be said by me now to start with and give up this co-operative business if you don't want to play the devil with yourself from the beginning."

Ralph shook his head.

"Keep a quiet tongue in your sconce then, but it's a bad beginning. And they're a bit suspicious of you because your father is mixed up with the movement. However, I'll see what I can do," he added, as he left the room. "I'll head Donaghue off asking you to join the League by telling him a young man on his first mission has a power of prayers to say. Ta, ta," he said, waving his hand.

"Well, Ann, how are you liking Bunnahone?" he said to the servant, whom he met in the hall.

"So, so," said Ann, grimly.

She banged the door after him. "It's a power of glasses I'll have washed after him before I've done," she said, as she removed the tray.

Ralph went on reading.

"All the same, I wish you'd wear nice shiny clothes and a natty silk hat, like he does. You aren't nearly respectable enough looking," she said aggressively. "I never seen a priest in Dublin in the likes of that little soft hat you wear."

"I'm only a country curate," Ralph said, smiling.

"It's I have to bear the brunt of it. 'Twas only yesterday the servant at the parochial house cast it in my face that the heels were worn off your boots, and Father Molloy always that spick and span," she said, "and Father Hardy like as if he came out of a bandbox. And the bishop's housekeeper tries to treat me as the dirt underneath her feet. It isn't much of a help you're to me to keep my head high among them," she said with a break in her voice.

"There's that bell again," she added, rushing off. "It never stops ringing from morning till night. They think that a priest has nothing to do but be always at their beck and call."

Ralph heard voices in the hall, Ann's in loud welcome, followed by a low murmur from the visitor.

"My God! my God! and me never to hear a word of it," Ann shrieked at the top of her voice.

Ralph felt it must be news of his father and rushed out. Ann was rocking to and fro, wailing, her apron held to her eyes with both hands.

"Shut up, woman, and have sense," Father Duff said gruffly. He held out his hand silently to Ralph.

"He wants to see you at last," he said gently.

"That's splendid," Ralph said, his face lighting up joyfully.

"But he's dying, I'm afeared," Father Duff added gravely.

Ralph watched the corded veins in the cold hand of the old priest. His eyes wandered to the aged face, purple with cold, the shrunken jaws shaking. What a grotesque old figure it was in the shabby grey frieze coat.

"You should have told me and not let it come on me all of a sudden like this," Ann said reproachfully from the background.

"Bear up, man. I've a car at the door. We have need to hurry," Father Duff said, shaking Ralph's arm.

He mechanically put on the coat Ann held out.

"Put on your hat," the old priest said.

"He took to his bed two days ago, and the change came this morning. I hurried to you as quickly as the old mare could go," the old priest said, after a long silence, urging the horse to his best pace.

Ralph's eyes were fixed on a gleam of light that turned the withered bracken to a bright yellow gold. He sought for the break in the murky clouds through which the light came and felt a sense of relief when he found it. He counted the stakes in a wire fence on the roadside. What a pretty pattern the bare branches of the beeches made against the leaden sky.

"Is there any hope?" he asked, as Father Duff slowed up to enter the gate at Inniscar.

"Except a miracle," he replied, flicking the horse with his whip.

"I'll run up and see how he is first. You wait here," said the old priest when they stood in the hall.

Ralph smiled at the phrase as he watched the old man climb painfully and slowly up the stairs.

He looked at some prints, which he had known from childhood, as if they were new.

Hilda came down the stairs quickly.

"God has heard us," she said. "Come at once. He asks for you every minute."

John O'Brien lay in bed, half sitting up, propped with pillows. Ralph was shocked by his appearance, aged, thin, black hollows under his eyes, a rough grey stubble of several days' growth on his cheeks and chin, his lips a blue purple. At the sound of footsteps he opened his eyes and looked round enquiringly: seeing Ralph he smiled faintly and held out his hand. He shut his eyes again, Ralph's hand in his, breathing stertorously and with evident difficulty. Hilda, standing beside Ralph, watched him anxiously. After a minute she pressed a little globule between his lips.

"His heart," she whispered.

Almost at once he breathed naturally and opened his eyes.

"Don't keep Eva waiting long," he said sharply.

Ralph looked puzzled.

"Eva Dillon," he said, "she's fond of you. Oh! I noticed it. She has been waiting for you and you've been avoiding her. There's no one else that you prefer?" he asked wistfully.

"No," said Ralph, conscious only of the expectant look in his father's eyes.

"There's no reason why you shouldn't marry at once," John O'Brien murmured, after a few moments' pause. "Your mother thought you would be a priest, but I knew better."

He sank back exhausted. Hilda grew livid. She turned to Father Duff, who stood by the window.

"Absolve him again, Father. It is some terrible mistake. He hasn't really forgiven Ralph at all. It is all too dreadful, too dreadful!"

She knelt beside the bed and sobbed aloud.

Ralph withdrew his hand from his father's clasp.

"Call the doctor. He's in the drawing-room," Father Duff said, bending over the bed.

"He's dead." The doctor said, after a long examination.

Hilda became hysterical. She clung to Father Duff's soutane.

"Say he's not lost, Father! God would not send him to hell after all my prayers. God understands that he wasn't quite in his right mind. It is dreadful! Not to forgive his son for becoming a priest!"

Father Duff tried to console her, saying that he knew no better man than her husband.

"Perhaps it's only purgatory, then!" she said, gazing at the dead body with a look of terror. "I shall pray and pray and have masses said that God may forgive him."

She was persuaded with difficulty to leave the room, but insisted on being allowed to go to the chapel, where she knelt in tears before the altar.

"Go and take a walk. I'll see to everything," Father Duff said to Ralph.

He wandered from room to room and sat for a long time in his father's study. Only momentarily, at long intervals, did he think of his father as dead, and then, vaguely and remotely, with a feeling not unlike that of a physical hunger. He thought of their long walks together around Dublin. The incidents of the night they were lost on the mountain stood out vividly. Why should religion separate a son from a father? What a lonely life his father must have led with those thoughts of Ralph's marriage shut up in his heart, unsuspected by Ralph himself or by Hilda. His father was right. He had avoided Eva Dillon. He had long since risen above those feelings that had troubled him so much in regard to her in the past.

He went for a long walk across country and home by the sands in a vain effort to shake off his depression.

It was dark when he got back to Inniscar. The bishop's victoria stood before the door. Ralph found him in the drawing-room having tea alone.

"Your mother wished to come in, but I wouldn't allow her. She's a great saint. I saw her in the chapel for a few minutes. Of course, you mustn't think of coming back to work until the funeral is over," he said. "You must have something to eat."

Ralph took a cup of tea.

The bishop resumed his artificial manner. "I suppose he had arranged all his affairs? The will, etc., all right?"

Ralph shook his head vaguely. "I don't know," he said, after a pause.

Dr Devoy looked at him keenly. "Naturally you will get the property," he said. "It will be a great responsibility. A priest can do a lot of good with a patrimony. Your first duty, of course, will be to the Church.... But we mustn't talk of these things now." He added, rising, "I had a verbal message from Father Duff asking permission for masses here. I thought I would show the respect I feel for your good family by coming at once myself," he said, as he buttoned his coat in the hall. "Your mother is a woman of great faith. She has commissioned me to get a great number of masses said. I shall say mass here myself tomorrow."

He turned back on the doorstep. "Miss Eva Dillon is a cousin of yours?" he said.

Ralph nodded.

"She entered the Mercy Convent this morning. But I suppose you have heard. She will be a great acquisition. Goodnight."

Ralph stood watching the carriage move rapidly down the avenue. "Thank God," he said aloud, as the glow of the lamps were hidden by the trees. "I'm glad my father was wrong."

The evening before the funeral, as Ralph sat in the study, Father Duff limped in. His face was drawn and he wandered about without sitting down.

"You shouldn't have come out again. Your rheumatism is so bad," Ralph said.

"I couldn't rest at home," he said, looking at Ralph, sadly. "It's your father's will. He made me executor. Driscoll, the solicitor, came to me about it an hour ago."

"What's wrong?"

"Everything is wrong. Everything is left absolutely to your mother and you're not mentioned in it. He tore up the old will, in which the place was left to you, about two months ago. I can hardly believe it of John."

Ralph looked thoughtfully at the fire.

"What does the will matter?" he said, turning to Father Duff with a smile. "He died good friends with me. I am glad everything is left to my mother. I shouldn't have disturbed her in any case, but it's much better that she should feel that the place is hers. I have about a hundred a year of my own and that's more than I need."

"It's well you have that itself, for it's very little of the place'll be left when it comes to your turn," the old priest said angrily. "She's throwing money round like water for masses already and there's no knowing where she'll stop."

Ralph frowned.

Father Duff looked at him pitifully. "Don't get vexed at anything I say. I'd be the last to cast a reflection on John's wife and I'd put up with her religious vagaries for his sake, but I don't like to see ducks and drakes made of Inniscar. What came over John I don't know. No one knew better than him that every penny your mother ever laid hold of went to the priests. They'll be after her like a pack of hounds. 'Twas only today the bishop asked me if your father remembered the Seminary in his will. He's her confessor, too, by the same token."

"As executor you'll be able to influence her," Ralph said soothingly. "I shall help you."

"Listen to me! She'd as soon as listen to the door-post. An old farmer, she thinks I am. And sure no one knows better than myself that I'm not much more. No, it's lads with oily tongues like the bishop she'll be said by. Signs on it she might find herself without a roof over her head some day."

Ralph felt hurt that his mother should be discussed in this way, but he could not stop the old priest without offending him.

"I'll go down into my grave regretting that you ever joined the Church.... But what's the use of talking now? My car is waiting for me. Poor John! he was like a son to me when he was a lad! and to think of him lying a corpse upstairs now and me that broken and cranky that I'm good for nothing," he said, limping out of the room.

The bishop and several priests said mass in the house on the morning of the funeral.

"It is somewhat informal," the bishop said, "but in the case of such an excellent Catholic as Mrs O'Brien, I dispense with the regulations.

"I have heard about your father's will," he said to Ralph. "I think it was very wise of him. After all, a property like this might prove embarrassing to you. Your mother will be sure to make good use of it. God will be sure to guide such a holy woman aright."

Ralph longed to have an end to the ceremonies. Everything seemed to jar on him. He almost lost patience with his mother, who had some question to ask every time he met her as to the effect of a mass on the duration of his father's sufferings in purgatory.

As he said his thanksgiving in the little sacristy, he heard Father Hardy whisper to Father Molloy, "Will they expect a free job on account of O'Brien being a priest?"

"Not at all," Father Molloy replied. "It'll be two pound a head at least for us and there'll be picking afterwards in the way of mass offerings from the widow."

"Hush!" said Hardy, "O'Brien there might hear you."

"No fear," said Father Molloy. "He's going about half-dazed like. I doubt it's because he has lost the place."

"It'd put any man in a temper," Hardy said.

"Let us trot out to breakfast. I'm half starved."

Ralph's thoughts went back to the first death he had witnessed. No string of priests had said masses for Mrs Reardon's soul. Did God discriminate between her and his father because in her case there was no one to pay "two pounds a head"? How his father would have smiled cynically at such a question! Why had he shut himself off from his father? Life had no place for vain regrets. There was no recapturing the past even if death had not intervened. Then this travesty over a soul! He saw vividly Father Molloy at the altar, vulgar, inattentive, rushing hurriedly through a mass.... He should never know the cause that led to his father's strange mania. Of one thing he was sure – there was no break in his affection for himself. In some blind way he was battling against a wrong.... He smiled as he thought of the result. Inniscar, that his father hoped to save from the priests, would go to them now.... He felt a profound pity for his mother. All her generous and kindly feelings were dried up by what was worst in the religion she professed. Fear had shut out love....

He went into the chapel and knelt beside her. He could hear her murmuring, her head buried in her hands, "Have mercy on him, Lord; have mercy on him." Father Sheldon was saying mass with grave reverence. Father Devine knelt in a side bench, his eyes fixed vacantly on the tabernacle in rapt attention. Father Duff sat near by, his elbows on his knees, his gnarled hands supporting his shaking head, his eyes fixed vacantly on the coffin, which stood on a bier in front of the altar. The bishop, in purple soutane and rochet, knelt erect at a prie-dieu within the sanctuary, reading his breviary, glancing now at his watch, again at Father Sheldon whose slow fervour delayed the mass. It was a wonderful Church, with its Molloys and Sheldons, its Hardys and Devines, its holiness and hypocrisy, its kindness and its cruelty, its faith and its indifference, its piety and impiety! Could the muddy waters ever be made clear? Could the poor crushed kernel ever be made free of the overgrown petrified husk? Was a synthesis possible? His father in some dim way had discerned the evil, had put off fighting against it and, when too late, had delivered a pitifully feeble stroke, vain and impotent.

Ralph stared at the bishop, cool and confident, typical of the worldly security of the organisation that must be revolutionised if the spirit of God was to grow. Was it possible to break down that dominion? To substitute holiness for power and service for authority? What had this purple magnificence to do with the religion that took shape in men's hearts beside the sea of Galilee? Yet ... he shuddered. The cold of the chapel, which made his fingers tingle, seemed to touch his heart. All that was hard and narrow and rigid - all that was evil - in the Church, had succeeded in hypnotising the great multitude into the belief that this man-made organisation was the sole depository of holiness, the fount from which alone the divine spirit flowed to the heart. Not only had it the support of self-seekers, of the wise of this world who sought careers, but of the ignorant many, holy and unholy, who accepted its claim without question, because it was put forward in the name of Christ. Father Devine would fight for it even more ardently than Hardy.

Why, he asked himself, had he become a priest? For the Way, the Truth and the Life. He clenched his cold hands. Then his duty was clear. Failure mattered nothing. God was with him. There could be no failure. He might break his head against the solid barrier of this organised denial of the spirit, but his own spirit would be free. The kingdom of God had one more adherent - and who could tell? The way might be opened to many others.

Father Devine met him in the hall near the dining-room door.

"God comfort you," he said, pressing Ralph's hand kindly.

They could hear Father Molloy's boisterous laugh from the dining-room and Father Hardy's squeaky "Hear, hear."

Ralph looked into Devine's honest eyes, wondering if he would ever understand.

Father Hardy said "Hush" as they entered the room. Father Molloy stopped in the middle of a story he was narrating with elaborate gesture. Two strange priests stood up and shook hands with Ralph, murmuring a few words of conventional sympathy.

"The lord is praying a long time," said Hardy, looking at his watch.

"It's that Sheldon takes half the day to say a mass," said Father Molloy. "The lord'll be in a nice temper at being kept waiting for his breakfast. I wouldn't be in Sheldon's shoes for a good deal, and he the cause of it. My time for a dead mass is thirteen minutes and for an ordinary, credo and gloria and all, sixteen minutes. I think that takes some beating."

"I can do it myself in a minute less," said Hardy, superciliously.

"You're a little wonder, you are," said Father Molloy, with a sneer. "Well, Devine, how do you like your exile in that country parish at the back of God speed?"

"I'm very happy," said Devine, simply. "The people are very nice to me."

"I was there for a spell," said Hardy. "I used to throw purgatory at them every Sunday, and I can tell you the mass offerings were pretty decent before I left."

The arrival of the bishop made a dead silence. Ralph slipped away quietly and with difficulty induced his mother to leave the chapel.

"There are no more masses," he said.

"In that case perhaps I may leave," she said doubtfully. "He must be feeling much easier after all the masses. I have had a talk with Driscoll and I am having twenty masses said by each priest in the diocese and a hundred by the Carmelites in Dublin. Driscoll tells me John left the place to me. I shall make the best use of it I can for the good of his soul."

She insisted on taking part in the funeral, and Ralph drove her. He was touched by the evident grief of the tenantry, who carried the coffin on their shoulders to the graveyard in the ruined church, which for many centuries had been the burial-place of the O'Briens of Inniscar. Marshalled four deep, with white scarfs and hat streamers, they bore the coffin in turns.

The bishop read the service at the graveside. Ralph supported his mother, who wept silently.

"He had the heart of a child," Teig Moriarty said, as the earth was shovelled into the grave.

"Poor woman! No wonder she'd cry, but sure she has her son left," an old man said aloud.

Ralph stared dry eyed into the fast filling grave. He felt his heart contract as he heard the words. Was his father in the grave nearer to him than his mother, whose body, palpitating with sobs, rested on his arm? His arm closed around her tenderly and the grave was blotted out in a mist of tears.

Chapter 20

BUNNAHONE HAD LITTLE charm in the brightest days of summer, but on wet winter evenings it seemed to Ralph to be the dreariest place on earth. The prevailing south-west wind raked the main street from end to end, driving a sleety rain before it in gusts. Dim lamps marked the outlines of the street but gave no help in avoiding loose flags in the paved footway. An incautious step and a squirt of icy water covered one from head to heel. Nor was the road, ankle deep in mud, any safer. Occasional efforts at street cleaning never went farther than sweeping the mud into heaps alongside the footways, to be dispersed again by the rain. The sole means of escape from the muddy water of the pavement was to step into the watery mud of the street. Yet on the wettest nights men braved the elements to escape from their dismal cabins, compared with which the public houses, dingy, dirty and depressing, were havens of light and comfort. They, at least, gave shelter from wind and rain and were the only social resource of the town.

During many a walk through the streets at night Ralph pondered the social problem of the parish. Every avenue of escape from the existing condition seemed to be blocked by a dead wall. The little town had no industries and lived by sponging on the surrounding agricultural population. Well-organised, educated farmers would do their own business instead of having their buying and selling done by Bunnahone shopkeepers inefficiently and at enormous cost. The farmers were waking up to this. When they were fully aware of it Bunnahone must disappear, or set up an industrial life of its own.

The vision of half a dozen men in every public house, sitting listlessly over half-emptied pots of porter, suggested a fresh line of thought. He had no puritanical objection to drink, but he knew the men whom he saw sitting there night after night. He knew their homes, their families and their wages. From a wage of ten or twelve shillings a week, a drink or two meant a wife or child going without a meal. A couple of drinks every night might bring serious consequences.

The thought of a club first struck him as he stood one wet night opposite Darcy's brightly lit public house. He felt, as he looked at the men drinking by the fire in the bar, that it was attractive and cosy. But it was too expensive for Pat Gallagher, who stood by the counter, waving a pewter pot and haranguing the men seated at the fire. He knew Gallagher did not care for drink, that he liked discussing what he called "affairs of the nation" and came to Darcy's for company. A workmen's club would give Gallagher and others like him the resource they needed without endangering the happiness and comfort of a wife and family.

Full of this thought Ralph went direct to John Byrne's cottage and found him on his work-stool mending a boot in the light of a shaded lamp.

Ralph enlarged on his idea. It would be a beginning, would bring the men together and enable them to exchange views. Immediately, it would probably lead to thrift. Common thought and action might lead to an improvement in the condition of the members – in housing, wages. They might become strong enough to influence public affairs. They might even start some small industries.

Byrne waxed his thread and sewed more and more furiously as Ralph spoke. When Ralph paused, he stood up and slapped his open palm with the boot he held in his right hand.

"That's the first sensible speech I've heard since I left Lee, Massachusetts," he said solemnly.

Ralph blushed.

"There's nothing new in it," Byrne continued. "It's a plan that's nearly as old as the hills in every decent country on earth except Ireland. You'll find books there," pointing to a small bookshelf by Ralph's side, "Ruskin and Carlyle and the like, that put the heart into many a working man. But sure no one reads a book in Bunnahone – the priests wouldn't let them."

"I'm not putting it forward as new," Ralph said, smiling. "You admit it's new in Bunnahone and we are concerned for the moment with Bunnahone. We shall pick ideas from your bookshelf – from everywhere. You think the scheme practicable?"

"That depends," he said, looking at Ralph keenly. "Do you want me to speak my mind open?"

Ralph nodded.

"I believe you, and it's few priests I'd believe. Tell me straight now. Is it your idea that it ought to be controlled by the priests?"

"Certainly not. I shall join as an ordinary member. The committee might be elected by ballot."

"So far so good," Byrne said sententiously. "I'm not saying that you haven't made good use of your time since you came to Bunnahone, but you have a thing or two to learn yet. Have you thought of the opposition?"

Ralph looked puzzled.

"The publicans'll fight the club tooth and nail ... and what the publicans will be against, the priests won't smile on. Are you prepared for that?" Byrne said, sitting again on his stool, his hands on his knees, peering at Ralph over his spectacles.

"If the club is likely to do good, I shall stand by it," Ralph said quietly, his jaw set square.

"You'll never be a bishop anyway, not that you're any the worse man for that. If there were only a few more priests of your kind around, who knows but I might be a good Catholic myself before I die," he added, laughing.

They went into details and Byrne promised to call on Ralph with some useful helpers in a few days.

Ralph sat late in his study that night making plans. He took notes of all the vacant houses in the town suitable for lodging the club. Bowen House, near the quay, would be the very place if he could secure it. Built by an ancestor of his father's friend in the eighteenth century it had been empty for over forty years, and he thought it unlikely that the family would again occupy it. He wrote to Bowen before going to bed, explaining his project and asking for a lease if the rent proved suitable.

He felt in high spirits next morning as he crossed the road to say mass at the convent. He had come to think of Reverend Mother as a dear friend and was eager to tell her about the club, in which he felt she would be interested. The leaden grey sky was touched with a faint yellow on the horizon as he crossed the bridge in the convent grounds. He stopped for a moment to watch the slow spread of dawn. A cock crowed in the distance. How his father would have liked the idea of the club. He hoped the nuns would not speak much of his father. They would be sure to speak of him, but Reverend Mother was tactful....

A bell tinkled as he opened the sacristy door, and he could see a nun lighting candles on the altar as he vested. The thin voices of the nuns as they chanted the end of the little office of the Blessed Virgin seemed to faint away in the small but lofty chapel and were lost in the gloom above the shaded lamps. He waited, chalice in hand, at the door for the nuns to finish. The resonant contralto voice of Reverend Mother saying the final prayer seemed to summon the first flush of morning light through the east window. The nuns responded "Amen", with a dying-away, effortless sound, as if their energy was already exhausted. The nuns in the stalls opposite were ghostlike in their rigidity, fixed, as it were, like statues in niches, their faces indistinguishable, brown patches between the whites of their dimitys and guimpes.

What was Eva doing among these phantoms? It was as if one in the flush of youth, the embodiment of all the life in the world, was stricken down in a catalyptic trance. Yet.... Surely all these women were not reduced to the uniform type of their dress. It was a mere trick of the eye. Behind each guimpe was a heart full of vague longing, striving it knew not for what, tending it knew not whither....

He recalled his mind to the sacrifice he was about to offer as he walked to the altar. Try as he would, his mind was distracted by the voice of the nun who gave the responses, by the shuffling of feet of some children at the back of the chapel, orphans probably? Were the little Reardons among them, shut off behind the rood screen? There was something artificial in making this great symbolic act for a coterie, in breaking the bread of life to a few who had cut themselves off from life....

His fingers trembled as he distributed the wafers to the nuns approaching the altar two and two. Eva came last. He noticed her hair escaping in wavy curls from under her little black cap. A postulant, she was dressed in a plain black dress with a little cape and a cap tied on with ribbons. The pink of her cheeks as he remembered it had taken on a deep red, mounting even under the curls on her forehead....

He finished the mass mechanically and unvested in the sacristy, almost without thought. He knelt at a prie-dieu and read over the words of thanksgiving.

He heard a cough and turned round.

Sister Veronica stood beside him, looking at him tenderly, her big brown eyes opened wide.

"Your breakfast is on the table, Father. Reverend Mother sent me for you. We are all so sorry for you."

She took his hand and stroked it gently.

"Why do you never come to the infant school now? We all ... I miss you so much."

She blushed prettily and held down her eyes.

"Thanks, Sister," he said, disengaging his hand and picking up his breviary. He murmured something about being busy and turned to go.

"You are always busy when I speak to you," she said, pouting.

He laughed as he walked along the corridor to the breakfast-room. Sister Veronica was not a wraith. What had Father Dempsey said of her? Nothing about her specially. How like Miss Julia Hinnissey she was....

Reverend Mother poured out his tea. She spoke at once of Eva Dillon. "I have asked her to come in for a few minutes. She was devoted to your father and felt his death very much. She is very shy."

He spoke of his club. Reverend Mother brightened. Her eyes had a singular look of youth when she was interested.

"I am so glad you think of doing something," she said gently. "It is better to work than to grieve. Anything that will soften the grey of their lives will be a help."

Her eyes grew sad and seemed to grope for something far away that avoided her vision.

She sighed and said, "Life is a great mystery.... You knew Eva Dillon well?" she added abruptly.

"She is a distant cousin.... I have really seen very little of her and can't say that I know her well," Ralph said hesitatingly. "She was generally away from home when I was at Inniscar during vacations. I stayed at Dillonsmount once – but that was years ago."

"Convents are not suited to everyone," Reverend Mother said, sighing again. Ralph looked at her enquiringly.

"She puzzles me," Reverend Mother said, passing her beads through her fingers and gazing at the fire opposite.

Ralph went on nibbling toast.

Reverend Mother sighed and looked at Ralph, doubtingly, over her spectacles.

"I can't make her out," she said, still trying to read something in the blazing coal. "Our other postulants differ so much from her, in class, in education, in their motives for entering. All she will say is that she wants to be a nun here. Why, she won't say. I've told her of other convents that would suit her better, but she persists in saying this convent suits her."

She paused, expecting Ralph to make a remark.

"I know so little about her," he said, ill at ease.

"I wish you would speak to her some time about her vocation and advise her."

"What could I say?"

"I don't think she will be happy with us," Reverend Mother said, ignoring his question, and still gazing abstractedly at the fire. "The older I grow – I am seventy-three, and nearing the end – the less certain I am about everything. You are very young and I am very old, but I can speak freely to you," she added, looking at Ralph affectionately for a moment, again withdrawing her eyes and fixing them on the fire. "You have said many things about religion that I have felt vaguely myself for years, but have not been able to put into words. You will understand what I say. Forty-four years ago I became a nun. I was twenty-nine then and heart-broken. I was a coward and gave up life. The convent seemed to offer me all I wanted. It was years before I allowed myself to think. When I did think, I was not sure that I had done rightly. I am not sure now. I have pottered along, doing what little I could – it has not been much. I am not sure that it could have been more elsewhere. Yet," she looked at Ralph, shrewdly, over her spectacles, "if a convent suits anyone, it suited me. Love had come to me for a brief happy moment. Before I entered the convent my heart was buried in a grave far from here. I had no illusions as to what I was offering to God ..."

She looked again at the fire. "It is different with the young," she went on. "Girls come in here, ignorant of themselves, of life, of religion. There is no fathoming the power of self-deception. Some are comparatively happy in a futile round of external observance. They live always on the surface of things, proud of having given up a life that had no attraction for them, vain of their supposed sacrifices, of this magnificent convent, of their dress. Others, flattered into being nuns at school by foolish nuns, enter with some vague ideas of sacrifice. Afterwards they wake up to life and see that the convent has nothing to offer them. Some leave. The majority stay on, miserable, discontented, unhappy women. Some of them make the best of things. Others ..."

She shook her had sadly and was silent for a while.

"I am sad for days when a girl comes and tells me that she wants to become a nun ... I don't want Eva Dillon to stay," she said, pulling herself together and looking Ralph straight in the face. "She is young, and she thinks – a fatal combination: too young by far to bury herself in a tomb; too thoughtful not to find out how foolish she has been."

She toyed with her beads. Ralph gazed gloomily at his plate. It was with convents, then, as with other institutions in the Church. They had outlived their time. In a vague way he had realised this before, but he had given the subject little thought. "Do you wish me to speak to Eva about this?" he asked.

"If necessary," Reverend Mother said, smiling. "We shall give her a chance first of finding out things for herself. You must see her. I shall send her in to you for a few minutes."

She left the room and returned after the an absence of five minutes alone.

"She wouldn't come. I didn't like to press her, she seemed so distressed," Reverend Mother said, somewhat disturbed.

Ralph laughed. "She was always obstinate," he said, rising to leave.

"I can't understand her," Reverend Mother said.

On his way to the gate, the eldest of the little Reardon girls overtook him, panting.

"Father, Mother Ann wants you in the school," she said, looking at him shyly.

"How do you like the orphanage?" he asked, as he accompanied her across the grounds.

"Middling," she said solemnly.

"Only middling? Why?"

"Every why!"

"How do you like the nuns?"

She considered this question gravely.

"The nuns are very nice," she said; "some are, and some aren't."

"You go to school every day?"

"I do then," she said with a sigh.

"And learn a lot of lessons?"

"No. Only science and things."

"Science?" he said doubtfully.

"Yes. We break glass and things."

He did not attempt to elucidate this and she trotted along happily by his side.

"Sister Veronica is going to give up Father Tom for you," she said, looking up at him eagerly.

"What?" he said, astonished.

"She is so," she said confidentially. "I heard her telling it to Miss Eva."

He blushed on meeting Sister Veronica at the school door.

"I don't think I ought to speak to you," she said with pouting lips.

"Mother Ann sent for me," he said, somewhat confused.

"Of course, like all the priests, you run after the mothers. She's only an old frump anyway," she said, frowning.

An affected-looking nun with a receding forehead and a long nose came out from the senior school and stared sternly at Sister Veronica, who said, readily, "I just saw Father O'Brien passing, Mother Ann, and came out to tell him how bad the attendance is in the infant school."

"I shall attend to that, Sister," Mother Ann said sharply.

"Yes, Mother," Sister Veronica said demurely, walking away slowly.

"Considering everything, she's not too unladylike," Mother Ann said, her eyes on Sister Veronica's receding form. "A publican's daughter from Lisslea. I had to give her a good training in the noviceship."

"You are the novice mistress?" Ralph said, feeling very embarrassed.

"Did you not know it?" she said, bridling. "But of course, you have met me only in the schools. It is a somewhat arduous task to combine the two posts, but I feel called on to do it. So few of the nuns belong to our class and I think it so essential that the novice mistress should be a lady. My father is a solicitor in Dublin, as you probably know."

Ralph didn't know, and was tempted to say he didn't care.

"You sent for me?" he said.

"Oh, it was only about the attendance. Perhaps you would call attention to it in the Cathedral on Sunday. But it's not important. I'm glad of this opportunity of a little chat. I have great plans," she said, waving her hands towards the convent.

"You don't know perhaps that it was I who got the convent built. The bishop – what a charming man he is? such beautiful manners! – is so kind as to consult me occasionally, always indeed, I may say, in convent matters. Reverend Mother – you must have noticed it? – is getting old and has old-fashioned ideas. Although you may not think it, she is of very good family."

"She is a most charming woman," Ralph said.

"Of course, of course. But no initiative. You must have noticed that. 'Past her work,' the bishop once said to me, and I had to agree. But she is an excellent figurehead."

"I thought her most capable," Ralph said emphatically.

"She impresses strangers," Mother Ann continued, volubly. "But as the bishop remarked, the convent would die of stagnation if it depended on her. Now, what did I want to say? Yes. I'm sure you'll be interested in my new plans. I want a boarding school for young ladies here. That will appeal to a cultivated man like you," she added triumphantly.

"I thought your work was confined to schools for the poor?"

"My dear Father! we must move with the times. There are so many girls like the Miss Darcys and the Miss Hinnisseys. Why not finish them in Bunnahone instead of in Dublin or London?"

"Is it wise to multiply that type of school?" Ralph asked, smiling.

"Why, of course. There is no better means of keeping up the supply of nuns. When a girl of that class is accomplished, can play and paint and embroider, naturally her somewhat vulgar surroundings at home dissatisfy her and she soon develops a vocation. I want to give girls a vocation for *this* convent. At present, girls from the neighbourhood are induced to enter the convents where they have been educated. I have very great difficulty in getting desirable girls to come here. If we had a boarding school everything should be different. I could have my eye on suitable postulants all the time and put various little inducements in their way. A constant word in season does a great deal."

"It's your belief that all girls should be nuns?"

"It is the higher vocation, of course. The great aim of every girl ought to be to become a nun. Besides, for the daughters of rich farmers and rich shopkeepers, it is the ideal life. The accomplishments they acquire at the convent schools would be wasted on them otherwise. Imagine a nice refined girl like Katie Hinnissey, or Julia, marrying a boorish shopkeeper in Bunnahone! Why, it's unthinkable. In the convent they will have nice genteel society, and will have scope for displaying their accomplishments in teaching other girls."

"To be dissatisfied with their homes," Ralph interrupted.

"Not at all," said Mother Ann, "to discern their real vocation. God provides many external helps for this purpose. Even dissatisfaction with one's home surroundings may be a real sign of a vocation."

"But you admit you make them dissatisfied?"

"Not at all. We only educate them."

"It seems to me that more girls become mothers than enter convents. Do you never attempt to educate them for that state?"

"God forbid!" Mother Ann said with a look of horror. "I hope nuns know their duty better. Of course, I know you are only drawing me out," she added, smiling. "As a priest you must agree with me, that it is the duty of nuns to endeavour to develop as many vocations as possible."

"But if all girls become nuns?"

Mother Ann blushed, lowered her eyes and puckered her brows in thought. "Of course, not all girls are suitable," she said hesitatingly. "A certain standard of refinement is necessary – I should myself be inclined to be stricter in this respect – and there must be a sufficient dot."

"Is an absence of dot a sign of lack of vocation?" he asked gravely.

She looked at him keenly, but he continued to look grave.

"I think so...." She hesitated a little, "Decidedly. Sometimes, of course, if a girl has marked accomplishments, these might counterbalance the absence of dot. But as a rule, when God gives a vocation He also provides the essentials. The more money the convent gets with postulants the more we are able to do for the honour and glory of God. I am glad to say we have been singularly blessed in this respect," she added complacently, pointing to the extensive convent buildings.

"Not all girls with a dot, however, become nuns?"

"Unfortunately not," she said with a sigh. "The temptations of a wicked world are very strong. Some give way to the disgraceful passion of love."

Her forehead seemed to recede still further under her dimity, she pursed her lips and a hectic flush tinged her high cheek bones.

Ralph looked at her in wonder.

"I see you agree with me," she said eagerly. "You will understand why I want a boarding school here. Without flattering myself I can say, from my experience as mistress of novices, that I have great success in putting the eternal truths of our faith before girls. I know the arguments that appeal to them. I have no doubt I could treble the vocations in this part of the country if I had the right class of girls under my influence in a boarding school. A day school has many defects – there are too many distractions. Besides, of course, the children of the richer parents don't come to our day school. They go to convent boarding schools elsewhere."

Ralph was fascinated by the little narrow head with its gleaming, grey, fanatical eyes. He felt the uselessness of arguing against her ideas. The nun continued to speak of the boarding school, going into elaborate details. Her sharp thin voice grated on his nerves and he made no attempt to follow her. His thoughts wandered. Mother Ann had the teaching of every girl in the district except the few who went to boarding schools at a distance. Convents were being set up in every little town and village, even in some country districts. If Mother Ann had the whole female education of Ireland in her hands, what would be the result? He shuddered. But it was too grotesque.

Mother Ann said confidently, in a lowered tone, "I am glad you agree with me. Reverend Mother's idea of course was absurd."

He hadn't the faintest notion of what she was speaking.

"I am against the teaching of these subjects. The organiser who came down wanted the nuns to take off their sleeves and mix flour in basins, bake cakes and do the washing and ironing. I told

Reverend Mother it wasn't befitting nuns to do such menial work in public. Why, the girls would lose all respect for them! Reverend Mother was so obstinate that I had to appeal to the bishop. He understood at once and upheld me. As long as I'm mistress of schools, or in any office of authority in the convent," she bridled primly, "the nuns shall teach only refined subjects. There must be the necessary subjects for examination for the common children in the National School, of course. But all the extras will be refined - music, painting, languages and embroidery. The nuns themselves don't need to know cookery, laundry and housekeeping - we have lay Sisters to do all that - and the boarders I have in view have servants."

"None of your education is practical then?"

"Of course it is practical, but not messy. Try to imagine a nun standing before a class with an apron on and her arms exposed or covered with flour! As I told Reverend Mother, it would be positively indecent. For the last few years a cooking class has been forced on us by the National Board, but I hide away and employ a lay teacher. Thank God, it is decided that there will be no unbecoming subjects taught in our boarding school."

"I am afraid I have to go," Ralph said, taking out his watch.

"Just one minute," Mother Ann said eagerly. "You must come and see a class I am forming that I hope to make the nucleus of our boarding school."

On their way to a distant classroom she said, suddenly, "By the way, I believe Sister Eva, our new postulant, is a cousin of yours. She is a great aquisition. We want nuns so badly of our own class, if we are to attract upper-class pupils. She actually speaks French with a Parisian accent - that is more than most convents can boast of - at least she was at a Paris convent."

The first person Ralph saw when they entered the classroom was Eva giving a French lesson. He recognised the back view of her hair. She did not see him until Mother Ann called sharply, "Sister Eva. Here is your cousin, Father O'Brien."

He noticed her start and then become rigid. A few seconds passed before she turned round. Her face was set and a blush gave way to extreme pallor as she gave him a limp hand.

"I was surprised to hear that you had entered the convent," he said nervously.

"Indeed!" she said coldly. She fixed her eyes on the band on his hat and her face relaxed.

"Poor Cousin John," she said softly and burst into tears. She turned away and hid her eyes in a handkerchief.

"What is this, Sister Eva?" said Mother Ann, sternly.

"My father," Ralph said, in a low voice. "She was very much attached to him."

"Self-control, dear Sister, is essential in a nun," said Mother Ann, coldly. "You must never give way to these feelings in class. Indeed, before you leave the noviceship you must have them under complete control."

"I really must go," Ralph said.

Eva gave him a grateful look and went back to her class.

"Some day you must hear her give a French lesson," Mother Ann said with a sigh. "The class is really a good one. I have taken it myself hitherto. Sister Eva has been only a short time in my hands, otherwise she would not have broken down so disgracefully. I insist on a calm and collected demeanour. I must go back and give her a little lesson."

Sister Veronica stood at the door of the infant school as he passed.

"You do look glum," she said. "But it's no wonder after such a long dose of old Ann."

He smiled at Veronica. She at least was human.

Chapter 21

THE CLUB WAS opened at Christmas. Bowen not only gave the house at a nominal rent but put it in repair. "Be sure he has some cute landlord dodge at the bottom of it," Father Hardy said.

Ralph told the bishop of the opening of the club. He shook his head doubtfully. "Clubs of the kind are always dangerous," he said. "However, if you, Father O'Brien, keep a firm hand on the members, under Father Molloy's direction of course, it may do no harm. It is always open to me to withdraw my permission in case difficulties arise."

Father Molloy said, "Fire ahead. It may keep some of these nuisances like John Byrne quiet. If it interferes with anything in the parish I'll put down my foot. I may drop in an odd time and play a game of cards with the lads myself."

Father Dempsey was enthusiastic. "It's the very thing to give the Irish language a start," he said.

Father Hardy declined to have anything to do with it. "I couldn't waste my time talking to fellows like Byrne," he said. "Too cheeky they are already. If they get any encouragement they'll be standing up and contradicting us next."

Byrne, a young carpenter named Tom Dunne and a small draper, James Haverty, were the leading spirits. Ralph got Bowen to give them a lease of the house as trustees of the club. By the opening night about two hundred members had joined, labourers for the most part, a few artisans and some small shopkeepers.

Byrne proposed that Father O'Brien should be *ex officio* president, but he declined. The committee, he suggested, should be elected by ballot and the officers appointed by the committee. He would be glad, if elected, to serve on the committee.

"Bedad, it's new times in Bunnahone when one of the clergy makes an ordinary man of himself," Dunne said, stroking his yellow beard thoughtfully.

In addition to the trustees and Father O'Brien, Grogan the schoolmaster and a farmer, Martin Grady, were elected on the committee. At its first meeting Ralph proposed Byrne as chairman.

"No, no," Byrne said.

"Whoever heard the like! Of course, the priest'll be the chairman," Haverty said, looking round the table.

"I'm not sure but the priest is right," said Grady, a grave, clean-shaven man of about forty, with strong, regular features.

"I'm only a curate here," said Ralph, "and I may be moved at any moment. I have no experience. For many reasons I should wish a layman as chairman."

After more discussion Byrne was unanimously elected chairman and Grogan secretary: it was further agreed that the club should be non-political and non-sectarian.

For a month or two Ralph had doubts as to whether the committee had any initiative. At the first few meetings none of the members except Byrne offered any suggestions, but referred everything to "the priest". It reminded him of meetings of the Church committee at which the only speakers were the bishop and Father Molloy, who proposed and seconded every resolution in turn, the lay members contenting themselves with an enthusiastic "Hear, hear". Once when a layman made a mild criticism of some proposal of the bishop, Father Molloy said, indignantly, "Have you the impudence to speak agin his lordship?" and the layman subsided meekly.

Gradually the men plucked up courage and spoke their opinions freely. One night, when Ralph found himself in a minority of one, on a question in which he recognised that he was wrong, he felt that something had been accomplished. By March things were moving so quickly, chiefly at the instance of Dunne and Haverty, that Ralph and Byrne had become a conservative and restraining influence.

Classes had been established in Irish, history and handicraft. There were debates on Thursday nights and popular lectures on Mondays. A thrift bank was started, which advanced small sums for the tilling of the neglected gardens of the labourers.

"I think the time has come," Dunne said one night, "when we might take a hand in the town affairs. I have been counting up and we have about a hundred members with votes. If we keep 'em together we ought to be able to make things hum."

"Take things slow but sure. If we go too fast we might get tripped up," said Byrne, cautiously. "There's a lot of grumbling going on already agin us."

"What did you hear, Mr Byrne?" asked Grogan, anxiously.

"The publicans are beginning to kick agin us taking away their customers of nights."

"But Father Tom didn't say anything," Grogan said nervously.

"He wouldn't look the side of the road I'm at, so it's not likely I'd hear what he thinks."

"Don't be afeared, Mr Grogan; sure we'll stand by you," said Haverty.

"It's dreadful power the priests have over a poor schoolmaster, surely," Grady said with a glance at Ralph.

"Wait till the people wake up," said Dunne, jauntily.

"Easy, easy, Mr Dunne. Maybe you'd find to your cost that they're not easily woke up. You might bring trouble on Father O'Brien here, too," Byrne said.

"Don't mind me," said Ralph, smiling. "What do you propose, Dunne?"

"It isn't anything to make bones about," said Dunne, "and sure I'd be the last to injure Father O'Brien. I was only going to propose that we'd try at the next election to get a few of our members on the Town Commissioners."

"We might do that same," said Byrne, with a sigh of relief. "I thought there might be something more."

"There is," said Dunne, "but I didn't like to spring it on the meeting all at once." He pulled a sheet of blue foolscap out of his pocket. "I borrowed this paper off Mr Grogan. It looks responsible like. I've jotted down a few things that we've been talking about here and that I've gone into with Father Ralph. He agrees with them, more or less, if we only take our time about them. And I don't propose that we ought take'em up all at once." He cleared his throat and read:

"'1. To get new street lamps and to have them lighted on moonlight nights.' The reason of that," he explained, "is that it's often as dark on moonlight nights as on dark nights, by reason of the moon being under a bank of clouds.

"'2. To mend the pavements and sweep the mud off the streets.

"'3. To raise the wages of labouring men to thirteen shillings a week.

"'4. To get all houses kept wind and weather tight.' I picked them words out of an old lease I have at home, 'or if not, to have them condemed as pigsties by the proper authority.

"'5. To have Mr Grogan's schoolhouse put in order.'"

"Ought we to interfere in that, gentlemen?" Grogan said appealingly. "Father Tom won't like it. Remember my little family. You never know what the clergy might do if they're roused."

"Sure Father O'Brien will protect you if anything happens," said Haverty.

"But it's Father Tom that is the manager and has the power. And he's a hard man. God forgive me for saying it," Grogan said, looking at Ralph timidly.

"There's something in what Mr Grogan says," said Byrne; "but it's a queer thing if the people of the town can't have a say in the education of their children."

"The point is that up to this they haven't, and I've no doubt at all Father Tom'll be furious," said Grady.

"The proposal is," said Ralph, "to endeavour to get the schoolhouse put in repair, not to interfere in education, not but I think that is even more necessary."

"Hear, hear," said Dunne.

Old Byrne smiled humourously. "You'll be stripped of your Roman collar if you go on like that," he said to Ralph.

In the discussion that followed, Ralph was interested to find the comparative unimportance attached to the secular proposals, the difficulties of which were recognised but were thought to be surmountable. The sharpest differences of opinion arose over the schoolhouse. Hitherto he had not fully realised the strength of the distrust and fear of the priests among the members of the committee.

"I don't care a pin, with all respect to your reverence, for the clergy," Byrne said, "but I do care for the club, and if I'm slow to act it's not through fear that they can do anything agin myself, but they might intrigue agin the club and smash it up."

Dunne urged that "they should strike a blow for freedom".

"That's League-meeting nonsense," said Byrne. "We must act cautious."

When tears trickled down Grogan's face it was agreed to defer action in regard to the school.

"But we'll have to face that and other questions in time," Byrne said.

Dunne waited for Ralph at the door of the club after the meeting and they walked through the streets together.

"Come in and have a smoke," Ralph said, when they reached his gate.

"If it wouldn't be intruding?" Dunne said timidly.

"Nonsense," said Ralph.

Dunne was a teetotaler but said he'd be glad of a cup of coffee. Ann served it with an air of a martyr.

"Sure I'm giving up all hope of him," she had said to Hilda of Ralph a few days before. "Sure it's all the riff-raff of the town he gathers round him – shoemakers, carpenters, labouring men and the like. I'd put up with the Miss Hinnisseys itself sooner than the company we have nowadays. They were at least on a level with me, but having to get tea and coffee and sandwiches for them that are beneath me! Only for the power of praying I do, I'd never be that humble to do it."

She glanced angrily at Dunne as she laid down the tray.

"I often thought of telling you, Father, I was near going to America before the club started," Dunne said as he lit his pipe.

"I'm very glad you didn't."

"Well, 'twas touch and go. I was sick of everything. I served my time in Dublin and had a few years as a journeyman at high-class work. It near broke my heart, after settling here, to have nothing to do but making coffins or some odd repairs. Outside my work there was nothing either, except spending the evening in some public house or other. I tried the League but it turned me against politics. They talked a lot about patriotism and Home Rule, but sorra much the Bunnahone branch cares for only their own pockets. I resigned when they boycotted Haverty, a decent poor man, because Donaghue, who runs the League here, set his eyes on a little farm Haverty had come by honestly, and wanted to force Haverty out of it and get it for himself. Not that these things were the worst either," he said, drawing long puffs of smoke from his pipe moodily.

Ralph nodded sympathetically, but did not speak. After a few moments' silence Dunne continued, "You being a priest I don't like to say anything against the Church; but it's the priests that dealt me the worst blow."

He looked at Ralph sheepishly.

"There's a little girl I was keeping company with; she's an assistant in the drapery side of Hinnissey's and lives in. Sorra chance we had of meeting except it was to have a walk in the evenings. Father Tom came on us as we were walking peaceably on the shore road one night, and if he didn't up with his umbrella and give her several licks of it on the head and shoulders. I made a grab at it and broke it across my knee. I near struck him with it, but I remember my mother telling me that it was the most unlucky thing in the world to strike a priest and I kept back my temper in time and pitched the umbrella on the rocks. He abused us at the height of his voice and called the little innocent girl a string of ugly names. Only she kept a hold of me, I'd have broken every limb in his body, God forgive me. The little girl was telling of the tale to Mrs Hinnissey and the nuns. They took away her Child of Mary's medal at the convent and persuaded her that she was heading for the devil. Mrs Hinnissey won't let her out at nights. They painted me like the devil himself, and as the little girl is very religious, she didn't know what to do; her heart pulling her one way and her religion the other. I saw her pining away before my eyes, but after all that was said to her, she was afraid to marry me. The evening Byrne told me about the club she wrote me a letter saying that she'd been to confession to Father Tom and that she could have nothing more to do with me. I had nearly made up my mind to leave the whole place to hell, but Byrne made me put it off for a bit, and I've got a new heart in me since. Doing real work at the club has made a new man of me, and it's telling on her too. She's coming round."

He smiled, a humorous twinkle in his eye.

"I wouldn't be surprised if Father Tom, though he has never forgiven me for smashing his grand silk umbrella, silver handle and all, would have to marry Bridget Carey and myself some day."

"I'm delighted."

"Thanks, your reverence," said Dunne, shyly. "Not but I have a good deal to thank you for. 'Twas your seeming to make much of me that helped to bring Bridget round. Women are queer enough," he added musingly, "and the way the priests get hold of 'em is wonderful. There isn't a woman in Bunnahone that doesn't swallow everything they say. But maybe I oughtn't to speak of religion to you, you being a priest?" he added enquiringly.

Ralph laughed heartily.

Dunne looked puzzled for a moment and then laughed. "It sounds queer," he said, "but you know what I mean. Not but that there's something in the way I put it," he added, knitting his brows in the effort to express some confused thought. "The last person the likes of me could talk to about religion is a priest."

Ralph shook his head.

"Oh, I don't mean you. Sure they say at the club you're as easy to speak to as an ordinary man, you're that open, but it's few priests are like that. I once asked a question of Father Doyle, that used to be in the Seminary, about a bad pope I read of that troubled me, and he turned on me fierce and told me I was no better than a heretic to be reading Protestant lies and slammed the confession slide in my face. That sort of way to treat people, Father, is a mistake. It's many another thing of the kind I've read since that has given me a mighty poor opinion of Father Doyle. Anyway, I've never carried any of my doubts to a priest from that day to this."

"You have difficulties, then?" Ralph said, handing Dunne the tobacco jar. He filled his pipe slowly.

"You're sure you don't mind my speaking out?"

"If I wanted your help in anything I should be open with you."

"Byrne said as much to me often, but I find it hard to get over the idea that the priests wouldn't discuss things for fear that they'd have to give themselves away too much."

"Try me."

"Well, the long and the short of it is, that I don't know whether I believe anything at all," Dunne said sadly. "My mother brought me up to believe in a lot of things, but one by one they've been going from me. Though I read books denying there's a God, and as clear as print they prove it, at the back of my mind I still have a hankering after Him and believe He's somewhere. The little girl, too, has such belief that I find it hard to think she's wrong. The little brains I have tell me religion is all nonsense, but I have some sort of feeling there's something in it. I can't stomach the sermons I hear at the Cathedral, and it's only a joke to me that a good Protestant'll go to hell, while a Catholic can rob and do mean, low things all his life and go to heaven at the end if only he gets a priest to raise his hand over him and say a few masses for him. It's little faith I'd put in a mass that Father Tom'd say. It's my firm belief hell was invented to make money out of it," he added excitedly. "You don't want to kick me out?" he added, after a moment's pause.

"Do many in Bunnahone think as you do?" Ralph asked.

"A good few, as far as I know. Maybe only half a dozen," he added doubtfully, "are bothered about it like me. There are a good many that don't believe, and don't care a fig one way or the other."

"But there are a good many like Bridget," Ralph said, smiling.

"There are," said Dunne, "and some of the best too."

When Dunne had exhausted all his crude rationalist arguments, Ralph spoke to him of religion as he felt it, admitting the force of what Dunne had said. He told him of his own doubts and difficulties and how he tried to reconcile them. Dunne listened open-mouthed for a while. He was interested, but not convinced.

"I'd like to believe like that," he said.

"I think you do," Ralph said.

"It's the first time, anyway, a priest spoke to me about religion as if I was a reasonable being and not an idiot," he said, as he rose to leave. He lingered for a moment on the doorstep.

"May I bring one or two of the lads? A talk now and again might do them some good."

"Nothing I should like better. Goodnight. God bless you."

"And you too, Father."

Ralph sat before the fire pondering Dunne's case. He had long suspected, from talks with Byrne, that there must be many young men with Dunne's difficulties in Bunnahone and elsewhere. Could anything be done to help them? Almost uneducated, destructive arguments appealed to them, enforced by inconsistencies and contradictions in the practices of the Church and in the lives of priests. They became anti-clerical to start with and eagerly snatched at any facile argument attacking the religion of the priests they hated. Dogma was a stumbling-block to the educated, but they could be trusted to find out that faith was independent of dogma. The great difficulty was with the growing body of men like Dunne and Byrne, for whom religion, faith, dogma, morality, obedience to priests and bishops and the most absurd practices of the Church were all so joined together that a doubt about one led to the denial of all religion. It was almost impossible to bring home to them any real sense of relative values.

He looked long at the dying embers. How was the Church made up at the moment? Of millions like Jack Devine, whose religion was active and living, but who were secure only until they began to think; of many like Dunne, who were on the verge of unbelief and who with certainty would be driven there one day; of many who had lost all faith; of a comparatively few who in spite of ecclesiastical authority had succeeded in reconciling the simple faith of the Jack Devines with the intellectual and moral needs of the age. And the ecclesiastical order? It reflected the beliefs of the laity. The Joe Devines who clung to the simple faith of their fathers; doubters who clung to an easy means of livelihood and turned their eyes away from difficulties; unbelievers; and the few who had grown and developed with the needs of humanity and were alive to difficulties.

As the fire died out the room became colder. Ralph shivered. The future seemed hopeless. What could a few priests and laymen do against entrenched power? By constant iteration and exercise of authority the Roman power had succeeded in persuading the simple millions that it was the sole guardian of faith. In any struggle to purify the Church, to state doctrine in such a way as to save the growing number of Dunnes, and men abler than Dunne, legalists, time-servers and career-mongers would be sure of the support of the simple believers. Good and evil in the Church would unite to kill the best....

A loud knocking at the front door aroused him. It was after two o'clock and the fire had gone out. He opened the door hastily.

"A sick call to the workhouse, your reverence," a voice said, out of the darkness.

As they stumbled in the ruts of the dark streets, Ralph asked, "Who is it?"

"My father, your reverence, Maurice Delaney. We were evicted over a year ago and had to go into 'the house' last week."

Ralph murmured an expression of sympathy.

"I'm afraid my father won't be too pleased to see a priest," the man continued in a flat, toneless voice.

"Why?"

"We were on the same farm for more generations than anyone could count," Delaney said in his curiously detached voice. "Father Molloy's brother had a farm near by; a waster he was, if ever there was one. He didn't pay any rent for years and was going to be put out. Father Tom got the League to back him and got my father and the other tenants to refuse to pay rent as a protest against the eviction of his brother. The long and the short of it was that we were all put out. There was a lot of hugger-muggering with the League and the landlord. Molloy got his farm back all right, and some of the others, but my father and two neighbours were left out in the cold and their farms were given to a cousin of Mr Donaghue's. There was some show of boycotting him for a couple of months, but it died out, and he's a leading member of the League now. We lived for the last few years on the money we had saved, but it's all gone now, and my father and myself were so broken in health that we could do nothing but come into the house. Father Tom wouldn't come next or nigh us, and my father lays all the blame at his door."

A sleepy-looking porter opened the workhouse gate, and by the light of a lantern led Ralph through cold, flagged passages to the hospital. Two nuns met him in the little chapel.

"It is a very sad case," one said. "You had better see him first before you bring the Blessed Sacrament. He does nothing but curse and blaspheme."

Ralph followed the nuns to a small room where an old man lay on a bed clutching the bedclothes with his hands, his eyes gleaming.

"We had to put him in here alone," the nuns whispered. "He was giving such scandal in the ward."

The old man fixed his eyes on Ralph.

"Go away!" he shouted; "another black devil out of hell come to tempt me to give up my land. It's Father Molloy with another face on him."

The son, who had followed Ralph, came to the bedside and said gently, "It isn't, Father; it's a decent young priest come to clear away your sins and give you the last anointing."

"They're all one, I tell you," the old man said, glaring at Ralph vindictively. "I paid my dues regular and paid twenty pounds for the Cathedral, but nothing'd do for them but to have me land and put me on the road to starve."

"But the young priest hadn't anything to do with it, and you wouldn't die without the Sacraments?" the son said pleadingly.

"Who said I'm going to die? Be off with you, you black devil!" he shouted at Ralph, making an effort to get out of bed. His son held him and, after a few moments' struggle, he lay back exhausted.

The nuns knelt by the door, praying earnestly.

The old man closed his eyes and breathed heavily with his mouth open. His hands relaxed and he seemed to sleep. After about five minutes he woke up with a start and gazed around wonderingly.

"I had a bad dream," he said in a weak voice, his breath coming in gasps. "Where am I? Is it a station day or what is it? And me in bed and not up to welcome the priest."

"Thank the Lord, God has touched his heart," a nun whispered.

"More like he's wandering in his mind," his son said.

"I dreamt a priest wanted to do me some harm," the old man said, putting a hand to his head, "but sure that couldn't be. Let me get up and bid the time of day to the people coming to the station."

"It isn't a station, Father. You're not well, and, to be on the safe side, we thought it better to have you anointed," the son said.

"Sure I feel as strong as a horse," Delaney said faintly. "But as ye have brought the priest, I don't like to disappoint him. But I'll be up the moment he's gone. And it's little I've to tell. Sure I was always a great hand at attending my duty.

"Beyond an odd curse at one of the cows, there's nothing since my last confession," he said to Ralph when they were left alone.

Ralph went to the chapel for the Blessed Sacrament. When he returned to the bedroom the old man was saying an act of contrition, slowly and with difficulty. He watched Ralph anxiously as he opened the oil case at the little altar which the nuns had hurriedly arranged.

As Ralph began the prayer for Extreme Unction, a growing look of horror appeared in the old man's face. He sat up suddenly, apparently without an effort, and shouted, waving his shaky hands in the air, "Stop him! stop him! He's reading away my land from me."

His head fell forward. When they lifted him up his eyes were glazed.

"I doubt but he's dead," his son said, laying the head back on the pillow.

The nuns were horror-stricken and prayed aloud.

Young Delaney turned towards Ralph and the nuns. He made a genuflexion towards the pyx, in which lay the Viaticum.

"I ask ye all to witness," he said, calmly and tonelessly, "that, in the presence of God, I call on His curse this night to alight on the priest that took away my father's land and broke his heart and his mind."

The nuns wept aloud, calling on God to pardon such blasphemy.

"I have nothing agin you, Father," Delaney said, turning towards Ralph, "nor agin the good ladies there, but I was always taught that God'd punish the wicked."

He looked tenderly at his father, and with bent head said, "May Heaven be your bed this night," and stalked out of the room.

"I am afraid he died impenitent ... and the son was terrible, terrible," one of the nuns whispered, awestricken.

"To know all is to pardon all," Ralph said mechanically. "He was a good man and suffered."

The nun looked at him doubtfully. "I suppose we can do no more," she said.

An old pauper attendant shuffled into the room and looked at the corpse critically.

"He's gone," he said. "Would either of ye have a couple of coppers upon ye to close his eyes with?"

Ralph replaced the Blessed Sacrament in the tabernacle of the hospital chapel and knelt for some time before the altar. He was full of a dull anger against Father Molloy for causing so much sorrow.

Outside the door of the chapel young Delaney stopped Ralph.

"I call back my curse; I leave *him* to God," he said, and turned away at once.

The sky was saffron-coloured as Ralph reached the road. The sun would soon be up and he had to say mass at the convent at seven. He walked through the silent streets of the town. The blinds were still down in Father Molloy's bedroom. No doubt he slept the usual untroubled sleep of which he boasted, Ralph thought resentfully.

Chapter 22

FOR SOME TIME after his father's death, Ralph paid frequent visits to Inniscar. Hilda refused to see any of her friends and was full of morbid ideas, which Ralph tried, with much patience, to dispel. She was not free from all fear that John O'Brien's soul was suffering the extreme torture of hell. If, in the mercy of God, he had escaped that penalty which she felt he deserved, he was certain to have to expiate his sin by intense suffering in purgatory. The duration of this it was fortunately in her power to shorten by fasting and abstinence, by continuous prayer and by masses for the repose of his soul. She increased her list of charities, but rigidly excluded all secular efforts. Through religious charities alone would John's soul be fully benefited.

At first she consulted Ralph as to her charities. One day she showed him a list: the Association for the Dissemination of St Francis' Cord, St Anthony's Bread, the Society for the Conversion of England to Catholicity, the Association for buying Chinese babies as a step to their baptism. He said they seemed rather footling. She was deeply offended and gave him a lecture on his lack of spirituality. She asked if he saw much of the bishop.

"Very little," Ralph said, shrugging his shoulders.

"What a pity!" she said. "He's a deep fount of spirituality. You are too much interested in secular things, Ralph."

Gradually she spoke less and less to him of her plans. When he asked her for a subscription towards providing a billiard-table for the club, she refused rather sharply. She seemed unhappy for a few minutes and then said hesitatingly, "I couldn't conscientiously give it; I am only a trustee for your poor father's money; I can never look upon it as my own. I am convinced now that it was some suggestion of grace, a hint from his guardian angel perhaps, that led him to leave his property to me. He had some prevision that he should need it for the good of his soul and he knew he could trust me to apply it as he, or his guardian angel, wished. I spoke of this to the bishop in confession, and he said that these mysterious dispensations of Providence were not at all unusual. You understand, then, that everything must go directly for the good of his soul. I cannot give to any merely worldly object. Besides, I never give anything without the advice of the bishop, my spiritual director. I wish you would place yourself more in his hands. He is such a consolation to me that I am sure he could help you too."

Having said mass at the convent on the morning of Maurice Delaney's death, Ralph went home for breakfast and found a letter from his mother awaiting him, asking him to come and see her at once.

He found her sitting in the study surrounded by legal documents.

"I wish all this was finished; it is too distracting," she said, smiling wanly at the papers.

"What is it?"

"I didn't wish to trouble you about it. Indeed, it wasn't necessary," she said, blushing. "Still, you ought to know, Driscoll says. I am selling most of the property to the tenants under the Land Purchase Act."

"I'm very glad. They told me that they have been anxious to buy for some time. I suppose you consulted Father Duff?"

"Yes," she said, frowning. "He was very kind in the beginning. In fact, he made all the arrangements with the tenants; but last night he was so rude that I decided to have nothing more to do with him."

"He's the kindest man I know," Ralph said, very much distressed. "Surely you must have been mistaken, Mother. He's the best friend we ever had."

"I never liked him," Hilda said stiffly. "I never could understand what you and your father saw in him. He's a farmer rather than a priest. He has no spiritual conversation."

"He's a good man."

"He's intolerable." She hesitated. "You don't claim any of the property, Ralph?" she said nervously.

"It is yours, to do what you like with," Ralph said, smiling.

"Of course, Driscoll told me that, so did the bishop, but I'm glad you agree so willingly," she said with a sigh of relief. "Father Duff worried me about it. He wanted me to invest the purchase-money in your name and mine. He's a horrid old man. He said it was my duty. I said my first duty was to your father's soul."

Ralph winced.

"I don't think Father Duff has any sense of religion," she continued; "all the comfort he offered me in the one object of my life now was to say 'fiddlesticks'."

She wiped away tears from her eyes.

Ralph smiled. "He has odd ideas. Don't mind him, Mother. I shall speak to him and make it all right."

"He gave in on that point. That was not the worst. He was almost insulting about the home farm."

"My father always took his advice on farming," Ralph said.

She looked at Ralph suspiciously.

"He threw that in my face, too," she said, her eyes glowing angrily. "However, I must bear things patiently. God knows how my life is devoted to your father." Her lips moved as if in prayer, her eyes bent to the carpet.

"I am sorry, Mother, if ..."

"It doesn't matter ... nothing matters now.... About the home farm," she added, after a short pause; "I am going to let it, at a very good rent to a most respectable man from Bunnahone, whom you must know. The bishop recommended him to me – a Mr Donaghue."

Ralph frowned. "Why, he's not a farmer, he's a gombeen man. He ..."

"I have heard all that from Father Duff," Hilda interrupted, in an icy tone. "He lost his temper and insulted the bishop and Mr Donaghue and me."

She again wiped her eyes with her handkerchief, and said, "I hope my own son did not come to insult me."

"I was only going to discuss ..."

"What's the good of discussing it? It is all settled," she said wearily. "Father Duff got on my nerves. I am sure I acted for the best. The bishop is so wise, so saintly. I was a little surprised that he knows so much about business, forgetting for the moment, as he reminded me gently, that bishops get special grace from God in regard to business, as it is a necessary part of their office. I thank God every day you are with him. It was an inspiration of the Holy Spirit that put it into your father's head to have you a priest in this diocese. Much will be forgiven him for it," she added, looking out of the window wistfully. "Be guided by the bishop, Ralph, in everything. I shan't ask you to stay to luncheon. This business has broken into my day and the order of my spiritual exercises is sadly interfered with."

Ralph cycled to Father Duff's. He found the old man sitting despondently before a large turf fire.

"You heard, then?" he said dryly, as Ralph took a seat.

"I feel a stranger in my own home," Ralph said sadly.

"Your home! It's very little you'll have to do with it from this out. I did my best." He stretched his shaking hands towards the blaze. "But I was never the kind of man to deal with a woman like her. She was bred, born and reared on religious pap. The more sugar was put in it the better she liked it. A priest with a soft tongue, with religious talk always on the end of it, could do what he liked with that build of woman. And there are priests enough of that sort knocking around.... I saw how it would be from the day ye settled here. I didn't know it was going to happen in this way, maybe. But the bishop had his eye on the place and he worked on your mother from the start. He had the devil's luck that things happened as they did and that she has the disposing of Inniscar. Poor John had a glimmer of it and he tried to prevent it, but his mind was too weak at the end, and he only made it all the easier."

"Dr Devoy couldn't possibly have foreseen my father's will. I find it hard to believe he has these designs," Ralph said doubtingly.

"He didn't know she'd have everything, but he guessed she'd have a good deal. What made your mother change her mind since the funeral?" the old priest said doggedly. "She was prepared to leave you everything then. She told me so. All I can tell you is that she has changed, and that the bishop is the cause of it. Sorra a week passed since but his carriage was once or twice at Inniscar. You'll see a good slice of that purchase-money go to the Seminary before long ... and you'll see other things too."

He took a pinch of snuff and sighed.

"Why, that is trading on my mother's religiosity?"

"I don't rightly know what the word means. It's trading on her whims right enough. The Church is a great institution. Sometimes I think the Holy Ghost is having a nap when some lads are made bishops. But them things are beyond me. The older I get the more I'd like things to be done a little straighter, but sure, God knows best ..." He gazed thoughtfully at the fire.

"The home farm rankles most in my mind," he said, after a short silence. "That's open trickery; any child except your mother'd see it."

"I don't," Ralph said. "Though the choice of Donaghue struck me as odd."

Father Duff looked at him affectionately.

"No wonder Inniscar'd be going as it is," he said. "Can't you see that that farm is the mainstay of the Inniscar creamery? Donaghue thinks he'll be able to wreck it by having the farm. Not that Donaghue ever thought of it - that's Devoy's or Molloy's doing, or maybe both of them. However," he sat up straight in his chair, "old as I am, I'm not dead yet, and that's a matter in which they'll have to reckon with me. In a matter of religion I'd give in to the bishop even if I thought he was wrong, but in a matter of farming I'd give in to no man."

The incidents of the preceding twelve hours kept running through Ralph's mind as he cycled home. The roads were rutty, greasy and covered with loose broken stones. He had so much difficulty in keeping his balance that connected thought was impossible. Indeed, he did not try to think. Detached images of the scene in the workhouse, of the bishop and his mother, of Father Molloy busy about affairs, floated on the surface of his brain. He saw Dunne throwing Father Molloy's umbrella over the sea wall....

He had a hurried lunch and tried to read, but he couldn't keep his attention fixed. When he had lost the thread several times, he shut the book. He felt very sleepy, but couldn't sleep. Thoughts of Father Molloy and the bishop kept recurring to his mind. He dozed for a moment and had a horrible feeling that the room was closing in around him. He woke up with a start. It was that tale of Poe's, not the bishop and Father Molloy. How foolish of him to associate them with that breathless feeling of terror. Was it so absurd after all? Was he doing any good in Bunnahone? Could he do any good? Everything that he thought good met with opposition. From whom? The ecclesiastical authority - from the bishop and Father Molloy.

He tried to justify the bishop. What was to be said in his favour? The building of churches and convents, a deep sense of the importance and dignity of his office. He could think of nothing else. It was a barren record for a representative of the Apostles. And Father Molloy? But why pursue this futile criticism? He was becoming a carping critic of individuals who, doubtless, had many good points. He couldn't see them. All desire for sleep dropped away from him. A feeling of responsibility came home to him. He was a priest, curate to Father Molloy and the bishop, curate of Bunnahone, a link in the great chain that bound the millions of Catholics throughout the world.

He got up, walked about the room and wound a small clock on the mantelpiece. It was five minutes slow he found on looking at his watch. He set the clock right.

Was he honest with himself? He shook his head doubtfully and pondered his childhood, his youth.... He could not see what other course he could have taken.

God revealed Himself in life, of that he was convinced. He was in everyone who had an ideal - an impulse that rose above self. History - science revealed Him. The Church was the great spiritual clearing house of the religious experience of the world.

Was it? He sighed. There was not much evidence of this in Bunnahone. He was strongly tempted to allow the glamour of past memories to colour his vision, but he put the temptation aside. The Church in Bunnahone was a dismal failure. All sense of its mission seemed to have been lost. It was a branch of a large administrative organisation, manned by indifferent officials whose sole aim was to keep the offices tawdrily gorgeous and to maintain or increase salaries.

"Hullo!" said Father Molloy, opening the door. "I found the front door open and came in. Having a snooze, were you? You were up late last night, I heard at the workhouse when I said mass there this morning."

He flopped into an armchair and carefully brushed a thin wisp of hair across his bald head.

"Old Delaney was a bit of a nuisance, the nuns told me," he said lightly, looking at Ralph keenly.

"He seems to have suffered a good deal," Ralph said coldly.

"He was babbling about his land, I believe. That's what I came to see you about. I believe that blackguard of a son of his put a curse on me, too," he added, his florid cheeks growing slightly pale; "not but that I'm used to curses. One more can't do me much harm," he said, nervously twitching his hat which he held in both hands.

"He withdrew the curse," Ralph said dryly.

"He did, did he?" Father Molloy said with a sigh of relief. "I've put the fear of God into them fellows' hearts. The idea of his cursing a priest! Wait till I see him, the lying scoundrel!"

"He seemed a decent man who was badly treated," Ralph said.

"Decent, indeed! Ask any real decent man in the town about him, any of our leading men, Hinnissey or Donaghue, or the like. Why, a Delaney couldn't recognise the truth if he saw it written in letters ten foot high on a blank wall. I'd scorn to defend myself agin him."

Father Tom had imported such a passion of sincerity into his voice that Ralph was shaken in his suspicions.

"He gave me names and other details. It is easy to investigate his story," he said.

"The Lord love your innocence. You might as well look for a needle in a bundle of straw as look for the truth of a story like that ... except from me and one or two others," he added, waving his hat in a little podgy hand. "Besides, I'm a forgiving man and I don't want to rake up the story now. If the tale of the old man dying like that leaked out, it'd make a lot of bad talk. The end of it'd be that young Delaney would be ruined past repair. I know things about him that'd knife him for ever; but I don't want to be forced to let them out. As I say, I forgive him if the old matters are let rest. I'd be even prepared to go farther and help him a bit," he said anxiously.

Ralph, who had for the first time closely watched the play of Father Molloy's features, was disgusted with the sly look that followed the anxious glance.

"In what way?"

"I could get him a farm under this new Act of Parliament. Just as good as the one he left."

"Why not get him back his own farm?"

Father Molloy frowned.

"That's where your want of experience comes in," he said. "There's the League to square."

"But surely one of the main objects of the League is to look to the interest of evicted tenants."

"Do you know what?" Father Molloy said, closing one eye and scrutinising Ralph with the other, "I like you for your innocent ways. Only they're so damn dangerous and might land me in a hobble, I'd get some fun out of seeing you trying to do things." He laughed heartily.

"The fault comes of your reading books," he said. "If you want to get on in a town like this you must be born with your eyes open. And it's men you have to read and not books. You get what you say about the League out of the little book printed about it in Dublin. Them lads in Dublin and in Parliament, that founded the League, may believe in what they print, or they may not – I don't know and I don't care. But sorra man in Ireland knows more about the League in Bunnahone that I do. And where did I learn it? Out of a book? Faugh! no, nor out of speeches on platforms either, but from strolling round and taking a drink in a leisurely way with a few of the lads in Donaghue's snuggery; and then passing over to Darcy's and having another with a few more of the boys. And you gather a lot from a game of cards, with the bottle on the table. Then a quiet chat with Mrs Darcy gives you a power of knowledge at times: there's little going that she doesn't hear. I wouldn't take everything she says as gospel, but by means of a little winnowing you get down to the truth. To come back to Delaney, take my word for it, the League'd be dead agin him if he tried to get back his own farm. By pulling a string or two here and there, I can get him one as good. There's no call on me to do it, but I can do an act of Christian charity as well as another man," he said complacently, stretching out his short legs.

"I shall speak to Delaney," Ralph said doubtfully.

"That's right," said Father Molloy, approvingly. "Tell him how unlucky it is to be going around talking agin the clergy. You might drop a hint that I'm wearing out shoe-leather going around trying to do him good. I'd speak to him myself, but he might say something that'd anger me. And if he makes a fight agin me now, I'd have to down him. A man must think sometimes of his own position," he said, setting his lips. "I'd see him before he has time to talk," he added as he was leaving the room. "If last night's story gets around, I'll have to act in my own defence. Anything for a quiet life, is my motto; but the man in this parish that'd get the better of me in a fight wasn't born yet."

Ralph felt intimidated by Father Molloy's overflowing self-confidence.

"Of course, I am being made a tool of," he said to himself, as he watched the fat priest, with squared shoulders, his silk hat set jauntily on the side of his head, swing down the pathway to the street, humming loudly a popular air.

Delaney would have no chance of success in a dispute with him! Donaghue and Father Molloy were "sworn friends", as Byrne once said. They would stand by one another. What could a pauper in the workhouse do against such a combination? Ralph thought as he set out to the workhouse to interview Delaney.

He found him sitting moodily smoking by the fire in the day room of the infirm quarters, a dirty bare room furnished with a few forms, on which a number of men sat listlessly, one or two reading old newspapers, a few smoking, the others watching the smokers' pipes greedily.

"Let's have a walk in the courtyard. I wish to speak to you," Ralph said to Delaney.

"Well, Father, and what may you be wanting with me?" he said as they walked across the paved courtyard. He was tall and broad-shouldered, with sunken blue eyes, cheeks drawn and sunken, covered by a few days' beard, nose thin and pointed and lips a pale purple that looked blue against his pallid skin. His head was huddled between his shoulders and his gait slow and shambling.

"I came about your land. Father Molloy thinks he could get you a farm."

"Our own farm?"

"No, another, but a good one."

The dull eyes that had brightened for a moment again became expressionless.

"I wouldn't take anything but my own and I wouldn't be beholden to him for that either."

"Father Molloy denies that he was responsible for your loss."

Delaney walked in silence for a few moments, and then said, abruptly, "Every word I told you last night is gospel truth. I've a mortal disease on me – the heart, the doctor says – and I may drop down at any minute. Do you think I'd tell you a lie, and me maybe to be called before my God the second after? But I suppose you all stick together and you'll likely believe Father Molloy," he added, in his curious detached voice, his eyes fixed on the cobbled pavement.

"But you have forgiven him?"

"I said I'd leave him to God – if there is a God, which I sometimes am doubting, and my father dying with curses on his lips that was a good man all his life, and my mother beyond there in the asylum a hopeless lunatic, and all brought about by the scheming of a priest."

"I didn't know of your mother. It is very sad," Ralph said gently.

"What good would a farm do me now, and I broken in health and spirits? And between you and me I don't believe I'd ever get it."

Ralph tried to persuade him to take the farm, but his reply to every argument was: "A broken man is best left in peace." He was silent for a while.

"Do you think, Father, now," he said eagerly, "there is any fear of my father's soul?"

"Surely you don't believe there is?" Ralph said, astonished.

"I don't know what to believe. I only know there oughtn't to be. He was a good man in his day."

"If God isn't kinder than you and I there is little hope for the world," Ralph said.

"You haven't a doubt my father is safe?"

"None whatever," Ralph said emphatically.

"Thank God for that," Delaney said, taking off his hat and looking reverently towards the sky. "His soul was troubling me more than the land since last night."

"Well, think of the land now," Ralph said. "You are young and you'll be well again soon."

Delaney relapsed into gloom.

"When I leave this it'll be to the little graveyard beyond. Didn't I hear the death-watch ticking this three nights. That might have been for my father, but I heard it again a while ago, and I sitting by the fire, and it was for me surely. The only land I'll ever have now I'll go to with my feet foremost and there'll be only six foot of it," he said, smiling for the first time. "I'm beholden to you all the same, Father. May God keep you and bless you."

Chapter 23

THERE WAS INTENSE excitement in Bunnahone when Dunne, Haverty and Byrne were nominated to fill three of the six vacancies for the office of Town Commissioner. As a rule, Bunnahone took little interest in elections of any kind. Candidates were always selected by the League and returned unopposed.

Pat Darcy met Ralph in the main street.

"May I have a word with you?" he said pompously, with an elaborate bow.

"What is the town coming to? An ancient town that has always held its head high. It's a disgraceful business, disgraceful." He grew very red and spluttered.

Ralph looked puzzled.

"A cobbler and a carpenter and a petty fellow like Haverty, the keeper of a little pin and needle stall! To set themselves up against the respectable shopkeepers of this ancient town! It's little short of a scandal."

"They are good fellows and very keen to have the town run well," Ralph said coldly.

"Ah, Father, you don't know the town yet. You are young. One of the best of priests, but inexperienced, I often say to the wife."

Ralph smiled.

"One of the best of priests, and why not?" Darcy said, rubbing his hands together. "Son of a house that has dealt with Darcy and Son since time out of mind."

"Byrne and his friends have votes. They are free, surely, to seek election if they choose."

Darcy seemed to consider this gravely.

"What would the country come to if every Tom, Dick and Harry had a say in affairs?" he said, putting his finger meditatively to his chin.

"But that is what the League wants."

Darcy smiled knowingly. "A little platform fireworks!" He took hold of a button of Ralph's coat and spoke confidentially.

"They may be violent elsewhere, but the Bunnahone League is a most respectable body. I have been in the League for years; indeed, I may tell you in the strictest confidence that I and Mr Donaghue are the League! Hinnissey has a voice, too, but he's weak in public affairs. A good business man, I admit; too sharp, if any, but a child in public matters. Now, will you tell me this? During all the years of agitation against the landlords, did one of us lose a single landlord customer? Not one, sir! We are the friends of the tenants and the enemies of landlordism. Though I say it myself, it was statesmanship in a small way, Father – to keep a solid front to the enemy and not a Bunnahone shop ever lost a single penny."

"What enemy?"

"Oh, the enemy, the enemy!" Darcy said, waving his arm. "Landlordism and England, the enemies of the people, you know."

"But what has this to do with the election of Town Commissioners?"

"Ah, that's the thin end of the wedge. Once you admit the riff-raff into any elected office, where are we, I ask you, Father? They have no stake in the town. Why, I wouldn't put it past them to turn against *us*, sir – yes, against me and others like me, Father, who have the best interests of the town always at heart. I may tell you, too, Father," he said, glancing around cautiously and speaking in a low tone, "that some of these men are not good Catholics."

"They are straight and honest ..."

"Ah, I knew it," Darcy said, striking his leg with his hand. "The wife often said that Father O'Brien was hand in glove with Byrne and the like; but I always said that, for certain, they didn't show the cloven hoof to the young priest. Be sure, I said, Bessy, when he'll find 'em out he'll give them the go-by. By the same token we are often a little jealous that we don't see more of you. We pride ourselves on being good friends of the clergy ..."

"Ah! the top of the morning to you, Pat," said Father Molloy. "What are ye colloguing like this in the middle of the street for?"

"I was dropping him a hint about the election," said Darcy. "Where in the world did you rise out of, Father?"

"I turn up everywhere, like a bad sixpence, even where least expected," said Father Molloy, boisterously. "Talking about the election, were ye? I've something to say to Father O'Brien about that. Leave him to me, Pat," with a wink at Darcy; "leave him to me. He's coming for a bit of dinner with me today and I'll talk to him."

When Ralph arrived at the parochial house, he found Father Molloy as usual stretched on the sofa in his sitting-room. Hardy and Magan were talking together by the window; Dempsey sat in an armchair by the fire.

"There's only one wanting now," Father Molloy said, looking at the watch he held in his hand. "It's past dinner-time. Where's Lanigan, Magan?"

"He ought to be here in a minute. He was taking a class."

"He might have cut it short. That must be he," he added as the knocker on the front door sounded. "Ring the bell, Dempsey. We'll have the dinner up at once. I'm dry and peckish."

A slatternly servant followed Lanigan into the room.

"The dinner's up now," she said.

"Come along, boys," said Father Molloy, jumping up and leading the way briskly to the dining-room, bare except for an immense marble-topped sideboard, a long mahogany table, on the upper half of which a cloth was laid, and rows of heterogeneous chairs.

"*Benedic Domine ...*" said Father Molloy, making a sign of the cross perfunctorily when he got inside the door. "The guests next me. Father Magan to the right, O'Brien to the left, and the rest as you like. You'd better sit opposite that dish, Hardy."

He took the cover off a dish at the head of table, disclosing a leg of mutton.

"The ducks are with you, Hardy. I think we'll all have some of that first as a tit-bit. The solid stuff here can wait. But I must have a pick-me-up first," he said, pouring some whisky into a glass. "Who says ditto?" holding up the decanter.

"Here," said Magan.

"Bedad, you didn't keep your five years' pledge long," Father Molloy said with a loud laugh.

"It's a weak stomach I've got," Magan said slyly. "I don't take it in front of the lord yet, but I will one of these days."

Magan passed the decanter to Hardy, who helped himself.

"The rest are ginger-pop, I believe," he said sneeringly.

"They'll learn sense in time," said Father Molloy. "Hurry on, Hardy, with them ducks. I've the appetite of a wolf on me."

Father Molloy did not speak while he was eating duck. While carving the mutton he said to Magan, "How's the Seminary doing?"

"Fine," said Magan. "That lay lad I picked up is the devil for work."

"And you let him have his belly full of it, I suppose," said Father Molloy, dryly.

"And why not? What else are we paying him for? We've to give him sixty pounds a year. These lay teachers are getting so damn stuck up, there'll be no standing 'em after a short time."

"That fellow Boyle that used to be in the Seminary is kicking up a fine rumpus with his rotten rag of a paper," Father Molloy said. "Not that I could see any harm in it myself. I tried to read it once or twice, but I couldn't make head or tail of it; but the bishop says it's going from bad to worse. The lord tells me the kybosh is going to be put on him soon."

"What's going to happen?" Ralph asked eagerly.

"I don't know that I rightly remember. It didn't sound of much importance and it went in one ear and out the other."

He paused, a slice of mutton on the carving-fork, his brow wrinkled in thought, "It's some Bull or other they're going to bring out of Rome. There's a lot of priests, it seems, in France and places that don't take Gury – or is it Perrone? – for gospel. They're going to be made toe the line or be pitched out: and papers like Boyle's that supports them'll be condemned."

"It's mostly dogmatic theology and philosophy they're wrong on," said Magan importantly.

"Hear the prizeman showing off!" Father Molloy said impatiently. "it's all one to me. There's more than enough in Gury for me, and maybe I know my way around as well as any of the guns," he said, eating his mutton.

During the silence that followed, Ralph was unable to eat. He did not attach much importance to what Father Molloy had said. Still, the bishop would probably know. If determined steps were taken by Rome to fetter thought, his own position might become untenable. He had already stretched his conscience to a limit that caused him much uneasiness. He was upheld, however, by the hope that the official Church was slowly realising her essential mission. But if she openly declared for what he believed to be error, what was he to do?

"Clear off the things quick, Mary, and bring in the hot water," Father Molloy said to the servant. "It's only wasting food to offer it to you. You haven't the appetite of a baby," he added to Ralph.

When the hot water was brought in Father Molloy made himself a glass of punch and passed the hot water to Magan.

"There's ginger-beer for anyone that doesn't want the hard stuff," he said, taking a sip of his punch. "Now we can talk of something more important than theology, and that's the election." He leant back comfortably in his chair.

"There'll be no election. The opposition of these fellows, that no one heard tell of in public life before, is only a joke," Hardy said.

"We'll soon know that," said Father Molloy, looking at Ralph keenly.

"If you refer to Byrne, Dunne and Haverty, they are quite serious," Ralph said.

"It must be put a stop to," said Father Molloy.

"Hear, hear," Hardy said, striking a spoon on his tumbler.

Magan looked at Ralph and laughed.

"I'm sure there'll be no difficulty about it," said Father Molloy, blandly. "We're all a happy family here and we'll work together. It's up to you, O'Brien."

"I haven't a vote. I hope they'll win though. Besides, I couldn't prevent them standing even if I tried," Ralph said.

"Tell that to the marines," said Father Molloy. "The whole town knows you have that club well in hand. Hasn't he, Dempsey? You're in and out there and you ought to know."

"I don't think he interferes," Dempsey said. "They seem very independent."

"My God!" said Father Molloy, "to let a nest of vipers like that grow up under my very eyes. I had more dependence on you, O'Brien, especially after the way you settled that skunk Delaney for me the other day."

"What do you mean?" Ralph asked.

"Mum's the word about that, but I don't forget it for you." He put a finger to his lips and winked at Ralph. "But this is sad business about the club. If you're not able to manage it, I must step in myself and take control. I'll soon bring these lads to reason."

"But he says he approves of their standing," said Hardy, maliciously.

"Maybe he had some reason for saying that, but I'm sure he didn't mean it."

"Of course I meant it. What do you take me for?" said Ralph, with some heat.

"Easy now," said Father Molloy, waving his hands. "I only took you for a sensible man, as, I'm sure, you'll turn out to be. There's more in this than meets the eye and I'm sure, when I've had my say, you'll come round to reason." He took a long drink of punch, and smacked his lips.

"I've never known the leading men of the town so vexed about anything before," he said seriously; "and no wonder, when a set of nobodies try to oust them out of their place. It's the principle of the thing they mind."

"It's none of our business, anyway," said Lanigan, yawning.

"Isn't it? It's little your Greek teaches you. I don't know where this town'd be if I wasn't at the helm. On one side in this dispute there's all the money in the town – the other side'd have some trouble in making up a pound between them. Now, tell me this: are the priests to be found fighting on the side of their pay or agin it? Let me tell you that this is very much of our business. Rightly or wrongly, I hope wrongly, it's spread through the town broadcast that some priests are supporting the fellows that are making all the trouble."

"Not me," said Hardy and Magan in a breath.

"I don't give a fig one way or another," Lanigan said.

"You might soon find yourself out of the Seminary," Father Molloy said sharply.

"I wish to the Lord I did."

"I like the candidates," Dempsey said; "I see a good deal of them in the Irish class. They are very decent fellows, but I don't interfere in elections."

"As I said before, I approve," Ralph said coldly.

"Are you going to canvass for them?" Father Molloy asked.

"No," Ralph said.

"He's drawing in his horns," said Hardy, sneeringly.

"I don't believe in priests canvassing," Ralph said.

"In that case we might be able to gloss it over," said Father Molloy with relief. "Myself and Hardy aren't that thin-skinned. We'll do a bit of canvassing all right. I'll have a go at the club to head the lads off if I can. There'd be the devil to pay if a priest was mixed up with them. There has never been a division between the leading men of the town and the priests since I came to Bunnahone. Damn me if it'll happen now. Look here, O'Brien, you're not going to fight me, are you, in my own parish?" He shut his lips and peered at Ralph through half-closed eyelids.

"I don't intend to fight anyone," Ralph said, smiling. "But since you have raised this question I may as well say what I feel: there is too much clerical interference in elections. These men have the right of any ordinary citizen to put themselves forward for election. We have the right of supporting or opposing them as voters, not as priests."

Father Molloy laughed harshly.

"An infant Solomon!" he said derisively. "Did any of ye ever hear the like, boys?" He gazed vacantly at the window and gave a long low whistle.

"We'll see, we'll see ... what we'll see," he said, finishing his punch. "One thing is certain," he said, frowning at Ralph. "It's my job to see that the dues of the parish aren't put in danger by any foolishness ... and the Seminary collection coming on, too, in a few weeks."

He left his seat suddenly and the party separated. Dempsey accompanied Ralph on his way home.

"The club was getting on so well, too," Dempsey said sadly. "Not a better Irish class within the four seas of Ireland."

"What are you so gloomy about?" Ralph asked.

"Molloy'll break it up and that'll be the end of all our labour," Dempsey said, shrugging his shoulders.

"Not he," said Ralph. "Byrne and Dunne will never give in. "You'll find most of the members will stick to them."

"I doubt it. Wait till Molloy sets to work in earnest. There's nothing he'd stop at when his temper is up. I know him well this many a year."

During the next few days Ralph frequently met Father Molloy and Father Hardy in the street. They avoided him as much as possible and were evidently making a house-to-house visitation. Once when Lanigan and Ralph were walking together, Molloy and Hardy passed them on the side walk. Father Molloy strutted along, his head in the air, his lips pursed, and pretended not to notice them; Father Hardy grinned triumphantly.

"You deserve a medal, O'Brien, for making Molloy and Hardy friends," said Lanigan, chuckling. "Not that it's only skin deep, I'm thinking. They're as thick as thieves now, but the moment they've cooked your hash, they'll hate each other like poison again."

"What are they doing?"

"Canvassing. Hardy told me this morning that they had the election already in their pockets, but that Molloy wouldn't rest a foot until he'd smashed the club and made it the laughing-stock of the town."

The club was full of rumours every night. Father Molloy had visited the reading-room and taken away a copy of Boyle's paper; Haverty had retired from the contest; a lot of members were resigning.

Ralph went to the next committee meeting with a heavy heart. Grady was the only member present at the hour appointed. Byrne and Dunne arrived five minutes late.

"Canvassing that kept us. It's only wasting good shoe-leather," Byrne said, "but we might as well fight it out to a finish." He looked round the room.

"We might as well begin," he said; "I don't think we'll have any more members." He laughed dryly, with a half-amused glance at the bundle of letters in front of him on the table.

"I guess what's in most of them. Haverty's given us up. He told me today. His wife wouldn't give him rest or peace since Father Molloy was talking to her. He's ashamed of his life - not a bad sort of poor weak creature."

He opened the other letters. "Grogan resigns ... one, two ... twenty-two resignations. Some without a word of explanation; others because the club is 'anti-national' or 'irreligious' or 'anti-clerical' or 'opposed to the best interests of the town'. Where's your programme of reform, Mr Dunne?" he added, laughing bitterly.

Ralph took the letters and read them over. The same phrases occurred in many of them One letter he knew to be in Father Molloy's handwriting.

"Don't be depressed, Father," said Byrne, kindly. "I had my hopes, too – the most hardened of us believe, one time or another, that a miracle is going to happen. But I have had so many ups and downs in life that a disappointment doesn't surprise me much."

"It's a shame the way we've been belied," said Dunne heatedly.

"Anyone who tries to do anything is belied. It's easy known you're young, or you wouldn't mind that."

"Some good has been done, anyway," Grady said quietly. "We've made a start for independence. They can't take the house away from us, and if only a couple of dozen of us stick together we'll make headway yet."

"What's that out of over two hundred?" Dunne said.

"Grady is right," Byrne said. "I don't mind a set back. All the same, things are waking up. The great change may not come in my day, but Dunne there is sure to see it. What do you think, Father?"

"Perhaps you're right, but I'm as disappointed as Dunne. There are so many of these men on whom I was certain we could depend," Ralph said, fingering the letters.

Resignations continued to come in every day. For several evenings preceding the poll the club was almost empty, while the public houses, Donaghue's and Darcy's especially, were filled with customers. "Free drink is flowing like water," Dunne told Ralph. On the eve of the election the club was reduced to thirty-one members. A crowd gathered in front of the club door and jeered the few members who entered. Ralph felt his coat tails pulled as he reached the door. He turned and recognised one of the men who had resigned.

"Well, Leary?" he said.

Leary gave a drunken hiccough and pulled Ralph against the jamb. "Don't go in, Father," he jerked out; "the dev – il's house – in there. Bad Cath – Catholics all of 'em.... Don't go sacra – sacraments. Good Catholic li – like me," he patted his chest vigorously, "wouldn't touch 'em ... forty foot pole."

"Go home, Leary. That's a good fellow," Ralph said quietly.

"Won't go home. Best drink in town ... Mr Donaghue, grand man, Mr Donaghue. Good Catholic, like me."

Ralph took his arm and led him home. He struggled to get into several public houses and grumbled all the way.

"Shame. Lots of drink ... quarts and quarts.... I'm good Cath –

olic. Father Tom says ... he says ... one of the best in the bloody town."

Ralph knocked at the door of one of the dilapidated cottages opposite Byrne's. A neatly dressed young woman opened the door halfway, held a lighted candle high and peered into the darkness. Her face was pale and had the marks of recent tears. The light fell on Leary, leaving Ralph in the shadow.

"Hallo, Kate, old woman," Leary said with a foolish leer.

"You drunken swipe!" she hissed, "shut your mouth and don't wake the child."

"Light as a feather," Leary muttered, stooping and attempting to open his boot laces. Ralph moved to prevent him falling and came within the glare of the candle.

"I beg your reverence's pardon," the woman said; "sure it's ashamed he ought to be for you to see him like this."

Leary, after a great effort, succeeded in removing his shoes and stumbled on tiptoe across the earthen floor towards a cradle by the fire.

"Sound as a bell," he said, smiling inanely and putting his finger to his lips, after he had peeped into the candle. He sank into a chair and waved his hand vaguely in the air. His head fell forward and jerked up and down.

"And we getting on grand!" she said, in a low voice to Ralph, holding the candle aloft and pointing to a few new chairs and a new dresser.

"Sorra drop of drink he took these three months, and Mr Byrne was to be thanked for it all. And now to turn agin him. I'll be ashamed to look him in the face ever again."

She wiped her eyes with the corner of her apron.

Leary fell forward off the chair and woke up. She put down the candle hastily, knelt beside him and put out her arms to lift him.

"Damn you! Let me be," he said angrily, pushing her aside.

"Don't heed that, Father," she said anxiously. "He's as good as gold when he hasn't the drink on him. Get up now, Tom, and let me put you to bed."

"Byrne ... old cobbler ... bad Catholic," he said; "Mr Donaghue ... good fellow ... good Catholic, best drink in town."

Ralph helped him to his feet.

"Vote for my religion," he said, nodding his head emphatically at Ralph. "The old Church for ever."

Ralph helped him to the little bedroom off the kitchen, where he threw himself on the bed and fell again into a drunken slumber.

His wife tucked him in comfortably. "Best let him sleep it off," she said.

"Them that brought him to that'll have no luck," she said, as Ralph left the house.

There was an unwonted stir in the streets as Ralph walked back. A small crowd in front of Darcy's shop were singing in varied discord, "For he's a jolly good fellow."

"Three cheers for Mr Darcy that'd never read a heresy paper," was shouted by someone as Ralph drew near.

"Old Byrne can hide himself in a sack after this," the same voice shouted when the cheers died down.

Ralph recognised half a dozen of the men. Three or four had been members of the club. One of them clung to a lamp-post in front of Darcy's door. He slapped Ralph on the arm as he passed by.

"Vote for Mr Darcy and Father Tom, the best men in Bunnahone," he shouted.

"Shut up, you fool!" a companion whispered.

Ralph went home disgusted. The club was the one thing in Bunnahone that had sustained his drooping spirits all through the winter. The enrolling of a new member gave him keen pleasure. He saw in it an awakening self-respect that gave him some hope of the future of the little town. He recalled the evening Leary joined. He had watched him loitering, his hands in his pockets, through the well-lit rooms and now remembered that he had said on leaving: "I'll never go home to Kate again with the signs of drink on me." There were others who, like Leary, had been addicted to drink and had given it up, attracted by Father Dempsey's Irish class or the reading-room or the general atmosphere of the place. Had they gone the way of Leary tonight? What he had hoped would be a bond of union had become a weapon of division and strife. For a while, as he sat deep in an armchair in his study, he felt that he had, in some obscure way, been the cause of all this trouble. He analysed his motives. As far as he could see his sole intention was to help others to bring decency and comfort into their lives and some freedom of thought and action.

The desire of the club to take a part in public affairs came afterwards. It had grown unconsciously and was due more to Dunne than to him. He approved of it. The more he thought of it now, the more he approved of it. The village was run in the selfish interests of a few. Byrne and Dunne were honest unselfish men and not self-seekers. And they were about to be crushed. By whom? He smiled grimly as he thought of the expression used by the man clinging to the lamp-post – by "the two best men in the town", Father Tom and Darcy. Public honesty was on one side, the Church and the gombeen publican on the other. Was this what the Church had come to?

The memory of all the good priests he knew and had known came back to him and he felt that even now a leaven of sanctity was in the Church. But here and now in Bunnahone, Father Tom was the Church in so far as it was a public institution. His will and the bishop's were evidently one.

He shivered as he lit a candle and went upstairs to bed. All night he turned feverishly. He huddled under the blankets, thinking they were a cooling stream, and then pushed them away, for suddenly they had become icebergs that threatened to crush him. He was fascinated by a picture of Father Tom standing in Darcy's shop, his foot on Byrne's neck, one hand raised aloft, excommunicating him, while with the other the priest turned the tap of a huge porter barrel high as the ceiling, from which Leary, stretched prone on the ground, drank with uplifted lips....

Next evening, a few minutes before ten, the poll was declared. Ralph heard the shouts of an excited mob that paraded the streets. Ann, who had been at the Cathedral praying, told him the result. Byrne and Dunne were at the bottom of the poll – hundreds of votes behind the successful candidates – with twelve and fifteen votes respectively.

Ann told him the news with unusual gentleness. She lingered, as if expecting him to say something.

"You're not troubled in your mind about anything?" she said anxiously, after a long silence.

He smiled.

"There's all kinds of talk going on," she said, fingering her apron. "I'm not given to gossiping with idle stravagers, but I couldn't close my ears."

"People must talk."

"I don't know that. They oughtn't bring you into it. Priests, too! May God forgive them their sins."

"I shall breakfast at the convent tomorrow," he said, looking pointedly at his watch.

Ann, however, was not to be repulsed.

"They say many of the men in the club are no better than Protestants – may God come between us and all harm." She turned up her eyes and made the sign of the cross.

"Don't listen to such nonsense."

"And," bridling, "that you're as bad yourself." She burst into tears. "They shouldn't be saying it," she said piteously. "And me rearing you by the best of good advices from Father Eusebius himself."

"Don't, Ann," Ralph said, patting her gently on the shoulder. "Does it matter what people say?" He felt near to tears himself. "Do go to bed, Ann. I don't mind talk of that kind."

He took up a book and pretended to read. She watched him for a few seconds and then turned towards the door.

"May God be their judge and a bitter one, too," she said, as she shut the door behind her.

Ralph felt unaccountably miserable. The print swam and he could not make out the words. After all, he had expected this result. He was making a mountain out of a mole-hill, he thought. There would be better results another time. A defeat was often success. Perhaps it was so now. He heard a single knock at the front door. It must be a sick call at this hour. He vaguely speculated whether it was to the workhouse or to some house in the village.

Ann entered and gave him a letter.

"From his lordship, the bishop," she said. "His man said there was no answer."

He turned the letter over and looked at the large red seal on the back on which the rather florid episcopal crest stood out distinctly. The motto was slightly blurred, but he deciphered the words "*Caritas et veritas*". "A good motto," he murmured aloud, as he opened the letter. He raked up the dying fire, and settled himself in an armchair with his feet on the fender. He held the letter open in his hand for a few seconds, watching the flickering flame, sighed as it died out, and read:

"The Palace, Bunnahone.

"Dear Father O'Brien,

"I am informed on unquestionable authority that much scandal has been given to devout souls in this parish by your connection with the club in Bowen House. It is a very great pain to me that one of my priests, in the premier parish of the diocese, under the shadow, I may say, of the episcopal palace, should be the cause of so much spiritual suffering to the faithful. Not only is it reprehensible in yourself, but it casts a stigma on the other priests of the parish, on religion generally, even on your bishop himself.

"I feel remiss in ever having allowed any club to be set up in the diocese except under responsible clerical control. Of course, I was aware of your lack of experience; but even I could not have foreseen that a club, in which a priest was one of the controlling spirits, would have countenanced the admission of members who had – remembered, I am speaking from information received – openly expressed hostile sentiments in regard to good and holy priests; were remiss in their spiritual duties; circulated newspapers of a noxious and quasi-heretical character; stirred up turmoil in a peaceful and orderly town by arrogantly attempting to force unknown and, as I have indicated, unscrupulous,and irreligious men into a position of civil authority, rightly reserved in a Catholic town for good religious citizens, whose adherence to the Church is a proof of their fitness for civic office. To atone for my remissness, if any, and for your own spiritual good, I hereby, as your bishop, order you: –

"1st. To resign membership of the club. Let it be known publicly – to correct any scandal that has been given – that your resignation is due to the facts I have enumerated. (N.B. For obvious reasons you will say that you resign of your own option and not under my direction.)

"2nd. That any influence you may have with these misguided men shall be used towards inducing them to hand over the club premises to Father Molloy, in whose wisdom and discretion I have every reliance. It will be for him to decide what useful purpose they may afterwards subserve.

"I have written to Father Dempsey, who is, I am informed, also a member, directing him to resign, and to Father Lanigan directing him not to frequent the building. Fortunately, the other priests were alive to the dangers likely to arise from such an institution and refrained from joining it.

"Believe me,

"Yours faithfully in Christ,

"† James Devoy,

"*Bishop of Bunnahone.*"

"P.S. – I wish to add informally that out of regard for the noble character and deeply religious spirit of your good mother, who has given many signal instances of her devotion to the Church – only today she munificently sent me £1000 for our new Seminary – I do not wish to deal harshly with you. On your full submission I shall be willing to forget the very grievous fault, if not worse, into which you have fallen, I pray, unwittingly.

"† J.D.,

"*Bishop of Bunnahone.*"

"P.P.S. – I delayed sending you this letter in order that, as I anticipated, my opinion in regard to the club should be confirmed by the votes of the good people of Bunnahone, who, with that zeal for religion which has always characterised them, have dealt a lasting blow to those who attempted to override the expressed wishes of the respected administrator. Of course I take no part myself in public affairs, but I watch the actions of my devoted people with an anxious eye in temporal as well as spiritual things.

"† J.D.,

"*Bishop of Bunnahone.*"

Chapter 24

RALPH READ THE letter twice. He felt benumbed. A feeling of resentment against the bishop was succeeded by one of anger against himself. The memory of Eva Dillon standing at the door of the drawing-room at Dillonsmount came back to him. She was right - he had no sense of humour. He laughed and stretched his legs. No wonder the bishop should try to treat him as a fool, for he was a fool. He had been shutting his eyes to facts all his life. Had he looked them in the face he could have foreseen Dr Devoy writing him the letter he held in his hand.

He lit a candle wearily, put out his lamp and walked towards his bedroom. He stood on the landing outside his bedroom door and leant over the balustrade. The candle cast a smoky light against the pale glow of the full moon that flooded the landing window. He flicked off a piece of burnt wick and the candle burnt brightly.

As he undressed he saw his life differently. Today was made up of all the past. His whole life was a preparation for this hour. His life was his religion. It burned, like the candle, now dimly, now more brightly. He had walked by the dim light he had made for himself, straying hither and thither, sometimes backwards, but always regaining the path, sustained by some growing strength within him. Ann, his mother, Father David, the grotesque Seminary, the still more grotesque Maynooth, even Father Tom, and now the bishop, had all helped to free his soul.

He stretched out his arms with a new sense of elation. That was it. His soul that was in bondage had a glimpse of freedom. He tried to think of the future, but it was all dark. The bishop's letter? That was easily dealt with if ...

He slept soundly and jumped out of bed at the first sound of the alarm clock. The sun streamed in through the open window. He drew in deep breaths of the fresh morning air. He dressed hurriedly and knelt to pray beside his bed. He said the formal prayers of his childhood. The bishop's letter came into his mind for a moment. "I must be honest about that," he said aloud as he arose.

He said mass at the convent with more than usual reverence. He lingered over the communion and felt it more than ever some mystic bond with all that was good in life.

At breakfast Reverend Mother looked old and tired. Her hand trembled as she poured out his tea. She put down the teapot with a sigh.

"I am not able even for this," she said with a faint smile.

Ralph talked of a book he had been reading, but she was evidently thinking of something else.

"The bishop was right," she said; "I am too old."

Ralph looked at her enquiringly.

"You have not heard? My term of office as Superior is up tomorrow. The bishop has let it be known that Mother Ann is to be Reverend Mother."

"I'm very sorry, Reverend Mother. But surely the nuns will elect you?"

"I am glad to be relieved of the office. I was never suitable. Of course, the nuns will elect Mother Ann. The will of the bishop is the voice of God," she said with a humorous twinkle.

"Is it always?"

"I am tired," she said wearily. "I don't understand new ways and new methods. Mother Ann suits the bishop much better. All I want is a quiet corner in which to be forgotten."

Ralph handed her the bishop's letter, which she read in silence.

"My poor boy, my poor boy!" she murmured at the end. "All the saints had to undergo trials."

"There is very little of the saint in me," Ralph said, laughing.

"I had heard something of this," she said musingly. "Byrne does some work for us. He's a good man. What will you do?"

"Of course, I cannot do what he orders. I am thrown back on my own conscience, poor thing as it is."

She sighed. "Think of the poor people for whom you might do so much."

He was silent for a few minutes. If he sacrificed his self-respect, his honour, his judgment, what help would he be to anyone? He must be honest with himself, no matter what he had to give up – the work, the people he loved. "It may not come to that," he said, following up his own thoughts aloud.

"I know the bishop," she said. "It is only a question of time; you will have to give in."

He shook his head and smiled.

"God give you courage," she said. "I never had it; I'm only a failure. I oughtn't attempt to advise anyone. All that is left to me now is to pray. I sometimes wish I was young again," she said wistfully.

She accompanied him to the door. "The will of God be done," she said, as she shook his hand warmly. "Who knows what may be in store for you?"

Ralph stood on the little bridge on the way to the gate, leaning on the parapet, thinking of what he should do in regard to the letter. Should he answer it or call on the bishop? An interview would perhaps be best. What would be the result?

"Ralph, I want to speak to you."

He was startled by the sound of Eva's voice. He had not heard her walk across the grass in her light house shoes. He turned quickly and saw her beside him, flushed and excited.

"Have you tired of avoiding me?" he said, smiling.

"Are you in any trouble, Ralph?" she asked anxiously, ignoring his question. "Sister Veronica has just told me that you are. Father Molloy was in the school for a few minutes this morning and told her that you have been doing dreadful things and that you were to be sent off to an out-of-the-way parish."

"I haven't heard that," he said. "It mightn't be a bad thing if I were," he added thoughtfully.

"They are very horrid to you. I know they are," she said vehemently. "If I stay much longer here I shan't have a spark of religion left in me." She looked at him appealingly, her hands clasped, her eyes glowing.

"What is wrong, Eva?" he said gently.

"Don't speak to me," she said angrily. "I ..."

She checked herself and said quietly, "Things have got on my nerves ... this treatment of you ... all the gossip about it. The nuns are talking of it. And then the putting aside of Reverend Mother. Why did I ever come to this place?"

"Why did you?"

"I don't know," she said hesitatingly. "Reverend Mother understood. She understands most things. Were it not for her I would leave tomorrow."

"Are you unhappy?"

She looked at him keenly and gave a short laugh.

"Mother Ann says I have all the signs of a true vocation," she said sharply. "But I didn't come to talk of myself. I hope you won't be made to suffer. Let me know what happens?"

He walked beside her towards the school. Mother Ann saw them coming and waited at the door. Ignoring Ralph, she said to Eva, "You should have been in your class for the last five minutes, Sister," and turned into the school. Eva bit her lip. "And she's to be the new Reverend Mother," she said bitterly. "Never mind, Ralph, they can't eat you. I believe they would if they could." She stamped her foot. "She knows you are in the bishop's black books – he spent an hour with her yesterday afternoon and now you are taboo."

"Hem, hem," said Veronica, from the infant school door. "Sister Eva! to your class at once! Don't be flirting with Father O'Brien," she laughed loudly.

Eva blushed, was about to make a retort, but walked away towards her classroom without speaking.

"I ought to be Reverend Mother," Veronica said, making a grimace. "I'd keep all the novices and postulants and some of the old ones, too, in great order." She came closer to Ralph.

"I have given up Father Tom. I told him so to his face this morning. I said I wouldn't have any tale-carrying about you; that you were worth a dozen of him and his Hardys and the dry old stick of a bishop, too."

Mother Ann appeared at the end of the corridor. Veronica vanished abruptly into the infant school.

Ralph gave a sigh of relief and went home, where he found Byrne awaiting him.

The old man seemed grave and preoccupied.

"Well," he said, with a slight American drawl that rarely appeared in his speech, "I guess we got a good whipping."

"I thought that the club members at least would have supported you."

"They were mortal afeard."

"But the secrecy of the ballot ..."

"In a small town like this," Byrne interrupted, "the people don't believe it's secret. It may be – still, things have a way of leaking out. There are more than twelve in the town would have stuck by me if they weren't in dread their names'd be known. Quarts of porter in front and the fire of hell lashing them behind wouldn't be enough if they weren't afeard of their bread and butter and the roofs over their head. But there's no use in crying over spilt milk now. What's to happen about the club?"

"We shall keep it open," Ralph said firmly. "We shall have twelve or fifteen members at least, perhaps more."

"I'm not so sure of that. A few might risk the ballot-box that won't have the courage to stick to the club in the face of the dead set that'll be made agin us."

"You are not afraid," Ralph said, smiling.

Byrne snorted contemptuously. "Me afeard? Of a few gombeen men and priests! They'll try to boycott me, I don't doubt, but I laid by a few pounds in America and I'll be able to wear them out. There are others that need to be more careful," he added, looking at Ralph significantly.

"Yes," Ralph said thoughtfully, "they might injure Dunne and ..."

"There's yourself, now," Byrne said.

"I'm all right. I am not afraid."

"I think we know that by now. All the same, we're afeard for you. We have been hearing things for the last week. Father Hardy has been boasting everywhere that the bishop is going to give you hell."

Ralph smiled.

"You know what I mean," Byrne said insistently; "a more real hell, maybe, than the other. I'm an old man and I've kept my eyes open. The trampling that the priests give the people is nothing to the trampling a priests gets who holds out agin his bishop."

"I shall do what I think is right. If I am unjustly treated I can appeal to the archbishop. There is such a thing as canon law."

"It strikes me it's going to law with the devil and the court in hell," Byrne said grimly. "They cling together like limpets to a rock. They'll hound down any priest that dares to hold up his head agin them."

"Nonsense!" Ralph said; "we are not living in the Middle Ages."

"I don't care what age we're living in. 'Twas often done in my time and 'twill be done again. You'd have felt the lash before this, I beg your pardon for intruding in your private affairs, only they want to make sure of your mother's money."

Ralph blushed. "Surely not," he said. "I wouldn't dream ..."

"You wouldn't!" Byrne said gently. "And that's your weakness in fighting agin the like of them. It was spread all over the town yesterday before the poll that your mother had given a lot of money to the bishop to show that she was agin the club; and that she had let a big farm to Donaghue to give him her countenance."

"The money was for the new Seminary and the farm was let before the election," Ralph said in surprise.

"I'm telling you what was given out, and it came from Father Tom. I believe there's something in it and that they're turning your own mother agin you," Byrne said doggedly. He saw Ralph's pained face and added hastily, "It may be only a lying report after all."

"In any case I shall stick to the club," Ralph said, tightening his lips.

Byrne held out his hand, which Ralph clasped. "Any man that'd tell me I'd have a weakness for a priest a year ago, I'd call him a liar. But there isn't any club to stick to," he said sadly.

"What!"

"Now let us talk sensibly. Dunne and myself decided to close the club after the poll last night. We hold the lease and we simply shut the door."

"It was highly irregular."

"It was then, I suppose," Byrne said dryly. "But we heard what was brewing agin you and we made up our minds that you wouldn't get into deeper trouble because of us. We don't want to lose you from the town. You may be able to do some good yet."

Ralph was silent for a few minutes. He was very much touched by Byrne's thoughtfulness. He knew the old man's fighting spirit and appreciated the sacrifice he had made.

"You are a better man that I can ever hope to be," he said gently.

"Pah," Byrne said, scowling. "Come and see an old man an odd time. You'll find me glued to the bench most times, now that the club is shut."

When Ralph was again alone the thought of what Byrne said

about his mother worried him and he made up his mind to cycle to Inniscar and see her. He had to make several visits to sick people in the town before leaving.

"It's a black day for the town that the club is shut up," one woman said. "When Jack is on his feet again, he'll be taking to the drink, now that he'll have nowhere to go of a night but to one pub or another."

As he was passing the parochial house Father Molloy, who was standing at the gate, crossed the street jauntily.

"I'm glad you're learning sense," he said "A little bird told me the club is shut. Bedad, but you acted quick. My lord'll be as pleased as punch. Come round tonight and see me. Now that I've shown you what I can do I don't bear any ill will. Besides," he added confidentially, "that fellow Hardy is getting too cocky. He thinks he did it all. As I told you before, I'd give his whole carcase for your little finger. If you'd only work in with me we'd have the whole place to ourselves. It bothers the life out of me to make out what deep game you're playing. Let us talk it out straight and I'll give you as much rope as I can ... if you stand by me."

"I am in a hurry to a sick call," Ralph said coldly.

"Don't be stuck up because you got beat. It does a young lad like you good to knock some of the cock feathers out of him at the start. Ta, ta. See you soon."

It was late in the afternoon before Ralph was able to get away. Cycling rapidly he had almost passed Teig Moriarty, grown bent and feeble, without recognising him. Ralph got off his bicycle and turned back.

"It's a cure for sore eyes to get a glimpse of you," the old man said. "It's queer doings up at Inniscar these times," he added, shaking his head.

"How is the home farm?"

"Of course you know Dongahue has it. 'You'll stay on and keep it for me,' he said to me. 'Not if I was to get a crock of gold every Lady Day, Mr Donaghue,' I said. And at that we parted. It near breaks my heart to go next or near the place, in the hands of a man who knows as much about farming as I know about trimming a hat. He'll bring the best farm in the county to wrack and ruin in a twelvemonth."

"You are not idle?"

"Is it me?" he said, straightening himself with an effort. "Sure I have my own few acres to look after and I give a helping hand to Father Duff. He's a great man for you. I had it always agin him that he wouldn't help on the Irish, but there's true stuff in him for all that. Donaghue thought he was going to break the creamery by keeping back his milk. 'I may have one foot in the grave,' the priest said to me, 'but my whole body'll be there before the likes of Donaghue gets the better of me. Call the boys together, Teig,' he said to me, 'I have a little plan to put before them.' He even spoke to me in Irish when we were alone. Do you know what he's going to set up now? A store, no less, where the best of manures and seeds and all sorts of stuff for the farmers'll be sold at cost price, good stuff and not the rotten things they get from Donaghue and his like. 'We'll soon make up for the loss of the Inniscar cows by increasing the number we keep ourselves,' he said, and I haven't a doubt in the world he'll do it," Teig said with enthusiasm.

"He's a good priest," Ralph said.

"He's a good man," Teig said, "and that's saying more. He pretends he likes a scrap and that he's only having it out with Donaghue, but sure I know he had this plan in his mind this many a day and was only biding his time until the people got some backbone into them. Sure it's thinking of their good he is from morning till night."

The bishop's victoria came through the Inniscar gate as Teig was speaking. The bishop had a faint smile on his lips, which deepened when he saw Ralph. He waved his hand perfunctorily as the carriage passed.

"That's how the wind blows now," Teig said sadly. "He might just as well own the place."

Ralph found his mother reading a devotional book in the drawing-room. Her mourning accentuated the pallor of her face. He noticed a change in the room. A large curcifix stood on the small table at her elbow. A statue of our Lady of Lourdes, a small silver lamp on the pedestal, filled a corner. In front of the statue was a prie-dieu, with some religious books on the ledge. There were some changes too in the pictures: devotional prints having been substituted for the secular ones he remembered. He had come in unannounced and he stood in the room for a few seconds without speaking. His mother's face had hardened, he thought, as he watched her reading, sitting erect in a stiff chair, the drawing-room a conventual setting to her nun-like figure.

As he walked across the room, she raised her eyes abstractedly and gazed at him. He was almost in front of her before she seemed to notice him. With a slight frown she carefully placed a marker in her book, shut it and laid it on her knee. She gave him her hand coldly, saying, "I am glad you have come," and motioned him to a chair by the tea-table.

"This is all very sad," she said, crossing her hands on her lap and looking at him sternly.

"May I have some tea? I've had no luncheon, and I'm as hungry as a hawk.

"What is sad?" he asked, as he sat down.

"The bishop has been here. He told me everything."

Ralph laughed.

"It is not a subject for laughing. However, we shall discuss it when the servant has left the room."

While the servant was bringing tea she sat silent, her eyes fixed on her hands.

When she had given him tea, and they were again alone, she said, "The bishop read me a copy of his letter to you. It was just the letter I should have expected him to write, kind, religious, fatherly." She fixed her eyes on the crucifix. "I am being punished for my many sins," she said querulously. "First the father, now the son - both turning against Thee."

"Mother!" Ralph said in a pained tone.

"I am an unhappy woman," she said, looking at him sternly. "And it is you who make me so. I dedicated you to God, I guarded you from temptation and sin, I fostered the vocation God gave you. And now you repay me by consorting with wicked men, encouraging them in evil and helping them in their opposition to our Holy Church."

"You have heard only one side."

"I have heard the bishop. He represents the Church and when the Church has spoken nothing more is to be said."

"Good Maynooth theology," he said dryly.

"I don't know anything about Maynooth, but I know what every good Catholic is bound to believe."

Ralph felt helpless. Hilda's hard face, the hard lines about the mouth, her narrow forehead, her cold eyes fascinated him. He searched her face anxiously for some sign of softness, for the motherly feeling that used to co-exist side by side with her narrow, religious views. All was hard, cold, repellant. He longed to throw himself at her feet, to lay his head in her lap, to feel her arms around him and her warm kisses on his head. He tried to rise, but her emotionless eyes unnerved him. He felt that they created a barrier of ice between them. How futile all argument was with a lifeless statue, he thought, and sighed. She gazed at him coldly, awaiting a reply.

"I acted according to my conscience," he said.

A look of horror came into her eyes. He noted it with some pleasure as the only sign of feeling she had displayed. It died away in a moment, and she said harshly, "You are adding blasphemy to disobedience. As if conscience, which is the mirror of God's will, could prompt you to do anything a holy bishop disapproved of."

"Don't let us bandy theological quibbles, Mother," he said earnestly. He stood up, pushed aside the table and laid his hands on her shoulder. He felt her quiver slightly and a faint flush tinged her cheek. It died away, and she grew rigid to his touch.

"I want you to love me. I want it so badly – more than anything in the world," he said vehemently.

"Sit down," she said, pushing him away.

He felt cold at the roots of his hair. A dull, cold, aching pain shot through him, as if he had been struck by some icy draught. He looked round anxiously, but the afternoon sun streamed warmly through the windows and a fire burned brightly in the large grate. He sat down wearily.

"You have more need of the love of God," she said coldly.

Ralph gazed at her with dull eyes. She was like a hard, frosty moon, motionless in a wintry sky, miles and miles away. Feeling had failed to bridge the distance – words were useless. They did not speak the same language.

"There are so many things I wanted to say," he said hopelessly.

"Make your peace with the bishop first. All he asks is repentance of heart. He spoke beautifully of it. 'We must not crush the bruised reed,' he said. I thought his letter gentle, but he is even more gentle. He will let bygones be bygones. He says that he will forget the letter, that you need not notice it. Submission of your will for the future is all he asks."

Ralph heard her vaguely. He was thinking of how she once loved him.

"All that is left for me is to make reparation for my own sins - and those of others," she added, after a pause. "There are too many distractions here. I have been too much bound to earthly things and earthly affections and I have been punished. I must go away. I have arranged to enter the Convent of Reparation. The bishop approves of it."

"And leave Inniscar?" he said with astonishment.

"Yes."

"Don't do it, Mother. Go out among the people; take an interest in their lives. You will find God in work ..."

"Don't be offensive," she said coldly. "I seek spiritual advice from spiritual people."

He bit his lip. "I didn't mean to be offensive. I ..."

"Pray for yourself," she said solemnly, "and I will pray for you. I shall let you know of my arrangements."

"Can I help you?" he said. She had risen and held out her hand.

"The bishop will see to everything. I am transferring the property to him in trust for religious purposes."

"You are young. You may not stay in the convent. You may need ..."

"I regret that you are growing worldly. I trust in God," she said, fidgeting with her book which she had again taken up.

He looked back at the house from the avenue. The windows relfected the sun in sheets of flame. The austere lines of the house were softened and it seemed to smile on him with friendly eyes. He lingered at the gate, his eyes dwelling lovingly on the fine old hammered ironwork. He pulled the gate to and it shut with a clang. He gazed at it resentfully. The sound seemed to snap something within him. He looked back towards the house hidden in the trees and saw smoke ascending lazily to the sky, and a feeling of loneliness overcame him.

Chapter 25

RALPH, FOR SOME time, was so absorbed by daily problems in connection with his work that he gave little thought to questions of theology and philosophy. Boyle wrote him letter after letter begging for articles, but he had no inclination for writing. The restatement of the intellectual position of the Church seemed of slight importance compared with the providing of work for men dismissed by Donaghue on the suspicion of having voted against him.

For days after the election the little town seemed to be a hot-bed of intrigue. Byrne called at the convent with some boots and was told that the new Reverend Mother had given instructions that he was not to call again. One by one half a dozen workmen were dropped by their employers and found it impossible to get work elsewhere.

Ralph was so worried that he forgot even his mother's antagonism. The bishop's letter had passed out of his mind when he got a short note from Dr Devoy, saying that he was called suddenly to Rome; as the club was dead he would defer further action in regard to Ralph until his return; meanwhile, Father O'Brien was to act entirely under Father Molloy's instructions.

The day after the bishop's departure Ralph made up his mind to call on Father Molloy and ask him to intervene on behalf of the unemployed workmen. After a long struggle with himself he reluctantly admitted that there was no other way.

Father Molloy's eyes gleamed.

"Did you try to get them work?" he asked, flicking some dust off his coat.

"I could get no one to take them."

Father Molloy rubbed his hands gleefully. "That's organisation for you. It's I can do it when I set about it," he said, hitting his chest with his closed hand.

"Will you get them work?" Ralph said.

Father Molloy pursed his lips and frowned. "A little starvation will do them good and bring 'em to their senses. However, I'll think about it. You see yourself now," he added, winking, "how the wind blows in this town?"

"Yes, I see," Ralph said dryly.

"Good. I'm glad you see reason. I'll make a man of you yet."

Ralph felt inclined to hit him and kept his temper with difficulty.

He had been penniless for some days, and these men, for whose condition he felt he was in some way responsible, would either starve or go to the workhouse unless they got work.

Father Molloy whistled thoughtfully.

"I won't lift a finger though for Byrne or Dunne. They may go to hell for all I care. I wish to God they were out of the town," he said angrily. "I'll have no man in the parish that won't go my way. I met that little Dunne yesterday and he had the impudence to cheek me. I'll make mincemeat of him yet."

"I dare say they can fend for themselves. What shall I say to the others?"

"Oh, let them come to me," Father Molloy said, waving his arms expansively. "I'll give 'em a hell of talking to first, and then, if they're rightly amenable - well - well," he drew himself up and pursed his lips, "I don't mind if I take 'em back. No one can say but I'm a kind-hearted man," he added complacently. "You're not going? Now that you're beginning to cut your wisdom teeth I want to talk to you a bit and give you a few tips."

Ralph said that he had to see the men at once.

"You're a queer chap. Making work, you are. Young colts take the bit in their mouths at the start, but they settle down. Sober and easy goes far in a day, is my motto. I was thinking of taking you down to tea with the Miss Hinnisseys and you might make it up with the old man at the same time. It'd make a good impression in the town, too, if we walked down arm in arm - it'd show that I had brought you round to reason."

Ralph felt relieved when he got to the street. A feeling of nausea that oppressed him in Father Molloy's room passed away. He walked some paces without thought, his eyes unconsciously noting impressions, a heap of mud on the street, a letter missing from Donaghue's signboard, two ragged urchins playing on the sidewalk. When his thoughts became active, he felt depressed. Failure seemed written all over his life. He had to go hat in hand to Father Molloy to save men from starvation. All countries had the institutions they deserved. Bunnahone had its Father Molloy. Surely that was only cheap cynicism, an excuse for apathy. The ideal remained after every temporary failure.

A drizzling rain fell. The intolerably dreary appearance of the town, with its discoloured house fronts and shabby signboards, made him shudder.

He called on one of the workmen, whom he found lounging at the door of his house. He listened to Ralph apathetically.

"I suppose I'll go to him," he said, when Ralph asked him to see Father Molloy. "If it weren't for the children, I might work my way to America. I'm told a man can call his soul his own there. But I don't know – I have my doubts."

A slatternly woman half opened the door in another house.

"Jimmy! Where'd he be but in a pub? It's you and your club did it all. I wash my hands of the whole of ye," and she slammed the door in his face.

He managed to see all the men. Life seemed to have been crushed out of all except one, who shrugged his shoulders and said, cheerfully, "It's all in a day's work. Better luck next time."

Ralph went homewards overwhelmed by a sense of defeat. The crushed souls of the people he had visited; the memory of his mother, cold, almost inhuman; Father Molloy's complacency in his use of the wonderful mysteries of Catholicism as a lever in local politics – was this the only result of that faith which was to renew men's hearts and transform the world?

There was Mrs Fahy! He called at a little one-roomed cottage a few yards from his own house. The door was open, a half door in front being hasped. He leant over it.

"You're as welcome, Father, as the flowers in May, may God Almighty bless you," a voice said from a bed in the far corner, beyond the fireplace. "And sure it's fine this rain is for the crops, may the Lord be praised."

An old woman in a spotless goffered cap was propped up in bed, a heavy shawl over her shoulders.

"Shall I shut the door? The rain is coming in," he said when he entered.

"Sure, a drop of rain does no harm to anything and there's more light when the door is open. My eyes are that weak that I must have the door as well as the window now. Not that I've anything to complain of," she said cheerfully, "for the Lord is very good to me."

"How is the rheumatism?"

"Fine, thanks be to God. Sure, He keeps it out of my hands and I'm able to work all day long." She was busily knitting a stocking. "I was able to limp round for an hour today and ready up. Sure, that was a great thing."

He sat beside the bed and she talked while she worked of the goodness and love of God. She had been practically bedridden for twenty years and was always cheerful. She had a small pension of five shillings a week from a former employer. "More than enough," she said, "and there's a penny over often for them that's wanting it.

"Work is the great prayer," she said. "Sure, I feel I have a grip of God when I have a knitting-needle in my hand. God has a way with Him," she said again, "and there's more people in heaven than people rightly know. Sure, He's not pernickity, or mean, with His eyes always to a keyhole. There's good in the greatest sinners I've known in my time, and you may be sure it's not there unknownst to God."

The rain ceased as she spoke, and a bright gleam of the warm sunshine that follows early summer rain fell across the bed and lit up her face.

"In some queer way as it looks to us, but you may be sure it's as clear as daylight to God, the good is working to the top in us all," she said, looking abstractedly at the sunlight.

The light was fading before he rose to go.

"If I only had the lamp lit I'd be as happy as a queen," Mrs Fahy said.

He lit it and laid it on a chest beside the bed.

"The whole world is wonderfully kind to me. May God be in your heart, Father, ever and always," she said fervently.

Bunnahone seemed brighter and more cheerful when he went into the street again. He stood at his own gate. Light gleamed on the wet roofs of the houses, sodden thatch glowing with myriads of jewels. Under these roofs, too, were mysteries of faith, hearts through which flowed that living stream that had fructified life ever since man felt the need of religion.

And the Church was deliberately putting itself outside it all. For power and money it was sacrificing the heritage of the saints. It no longer made any effort to express this living faith. For a religion that embraced all life it was busily substituting formulas to buttress its own power. The living experience of the saints of God was ignored....

It was worse still when one considered the concrete – the relations of the Church in Bunnahone, for instance, to the people.

"It's a grand colour, surely."

Ralph started at the sound of Dunne's voice. He had been looking at a clump of fir-trees behind which the sun was sinking into the sea.

"It is very beautiful."

"I hope it'll shine on a better place for me than Bunnahone when I follow it west," Dunne said sadly.

"You're not leaving?" Ralph said in surprise as he opened the door.

Dunne nodded. When they were seated in the study, he said heatedly, "Do you know what happened a couple of hours ago? Father Tom went into the Emporium and had a talk with Mrs Hinnissey. Bridget Carey saw it all, and that the poor woman was flustered like. With that the priest goes over to the drapery counter: 'You're keeping company still, I hear, in spite of all my warning, with that blackguard, Dunne,' he said. The breath was nearly knocked out of Bridget, but she admitted that she was. 'If you don't give him up Mrs Hinnissey'll give you the sack,' he said, as mad as a March hare. With that Bridget fired up – lately she has been getting great pluck. She went for him in great style. She didn't leave a word in him. But the minute he turned his back, she sat down with her head on the counter and cried her fill. And there Mrs Hinnissey found her when she gave her an hour's notice and her money. The old woman cried, too, but she said she wouldn't keep anyone in the shop that was disrespectful to the clergy. In ten minutes Bridget's box was in Hinnissey's backyard and she came straight to me where I was making a coffin in the workshop. There were the signs of tears on her and she said to me, shy like, 'Will you marry me now, or will I get another situation?' Without letting another word out of her

I took hold of her and told her the first situation she'd mentioned was hers as soon as we could get a priest to marry us. Then she out with it all. I used some language, but she shut me up. She said she wouldn't listen to a word in cold blood agin a priest; that she had said enough herself for two, and she in a temper. I let it go at that and found some decent lodgings for her for a few days. The minute the knot is tied, we're off to Queenstown - then the first boat to New York."

"Why not stay on in Bunnahone?"

"If there was only myself to think off, sorra foot I'd leave it," Dunne said, frowning, "but there's the girl to think of. Father Tom has his knife in me and wouldn't give us rest or peace. It'd break Bridget's heart in a year."

Ralph walked up and down the room. His first impulse was to go straight to Father Molloy and tell him what he thought of his conduct. He would only laugh. It was intolerable.

"I don't know what to advise," he said helplessly.

"Don't let it bother your head, Father," Dunne said more cheerfully. "With things as they are here and the skelping Father Tom gave us at the election, it's with no light hand he'd deal with me if I crossed him again. To tell you God's truth, I'm a bit sick of making coffins, and it's all there's ever likely to be done in the way of carpentering in this town."

"But to be driven to emigrate by a priest ..."

"God help us, but that's no new thing," Dunne interrupted with a smile. "It's many a man and woman I'll meet in New York that's in the same boat. Many's the one Father Tom drove across the water in my own time. But I'll say no more," he added, shrugging his shoulders. "I promised Bridget not to be bitter agin him."

Dunne fidgeted with his hat. "Might I make bold to ask you to arrange about the marriage for us? If I go near Father Molloy we're more than likely to have a row and Bridget is afeard of her life of him. If he charges us too much I don't know what we'll do at all. After selling the few boards and things I have, there won't be a great deal over when I've paid our passage money."

"I shall see Father Molloy at once," Ralph said. "He told me he would be at home this evening. Stay here till I come back."

He felt so resentful against Father Molloy that the prospect of an interview was distasteful. His nerves tingled: he stood for a moment at the gate and made an effort to control himself. The sun had gone down and the ragged black line of the pine trees stood out against a gorgeous background of gold and red. A deep peace brooded over the town, solemn, still, beautiful. The half light hid the meanness of the houses. Petty quarrels seemed so trivial beneath that mocking beauty.

The servant who opened the door of the parochial house hesitated a moment and said, pointing to the dining-room, "You'll find them all in there."

He opened the door, and was about to close it again, when Father Tom said, "Come on, man. Don't be a spoil sport."

The table had been removed, the floor waxed. Standing by the walls were groups of men and women. In a corner sat the local fiddler taking his fiddle from its case. In the centre of the room was a group of eight about to dance, awaiting the music, Father Tom at the top, with Miss Katie Hinnissey on his arm. Father Hardy frowned when he saw Ralph and looked anxiously at Father Tom.

Ralph stood astonished at the door, his lips parted.

"Shut the door, man, and come in. How did you get wind of it?" Father Tom said boisterously. "I'd have invited you, but it was got up very sudden."

"Oh! he's too prim for anything of the sort," said one of the Miss Darcys.

"I am afraid I have come on business," Ralph said, blushing furiously. "Could you spare me a moment, Father Molloy?"

Father Molloy grimaced. "I can never get a minute to enjoy myself in this blessed town. You wait for me, Katie. Let the rest of you be going on. I'll be back in a minute."

"That fellow'd freeze any company," Father Hardy said, as Ralph followed Father Molloy out of the room.

"Sure, no one could freeze near you, Father," his partner giggled.

"What's all this about?" Father Molloy said, opening his sitting-room door. "I thought you were coming to the dance. It's not a real dance," he winked; "that would be agin the statutes. It's only a little private hop and that's allowable when the lord isn't nosing round. Not that he's very particular about trifles of the kind."

"I called about Dunne."

"I gave that lad a wipe in the eye today. Has he come whining to you about it already?"

"He wishes to get married to Miss Carey."

The jocose look in Father Molloy's face gave way to a frown. He bit his nails, his eyes fixed on the floor.

"It's wishing it he'll be then, if I can stop it," he said decisively, after a short pause.

"There is no reason why they shouldn't marry, and I have promised to arrange it for him," Ralph said firmly.

Father Molloy looked at him keenly. "Do you know you're interfering in my business? I let you down easily over the election, but I'm going to be master in the parish. Have some spark of sense in you and let this alone. Tell Dunne to come to me and I'll soon settle him."

"You can't refuse to marry him. I may tell you that I mean to see this through."

Father Molloy's eyes gleamed. "You want to fight, do you? Well, you'll have your belly full before you're done with me. What can you do if I refuse to marry him? And refuse I will." He spluttered the last sentence and hit the table by his side with his closed fist.

"I must go to the vicar-general, then, as the bishop is away," Ralph said quietly.

"That's the last straw!" Father Molloy said furiously. "To threaten me with Doyle, as if I cared a fig for him." He walked to and fro excitedly. "You've been crossing me ever since you came into the parish. I'll be damned if I put up with you much longer. As soon as ever the bishop comes back I'll see that you get your walking papers."

"Am I to go to Father Doyle or will you marry Dunne?"

Ralph's coolness seemed to irritate Father Molloy to a high pitch of excitement. His florid cheeks grew pale and he puffed and spluttered widly.

"You be ..." He checked himself, strummed with his fingers on the mantelpiece, with his back to Ralph.

"Doyle might spite me in this," he muttered, thinking aloud. After a few minutes he turned round and listened to the laughter and music that reached them from the dining-room.

"They're having a great time in there," he said with a wry smile.

"Where did you say the fellow was going to live?" he said, taking a book of dispensation forms out of his desk.

"In America."

"Why the hell didn't you say that at first? Bunnahone will be well rid of him. There's the dispensation in banns. Charge him ten pounds. You can do the marrying. I wouldn't demean myself raising my hand over him."

"I shall take whatever he offers."

"You'll take ten pounds or pay the difference yourself," Father Molloy said angrily.

Ralph shrugged his shoulders and looked Father Molloy squarely in the face. "You ought to make an apology to Miss Carey for what you did today," he said.

Father Molloy backed away a step and laughed harshly. He drew himself up and said with as much dignity as was compatible with his squat figure, "Is it the administrator of the Cathedral apologise to a shop girl? And a street walker at that," he added viciously.

Ralph looked at the mean face with its leering eyes in astonishment. Father Molloy laughed.

"I doubt they're not getting married before they needed it," he said. "I hope they'll get to America before the christening."

"May God forgive you!" Ralph said, looking at him pityingly.

Chapter 26

ONE DAY IN June Father Lyons called on Ralph.

"I have had a letter," he said, looking grave and worried, "from one of our Dominicans in Rome with very sad news. One of these days we are to have a new syllabus. The Jesuits are at the bottom of it. The efforts of the ablest and most devoted men in the Church for the last twenty-four years are to be condemned."

"The Pope will never consent to it," Ralph said. "He's a good man."

"His goodness and simplicity make him a dangerous man. He's thoroughly frightened by the wirepullers. He doesn't understand the problem our friends have tried to face. They have been misrepresented to him. He now believes, I am told, that he has a divine mission to save the Church. One of the best of men, simple and conscientious, will go down in history as one of the worst of popes. His attempt to save will probably lead to the annihilation of the Church. It has been heading for the rocks for years - he is going to drive it straight on."

"We shall be in a difficult position," Ralph said thoughtfully. "However, we shall at last know where we stand."

"All I want now is to be let die in peace," the old man said wearily. "I've been on the shelf for years. I've given up bothering about decrees as far as they affect myself. I know too much of how they are made - I was in Rome during the Vatican council - to think that they can either damn or save me. I had hopes, though," he added sadly, "that when I died I'd leave a living Church behind me instead of a dead one."

His actions contradicted his words. He was evidently deeply affected. He sat for some time absorbed in his thoughts, his thin face bent almost to his knees.

"I was dreaming," he said, standing up. "You are young; you may see better times."

By the next post Ralph had a letter from Boyle.

"The Roman bomb is about to burst," he wrote. "It is the end, and this will be the last number of *The Dial*. There is nothing more to be done within the Church. Every thinking man is to be muzzled or driven out. The poor old Church is going to bury her head in the sand. There I, and I expect many others, will leave her. I have got a job on a London paper and shall run down to see you before I go for good – if you don't think me a lost soul!"

In a few days the decree *Lamentabili Sane* was published. Ralph had awaited it with much anxiety and procured an early copy. It more than confirmed his worst fears. He had tried to put Father Lyons' warning and Boyle's letter out of his mind, but there was no avoiding the sixty-five propositions of the decree. Religion, as he understood and felt it, was condemned as heresy. Life and growth and development were anathema. It was madness! But there it was, staring him in the face.

An encyclical was to follow, he read, in which directions would be given for guarding the faithful from these damnable errors. Boyle was right, then. In a short time he should have to decide whether he would accept the teaching of this decree or.... What was the alternative? To give up his service among the poor at Bunnahone, to be driven out of the priesthood, out of the religious communion in which he had been born....

Panic seized him. He lost all power of thought. He felt a passionate longing for the ritual and practices of the Church. He clung desperately to something vague that was being forcibly taken from his grasp.... A succession of detached memories made him calm: the little blue and white altar of the Virgin in his nursery; his first rosary beads, with Ann Carty explaining how he was to say the prayers. Of course Ann was somewhere in the house now. He was safe. Then, kaleidoscopically: Clarendon Street Church, the smell of incense, the priest saying mass at the altar, the lay brother lighting and quenching candles, a hill with the sea at his feet and his father, his kind face set sternly, saying that the O'Briens were always Catholics; his first mass, a long blank, and he found himself sitting by Mrs Fahy's bedside....

It faded away. He felt cold, stood up and looked at a thermometer in the hall. It was seventy-nine in the shade. He strolled to the garden and blinked, hatless, in the glare of the sun. His eyes sought the sea in the distance. Long white waves were breaking on the rocks. They gave him a feeling of impending calamity. He gazed, fascinated, for a minute, and turned back to his study with a sigh. He took up the paper off the floor where he had dropped it and put it in his desk. He wandered round his bookshelves and read the titles. He counted a book here and there, "One, two – ten, twelve. All condemned. Muzzled or driven out, Boyle said."

He fingered a book lovingly. He opened it, read a few sentences and gave a sigh of relief. That was as near as words could get to the expression of his own religion. Condemned, too! Well, he should not be quite alone....

For days he went about his work with renewed zest. It had never before seemed so attractive. The feeling that he was about to leave it all had taken possession of him. There was no longer any questioning. It seemed inevitable. He paid a visit every day to Mrs Fahy. Surely there was more in common, he thought, as he sat listening to her voice and the click of her knitting-needles, between her religion and his than between either and that of the writer of the decree *Lamentabili*. The decree could not deprive him of his faith. He would miss many things, most of all the mass, which had always been for him the symbol of brotherhood with those who tried to live Christ's life. He said every mass now as if it was to be his last.

One evening Mrs Fahy said she would die happy if she could see a mass in her own house. Father Molloy was away for a few days and he got the necessary permission readily from Father Dempsey, who was in charge of the parish.

"When the bell went at the consecration," Mrs Fahy said afterwards, "I caught a glimpse of the young priest's face, and there was that suffering in it that'd near break anyone's heart."

Often, during mass, a feeling of desolation overcame him, as if he were going out alone into a desert where only bitterness and death awaited him. It was a feeling beyond the power of his will. He tried to reason himself out of it, but the effort was useless. It recurred again and again....

At times he thought he was worrying unnecessarily. No one in Bunnahone, except Father Lyons, seemed to have heard of the decree. Ralph spoke of it to Father Dempsey.

"Sure, they have nothing else to trouble them at Rome," he said, "but making decrees. If it was a decree, now, ordering the study of the Irish language, there would be some sense in it."

Father Lyons refused to discuss the matter. His spirit seemed broken. He had shut up his books in a cupboard and seemed frightened when Ralph mentioned the decree.

"I want to die in peace – a Dominican as I have lived. I want to die in my cell with my habit on me. They wouldn't search an old man's room and turn him out into the street," he said in a whimpering voice. "I won't tell a lie if I am asked," he added, straightening his bent back, "but they'll forget an old man who has retired to his cell and wants only to be let die in peace."

The breakdown of the old priest made Ralph resentful against the whole system of back-stairs intrigue at Rome, that gave no thought to the misery it brought to so many like Father Lyons, upright but timid men. None would suffer through this preposterous decree but the most devoted children of the Church....

Boyle, who came by an afternoon train, was in high spirits.

"Bunnahone does not seem to be on fire with the revolutionary decree," he said as he walked with Ralph through the almost deserted streets.

"It has broken old Father Lyons' heart. I saw him today. It was one of the saddest things I have ever seen – no one else seems to mind. Is there any hope of an effective protest being made?" Ralph asked anxiously.

Boyle shrugged his shoulders.

"None that will matter. There is a rush already to toe the line. Cardinals and bishops who coquetted with modernism when it seeemed a growing movement are falling over each other in their professions of loyalty. No words are strong enough to express their abhorrence of the views they held a month ago, or fulsome enough to express their admiration of the wisdom of the poor Pope."

"Not all, surely?"

"Well, I suppose there are a few fools even in the priesthood," Boyle said cynically. "Not one as far as I see," he added, laughing, "that has reached the rank of bishop."

Ralph had asked Father Sheldon to meet Boyle at dinner.

"You should not have stopped *The Dial*," he said, hesitatingly, on greeting Boyle.

"Would you have written for me?" Boyle asked, lifting his eyebrows.

Father Sheldon looked sadly at the empty grate.

"I deserve the reproach," he said gently. "My own conscience is my worst accuser, but I cannot leave my parish. For the first time in my life I am going to temporise. It's not all selfishness," he said appealingly. "It is impossible to explain, yet I owe you both an explanation. I encouraged you and now I hold back." He did not lift his eyes. After a short pause he went on: "I have been in my parish thirty years. Most of the people I meet on the roads and at their firesides, I baptised or married, sometimes both. I promised many a mother and father on their deathbeds to look after their children. My heart is chained to the place. You are young and can make new ties. You may be too young to understand, but God knows an old man's weakness."

"Or his strength," Ralph said, clasping the old man's hand warmly.

"Who knows?" Boyle said, taking the priest's hand in turn.

Tears welled in Father Sheldon's eyes. He sat dejected and silent until dinner was announced.

"What will you do?" he said to Ralph, when Ann had left the dining-room.

"It will depend on the practical steps that are taken to enforce the syllabus."

"It is well known what these will be," Boyle said.

The two priests looked at him enquiringly.

"Universal delation, prohibition of books and discussion, local ecclesiastical policing and an anti-modernist oath for all teachers and suspected priests," Boyle said, ticking the items off on his fingers; "my information is, I think, authentic. This very discussion would be subject to censure."

"I anticipated this," Ralph said calmly. "I haven't your ties," he said, turning to Father Sheldon. "If I am asked to take the oath I must go."

"There is no such system as that which the syllabus condemns," Boyle said tentatively. "The lawyer who wrote it over-reached himself. In his desire to make a case he has descended to the worst traditions of the old criminal prosecuting counsel. No man ever held the farrago of opinions condemned in these sixty-five propositions."

Ralph shook his head and smiled.

"That is true, of course. Still, as I hold many of them, I don't see my way out."

"You may not be asked to take the oath," Father Sheldon said.

"In that case," Ralph said, "I shall have to reconsider my position."

"Don't leave if you can at all help it," Boyle said solemnly. "A layman like me can slip off and be little the worse for it, but they make it hell for a priest."

"True, true," Father Sheldon murmured.

"The days of the Inquisition have passed," Ralph said, more lightly than he felt.

"Have they, indeed?" Boyle said, laughing bitterly. "There are worse forms of torture than the rack. The Church has reduced social torture to a fine art. Why, even a layman like me can only escape it by burying himself somewhere. Do you think I could live in Dublin, or anywhere in Ireland, once the Church had definitely attacked me? I have already had some experience while running *The Dial*. I feel a new man since the chance was offered me of escaping it all – innuendos, secret accusations, efforts to prevent my getting work, defamation and calumny, persistent, continuous. My God!" he said excitedly, "I have come to believe that the organised Church is itself the devil with whom it is always threatening people."

Father Sheldon listened with his eyes fixed on his plate.

"Don't forget, Boyle," he said gently, "that what you say, true as I feel it is, may be due to perverted zeal. Somewhere beneath it all there is an ideal."

"I'm tired of looking for needles in haystacks," Boyle said bitterly.

Ann came in and removed the plates. Ralph thought of Father Doyle's accusations against Boyle in the old days at the Seminary; and Father Molloy's sneer at Dunne and Bridget Carey still burned in his memory.

"I didn't intend to speak of myself," Boyle said, when Ann had again left the room. "I was thinking of you, Ralph. I want you to realise what you are in for, if you go."

"There is much to stay for," Father Sheldon said. "All hope is not lost yet. I believe that the Spirit of God will yet sway the Church. The holiness and sanctity that I know are in it must prevail. This foolish decree has only the ignorant authority of its authors."

Ralph and Boyle listened in silence while he dwelt on the spiritual needs of the people, on the duty of sacrificing opinion, which was passing and fallible, to service. A few years' silence and all would be well.

"I don't blame Sheldon," Boyle said when the old priest had gone. "He has always had to deal with a simple people who are not troubled with intellectual and moral difficulties."

"They are among the best, too," Ralph said thoughtfully. "It will break my heart to leave many of the same kind in this parish."

Boyle smoked in silence. After a short pause, Ralph said, "All my life, Boyle, I have been the play of some external force. In some vague way I was always looking for some intimation of the Divine Will, invariably outside myself. First it was from Ann. When I doubted her infallibility, from someone else. It has been like walking through a bog – one jumps for safety to a green tuft, and when that gives way beneath one's feet, to another; only in my case I left the choosing to others. At last I have got some foothold. Any step I take now will come of my experience of myself and the world, of God revealing Himself to me through them. I can only help others by following my own judgment and conscience. I shall make mistakes, but, at least, I shall make them honestly. If I assented to that document," pointing to the syllabus, "I would be lost."

Boyle had taken his pipe from his mouth and held it in his uplifted hand while he listened attentively.

"I have only now found my feet," Ralph continued; "not very firmly even yet. But I must not yield. If that decree is enforced I must go. It is a choice between my faith and entire scepticism."

"I thought so," Boyle said gently. "You will feel it?"

"Feel it? I shall go out like a shivering deserter. I feel at this moment as if everything that bound me to life was about to snap. My whole life has been built up on illusions, and they have left their mark on me. I have to face a reality at last. Religion, duty, honesty force me to it, but I shall feel in doing it as if I was committing some unthinkable crime."

"Don't, Ralph! It is horrible," Boyle said appealingly.

Ralph rapped his pipe against the grate. He went on rapping it mechanically long after it was empty.

"There is some tobacco," Boyle said roughly. "Don't give way, man."

Ralph smiled, filled his pipe slowly and lit it.

"That is good tobacco," he said, and lapsed into silence.

"You don't know, Boyle," he said, after a pause, "how I looked forward to the priesthood. I hoped to do so much. I worked hard to understand the difficulties that beset people in matters of faith. I saw that in the Church itself was the great difficulty, but I clutched at every straw. There were signs of change. Even in my time I hoped that the Church would be the city on a hill whose holiness and charity would draw all men to its fold. Then there were other things – great things that a priest could do for the people even outside his spiritual duties. I was full of these movements of Clayton's and Dillon's. But everything I put my hands to failed. The club, too, you've heard of it?"

"You wrote to me."

"And now it has come to this. I shall always be a Catholic. They can't take that from me," he said musingly.

"Can't they?" Boyle said doubtingly. "My dear O'Brien, we are only a coterie. The moment you take off that Roman collar you will be branded as a heretic. Publicly ignored, perhaps, but privately hounded down in a hundred subtle ways. I hope you fully realise what you will have to face."

"I shall have the support of my conscience in any case."

"It's about all you will have. The very people here with whom you have most in common will look upon you with horror. All your Catholic friends will desert you, some sincerely, others because they wish to keep in with a powerful organisation and have no desire to compromise themselves. So much mud will be thrown at you that some of it is sure to stick. You will be accused of every sort of moral obliquity. You talk of conscience. It will be whispered here and there that you never had one."

Ralph stared at him in astonishment. "I cannot believe it," he said.

"My dear fellow, they would burn you, only that the temper of the times is a little against it. If you are right in going, then the authorities of the Church are wrong in forcing you to go. To prove themselves right they will blacken you past all recognition."

"But the morality of it?"

Boyle laughed harshly. "Have you experienced these fine shades of a lofty morality in the ecclesiastical authorities of Bunnahone?" he asked bitterly. "If you have, Molloy must have changed his skin since I knew him."

Ralph laughed uneasily. "No, he hasn't changed. But the whole Church isn't made up of Molloys."

"Perhaps not; but they lead the pack on occasions like this."

Ralph gazed at the picture at the end of the room as if he were searching for his own thoughts in the glass.

"I have made a mess of my life and I must take the consequences," he said wearily.

They sat up till two o'clock talking. Boyle was pessimistic. The decree was the worst blow ever struck at the Catholic Church. It came when thousands of priests in many countries were awakening to a real sense of religion. The best would be driven out of the Church. Some good men, like Sheldon, would stay, but they would be as powerless for good as those who went. The great majority of the priests who were influenced by modernism would accept the new decree from sheer cowardice.

"I know the feeling," Ralph said. "I find it hard to blame them."

Boyle shrugged his shoulders.

"Frankly," he said, "I have given up all hope of the Roman Church. To use its own language, it has committed the unforgivable sin, it has sealed its ears to the voice of the Spirit. It has given itself up to the loaves and fishes. The best priests left in it, after this débacle – always barring a few like Sheldon, who come under no law – shall become the worst, for they see the light and haven't the courage to follow it: their inevitable end is hypocrisy and time-serving."

Next morning Ralph took Boyle with him to the workhouse for mass. On their way home to breakfast they were both silent. At length Ralph spoke, "We shall be cut off from all that."

"I feel it, too," Boyle said. "I don't deny that much remains. There are springs of holiness, but the official Church has ceased to draw from them."

As they passed by the convent gate Father Molloy came out. He stared at Boyle and turned away without speaking.

"Molloy after all is the typical priest," Boyle said, laughing. "When a Church loses all sense of its divine mission and becomes a mere business organisation the Molloys keep it going. Make up your mind, Ralph, the Molloys rule the Church – pull all the strings."

Boyle's bitterness, which increased during his stay, produced a reaction in Ralph. After bidding him goodbye at the railway station, Ralph wandered along the streets towards the sea. The tide being out, he walked on the sands beyond the rocks and watched the glitter of the sun on the rippling water. He felt an intense longing for a simple dumb faith that needed no articulate expression. If only he could get away to some country parish and were allowed to work there without being asked to make professions of faith....

Far away on the horizon appeared the dim blue outlines of an island hanging mysteriously between sky and sea. A slight breeze swept across the bay, the island became a wisp of grey cloud and was soon blotted out altogether by an approaching bank of fog. Was it so with life? he thought.

Late that night, as he was about to go to bed, Father Dempsey called. He stood by the study fireplace, refused to sit down and said, hesitatingly: "I only called to warn you. There may be nothing in it. Magan has got hold of that decree you were talking of and was giving out a lot about it at dinner in the parochial house today. Lanigan, by the way, of no harm, said you held a lot of the views that were condemned, that he often heard you talking of them at Maynooth. Molloy pumped him dry and said at the end that it was easy known that you weren't a right priest, having that heretic Boyle to stay with you. He was hugger-muggering in a corner with Magan all the evening. I'm afraid they're up to mischief, for I heard them both chuckling and Molloy saying, 'We'll have O'Brien in the hip after this.' I hope to goodness there's nothing in it. I told Lanigan, and he's very much put out about it, and he's afraid they'll go to the bishop with some tale when he comes home in a few days."

Ralph hardly listened. "I had another dream all day," he said with a smile.

Dempsey stared at him. "There's nothing to fear then?" he said.

"It had to come sooner or later," Ralph said. He looked at

Dempsey's anxious, sympathetic face and took his hand impulsively. "You are a good fellow, Dempsey," he said; "but we won't talk now. I must think."

Dempsey went away reluctantly. "I can't believe there's any fear of you, and you a good priest, too. I wish to God them decrees were all burned. It's a queer world entirely, and queer defenders of the faith we have, too, in Molloy and Magan," he muttered on the doorstep.

Ralph went back to his study and filled a pipe slowly. He held a lighted match in his hand, looked at it curiously and laughed. He threw it into the grate when it burnt his fingers. He drew a book from a shelf at random, drew a lamp towards him, sat down and lit his pipe. He opened the title page and read *Alice in Wonderland.*

He laughed again rather hollowly. "It's as good as any other," he said aloud. "If I tried to think I might become the mad hatter."

Chapter 27

FOR SOME WEEKS Ralph was busily occupied. An epidemic of typhus broke out in an outlying district of the parish. There were two nurses for seven houses and it was impossible to get any attendance, as the people in the neighbourhood were panic-stricken and would not go near the infected houses. Father Hardy was on vacation and Father Molloy said he was too busy over the Seminary collection to do any sick calls. Ralph and Father Dempsey took turns in helping the nurses, often staying up all night.

The bishop arrived home and was received at the railway station by the brass band. Darcy read an address written by Father Molloy. The bishop in reply made a glowing speech on the wisdom of the Pope, whose unceasing care of his people would be manifest when the great encyclical, a copy of which he had the happiness to have in his pocket, was read in the churches. It would gladden the Pope's heart to hear that the bearer of his encyclical had received such a magnificent welcome, worthy alike of the great occasion and of the holiness of the people.

Ralph, who had spent the night in one of the fever houses, heard all this next day from Father Dempsey.

"Your absence was remarked on by his lordship. I said you were on a sick call, but he was none too pleased. He said it showed a lack of zeal not to be present to welcome one's bishop after a long absence."

"Have you heard what's in the encyclical?"

"Not a word, only Molloy said this morning that it was a great document for keeping young cubs on the leash."

At night, when he opened a newspaper, Ralph found the encyclical in full, sharing the front page with "Princely Reception of the Bishop of Bunnahone in his historic diocese". He read the encyclical through. It was on the lines outlined by Boyle. He sighed hopelessly when he came to the end. He was tired from want of sleep and he had some difficulty in keeping awake. The paper fell to the floor and he awoke with a start. He was not asleep then! There would be some days yet. He could not leave these people who were ill. If there were no fresh cases, all danger would be passed in less than a week.

He slept badly all night. He sat up once thinking he heard a knock: it was only a window rattling. Half asleep, he seemed to be working desperately against time to get something done. He tried to think what the work was or what was the danger that threatened to prevent it; turned restlessly from side to side in a vain effort to remember, until at last he fell into a dreamless sleep.

He awoke refreshed and lay quite still, without thought, listening to the swish of the blind, moved to and fro by the wind through the open window. He drew the bedclothes tightly round him, feeling vaguely restless. The fever patients of course! He jumped out of bed. The crisis was expected today in the last bad case, John Feeney. While dressing, he thought of his mother with a pang. He felt a dull, physical aching all over him.

Did she care for him? Something in her eluded him. She had loved him so much. What had come between them? Religion? That would have drawn them closer.

He sat with a boot in his hand for fully five minutes, his eyes fixed on the sunlight, making curious patterns on the wallpaper. His mind went back over all their relations in the past ...

He felt hard and resentful for a moment, then a wave of pity swept over him. Her heart had become as flint. Fear had driven out love, had crushed even her mother's love for her son. He recalled incident after incident that marked crises in her life – the growth of her idea of a tyrannical God ...

He stood up and clenched his fists. He wanted to pull down something. The shadow of the waving branches of the tree outside the window danced gaily on the wall and seemed to mock him. The room was stuffy, stifling. He threw up the sash from the bottom and drew in deep breaths of air.

The Church to which he had offered his life had done this. It had separated his mother from him. It had so influenced her gentle timid nature as to dehumanise her. Fear of the God it had given her to worship had narrowed her interests, first to her family and then to herself ... She would sacrifice her husband and her son to propitiate the anger of a monster....

He saw her grovelling before a colossal stone idol with a malignant grin on its cynical deformed face....

He felt that he must have more air. He hurriedly finished dressing and went out. Unconsciously he took the road to Feeney's house. His feeling of resentment against the Church gave way to an intense longing to be with his mother....

A fresh warm wind from the sea was like the touch of a soft hand on his face. He was back again in the nursery cuddling on his mother's knee, his cheek on her hand, her fragrant breath deliciously fanning his hair....

No decree should keep her from him. She could never cease to love him....

The nurse met him on Feeney's doorstep. The crisis had come in the night, quite normally. He was now sleeping quietly.

Ralph looked at his watch and suddenly remembered that he was to have said mass at the convent at seven o'clock. It was now after eight. He muttered some excuse to the nurse and ran rapidly along the deserted road. He met the old Reverend Mother on the bridge in the convent grounds. She looked keenly at him over her spectacles.

"You are too late. We waited an hour; the nuns have had breakfast."

"I am very sorry, Reverend Mother."

"Sister Elizabeth now," she said with a faint smile. She continued to look at him. "We shall walk here for a few minutes," she said with a sigh, turning down a side-path along the river. She fingered her beads, as she walked slowy and with difficulty. She stopped at a seat and sat down.

"There is a lot of gossip in the convent," she said, her eyes on her beads.

"That is nothing unusual," Ralph said uneasily, with a smile.

"Don't," she said gently, "I feel it too much." She drew her spectacles up over her clouded eyes.

"The bishop told Reverend Mother. He was here yesterday and was very angry. You are to be punished. Poor boy, poor boy," she added, under her breath. "There is to be a special conference next

Thursday, Reverend Mother says. He will then make known his decision, not too severe because of your good mother, he said."

"You seem to know all about it," Ralph said harshly.

"He tells Reverend Mother everything," she said simply.

His face had grown rigid. She looked at him anxiously. "You will bear up ... and not be proud."

He laughed, but seeing her pained look he said gently, "You have been very kind to me. Wherever I go I shall always remember it. I am probably leaving...."

"This parish?" she asked eagerly.

"The priesthood - the Church, as far as the Church is concerned." The words, in his harsh staccato voice, sounded to him as if someone else had spoken. He had taken the decision for granted since last night, but had not put it into words. He felt numbed.

"My God! my God!" the nun said, swaying on the seat.

He was acutely conscious of the sounds which burned his brain, the murmur of the stream, the sobbing of the nun, voices from the school in the distance, twittering of the birds on the lawn.

"Oh, dear God, save him!" He felt the touch of the old nun's hand on his. He returned the pressure.

"You haven't lost your religion?" she said timidly.

A lark rose across the stream and seemed to flood the air with melody.

"I am only trying to find it."

The nun sat absorbed in thought, or prayer, for she fingered her beads rapidly. Ralph's eyes wandered over the grounds in front. Sound and sight were no longer painful. He drank in the beauty of the wonderful autumn colouring, brown and gold against the light green of the well-mown grass and the harsher green of evergreens gleaming in the sun. The autumn day had all the freshness of spring and the genial warmth of early summer. A weight seemed to have fallen from his spirit....

"Where will you go?"

"I don't know. Anywhere." He restrained himself because of the sad tone in the nun's voice. "Where I can breathe and live." He felt inclined to sing. It was joyful to be alive. "I was dead and now I live," he said under his breath.

His eyes fell on the old nun's face, drawn and aged, and the joyful mood passed away.

She shook her head sadly.

"I am too old to understand. There is so much to do in Bunnahone...." Her voice trailed off in a murmur.

"Mother, if I could stay I would. All I see clearly is that I must go – all the rest is dark enough, God knows," he said drearily.

"Poor boy!" she said. "I suppose we must all seek God in our own way."

His eyes roamed round the grounds. It was all so peaceful – late purple and scarlet flowers against the green, the faint drone of the voices of two nuns saying the rosary along a path near by, a hoarse murmur from the schools, a deeper chord in harmony with the voice of the stream. It was the peace of the old, of death....

A clock chimed the hour. "I must go," she said. She held his hand gravely. "There were so many things I intended to say, but somehow I cannot say them. The soul of another is like a trackless wood at night – impenetrable. I won't meddle, but I will pray. May God be ever with you."

He crossed the road and opened the door of his house in a dream. Some letters were on the study table. He opened one with the episcopal seal in Father Magan's handwriting – a formal announcement of a special conference to consider "the recent important pronouncements of the Pope, and to take steps for their enforcement". He dropped it idly. Ann came in and asked if he had breakfasted. He stared at her a while, seemed to consider the question with great gravity, and said "no" solemnly.

"What's coming over you?" she said, looking at him suspiciously. He didn't reply, and she left the room grumbling.

He took up his letters again and read them with little interest. He ate a good breakfast, wandered about his rooms, opened a newspaper, glanced at the headings and put it by. He went to the bookshelves. There was nothing to read. He lit a pipe, strolled into the garden and lopped off some dead flowers. He had a restless feeling that he had a lot to do, but he did not know where to begin. Thursday was the conference day. Why put off his preparation for leaving till then, since he had already come to a decision? Ought he to see his mother now or wait till after Thursday? There was Ann to consider. What was to become of her? He shrank from considering anything.

Father Dempsey called and was full of the coming conference. The bishop was writing a loyal address to the Pope, which Father Molloy was to propose and Magan to second. There was some plan to have some of the young priests sign some document. "Sure no one ought to mind," he said anxiously, "about signing a thing like that. What is it but a little bit of paper? There isn't much meaning in theology anyway. I read over that decree myself and it is only a lot of bother about trifles. It might be the soundest theology in the world that's condemned in it for all I can remember of my reading in Maynooth. You'll sign anything you're asked?" he said eagerly. "If for nothing else but to spite Molloy and Magan, who think you're in for a fall."

Ralph smiled at the naïveté of the priest, whose simple face glowed with sympathy. He would have told him of his resolve but he wished to avoid endless talk with no common basis of argument and no possibility of agreement or even of understanding. He turned the conversation to the Irish language, in his zeal for which Father Dempsey soon forgot Ralph's troubles.

During the days preceding the conference he hated being alone. He was glad of any routine work that gave him no time for thought. He haunted the workhouse, the asylum, the schools, and visited most of the old people in the village. He begged Father Dempsey to spend the evenings with him and to accompany him on long walks across country. Except Father Dempsey, who soon saw that Ralph did not wish to discuss his position, he avoided everyone he knew with any intimacy. Father Dempsey told him, "It has gone the rounds of the town that you are in some trouble," and he was conscious of curious looks cast on him in the street. One old woman, who begged him to help her to pay a fine she had incurred at the petty sessions court for drunkenness, offered him her sympathy, saying, "We're all liable to trouble from the drop of drink; sure I'm sorry to hear you have got into the same trouble yourself."

The conference met in the bishop's dining-room. When Ralph arrived, within a few minutes of the appointed hour, most of the priests had already come and stood around the large room in groups. Father Duff was sitting by the fire surrounded by several priests.

"Molloy tried a march on me," he said, loudly, so as to be heard by Father Molloy, who sat at the head of the table next an armchair evidently reserved for the bishop, "but he overreached himself. These town priests think they're very clever, but sorra bit they know of the country, no more than a child in arms. Unless they change their tune and give up being bill servers for gombeen men, the people'll give them the go-by."

"Right, Father Duff, right," a little apple-cheeked priest shouted joyfully, slapping his leg. "What do you say to that now, Molloy?"

Father Molloy flushed and pretended not to hear.

"Hush," said a tall sardonic-looking man, "don't you see that he's busy studying the decree?"

"He'd make as much out of it as a pig would out of the alphabet," said Father Duff, contemptuously.

"The Miss Hinnisseys gave him a lesson on it last night. Hardy, who is dead jealous of him, told me," the sardonic man said solemnly.

"I never said a word of the kind," Hardy said heatedly.

"I have it on the best authority," the apple-faced man said, "that Hardy is getting inside Molloy there. He turns the music for Miss Katie. Molloy was never able to do that as he couldn't tell one note from another. Miss Katie used to have to tread on his toe when she wanted a page turned over."

There was a general laugh. Father Duff caught Ralph's eye.

"Come here, Ralph," he said loudly. "There has been some whispering going on agin you, behind backs. I want to let the people know who are doing it," he glared at Molloy and then at Magan, who was shuffling uneasily by the fireplace, his face a deep purple, "even if they are precious relations of mine itself, that if I hear any more of it, I'll read their characters for them."

"Do you hear that now, Molloy?" the apple-cheeked man said. "I know I wouldn't have Father Duff's tongue agin me for a good deal."

Father Molloy turned the papers in front of him nervously. "I only do my duty," he said aggressively.

"Molloy and duty!" said the sardonic man, mockingly.

Several priests laughed.

"What's this decree about, anyway?" the apple-cheeked man said.

"I don't know what it's about," Father Duff said angrily, "and I care less, but I won't have it made a handle for Molloy's spite."

The bishop entered and all the priests stood up. Having said the "*Veni sancte Spiritus*", he took his seat at the head of the table. Ralph sat between Father Duff and Father Devine, half-way down the long table.

"Reverend Fathers ..." the bishop began.

"My lord, I beg leave to interrupt your lordship," a chinless florid pricst said, standing up. "Gentlemen, this is the first opportunity we have of welcoming, all of us together, his lordship the bishop on his return from the Holy City of Rome. Our hearts were filled with woe and sorrow during his long absence and are bursting with joy now that he's come back among us again. Our consolation is that he was giving the same good advice to the Holy Father that he's always ready to give to us. In the name of all your devoted priests, my lord, I bid your lordship a hearty welcome."

Several priests rapped the bare mahogany table loudly with their knuckles.

"And I might be at home getting in my potatoes on a fine day like this. And the frost coming on, too," Father Duff said across the table to Father Sheldon, who sat with his eyes closed, his clasped hands resting on the table in front of him.

"Muldoon is making a bid for a parish," the sardonic man said in a stage whisper. There was a jeering laugh at the end of the table.

"Gentlemen," the bishop said. "This eloquent expression of your devotion touches me deeply. It is a fitting prelude to the business we have in hand. You have all read the decree *Lamentabili*?..."

"I never saw it," Father Duff said gruffly. "Nor I"; "Nor I"; several voices repeated down the table.

"You have all read the decree *Lamentabili*?" the bishop said firmly.

"Of course we have, my lord," Father Muldoon said eagerly.

"Whist, man," the apple-cheeked man said under his breath, "sure it's a book about card playing - I wouldn't let on I read it if I were you."

"And you join with the Holy Father and every good priest and bishop throughout the world," the bishop continued, "in detestation of the errors condemned by it."

"What are they, my lord?" Father Duff asked.

"This facetiousness should be reserved for a less solemn occasion," the bishop said testily.

"It's like buying a pig in a poke," Father Duff said fretfully to Ralph. "Do you know what he's talking about?"

"May I read the address now, my lord?" Father Molloy asked.

"Yes, yes," the bishop said hastily, having apparently lost the thread of his remarks, searching among his papers for his notes.

Father Molloy stood up, cleared his throat, and read:

"We, the priests of the diocese of Bunnahone in conference assembled, having carefully considered the propositions condemned in the Bull *Lamentabili*, and the remarks of our Holy Father, the Pope, thereon in the Encyclical *Pascendi Gregis*, wish unanimously to place on record our horror that such blasphemous views as those condemned by the Holy Father should be held by any who call themselves Catholics. We wish at the same time to assure his Holiness that those errors are unknown and unheard of in this historic diocese, where all the priests and people, under the direction of their devoted bishop, think and act only in accordance with the mind and will of the Holy See."

"I second it," Father Magan said, popping up when Father Molloy sat down.

"That is satisfactorily done," the bishop said, rubbing his hands together. "Ours will be one of the first in. The Holy Father will be delighted."

"It's easy pleasing him then," Father Duff said, yawning. "Would you tell me now, Ralph, what it's all about?"

"Nero fiddling while Rome burns," Ralph said shortly.

"It's joking you are."

"Not at all. Someone will be thrown to the lions presently."

"Well, I'm glad to see you in good spirits anyway, even if I can't understand you."

A pained look crossed Father Sheldon's drawn face. He understood, Ralph thought. His eyes wandered round the table. The bishop was speaking in a low tone to Father Molloy. Two priests next Father Sheldon were discussing the price of cattle. The apple-cheeked priest, grown serious, asserted loudly that tenants who had purchased their land ought to pay double dues to the priest. Father Hardy whispered behind his hand to Father Muldoon, "Drop in at the parochial house before you leave; there's sure to be a game on with all the lads in town."

The bishop rapped the table and said, "Silence. There are just a few more formalities and I think we shall have done a memorable day's work. First I wish to appoint a board to act as censors of books and to carry out generally the wishes of our Holy Father embodied in his encyclical; they are the vicar-general, Father Doyle, the president of the Seminary, Father Magan, and the esteemed administrator of this parish, Father Molloy. The best interest of the Church may be safely entrusted to their wisdom and learning."

"Can Molloy read?" the sardonic-looking priest said gravely to the apple-cheeked priest.

"He makes a boast of reading the newspaper, and he was once seen reading a penny dreadful."

"Gentlemen, this business is most serious," the bishop said, again rapping the table. "There is only one other matter. I have drawn up a declaration, repudiating all the so-called modernist errors, which I shall ask all the young priests, under five years ordained, to repeat after me. Priests of longer service are too wise, I am sure," he looked meaningly at Father Sheldon, who still sat with eyes closed, "to hold any views condemned by our Holy Father. Young priests sometimes lack discretion. Would you stand up please, gentlemen, priests of under five years on the mission."

A dozen or more priests stood up. Ralph remained seated. Devine, who was standing beside him, pulled his sleeve.

"For the love of God, stand up," he said anxiously.

"There'll be some fun now," Hardy whispered joyfully to Muldoon.

Father Molloy whispered to the bishop.

"You are not five years ordained, Father O'Brien," the bishop said suavely.

"No."

"Do you refuse to make the declaration?"

"Yes."

"For God's sake, think of what you're doing," Devine said, in an agonised whisper that was heard all over the room.

"Crikey!" said the apple-cheeked man, "Think of anyone taking that gibberish seriously."

"You leave me no option but to suspend you from the exercise of Orders until you come to your senses," the bishop said with a frown.

“For shame, my lord! the poor lad,” said Father Duff.

“If you don’t respect your own years, respect your bishop, sir,” said the bishop angrily.

“He’s very young. He’s sure to do what’s right. Maybe like myself, he couldn’t make head or tail of the whole thing. To suspend him now! Think of the disgrace of it and he partly of my own rearing too,” the old man said feebly.

“Silence!” the bishop said loudly. He glared at Father Duff, was about to speak, but checked himself. He bundled his papers together and stood up.

“You didn’t read the declaration, my lord,” Father Molloy said.

“In view of our address to the Holy Father, I don’t wish to mar the harmony of our meeting. This matter is adjourned.” He knelt on his chair, said a prayer hurriedly and left the room.

“You’ll give in. It’s going against God Himself for He speaks through the mouth of the Pope,” Devine said eagerly to Ralph.

“I don’t understand it at all,” said Father Duff, weakly. He passed his hand over his eyes. “Sheldon’ll be able to tell me. He knows a power of things.”

Father Sheldon seemed to wake up from a dream. He crossed the room and put his hand on Ralph’s shoulder.

“I never found it harder to keep silent. You believe me and forgive me?” he said wistfully. “If I spoke I should have said too much.”

“Yours is the harder part,” Ralph said, holding out his hand.

“Is it the end?” Father Sheldon’s voice trembled as he put the question.

“Yes ...”

Father Sheldon pressed his hand.

Chapter 28

As Ralph left the room he was conscious of the curious eyes of a group of priests by the door. Two, whom he knew rather well, turned their backs on him. When he passed there was a jeering laugh, followed by "That will be a cooler for him, anyway." Another voice said, "Young pup, setting himself up as better than his neighbours. I hope the lord'll give it to him hot."

There was some delay in the hall while Father Duff was putting on his overcoat. "I'm well rid of him," came through the open dining-room door in Father Molloy's voice. "You see what happens to any man that stands up agin me. I flatten him out sooner or later." "The widow will shut her purse now," another voice said. Father Molloy laughed. "No fear; the lord has her in his fist."

"I'll tell that skunk what I think of him," Father Duff said, furiously angry, advancing to the door with his overcoat half on.

Ralph pulled him back. "It's not worth while; much worse will be said later."

"I'm afraid so," Father Sheldon said sadly.

They restrained Father Duff with difficulty.

"I'll not come back for any dinner here," he said; "it would poison me. Did anyone ever hear the like?" he added, standing on the sidewalk; "to suspend a man for nothing. If it was drink now, or women, there'd be some meaning in it! But theology! I often heard it said that theology never did a man any good, but I never thought that it could do any harm. You give us a bit to eat, Ralph, and I'll see if I can't set all this to rights."

Ralph glanced helplessly at Father Sheldon, who finally prevailed on Father Duff to go home with him.

"Let it be as you say," he said reluctantly. "I hope ye aren't keeping anything back from me. You ought to know by this, Ralph, that I'd give my heart to serve you."

When the two priests had gone, Ralph walked home slowly. He

hesitated at Mrs Fahy's door but decided not to go in; even her broad charity would shrink from him when she found out that he had given up the priesthood.

In his study he felt lonely and bitter; not even Father Duff would understand. He laughed cynically at the recollection of the conference. His dream had ended in a farce. His protest would furnish an idle laugh for one of Father Molloy's card parties.

What was he to do? Give up this house. The furniture belonged to Inniscar; his books he would try to keep. There was Ann; he shrank from an explanation with Ann. Would she be as hard as his mother? He was wrong in thinking that his mother could be hard; when she knew that he was in real trouble her heart would soften towards him again.... But she was going into a convent; would she give up the idea and live with him? The memory of her look - hard, implacable - as he left the drawing-room on his last visit came back to him; a feeling of fear overcame him. He struggled against it. She could not hold out against his love. He would break down that iron wall that stood between them. He said aloud, "I will see her. She will understand; she is my mother." He sank back exhausted in his chair. He looked at his hands, which felt nerveless, half expecting to see them bruised, so vivid was his sense of having battered at a wall.

He went out and walked to and fro rapidly in his small garden. He tried to shake off the depressed feelings that prevented any effort to think out his position clearly. His mind was such a poor thing, he thought, almost powerless against the dumb, overwhelming forces of its own background, a fitful light shedding a stray gleam here and there through the wrack that seemed to envelop it.

He plunked idly at the dead leaves of a rose tree. The blooms had long since gone, the leaves had withered, yet in the spring the tree would again renew its youth. This procession of life was universal, in religion as well as in the rose tree. His whole life had been a slow awakening to this truth. Use and habit and memory made him cling to the dead leaves while as yet the new buds had not forced them to fall.

There was no conflict between the new life and the old. He would take with him all the religious values that meant so much to him. He was simply choosing life instead of death....

For that was what the Church was doing - cutting itself off from the sources of life: in a few years it must wither and die....

A feeling of peace stole over him and he worked for a while selecting the books he would take with him. He piled them in a corner of his study, sat at his desk and began a letter to the bishop resigning his mission. As he wrote the opening sentence the lines became blurred and he sat helplessly staring at what seemed to his clouded eyes a blank sheet. An intense longing to stay came back to him. His justification of himself was a string of meaningless words. Others, better than he, were staying. It would regain for him his mother's affection. He saw a vision of an ideal Church with which he was at one....

It faded away almost at once and his mind dwelt on the actual Church as he knew it. His one hope of its regeneration had been crushed....

He took up his pen and finished the letter, formally resigning, and added that henceforward he considered himself a layman. He took it himself and handed it in at the bishop's door. He heard the sound of loud laughter from the dining-room and the clatter of plates. As the door closed on him he had a feeling of having done some necessary work, and a desire for food. He hurried home and got Ann to cook him a hasty meal.

"Why aren't you at the big dinner at the bishop's?" she asked, as she served him.

He hesitated a moment. "I am leaving," he said.

"To see your mother belike."

He explained incoherently. When she grasped what he meant, the plate she held in her hands fell to the ground and she stood transfixed, with her hands extended as if she still held it. Something comic in her attitude provoked a smile, which froze on his lips when he saw the horror on her face and her glazed eyes staring at him.

"The disgrace of it," she said feebly. "I once knew a silenced priest in Dublin who used to hang round the public houses begging for drinks."

His head sunk between his shoulders. He wished he had gone away silently. He should have to pay a bitter price for his freedom in the pain he inflicted on all who loved him. He suffered, but they suffered too, and the thought of their suffering was his heaviest blow. He could feel resentment against the ecclesiastical machine, against its time-servers and self-seekers, but not against those who, unquestioning, regarded it as the voice of God. Acts of authority might seem cruel to them or unscrupulous, but they were God's actions and must be right.

She put her apron to her eyes and began to cry. She fell on her knees, stretched out her arms and said passionately, "I reared you as if you were my own son. Don't go agin me and God now."

He shook his head sadly, deeply moved. "Have pity on me, Ann. I must go," he said, holding out his hand appealingly.

"Ask God to pity you," she said sternly. "Though I doubt but He's hardened His heart agin you."

She left the room and he sat staring at the table, forgetting the food. After a while she came back and removed the things with a set face, without speaking. He sat on, staring vacantly in front of him. A few vague, unconnected memories passed through his mind. He heard a coal fall from the fire and waited for another to fall as if his fate depended on it. Ann came in and said, "Father Devine is in the study. He wants to see you."

He stood up, hesitated and sat down again. "I can't go through this again," he thought. "I should only say things that would pain him."

"Tell him I can't see him," he said to Ann. "I'm not at home to anyone."

"And you sitting there," she said, bridling. "He's a good priest and might put the fear of God into you," she added more gently.

He smiled wearily, saying, "I'm not at home to anyone."

He heard Father Devine protesting in the hall and Ann's voice: "Leave him to God for the present at any rate. They're a queer, obstinate lot, the O'Briens, when the fit is on them."

After dark he went for a walk. He tried to make plans for his future, but his thoughts wandered. He must leave Bunnahone at once: but he must see his mother first – came back again and again like a refrain. There was Ann to arrange for and he must get some secular clothes and some money. What he should do after leaving Bunnahone he shirked thinking of. It would depend on his mother. He thought of her now in a detached, disinterested way, without fear or hope....

Exhausted from want of food he looked round him curiously and in the dim light of stars recognised the Inniscar gateway. He stood at the gate for a few minutes. It was too late to call now. He sighed and turned back. Hunger made his thoughts clearer. Should he fit in anywhere in the world of which he knew so little? Almost as unknown to him as the twinkling stars that crowded the dark blue vault above his head. Would he ever again get in touch with people?

It was late when he got home. Ann had not gone to bed and he found a tray in his study with some supper. He ate heartily and was sitting down to smoke when Ann came in.

"Will you be wanting hot water for an early mass tomorrow?"

He winced. He had said his last mass.

"The usual time. I am not saying mass," he said brusquely.

"The whole town is full of your going," she said angrily. "It's soon they scattered it. 'Twas an unlucky day you came among the likes of them. If you'd only been a Carmelite, it'd be a different story today. If you'd only go to Father Eusebius and let him lift a hand over you, you'd be made right yet, maybe," she said eagerly, her voice softening.

He made no reply.

"You're going, then?" she said dully.

He nodded.

"I'll never hold my head high again," she said sadly, lingering by the door.

He told her that he was about to arrange for a small annuity for her.

"You'll do nothing of the kind," she said angrily. "I've enough laid by to see me to my grave without trenching on the little you have. Besides, it wouldn't be lucky money. All the same, I'm glad you made the offer," she added with a break in her voice. "I'll pray that God'll give you grace to repent."

At breakfast next morning Ann handed him a letter.

"Larry Gallagher has just rode in with it. It's from the mistress. Larry wanted to see you right or wrong. He knows there's something up, but I wouldn't gratify him that far. I sent him skiddaddling."

Ralph opened the envelope, which bore no name, and unfolded the letter nervously. It ran:

"You have broken my heart. The bishop drove out yesterday evening immediately on getting your letter and broke the dreadful news to me. My son is a priest. When you have again made submission to our Holy Church, which you have outraged and scandalised, a mother's heart will be open to you, but, until then, I have no son. If you have forgotten your duty to our holy religion, thank God mine has become clearer to me. As some reparation to God for your wicked action, I have made a vow neither to see you, nor to write to, nor receive letters from you, while you persevere in your impenitence and hardness of heart. It rests with you to make that time long or short, as your kind bishop is ready at any time to receive you back on your making full submission and expressing regret for the scandal you gave at the conference. His kindness of heart and gentle, tolerant spirit in the whole matter should move even you.

"In a few days I hope to begin my life of reparation in the convent. I shall pray for you constantly. It is a consolation to me that Inniscar will be turned into a house of prayer, as the saintly bishop has consented to accept it as his residence, so that holy mass will be regularly celebrated in the chapel. May God in His mercy bring you back to the true fold.

"In Christ,

"Hilda O'Brien."

He read the letter twice before its import came home to him, and even then he grasped it only vaguely. He finished his breakfast, looking at the letter which lay open beside his plate curiously from time to time. His emotions were all dried up and his mind reacted feebly to external impressions. He stared at the signature, "In Christ, Hilda O'Brien" – his mother? he thought wonderingly. Suddenly he began to cry. His whole frame was shaken by sobs. He experienced a feeling of utter loneliness, a miserable aching feeling of absolute desertion. His mind became clearer. The thinking half of him seemed to consider the feeling half with curiosity. He had not cried since his childhood. He had no recollection of ever having cried at all. Why did he cry? Did tears always bring this feeling of desolation? He exerted all his will-power fruitlessly to stay the sobs that hurt him physically. He ceased to think and to will and the sobs slowly died away.

He got up from the table and again took up the letter and read it. He laughed bitterly. It reminded him – he wondered vaguely why – of the glossy stuff of which the bishop's coats were made: it was so smug. It was Hilda O'Brien in Christ, with the bishop at her elbow, who wrote the letter, not his mother. Was it possible to save her from the meaningless jumble of words with which she had fettered her heart?

He got his bicycle and rode rapidly to Inniscar, determined to make an effort to see her. He would pierce the artificial barrier that divided them. He turned over in his mind the arguments he would use, even the appeals he would make to her feelings....

The maid who opened the door looked confused.

"My mother, Kate. Where is she?"

The maid began to cry. "She told me to say if you came that she wouldn't see you, Master Ralph – Father Ralph, I mean. I don't know what's up with her at all at all."

"Where is she?"

"She's in the chapel, but you can't get in. She has the door bolted on the inside."

He walked rapidly down the corridor that led to the chapel and turned the handle of the door. It did not yield. He shook the door impatiently. He could hear the swish of a skirt on the carpet and he knocked loudly.

"Who's there?" His heart stopped at the cold sound of his mother's voice.

"It is I, Mother – Ralph. I must see you."

There was a few moments' silence.

"Have you submitted to the bishop?"

"Let me see you, mother. I shall explain everything. You must understand, you will understand."

"Have you submitted to the bishop?"

"No, but I can explain. When you understand, everything will be all right."

"I cannot break my vow. I shall pray for you."

"It may be the last time we shall see one another. You won't refuse me?" he said despairingly.

He listened intently and heard the swish of the skirt receding. After a few moments there was no sound except the beating of his own heart and the ticking of a clock in the corridor.

He called again, shook the door, beat on it with his hands, but there was no response. He lingered at the door for a few minutes, turned away, came back again and turned the handle gently, and finding it still unyielding, sighed and walked towards the entrance hall. The maid stood red-eyed where he had left her.

"I could have told you, Master Ralph. She won't stir out until I tell her you're not in the house."

He nodded to her absent-mindedly and, mounting his bicycle, rode rapidly home. His one thought was to get away from everyone, from everything. There was the midday train. He could catch that....

Ann opened the door. She had been crying and looked angry.

"I'm leaving by the next train," he said.

"I'm not sorry. If it was only to the Carmelites I'd die happy," she said, raising her apron to her eyes. "I had to go down the town and I could hear the track of Father Molloy's tongue. It's a queer world, and he's a good priest, and you're a bad one. My head is moidered with a power of thinking," she said weakly.

He packed quickly; wrote, rapidly but clearly, minute directions for Ann as to the disposal of his things and had, after sending his bags to the station, some minutes to spare. He walked round the garden, touching unconsciously, as he had once seen an infant touch flowers, with the top of his fingers, rose trees which he had himself planted. He was troubled for a moment about some chrysanthemums now in bloom which an early frost would kill. He looked towards the sea and suffered a keen disappointment that the mountains in the distance were hidden by clouds.

He rang for Ann,and handed her the paper of directions, his address in Dublin and Boyle's address in London.

"It must be goodbye now," he said, holding out his hand. "I'll write."

"I'd like to kiss you once," she said brokenly. "I was a hard woman by religion when I used to carry you in my arms. And I don't believe I ever kissed you, but I'd like to do it now."

She threw her arms around him and pressed him to her heart, weeping bitterly.

"It's queer that I never felt for you before as I do now, and you going wrong too. But I'll never believe that you're bad through and through. If you'd see Father Eusebius, he'd make you as good as new."

He pressed her hand warmly and rushed off. He had barely time to get his ticket. Through the ticket-office window he saw Father

Molloy sitting, dangling his short legs, on a high stool. He asked for a single ticket to Dublin.

"Isn't it a return you want, Father?" the clerk said, looking at him curiously.

"A single ticket, please," he said shortly.

Father Molloy laughed.

Ralph had a momentary feeling of resentment which passed away before he reached the platform. He met Darcy at the door and said "Good morning," cheerfully. Darcy half raised his hand to his hat, dropped it and turned away deliberately, without speaking. Ralph gazed after him in astonishment. Boyle's warning recurred to him and he smiled faintly. A small troup of men standing between him and the door of his carriage, a few of whom he knew intimately, turned their backs and sidled away as he approached. "Didn't you hear that he's turned a Protestant?" he heard someone say behind his back. This, then, was the beginning of the boycott, the innuendo and calumny of which Boyle had warned him, he thought as he took his seat. As the train was about to start old Byrne put his head, breathlessly, into Ralph's compartment.

"Oh. Here you are. I was afeard I'd miss you. I only heard a few minutes ago." The whistle sounded and the train began to move. He grasped Ralph's hand. There was a hiss from the group standing near. Byrne turned round and faced Father Molloy, who had appeared at the booking-office door. "It's a blasted shame," he said angrily, "and I don't care who hears me. And you're only a lot of damned cowards," he added, turning to the group that had hissed.

Ralph was alone in the compartment. He sat still for a while, his eyes fixed on the bay, along which the train skirted, and the mountains rising sheer on the far side. The throbbing of the engine seemed to prolong the hiss. He stood up and stretched his limbs. If that scene on the platform represented his country, and with a pang he felt that it did, he was without a country. The speed of the train increased and the mountains, clear in the autumn sunlight, seemed to fly past. Cut off by his family, by his Church, by his country – the voice of the train dinned in his ears in a rapid ceaseless refrain. The sounds mocked him. The mountain, in the pale watery sunlight, seemed to wear a sneer. He sat down again, hunched in a corner, oppressed by a sense of overwhelming defeat and failure. Gone,

gone, gone, family, Church, country, gone, gone, gone ... seemed to pierce his brain and sear it ...

He got through his business in Dublin in a sort of dream. In the eyes of tailors and outfitters he read a mute accusation ...

One morning, as he was buttoning his Roman collar, his eyes fell on unopened cardboard boxes piled on a chair at the end of his room. He unpacked the boxes and laid a lounge suit with a tie and collar on the bed.

He took off his clerical collar and proceeded to dress in the secular clothes. He made several efforts to knot his tie. It was years since he had worn one and he had forgotten how to knot it. Every new effort resulted in a more hopeless failure. He shut his eyes at length and trusted to the memory of his fingers with complete success.

In some obscure way the incident helped him. His languor passed away. He finished dressing with a new sense of power. For the first time he noticed the view from his bedroom window, the pond in Stephen's Green, the Dublin mountains looming blue and mysterious beyond the intervening houses and smoke. He looked again at the pond; a small boy was throwing bread to the ducks and the memory of his own childhood came back to him. He felt young again and had a momentary impulse to join the little boy and feed the ducks, too. He laughed joyously.

He took up his clerical collar and looked at it curiously. He smiled as he thought of how he had dreaded laying it aside. And now, there was only a sense of escape from bondage, of freedom ...

He stood on the deck of the Holyhead mail boat, his eyes fixed on the receding Irish coast. The sands at Merrion, Howth Head, Bray Head, the Wicklow mountains, recalled youthful dreams. In the blind groping way which is the way of life, he felt that he had been true to them. Life was larger than his vision of it, and where he had read failure life marked advance.

He walked the deck with a springy step, breathing an east wind, that made his face smart, with a sense of victory.

"I have found myself at last," he said under his breath. His blood surged through his veins, and he went back to the stern. The sun, falling slant-wise on the foam in the wake of the boat, made a track of molten silver. On the horizon land had faded to a blue outline. He gazed at it longingly until the last faint grey disappeared and the sea everywhere met the sky.

He turned round and braced himself again to the east wind. Only one dream had faded into the sea, he thought....

And then?

FICTION FROM BRANDON

John B. Keane *The Bodhrán Makers*

"This powerful and poignant novel provides John B. Keane with a passport to the highest levels of Irish Literature ... an important and valuable book which must be read by all who love Ireland." *The Irish Press*

William Cotter Murray *Michael Joe*

"Michael Joe is a shopkeeper in a small Irish town. He's bitterly submissive to Mother and Church. Lusting after girls. Cocky about football prowess. Muddled by drink, vanity and jealousy. Mr Murray conveys a human history and view of Irish life with the quicksilver words of a story-teller." *New York Times*

Tom O'Flaherty *Aranmen All*

"A valuable personal account of life in Aran at the turn of the century." *Sunday Tribune*

Brian Cleeve *A Woman of Fortune*

"In almost Dickensian detail, Cleeve gives an engrossing description of the transition of Dublin life from the puritanism of the 1930s to the surface-deep liberalism of more recent times." *The Irish Times*

Donall Mac Amhlaigh *Schnitzer O'Shea*

"This delighful novel is a satire on poets and their adopted lifestyles, on Irish intellectuals and perhaps on English landladies... Mr Mac Amhlaigh is an excellent master of English prose." *Daily Telegraph*

Mary Maher *The Devil's Card*

"In this unusually accomplished debut novel... Maher marvelously evokes the atmosphere of late-19th-century Chicago... She uses a true crime to reveal the tensions dormant in the city." *Publishers Weekly*

Gerry Adams *The Street and other stories*

"The Street is not so much a fictional microcosm of Adams's world, it is the world itself... a small world, but a rich one, and lovingly recreated by Adams in small-scale, understated and domestic stories."

Times Literary Supplement

Pádraig J. Higgins *Ballybawn*

"Religion and sin, the power of men, the weakness of women... an enormous concoction. All the characters are introduced with great irony and lots of tongue-in-cheek humour and I must say I found myself just laughing outright." Mary O'Donnell, *Bookpack*, RTE

Brian Leyden *Departures*

"Brian Leyden speaks very directly to a culture in transition from pre-modern to post-modern. With tremendous economy he is able to articulate a whole culture... and he is stylistically superb."

Professor Thomas Doherty, *Booklines*, RTE.

Peter Tremayne *Aisling and other Irish Tales of Terror*

"Deliberately calculated to give nightmares to anyone whose veins contain one drop of Irish blood." *Times Literary Supplement*

"The author has plundered the eerier elements of our rich and varied folklore, and used them to craft a superb series of stories in one of contemporary literature's most popular idioms, the thriller." *Cork Examiner*

Kathleen O'Farrell *Kilbroney*

"A beautifully written book with a cornucopia of historical details so seamlessly woven through the fabric of the narrative." *Newry Reporter*